SAINT SEBASTIAN'S HEAD

LeAnn Neal Reilly

ZEPHON
BOOKS

Boston

Zephon Books USA
3 Billings Way
Framingham, MA 01701

First published in the United States by Zephon Books in 2011.
First paperback edition: November 2011
First ebook edition: November 2011

The characters and events portrayed in this book are fictitious. Any similarity to real persons, living or dead, is coincidental and not intended by the author.

ISBN: 978-0-982-6875-2-9 (paperback)
ISBN: 978-0-982-6875-3-6 (ebook)

Library of Congress Control Number: 2011935153

Book design by LeAnn Neal Reilly

Front cover image by Massimo Merlini/ iStockphoto

Text set in Cambria.

Printed in the United States of America.

For Mom,

Who always knew I would

ACKNOWLEDGMENTS

It's a truth universally acknowledged that books aren't conceived and written in a vacuum (even that line owes its existence to Jane Austen). I'd like to thank everyone who supported me with their love and friendship, both during and following the writing of *Saint Sebastian's Head*. In particular, I'd like to thank Michele Gutlove for introducing me to her beautiful glass art, for serving as the model for Tom Paul, and finally, for suggesting *pâte de verre* as his medium. I'd also like to thank Chris Hughes, who has been putting up with my writing (and me) for decades—nothing can adequately express my admiration for your insight and patience. Others who deserve appreciation for plunging in and reading an early version of the novel include Mary Flanagan, Lana Saksanov, Howard Beale, Paula Jacobs, and Raffaella Agostino. Last, but never least, I want to express my eternal love and undying gratitude to my husband, Scott Neal Reilly, who convinced me that Weeble's story should see the light of day.

We do not truly see light, we only see slower things lit by it, so that for us light is on the edge—the last thing we know before things become too swift for us.

—*C.S. Lewis*

One

▼

WHENEVER I VEER TOWARD CHUCKING IT ALL, draining my savings account, filling my tank, and driving toward Mexico and sun-drenched oblivion, I invariably catch a glimpse of Flat Stanley lying in the window, eyes squinted and licking his stump. Watching him quiets my mind and slows my breathing enough to remind me that it's not about me, this story I've got to tell, the one that's burning a hole in my heart. Flat Stanley always stops grooming himself when he feels my gaze and his eyes slide open to study me with such wise compassion that I wonder what gives me the right to despair. Then he rises onto his three legs, stretching and yawning, and drops to the floor to lope toward me, his footsteps delicate and determined. In the face of Flat Stanley's hope, I'm ashamed.

Today Flat Stanley lurks underfoot as I pull on my running shorts and sports bra, a pint-size trainer urging me to keep moving. On my bed feigning sleep lies Flat Stanley's lieutenant, Hero. All I've got to do is move to the living room where the leash resides and Hero drops his act and springs down as if he'd been on full alert the whole time. I don't know how I ever managed to get myself through work or school without these two drill sergeants. How I ever thought I was the one rescuing *them*.

Hero waits next to the sofa while I spoon out canned food for Flat Stanley and scoop up his kibble, but he crunches through it so fast I suspect he thinks I'm going to sneak away while he's busy. I mix up some chocolate milk and peel a banana, reviewing the route from my apartment to the path along the Charles River while I eat. It's early and cool, and I'll have to ignore the gooseflesh on my thighs and the tightness in my calves, at least until my blood starts flowing and sweat forces me to tie my jacket around my waist.

I pull on a baseball cap and click the leash onto Hero's collar. Eagerness pricks his gait, but he waits for me to slip on my headphones, grab a plastic bag, and lock the deadbolt before towing me towards the stairs. It's quiet but not deserted out on the street: at least four others run along the liquid gold of the sidewalk toward Memorial Drive, their faces serene and their breathing rhythmic. I turn into the sunlight for a moment, its warmth on my cheeks making me forget the April air, and then I wrap Hero's leash around the railing and sprint up and down the steps before stretching out. Hero doesn't watch me, but his ragged ear, torn when his former master let another dog attack him, flutters in the breeze.

I didn't always run. Far from it. I spent most of high school in my bedroom reading or taking walks through the park when Mona thought I'd gone to a friend's house or stayed after school for some club or other. I should've taken up running when I got to Cambridge, but running seems so East Coast, not something a poor biker's daughter from Missouri does. Only nightmares waking me before dawn and a desperate search for coffee at six a.m. during finals week led me to the solution for my never-ending insomnia. On that fateful morning four years ago, as I stumbled toward the café a few blocks from my apartment, a runner brushed past, his eyes focused ahead, the valley of his spine blotchy wet and his bare forearms shining. I stood and watched until he'd grown too small to distinguish on the dark horizon, but something told me this was what I needed.

Running doesn't come easily for me. I had to fight for it. Just like I've had to fight for everything every day of my life. I fight, even when it does no good. But this time it got me through. Through my chest burning as I ran. Through my legs twitching and sobbing for mercy when I lay down at night. Back then, I'd been right though: those first couple of weeks, I fell into bed so exhausted no ghosts stirred to torment me.

At last my hamstrings loosen and moisture beads my forehead. I'm ready to set off on an easy jog for the first two blocks. Hero matches my pace and it's only moments before we're running, Joan Osborne's *If God Was One of Us* winging through my mind. Her lyrics are my anthem, her sultry voice my confessor:

> *If God had a name, what would it be*
> *And would you call it to his face*
> *If you were faced with him in all his glory*
> *What would you ask if you had just one question*

I find myself humming and picking up my pace as she sings "God is great, God is good" and I'm flying, my legs pumping in rough synchronicity to the rhythm of the chorus. The next verse twists an ancient hunger, propelling me on a quixotic quest.

> *If God had a face what would it look like*
> *And would you want to see*
> *If seeing meant that you would have to believe*
> *In things like heaven and in Jesus and the saints and all the prophets*

I push away from these questions, the strength of my discomfort lending angry energy to my stride. Confidence burrows through my ear canal and into my brain and I know I'll do it. I *will* finish my sprint training and run in the Boston Sprint Triathlon in September. Marcie's always after me to set goals, envision where I want to be in ten years, that sort of thing. Next time we have lunch together, I'll steer her clear of my love life, or lack thereof, by telling her how well my training's going. Ahead and just to my side runs Hero, his tongue dangling and his hair fluttering, joy sparking from him each time his paws hit pavement. I forget I had to drag myself out of bed this morning, that my throat is sore and my calves are tight as a drum, that I'm five eight and built like a brick shithouse as Frank always said. I'm flying over the pavement toward the rising sun and everything is perfect, if only briefly. Just over the horizon, I'll meet God and ask Him the only question that ever mattered to me: *why*.

From long habit, I estimate my velocity and predict how quickly I can pivot and change the angle of my run, how quickly I can stop without momentum carrying me another step or two. I begin translating the shock in my feet to the shock in my knees and up to my hips. I calculate on the white board of my mind the force per square inch of bone, the wear and tear on joints. I re-engineer ankles with shock absorbers to transfer energy from my stride to an imaginary water heater wrapped around a thermos at my waist. I focus on the number of steps it should take to heat up a cup of coffee. I can't be sure, but I tell myself that it's exactly the number of steps it takes to finish my run.

More runners and bikers merge into the human flow along the Charles River, but traffic on Mem Drive is light. I watch the crew teams rowing along the sun-fractured water, the muscles on their shoulders rippling and bulging beneath their t-shirts. They are beautiful in their discipline, silent and terrible as arrows slicing through air. I can't help but think the coordinated dips and sweeps of their oars hark back to some ancient practice, back to Sparta's fierce training or Rome's legions marching in jingling unison. Even if it's not true, I sense history and nobility in those crewmen flying down the river away from me. It's no surprise none of the corn-fed boys of St. Joe, their minds occupied with Friday night football and cheerleaders' thighs, ever saw anything worth conquering in the muddy waters of the Missouri.

By now, I'm no longer thinking about my route, body mechanics or sore muscles. The thumping of my feet and the sound of my breath don't deserve any more attention than the beat of my heart. Instead, I think about the letter from the foundation. I can't quite wrap my head around what I've gotten myself into. Marcie would tell me I'm in shock because I never give myself enough credit; I always expect the worst. She's probably right, but I don't come from a place where people get fifty thousand dollars to spend a year working on personal projects, no matter how important those projects are to them.

Lauren, if she'd ever had the chance, she'd have gone for the money and not looked over her shoulder at all, wondering if anyone would peg her for a fraud. We might've been born in the same town, but Lauren always looked at where she wanted to go, not where she came from. Lauren isn't the one who made it out of St. Joe though, so I'll just have to do what I can and hope it isn't an insult to her memory.

No matter where my mind strays on my daily runs, however, my internal warning system stays on high alert, scanning the sidewalk and street a hundred and eighty degrees around me. I've survived this long—I've managed to eke out a superficially normal existence— only because my ever-vigilant guardian never sleeps when I'm outside the safety of my apartment.

Almost as soon as the glossy-brown curls appear over the lip of a dumpster thirty feet in front of me, horror shuts off my thoughts. Adrenaline lurches through my veins. I urge my burning thighs to force more speed into my gait. I've only covered a quarter of the distance before the curls rise to reveal a man's face, suspended Kilroy-like over the rim of the dumpster. His dark eyes attract my own so strongly that I can't look away. Heat suffuses my chest and cheeks. I'm aware of the sweat coating the back of my neck beneath

13

the arch of my ponytail. As he jumps over the side of the dumpster to land as softly as a cat on the pavement, I continue several paces before lurching to a halt. Hero, instead of growling a warning, stops and watches the stranger.

The stranger studies me. I notice he's got a stained canvas bag slung over one shoulder. Evidence? Ropes? Duct tape? Knives?

"You look like you've just seen a murder." His voice when he speaks matches the depth of his gaze.

I twitch.

Something flickers across his face. His eyes narrow and his forehead furrows, as if he's trying to figure out what planet I'm from. Or as though I'm a loved one who's just returned after being gone a long time and he's trying to understand the changes my absence has wrought. At last, he smiles, a cock-eyed curl that turns his brown eyes into half moons.

"Nope. You got me wrong. I was just dumpster diving. May I?" He touches fingertips to the canvas bag.

I look at the bag, trying to discern its contents by the outlines. Do I see any dark, wet blotches spreading over its surface? No. I give a slight nod.

He watches me as he drops the bag. Hero sits with his muzzle tilted, curious. The stranger squats and works the drawstring open. My heart flutters as he reaches in. I twist and lift my foot to step backwards. He doesn't seem to notice, instead drawing out a large, blackened object and setting it on the ground.

It's a wok of heavy-gauge aluminum—an expensive item from an upscale kitchen store.

"Isn't it a beauty?" He runs calloused fingers over its rim. "Can you believe what some people will throw away?"

"Yes, I can." The bitterness in my voice stuns me.

The young man looks up; his eyes, so alive, squint as though the sun pains him. The world-conquering smile is gone. He lifts tentative fingers toward me but makes no effort to rise. "I've never seen an aura so dim, so shrunken. Who wounded your spirit so savagely?"

My mouth opens. Shuts. Opens again. Some part of my brain notes how much I'm acting like a fish stranded on a sandbar, but for the life of me I can't grasp the nature of my accident.

And then, without allowing me to utter a word, the pistons of my legs pump and carry me away from him. I feel his gaze on my back as Hero and I pick up speed and run flat out. His eyes. His eyes stay with me as I run. They'd been so warm, so open. So discerning.

* * *

I've been Weeble for as long as I can remember. It's not my real name, but it's more real to me than anything else I've been called in my twenty-five years. Names like slut, whore, cunt, bitch. Those names define a whole class of woman; they aren't specific or personal. Weeble belongs only to me. I earned it when I was three and Frank, my father, got tired of waiting for Mona, my mother, to get home from a girls' night out and sent me to the refrigerator for a Budweiser. The way Frank told it, I was "prouder'n shit" to get my daddy a cold one and tried popping the top for him as I walked to his La-Z-Boy.

Frank laughed his bear laugh and reached for the can. "Gimme that before you break the tab and I have to pry it open with a screwdriver."

He was watching *Kojak*, grunting, either in mirth or approval, and smoking as enthusiastically as Telly Savalas, but nothing in the show interested me. I played for a while with some toys in the corner, but Mona had thrown out the Play-Doh when I'd mashed a pancake into the shag carpet so I couldn't use the Dough Machine and I'd long since lost all the magnets for Mr. Magnet Man. So I squatted down next to the recliner and wrapped my arms about my knees, keeping an eye out for Miller, the cat, who had a love-hate relationship with me. Frank said he never noticed me drinking from the first can. Or the second or third. He just kept sending me to the kitchen for more

15

beer while the empties multiplied on the floor. I remember stacking and knocking them down, over and over, until Frank bellowed at me "to quit makin' a fuckin' racket."

It wasn't until his friend Ricky showed up to bum some weed that Frank realized just how soused I'd gotten. Ricky came over to our house for years, gray stubbling his chin and loose cheeks, cackling over his arrival that night while dragging on yet another joint bummed from Frank.

"I ain't never, I repeat, never, seen anything so damn hilarious in my life, Weeble. Not before, not since. There you were, rocking back and forth on those stubby little toes of yours as you toddled off into the kitchen, and damn if Frank wasn't completely unaware of it! I just stood there in the doorway laughing my ass off at the two of you. Frank, he just turns his head in his chair and tells me to shut the fuck up, *All in the Family* is on."

What Frank didn't or couldn't tell me about the next hour, Ricky more than happily told me. I imagined the rest.

He persuaded Frank to ignore the TV long enough to let my drunken state sink in and then Frank howled as loudly as Ricky at my determination to stay on my feet. Frank directed me to the kitchen to get Ricky a Budweiser, as much to watch me wobble as to be a good host. Ricky, kindhearted fool that he was, let me have the first sip from his can. At that point, it became a game to see how long I could stay on my feet as I walked between the two of them, sipping and belching from their beers.

"She's got a stubborn streak as wide as the racing stripe in your Fruit o'the Looms, Frankie." Ricky guzzled his beer as he watched me, a lit cigarette clouding his view. "I believe she'll fall down on her face before she gives up."

Frank lit a joint and inhaled. He said nothing as I wobbled away from him and then he blew hot, weedy smoke toward me. "She's one of those damn toys, what are they? You know the ones, the ones in the commercial that don't fall over no matter how hard you push them? Weebles? She's a goddamn Weeble, that's what she is. What do they say? Weebles wobble, but they don't fall down."

I still hadn't fallen down when Mona arrived and brought hell with her. I swear the heat from her melted paint on the walls and peeled the laminate from the coffee table. She marched right up to Frank and slapped him as he lounged, stoned, and then she tore into him with her tongue, sharpened on Jack and Coke. "Tore him a new asshole" as Ricky so delicately put it. Frank said and did nothing until her anger burned itself out. Then he passed her a joint. I no longer wobbled around the room. Instead, I stood clutching the frame of the kitchen door, blinking fiercely as I tried to keep my eyes open.

"What the fuck do you think you're doing?" Mona repeated before taking her first hit. "Frankie, I can't leave you alone for two hours and you're feeding beer to the baby?" She passed the joint back to him, silent long enough to retain the potent smoke inside her chest. "Where the fuck is Tim?"

Frank, whose gaze had wandered back to the TV, waved his hand toward the front door. "Out harassin' a couple of girls down the street. Told him to be home when it got dark."

"It *is* dark, Frank. Do I hafta do everything around here?" Mona stood up and walked to the screen door, which she held open. "Tim! Tim! Get your ass home. I see you and your friends there don't think I don't. I'll march right down there and plant a boot in your ass if you don't get here in five minutes."

She came back and sat on the arm of Frank's chair and took the joint from him. "How much did you give her?"

Frank looked at me and shrugged. "A few sips here and there. Didn't matter, though. Just helped herself when I wasn't looking."

Mona laughed. "That's my girl. Looks like she can hold her liquor, too."

"Just like you, Moan." Ricky chuckled and took a hit.

17

"Yeah. We were just thinkin' she looked a bit like those toys, the Weebles. She's a Weeble if I ever saw one."

"'Weeble'? Hm." Mona didn't give the name a second thought, but from that moment on, that's what everyone called me.

I lived up to the expectations inherent in my new name, constantly climbing, balancing, and hanging in a serious effort to test out its appropriateness over the next several years. By the time I was six, I routinely scaled the kitchen cabinets in search of a clean cup for my Tang, that orange-flavored beverage of astronauts that fueled so many of my dirt-crusted activities. Of course, one thing led to another. I found myself estimating the physics of my actions in the world, always with the goal of remaining on my feet. In some perverse and tangled way, Frank planted the seed for my training as an engineer the night he let me get drunk on Budweiser.

According to Mona, the night I earned the Weeble name is also the night she and Frank created Annie, my younger sister. Up until that point, I'd been the baby, mostly ignored but lavished with attention when either Frank or Mona felt affectionate. In those days, when they had some extra cash, they'd make a run to Church's Chicken downtown and pick up fried chicken, jalapeños to cut the grease, coleslaw, and biscuits with honey butter. Most of my early childhood is lost in the white blankness of forgetting, but the smell of fried chicken and the feel of Coke burning down my throat while marijuana fogged the air will stay with me forever.

Annie's arrival changed my status profoundly. At the same time I realized Frank and Mona had abandoned me for diapering and giving bottles to the squirming, wailing, stinking bundle I often saw in their arms, I became aware of Tim, Frank's son from his previous marriage. He was a new class of person, unlike Annie who was simply a demanding creature. Tim was a person bigger than I was but not as big or powerful as Frank and Mona. I soon discovered it didn't matter that Tim had less power than my parents: what mattered was that neither Frank nor Mona expended any of it protecting me from him.

I suspect Tim ignored me while I was the baby of the family because he feared Mona, who'd taken to her role as his stepmother with relish. Or at least she'd taken to the role of enforcing peace and quiet, with a loud backhand if necessary. But as soon as I lost status as the baby, Tim adopted the role of vigilant instructor in minor, if unimaginative, cruelties. One day I might wake up to find peanut butter in my sandals or toothpaste in the bottom of my milk cup. I quickly learned Mona had more to keep track of than who was responsible for the sand on my sheets. Nothing he did convinced me of my new place in our family hierarchy, however, until he mutilated my fifth birthday present, a Weebles family and their cottage playhouse. He'd taken something sharp and etched the clear shell over the girl Weeble's face so her features were blurred. When I complained to Mona, she told me to quit running to her for every little problem I had.

"There's nothing wrong with that toy, Weeble. The next time you complain about those retarded plastic eggs when I'm making dinner, I'm goin' right outside and throw them as far as I can across the field toward Spring Garden. Now go on, go play and take those stupid toys with you."

I looked into the family room where Tim sat on the sofa, his sneakers propped on the worn coffee table while he watched *Laverne and Shirley*. He turned his face toward me, his slow, sly grin chilling. After that, if I didn't find a place to hide my Weebles and their cottage, Tim would steal and mar them, moving from scratching deeply to drilling holes in their bodies. The worst came when he stuck a hot match into the girl's plastic body until it shrank and contorted so the face was unrecognizable. I continued to bring them out when he was gone to school or with his friends, but my pity and sorrow for the Weeble girl had forever taken the joy out of my play.

19

Instead, I held these Weebles gingerly, aware that for all their ability to remain upright, they were still vulnerable inside.

* * *

St. Joseph, Missouri, is what happens when opportunity knocks on someone else's door. Or when opportunity is seized right out from under you.

Before the Civil War, St. Joe was the farthest point west the railroad reached, and it was a bustling outpost where hopeful pioneers and rough outdoorsmen all converged to stock up on supplies before heading into the Wild West. Like many other places where busy cities have sprung up, St. Joe began its life on a river, the Missouri. In the 1820s, Joseph Robidoux, a canny French fur trader, set up a trading post in the Blacksnake Hills not far from the site where he later created St. Joe, whose streets bore the names of his eight children. Less than twenty years after Robidoux sold lots for his town, St. Joe grew and prospered, with a population greater than the rival town just down the river thirty miles or so.

But sly old Robidoux lost out in the end to the younger, more visionary founders of Kansas City. After the Civil War, three prominent Kansas City businessmen had the foresight to see the importance of linking Chicago and Texas. They persuaded the Hannibal and St. Joseph Railroad to build a cutoff from Cameron, Missouri, to their city, leading to the first bridge across the Missouri River. For a while after this, both St. Joe and KC grew rapidly, but by 1900 Kansas City had outstripped St. Joe, whose own population peaked that year.

St. Joe still has the air of the place that got bypassed, a place time forgot. It isn't a place people go *to*, it's a place they flee from, if only to migrate to the larger, more cosmopolitan Kansas City metro area. In other places, when the downtown dies, immigrants move in and bring a measure of life. Not in St. Joe. No, in St. Joe, downtown has the air of a ghost town or the empty feeling of a movie set. A 1950s movie.

When I was a kid, I heard talk of revitalizing downtown. The city fathers tried closing off the streets and installing a walking mall. They brought in the Civic Arena for concerts and conventions, built a new Holiday Inn, and established riverboat gambling, but nothing revived the lifeless area and now growth is on the fringes of the interstate north of the city where Wal-Mart first broke ground. The lifeblood of St. Joe, once dependent on the Missouri River where fur traders, pioneers, and the Pony Express all crossed over to the frontier, has shifted north and east. Now the city subsists on chain restaurants, banks, and big-box stores. The state college, Missouri Western, offers one of the only sparks of life outside the closed system that St. Joe has become.

None of St. Joe's early promise mattered to me on the evenings Frank took me along when he went to score some pot. We might drive through the streets behind King Hill looking for a particular dilapidated white house with a sagging front porch. On those occasions, Frank made me wait in the truck while he went inside to haggle. I'd lean against the door and look out the open window at the sky, lushly honeydew. Voices filtered down the block from open windows where fathers watched the Royals on TV and children shrieked between houses in endless games of hide and seek. Screen doors banged shut. Pots clanked onto stoves. Sometimes a dog barked or a woman yelled at someone to "get on home" for dinner. I blocked those domestic sounds, focusing instead on the sound of tires on pavement or the movement of air through leaves. At eight, I thought magic still existed in the world and summer evenings offered a doorway into it.

After Frank concluded his business, he'd come whistling out the screen door, letting its wooden frame fall without a backward glance. It slammed satisfyingly and the sweet, burned-herb smell of the joint he'd shared inside fogged a nimbus around his upper body. He'd start the truck and rock music shattered the evening's peace as we pulled away, the truck's exhaust rumbling. Then he'd head down

King Hill to the DQ and buy me a peanut-buster parfait and get himself a Coke float and we'd sit in the truck bed watching the sun set near Lake Contrary.

Sometimes we'd drive east into the boondocks and the smell of road dust, the sound of crickets, and the cool air filled me with joy. Frank would pop in an eight track of *The Hotel California* and sing, his cigarette-rough voice a nice counterpoint to Don Henley's polished tenor.

> *On a dark desert highway, cool wind in my*
> *hair*
> *Warm smell of colitas, rising up through the*
> *air*

At these times, I sensed something larger in life, some hint of purpose or meaning beyond my understanding that teased me with its infinite possibilities. The twilit sky stretched farther than the horizon on all sides, hiding the stars behind an opaque blue curtain until the setting sun dragged the curtain away.

This dealer lived in a white farmhouse with a split-rail fence and cornfields. Behind the house stood a barn where chickens chuckled in the last light of day from the open door. Cows bawled along with the chatter on the TV and the smell of pig shit blended in an oddly comforting way with the odor of frying chicken. Frank's dealer would meet him at the bottom of the porch steps and they'd take a walk away toward the far side of the fields. After they disappeared, I'd get out of the truck and sit on the steps where I could stare at the horizon as the sun melted like a cherry Popsicle. A woman in a flowered cotton dress usually came out on the porch and gave me a glass of iced tea and some iced oatmeal-raisin cookies, but we never spoke.

By this time, Tim had ramped up his cruelty to me, but I had the astounding ability of youngest childhood to forget hurts from the recent past and focus on the here and now. When I think back to those days riding in Frank's rattling Chevy truck, my heart aches for

22

the happy innocence that underlay the whole of my young life. I waver between wanting to take that little girl into my arms and protect her trust in the essential goodness of the world and wanting to take her chin in my hands to force her to stare at the monster lurking under her bed even in the daylight hours.

Two

▼

TRIATHLONS AREN'T FOR WIMPS. They're not for people who hate to push themselves, who've got no stamina, who swim like wounded seals. An image of a great-white shark blasting out of the pool behind me, its rows of triangular teeth vivid against the angle of its head, motivates me for half a lap, but then I resume a leisurely crawl. I won't win any races, but it's okay. I'm not in it to impress anyone. I'm in it to finish. To exert my will over my body, to reclaim it after all these years.

I slow down even more to look at the clock on the wall. It's only been ten minutes. I'm only halfway through my training. Some people, Marcie included, would call this torture. I don't. I know better. My body hates it, whatever word I'd call it, but I relish its agony. The rebellion, the resentment of my muscles— they're nothing but the prickly feeling you get when your feet have fallen asleep and you stretch the toes and rub the soles to wake them up.

Despite being determined to push my pace, I swim so slowly that the swimmer behind me passes me in an irritated burst. The sudden rush scares me and I gasp a mouthful of water. I flail for a moment, a moment that lasts forever, but I manage to crawl to the end of the pool before drowning and dangle off the edge while I cough my lungs clear. Across the pool, the lifeguard watches me, but I shake my head at her when she starts to dismount her platform. After a couple of minutes, my lungs are clear and my heart beats normally. I've looked around and studied the other swimmers and I know that the only dangerous person in the pool is me.

I finish my laps and get out of the pool in a sour mood. This is going to be a long training season if I keep this up. So far, biking has been easy. Maybe when I'm done with the triathlon, I'll replace running with biking, at least when the weather's good. I won't be able to maneuver away from threats as easily as on foot, but the speed more than makes up for it. Distance is almost always the right choice.

When I get home, the apartment smells musty mixed with the rancid odor of dirty dishes in the sink. Even so, my stomach rumbles. The granola bar I ate after my laps only made me hungrier. Flat Stanley slinks around the arm of the sofa and mewls as he limps toward me, only to be knocked over by Hero as he dashes toward the door from the bedroom. I ignore him and rescue Flat Stanley.

"You're really going to be flat if that dumb dog keeps running into you."

Flat Stanley purrs and settles into the crook of my arm. In the kitchen, I cradle him while I pull out bagels and cream cheese. He doesn't notice when I drop crumbs on his forehead as I eat.

I can't say when I first read the Flat Stanley children's book or exactly why that name came to me when I saw my three-legged cat at the animal shelter. I'd gone down looking for a kitten, something tiny and spitting, with claws as fine as a fishhook, but I came home with an orange tabby whose rear leg had been amputated after being crushed under the wheel of a car. The thing is, Flat Stanley should've been the one spitting, his ears flat and his eyes narrowed, but he wasn't. He kept rubbing against the cage door and mewing loudly, so enthusiastic in his bid for my attention that he fell over repeatedly.

I swipe my index finger around the inside of the tub and lick the cream cheese off. Not too refined, but there you have me. When I can't eat any more, I put off showering to clean the kitchen. Really clean it. I wash all the dishes, wipe down all the counters and chisel bits of onion and pepper off of the stovetop, and finally carry out the garbage and recycling. Even then, I drift to the mail stacked on the end of the breakfast bar and sift through it for any bills that must be paid in the next two weeks. When the phone rings, I'm relieved. It's Jana.

"You going to Mark and Michelle's party?"

"No, I got rid of my car a few months ago."

"Seriously?"

"Yeah, I pretty much putter around Cambridge these days. Couldn't afford the insurance and gas right now anyway."

"So you really quit working."

"Kinda had to, you know. The grant has pretty strict deadlines or I lose it. In fact, I was just getting into the shower so I can hit the keyboard."

"On Saturday? C'mon, you gotta go to Mark and Michelle's. It's an engagement party for godsakes. You can't skip out on that. I'll come and get you."

"I'm too out of your way. I wouldn't feel right asking you to come in to get me."

"You're not asking. Anyway, I'm spending the day on Newbury Street at a salon. You could come with, and we'll get some lunch, get our nails done, buy some new slings. Then we'll head out to the party."

"I told them I wasn't coming. I can't crash an engagement party."

"Crash-smash. That's bullshit. You know they'd be thrilled to see you. You're such a recluse these days."

"Look, Jana, it's not you. Or Mark and Michelle. I sent them a crystal bowl from Lux, Bond, and Green. I just need to work right now on this."

Jana is nothing if not persistent. She's the girl in college who chose an unassuming and dedicated med student and pursued him until he married her between college and medical school. She has two children, a boy and a girl, and she volunteers at their daycare and for every fundraiser while working on her master's in education. Marcie always holds Jana up as an example of clear-eyed goal setting.

"So work! Put in a couple of hours and I'll pick you up later this afternoon. We'll still have time to get our nails done so you don't look so shabby, and then we'll arrive fashionably late. There'll be some friends of Mark's from law school and that guy James—you know, the one with the Spanish good looks. I hear you caught his eye."

I shudder, whether from fear or temptation, I can't say. Out of nowhere, the dumpster diver's brown eyes appear in my memory. Had I caught his eye too?

"No, I can't. I've got to walk Hero and I can't be out late." What I don't say is I can't be out after dark unless I've had too much to drink. Or with a guy. Preferably both. "I won't crimp your style."

"Style? What style? I've got a babysitter. I've gotta be home before she turns into a pumpkin."

The restlessness has evaporated, replaced by my own brand of stubbornness. I'm also not above deceit.

"Not interested in hobnobbing with the dewy-eyed. I'm the class slut, remember?"

Jana's unfazed by my crudeness. "No, you're not. It's time you turned over a new page, anyway. These are fabulous guys, smart. Going somewhere. They're not the guys you brought home from the restaurant."

"Oh, they're *all* the guys I brought home from the restaurant, bar, nightclub. Laundromat. Why're you so eager to set me up? Where's Julius anyway?"

There, that's it. It's hard to say how Jana does it over the phone, but an ice sheet descends between us. It isn't the first time, so I'm not worried. She'll just call Marcie and bitch. And Marcie will find some way to smooth it over for me. The trick is to know just how much of the truth to wield.

"He's working the ER rotation. 72 hours on, 72 hours off."

"Ah. So maybe this isn't about hooking me up with Spanish-eyed James or whatever his name is. Maybe *you* should hook up with him? Better go without me."

Jana huffs. "I'm married. I'd never cheat."

"No. You wouldn't." What I don't say is that she probably should.

"I've gotta go. Jacob's pulled all the feathers out of Juliana's boa and she's sobbing. I'll call you later. We'll have lunch next time I'm in Cambridge."

"Sure. Tell Mark and Michelle I said congrats."

Jana mutters something that sounds like "tell them yourself" before she hangs up.

I pick up Flat Stanley and carry him to my bed so he can keep me company while I get ready. His fluffy orange form rumbles, purring accompanying each rise and fall among the nest of sheets. No matter who I piss off, Flat Stanley's got my back.

When I finally sit down at my desk, I compress my lips and squint at the screen, surfing through a sickening number of links. I've seen some of these pages before, read some of their stories, but even though my eyes radiate enough heat to blind me, I don't cry. Once I've glued my butt into my chair, I don't get up. I wade through detailed descriptions of crime scenes, evidence, and shattering loss. I read them all, but I write down only four names, three girls and one boy, on the pad of paper next to my mouse. These children are the ones I'm going to start with. These are the victims that I'm going to get to know. It's not something to cut corners on. I can't gloss over their lives.

They are all so different from each other, so different from me. One lived on a farm in Minnesota, two lived in the suburbs. The last one, the girl with the Shirley Temple hairdo and the gap-toothed smile, Leslie Ann, she lived in an apartment. Something about her reminds me of Lauren and I find myself returning to her page. There's so little written for Leslie Ann. Just a paragraph six sentences long. It happened so long ago and no one thought to write more for her.

I print her page out. I can't pick her yet; I can't elevate her above the others without reading more, making phone calls, and asking questions I really don't have a right to ask. I suspect Leslie Ann's family and friends will be hard to track down and maybe harder to interview, but in my gut I know that she's the one. She's the first story in the larger story I've got to tell.

* * *

The first time Tim touched me, I was eight. It was a summer day like any other before and not too different from the ones that came after. Even so, I remember it. Our cousins, Missy and Joey, came over in the afternoon while my Aunt Susie waitressed. Missy was twelve, almost the same age as Tim, and Joey was nine. Annie and I'd been outside for most of the day, but I'd come in to watch some TV just before they got to our house. Mona stood a couple of feet inside the arched doorway to the kitchen, talking on the phone. Missy strolled in, followed by Joey, who carried a water gun.

29

"Why does it always stink of cat piss in here?" Missy's nose crinkled as she sat on the sofa next to me. "Cat piss and dust. Gross."

I looked at her. "I don't smell cat piss." I smelled her, though. Perfume from a tester and something metallic when she shifted her legs.

"You wouldn't."

Mona's head peered around the arch.

"You kids better get yourselves outside before dinner. I can't have ya'll inside and underfoot while I cook. Take Annie with you."

Missy grumbled, but Joey ran for the crooked screen door and let it slam behind him.

"Don't slam the door, you little fuck!" Mona yelled from the kitchen.

I knew enough to let Missy go outside ahead of me.

"Where's Annie?" she asked over her shoulder.

"Watching Dad."

Outside, Frank lay on the gravel driveway with a wrench and squinted at the rear of his Harley. Annie sat along the edge of the gravel among the foot-high weeds, her thumb in her mouth.

"Get your thumb out of your mouth, dork!" Missy said.

Annie turned to look at Missy and raised her middle finger.

"Uncle Frank, Annie just flipped me off!"

Frank clutched the wrench to his chest and glared at us. "What the fuck are you botherin' me for, Missy? You always gotta get your nose up everyone's ass and then get all prissy when they don't like it. Leave her be." Frank craned his neck around and looked at Annie.

"Your cousin's right. Get your thumb outta your mouth."

Annie let her thumb drop from her mouth and pulled at the weeds. I followed Missy, who stomped to the backyard. Joey was already there, squirting water at ants that swarmed over our

30

rickety wooden picnic table. Missy plopped down on one of the benches and crossed her arms across her chest.

"I don't know why the fuck I can't stay home. There ain't nothin' to do here but play with dolls or pick my nose." Her scowl kept me away. "Quit squirting that gun, dickweed, or I'll shove it up your ass."

Just then Tim sauntered around the corner of the house. He wore a black Led Zeppelin t-shirt, torn blue jeans, and scuffed Converse sneakers.

"Hey, dimwits, what's up?" He stopped five feet from us; his legs straddled the yard as if he captained a pirate's ship. "What the hell are you doin' out here anyway?"

"Hidin' from you." Missy turned away. "Guess it didn't work."

Tim came over and sat on the picnic table, which groaned under his weight. "I got somethin' to show you idiots. After dinner."

"Show us now," said Joey. "We wanna see it now."

Missy snorted. "You're so full of shit, Tim. No one's impressed."

"Is it your tattoo? Show it." Joey looked at Tim with a dog's eyes. "Please."

Tim twisted on the table and ran his hand through his ragged dirty-blond hair. I expected him to explode, but instead he pulled up his sleeve. He looked at Missy, who still had her arms crossed over her chest, but now she'd swiveled to look at his tattoo.

"Cool!" Joey exclaimed when the skull with a bloody nail through one eye appeared on Tim's thin upper arm.

He squeezed his bicep in a lame attempt to expand the tattoo. The skull laughed at him. "See what big boys get." He said it to Joey but kept his eyes on Missy.

She didn't look away or scoff. Tim dropped his sleeve and pulled out a pack of cigarettes from his jeans pocket.

"Let me have a drag," Missy said.

31

"Think you can handle it?"

"Yeah."

After Missy had sucked on Tim's cigarette, Joey begged a turn. I didn't want them to offer me one, and they didn't.

"No," Missy said to him. "You ain't old enough."

"Neither are you!"

"Shut the fuck up."

Tim laughed until a cough interrupted him. "He's gettin' too big for his britches."

Annie materialized at the corner of the house. Her green t-shirt, which rode up to show her belly button, sprouted multiple stains like lichen. Her once-beige shorts dangled a lifeline of thread to the dirty, jagged edge of her toenails. Somewhere between her weedy perch in the front yard and the corner of the house, she'd wedged her thumb back into her mouth.

All five of us stayed in the backyard for another half an hour; Tim and Missy smoked and talked while Joey, Annie, and I dug holes in the weeds behind the picnic table. We collected several rocks and stacked them next to the holes according to some plan of Joey's.

"Get your asses in here," Mona called from the kitchen window. "Tim, you'd better in the hell not be smokin' cigarettes back there."

Missy hid the cigarette in her hand behind her back. "We ain't."

"Don't lie to me, you little shit. I can smell the smoke. Wait'll your mom hears."

"Whatever," Missy said.

After Mona's head disappeared, Tim grabbed the cigarette from Missy and stubbed it out on the picnic table. He plucked up all the butts from the table around them, stuffed them into the empty cigarette package, and then jumped off the table.

"Get the fuck outta my way," he said to Annie and Joey.

"Hey!" Joey said. "That's our hole!"

"Not anymore."

Tim dropped the cigarette package and what was left of the book of matches into one of the holes near Joey. He scuffed the toe of his sneaker around the loose dirt, burying the remains of the cigarettes. When the hole no longer showed, he rolled several of the rocks over it with his foot, resting his foot on top of the rocks afterwards.

"Don't say a word."

Mona stormed into view. Tall and sunburned, she wore faded jeans, a thin white t-shirt with no bra, and a red bandana in her red-brown hair. She walked over to Tim and cuffed him. Tim didn't make a sound, but his eyes glistened and his chin rose.

"You little fuck, you know better than to steal my smokes. Where the hell are they?"

"I don't know what you're talkin' about."

Mona cuffed him again. "Yes, you do."

He said nothing.

"Where are they, Missy?"

"What?"

Mona whirled and glowered at her niece, who couldn't meet her eyes. "You know what the fuck I'm talkin' about. Never mind. I'll let Susie deal with you."

She looked over her shoulder at Joey and Annie, who stood with her thumb in her mouth.

"You pussy, Tim. You got these little kids scared shitless, don't you? Well, you're grounded. No goin' out after dinner with your friends. No stereo or TV, either. Now get your ass inside. Dinner's ready."

She stomped off, leaving a jet trail of heat behind her. Silence followed like a thunderclap. I waited for Tim and Missy to move. They didn't. After a moment or two, Annie scampered after

Mona, and then Joey, glancing over his shoulder at Tim, sprinted after her.

"That bitch," Tim said. "I'm gonna piss in her coffee one-a these days."

"Let's go inside," I said.

"I ain't goin' anywhere near her."

Missy stood with one hand on her hip and her lower lip caught against her teeth. She glanced at me and shrugged.

Tim also looked at me. "You go on inside, Weeble. This ain't your fight. Bring me and Missy back somethin' to eat."

"Okay."

I hurried into the house. Mona and Frank occupied the sofa and single recliner in the living room. They already had plates in their laps and bottles of Miller in their hands. Smoke spiraled from multiple cigarettes, winding white trails to the ceiling where it spread out into a thick fog. Annie and Joey clustered in the kitchen near where the table met the far wall; presumably they had found the food.

"Where's Timmy?" Mona asked.

"He told me to bring him some food."

"That little fuck."

"Leave it," Frank said to Mona. "Let him stay outside. I won't get heartburn from you two fightin' then."

I shuffled between the coffee table and Frank's outstretched legs to the kitchen. Joey and Annie had filled paper plates with hot dogs and chips and baked beans; each clutched a cold bottle of Pepsi—although Annie's grip looked pretty insecure. They squeezed past me and navigated the narrow path through the living room back outside. I saw them through the front window squat in the rough weeds in the patch of ground that constituted a front yard. I wished that I could join them. Instead, I grabbed two hotdogs and a bottle of Pepsi.

Out back, Missy and Tim leaned against the picnic table; Missy gripped the table's edge and scuffed at the dirt in front of her with a worn sneaker. Tim held his arms across his chest, his legs crossed in front of him. They stopped talking when they saw me. I handed off the Pepsi and hotdogs and made a beeline for the kitchen before they could give me any more orders.

Later, when the sun had finally gone down and the heat had subsided a bit, we returned to the house to find Annie and Joey watching TV alone in the living room. In the back bedroom we could hear adult voices. Sometimes laughter pierced the closed door and once or twice we heard the clink of beer bottles. Tim's sleepy eyes slid over toward the door, narrowing even more and he smiled a little.

"C'mon!" He went into the kitchen where dinner's remains lay on the table. "Now that fuckin' bitch's busy gettin' stoned, we're gonna have our own party."

He reached into his pocket and pulled out a small sandwich bag with something that looked like Italian seasoning. For all of Frank's buying trips, I hadn't seen marijuana before, but I knew what it was. Tim pulled out a small booklet of papers and some matches. While Missy and I watched, he pinched some of the weed between his thumb and fingers and sprinkled it along the edge of the paper. After rolling the paper around the weed, he licked and sealed the lumpy joint. He lit and inhaled before offering Missy a hit. After a long moment, its peculiar odor billowed out of their noses as they gasped for breath. Missy giggled.

"Good shit," Tim said. "Here—take a toke, Weeble."

"I don't wanna."

"Take a toke, Weeble."

"No." It smelled horrible.

Tim took another drag on the joint; smoke from its burning end curled around his face and fingered at the long strands of hair over his eyes. He opened his mouth a little and hot white vapor escaped on the stream of his breath.

"I said, take a toke, Weeble. And that's what I meant." His eyes cut through the smoke.

"Just do it, Weeble." Missy looked at me. I couldn't tell if her eyes warned or sympathized.

He passed me the joint and I stuck it between my lips.

"Suck, moron. Like through a straw."

When I inhaled, the hot smoke stung the roof of my mouth and I coughed. Tim hadn't noticed; instead, he was picking bits of chips off the table and eating them. I passed the joint to Missy and wiped water from the corner of my eye.

"Let's go over to Spring Garden and have some fun," Tim said, little flakes of dried potato clinging to the corners of his mouth. Spring Garden was the middle school near our house.

"What're you thinkin' about?" Missy asked.

"Shh, dipshit! Nothin' much. I just wanna look around. Weeble, go see if Mona's out there."

I went into the dark room; the harsh light from the TV illuminated only a couple of feet in front of it. Annie and Joey leaned together like weary travelers before a campfire, eyes unblinking before the wonder of *Dallas*. I paused long enough to watch Bobby Ewing taking on his nasty brother, J. R.

I returned to the kitchen where Tim and Missy, having finished the joint, stood eating baked beans with wooden spoons from the pot on the stove. When they saw me, they giggled around a mouthful; Missy spewed some beans across the kitchen and Tim slapped her on the back, laughing even louder. He wiped his mouth with the back of his hand and set the spoon back in the pot. I shook my head at the question on his face.

"Aw right then, let's go."

The three of us walked out the front, avoiding beer-bottle bombs and ashtray landmines on the way. Missy placed the screen door against its frame without a squeak and we walked down the gravel drive without a word. Along the western horizon, colors of cherry and orange Kool-Aid drained away into the dark treetops and the sky darkened. Overhead, stars pricked the deepening blue like tiny sequins.

We walked down the dark street toward Spring Garden, Tim and Missy singing and joking now that they'd left our yard. Open windows let out a stream of neighbors' conversations and the canned speech of TV shows. One street over a dog barked and we heard children's voices and the sounds of bicycle tires on pavement. As we neared the end of the street, we saw a dark figure on a porch smoking, only the hellish tip of the cigarette clearly visible.

"Goddamn kids! Stay the hell away from my property!" a hoarse voice said. I couldn't tell if it was a man or a woman.

"We ain't on your property," Missy said.

"Just stay the hell away." As we started walking, the voice went on even louder. "Goddamn kids, don't respect nothin'. I'm gonna tie tin cans to your asses and light fire crackers in them. We'll see how fast you run then."

"Crazy old coot," Missy said just loud enough for Tim and me to hear.

We crossed into the field at the end of the street; about two hundred yards away, the middle school's dark bulk squatted. My heart thudded and sweat prickled my palms. What did Tim want to do here? I followed them. They'd grown quiet once we entered the field. Without the lights from the neighboring houses, the darkness became thick around us. Halfway to the building, Tim stopped. Missy and I halted near him.

"Let's vandalize it," he said. He didn't whisper.

"What's vand'lize?" My voice trembled a little.

"Let them know we were here," Missy said. She looked at Tim. "You ain't got the balls to do it."

37

He bent over and started feeling around on the ground. He stood up and then I heard a crack from the school's wall. I just stood there, but Missy started flinging objects at the school too. I watched as they tried to find ways to pummel the indifferent cinderblock of the school. While they grunted and snarled curses, I wished that I'd stayed home and watched *Dallas*. At last, Tim, panting, hunched over with his hands on his thighs.

"Goddammit! Next time we're comin' with spray paint."

"No shit," Missy said.

We headed back home while Tim muttered about teachers who were bitches and boring homework and how school was a "fuckin' prison." We passed the house with the crazy person, but no dark form or demonic red-tipped cigarette accosted us. As we got closer to home, we spotted my Aunt Susie's black Ford in the street and heard her talking out front to Mona, who held a Miller in one hand and a lit cigarette in the other. When Mona saw us, she stopped talking.

"Where the hell have y'all been?" she asked.

"Just out for a walk," Tim said. "Why?"

"I'ma gonna slap you upside your head, that's why. I told you once, I told you a thousand times: you need to say somethin' before you go traipsin' off, especially in the dark. Susie's been here twenty minutes worried about Missy."

"It's okay, Mona. What kinda trouble could the three of 'em get into 'round here?" After Aunt Susie said this, I looked at the other two, whose faces stayed blank.

Mona still looked ready to bite the head off a squirrel, chew it, and spit it in Tim's face. "You ain't s'pposed to be out anyway. Susie, I caught these big 'uns with some smokes earlier. Missy here gave me some lip, but I left it for you to deal with."

Aunt Susie's eyes glistened in the dim light from the house. "That right, girl? Don't lie to me. You know I can't stand your lies."

Missy's shoulders hunched and her head tilted down. "It's Timmy's fault. He brought 'em out. I didn't wanna, but he threatened me. Then he made us go up to Spring Garden and throw rocks at the school."

"Well, goddamn!" Mona's hand snaked out and almost decapitated Tim. "Get the fuck inside."

Tim slouched away to the house. He let the screen door slam shut behind him.

"I'd lay money your arm wasn't twisted too hard," Aunt Susie said to Missy. "I'll deal with you later. Get yourself into the house. I gotta talk to Mona."

It was Missy's turn to slam the screen door. We heard Frank curse all the way from the street.

"Weeble, you ain't big enough to tag behind those two," Mona said. "Go inside and get a Popsicle with Annie and Joey."

When I got inside, Annie and Joey sat on the living-room floor sucking on Popsicles and watching TV. Frank reclined in his chair, a beatific smile on his face, Miller in his lap. Missy sulked on the sofa. Tim was nowhere to be seen.

I went to the freezer and took the last lime Popsicle. I sat eating it on the floor next to my cousins and watching TV.

That was the last innocent act of my childhood.

Tim came out of the bathroom. His face was blotchy and fingerprints reddened his cheek. He stopped and stared at Missy.

"You stupid cunt."

She glared at him. "Watch your fuckin' tongue. You wouldn't know what a cunt was if you saw one."

"I can smell yours all the way over here."

Missy sat upright. "Well, that's all you're gonna do. Tattoos and joints don't make up for a limp toothpick for a dick. You couldn't find a naked woman's hole if she stood in front of you."

I turned to look at them. Frank also looked up.

"You two had better shut the fuck up or I'm gonna end this conversation with my boot on your asses. Tim, you just sit the fuck down."

Neither Tim nor Missy spoke again, and I forgot the look on Tim's face until later, in the middle of the night. Aunt Susie took Missy and Joey home after Annie and I had fallen asleep, Annie on the sofa and me curled up on the floor. Frank carried Annie off to our bedroom, but I had to stumble to bed on my own. I crawled into bed without changing clothes or going to the bathroom. When Tim came in later, I didn't wake up right away.

The sour smell of beer and the heat of his breath woke me—that and the weight of what I thought were too many blankets. I started to struggle out of them and to whimper, when fingers tasting of dirt and cigarettes clamped over my mouth.

"Shhh. Don't wake Annie."

I stopped moving, confused. Rough fingers gripped me. Tugged at my shorts. I began to squirm again. Tim put his forearm on my throat and leaned on me until I stopped moving. Dizziness made the room spin and tears trickled out of the corner of my eye.

"Gonna stay still now?" His whisper hissed in my ear.

I nodded. I had no idea what he was doing, but my heart beat like a caged bird.

He slipped his thumb under the waistband of my shorts and yanked them down around my knees. I felt him moving above me, rolling awkwardly from side to side, but I had no idea what he was doing until I felt the hot, hairy flesh of his upper thighs on mine and something hard and moist on the tender place between my legs. His lower half moved and the hard bit of him pushed against me. I was as stiff as a board and shaking.

Nothing happened for what felt like forever. Tim's breath bathed my forehead and he grunted a bit, but I could feel the

40

hardness turning soft until it was only an odd lump against my bottom.

"Goddamn it. What the fuck." Tim pushed himself up onto his forearms.

My bladder ached, but I didn't move. The heat from Tim's body radiated, smothering me.

"I know. Sit up." He moved off of me.

I pushed myself into a sitting position. Annie rustled and muttered in her sleep. Tim's hand covered my mouth again. I felt his lips against my ear.

"If she wakes up, don't say nothin'." His other hand pinched my side and twisted, hard, but my cry of pain died behind his palm. "Now get off the bed and suck me."

I slid off the bed so confused and frightened that tears blinded me. I stood next to him until he put his hand on my shoulder and forced me to my knees. When I still didn't move, Tim punched the side of my face. While stars spun around my vision, he grabbed the back of my head and pulled my face down.

What happened next was like every other night that Tim snuck into my room, although perhaps more terrifying and surreal. I remember most of the other nights, but they're alike in their mundane similarity. I was no longer so stupid and scared, no longer needed a punch or a suffocating hand. If I try to recall the details from that episode, my mind draws a blank. No matter how hard I try to dredge up the first time, I can't. At least not until I recall the hot urine running down the inside of my thighs. Tim didn't notice until it pooled on the floor around his feet.

"What the—" In his surprise, he forgot to whisper.

Annie startled and woke. "Whosit?" She started sobbing.

"Christ." Tim shoved me away from him and stood up. He moved around for a few seconds and I realized he'd pulled his shorts up. "Not a word, got it?"

He was at the door when Mona got there.

"What's goin' on?" Her voice, always raspy, sounded even rougher with sleep. "What the hell are you doin'?"

"I heard Annie crying," Tim said. "Just wanted to see if she's okay."

Mona moved past him and came toward Annie, who sat up.

"What's up, baby?" She sat on Annie's bed, blocking the moonlight from the window.

"Monster, monster."

"No, no. There's no monster. It was only a nightmare."

Yes, I thought as I knelt on the floor in the cooling urine. *A nightmare.*

Mona smelled it. "Weeble? Is that you on the floor? Sweet Jesus, what are you doin' there? Turn on the light, Tim."

The overhead light popped on, dazzling me.

"Oh, Weeble! Where's your underwear? Why're you on the floor?"

"Looks like she pissed herself."

I looked at Tim, who grinned a Halloween grin.

"Don't just stand there, moron. Get a towel and clean her up. Annie, Annie, it's all right. Weeble just had an accident, that's all. Shush now, go back to sleep."

Mona snuggled Annie against her chest, where I would have given anything to be right then. Instead, Tim brought a towel and scrubbed my bottom until it burned. Then he tossed the towel at me.

"Clean up the mess, Weeble. I'm too tired."

He shot Mona a look, but she hadn't heard him. Annie had settled onto her shoulder and, although dry sobs still wracked her, she no longer cried. Tim grinned again and left the room. I bent over and blotted at the cold urine until the towel was soaked. Then I dropped the wet towel in the hall, pulled my shorts back on and slid under my sheets. I almost remember Mona's kiss before she turned out the light.

42

For the next two years, I wet the bed several times a month, with or without a visit from Tim. That's when the first nightmares started, nightmares of evil grinning monsters. I never screamed, however, or made any noise to rouse Mona or even Annie, across the bedroom from me. In the first months, Mona came in to find me sleeping next to Annie, pressed up next to her sturdy body and my wet underwear on the floor. She'd pull me out from under the covers and lead me to the bathroom to shower while Annie slept on.

The fourth time she found me in Annie's bed, she quizzed me while the water heated up.

"Weeble, don't you go to the bathroom before bed?"

I nodded.

"No more pop after dinner."

"Okay."

But Mona didn't yell at me when I still wet the bed even though I had nothing to drink with dinner. One time, I came home from school to hear her talking to Aunt Susie on the phone.

"She never wet the bed, Susie, never. Not even when she was two and we ran out of diapers and she went all night without one."

I stopped in the living room and waited to hear more.

"Yeah, I think that little shit has somethin' to do with it. He's the creepiest little prick, but I never see him even look at her." Pause. "No, he hasn't touched any of her toys in a long time, not that she's said. I don't know." Pause. "Yeah, maybe I'll ask her."

That's when I started waking up in the morning before Mona could find me. I washed off with a washcloth, and then rinsed out my underwear and shorts and hid them under my bed until they'd dried enough to put in the laundry. I waited for Mona to ask me. I planned what I'd say about stealing Pepsi when she wasn't paying attention. But my deceit paid off because she never did ask if Tim had anything to do with my nightmares.

I wish I'd told her. I wish I hadn't hidden anything from her. If I'd gone to her, perhaps what happened later wouldn't have. But I feared Tim's punch, his suffocating hand. What would she do to him? Yell? Smack him upside the head? Ground him? What could she do to him that would keep him out of my room at night? These are really pointless questions, the kinds of questions that adults ask. An eight-year-old child knows better. She knows that you don't question. You just keep your head down and survive.

Three

MARCIE HAS A BUILT-IN RESCUE TIMER. Why she bothers trying to rescue me is both perfectly clear and downright maddening. She collects damaged people like some guys collect baseball cards or women collect stuffed animals. I don't want to be rescued. I'm a waste of time. That doesn't stop me from feeling relief when she calls during my research. I barely get the receiver to my ear before she grills me.

"When was the last time you got out of that apartment?" Her fast accent no longer daunts me. Hasn't daunted me in years, but I still notice it. It's not my accent. I'm the stranger here in a strange land.

"This morning as a matter of fact." I swivel away from my monitor so I won't stare at the black-and-white crime scene photos. So I can concentrate on the living person on the other end of the line.

"I don't mean running through the streets of Cambridge. I mean talking to real people, looking them in the eyes. You know, having a conversation."

"Isn't that what we're doing now?" Even as I ask this, the intense dark eyes I'd been seeing in my memory for days reappear in my thoughts. I'd looked him in the eyes and now it haunts me.

Marcie sighs. "Jana's right. You're impossible. What're we going to do about you?"

"Nothing?" I ask. I know better.

She continues as if I haven't spoken. "You gotta get out of there. Come see us this weekend. Evan's got a paper to work on, so we'll have lots of time to catch up."

"I don't, Marce. I really need to stay focused." I crane my neck so I can look back at the screen and shudder. "I've narrowed the first biography down to a couple of choices. I've got to start phoning people. Traveling maybe."

"All the more reason to see us this weekend first. Take this in chunks. You can't plow through stories of the dead without spending time with the living. It's not healthy."

I'm quiet. She rightly takes that as my acquiescence.

"Evan'll be there at two to get you and your furry friends. I'm giving him orders to pack your bag if need be."

"I've been forewarned," I laugh. It's impossible to stay sour around Marcie. "If you're making me come out, I'm making dinner."

"Italian?" I hear the eagerness in her voice and laugh again.

"Certainly. You make the espresso?"

"Deal."

I abandon all hope of working for the next thirty-six hours and head into the bedroom to pack so Evan won't have to. For such a short, sweetly plump woman, Marcie would make an autocrat proud. Velvet over a steel chassis, that's what Evan always says, usually to her face. She just grins and issues more orders. In my bedroom, I avoid looking at myself in the mirror. I don't really want to see what Marcie's going to see in a few hours. No point in going over my haggard appearance more than once today, especially when she'll do such a stellar job for me. I

46

glance out the window. Sunny, but I know there's still a chill in the air. I'd seen my breath as I ran this morning. Better put on a fleece before I head to the Bread of Life Co-op to pick up groceries for dinner.

I brush my hair, twist a band around it, and consider whether I should grab a cap. It's not that I care what people think when they see me. It's whether I'd draw any stares with or without a cap. If I could be invisible, I would in a heartbeat. That decides me. I pull a BU cap from the rack on the back of my closet door and skewer it to the top of my head.

I return to the living room and see Hero on the loveseat. He doesn't raise his head, but his tail thumps hopefully anyway.

"Sorry, ol' boy. I gotta go out." I step closer and ruffle his ragged ear. Every time I touch it, my breath catches. I'd seen the pictures from the rescue group. I'd seen the scars hidden in his long white fur. I know how close Hero came to dying after the Rottweiler ravaged him. His trusting brown eyes hold mine, and then look away. "I'll be back in an hour with a treat."

Flat Stanley watches me leave from his perch on the kitchen counter. I hate leaving them alone, but I know that it's only *me* who fears I might abandon them. Their love for me almost makes me angry sometimes.

When I get to the Bread of Life Co-op, I slow down to consider the incongruity of a market in the heart of Cambridge surrounded by storefronts and redbrick sidewalks. Back home, farmers sold fresh corn and tomatoes, peaches and blueberries from the back of rusty pickup trucks in sun-scorched parking lots. Grocery stores dominated strip malls, and if they had produce, I can't quite convince myself I ever saw it. This market, the size of an antique store or dance studio, reminds me of my alien nature every time I cross its threshold, as if I've gone down the rabbit hole or through a looking glass. Even so, I expect to feel better, more hopeful. As I enter, I blink in the fluorescent light, breathing in the tangy scent of apples, greens, and dusty floor which envelopes me.

Every time I shop here for ingredients, I imagine Lauren prowling the aisles with me. Lauren wouldn't feel out of place in Cambridge, in a community-owned market where dried beans and spices wait in plexiglass bins, scoops dangling. She'd recognize the resemblance to the general store in *Little House on the Prairie*—our literary antecedent—and laugh at me.

"It's just food," she'd say. "We eat the same things. We're not from another planet, Weeble."

With her imagined laughter in my ear, I cruise the produce section for tomatoes, fresh basil, and Portobello mushrooms before going in search of buffalo mozzarella and Arborio rice.

I'm studying the tomatoes when he speaks to me, right at my side. I hadn't heard him approach. My heart stutters and then races.

"Those just came in today. Not as ripe as these." He points to a display of Roma tomatoes. "Not as good as the Zebras and Brandywines we'll get later in the summer, though."

Zebras and Brandywines. What are they? He's just spoken to me in a foreign language, but I don't acknowledge that. Instead, I keep my face angled down, hidden under my hat. "Those don't taste as good in *insalata caprese*." My voice comes out almost as a whisper. Did I pronounce the words right? Do I sound like the parvenu that I am?

"Ah. Try these, then." He reaches for a cluster of tomatoes still attached to a vine. "We don't have many. Is this enough?"

I nod and start to reach for them. My fingers brush his, sending a jolt through me. Without meaning to, I look up. "Thanks." His eyes recognize me. The polarity of his gaze attracts mine and I'm unable to look away. Apropos of nothing, I realize that his irises have flecks of light adding depth to them. I feel I am drowning and flying all at the same time.

48

"Hey," he says and smiles the half-smile that's tormented me for days. "It's you."

"Yes," I say as if his statement made sense. As if my answer did too.

"I've been looking for you." He laughs. It sounds wry. For half a heartbeat, I believe he meant that he'd been looking for me all his life. "I wanted to catch you and apologize for scaring you. You looked like you thought I was going to hurt you."

I flinch at his words and my mouth goes dry. "No," I say but it comes out in a harsh bark. I swallow, trying to moisten my tongue before I speak again to deny his suspicion. "No, no. You just surprised me is all." I wish I could laugh at myself, but I can't. I tear my gaze away toward the herbs and think *basil. I need basil.*

I step toward the display and he follows me. He smells like the market: piquant greens and tart fruit, edged with a little dust. Like some mysterious generative force had crafted him from elements of each, he exudes an energy that is entirely greater than their sum.

He speaks again while I study bunches of herbs before me. How can I distinguish among their tiny leaves? None of the signage makes sense to me right now.

"Dumpster diving *is* rather odd. My mother shudders every time I tell her about the items I've found. My sister Zandra snorts and rolls her eyes. She thinks I'm rather mental and *she's* known me all my life."

Why is he telling me this? "That's not a good thing. You know that, don't you?" I ask against my better judgment. I should be scuttling away from him, not engaging him.

He laughs. It's such a pleasant sound, a sound that I want to hear again. "Just getting it out there."

"It's okay," I assure him. "You don't owe me anything. I've forgotten it already." That was a lie, but I don't owe *him* the truth.

49

He waits while I pluck a bunch of basil and stick it into my basket. Not wanting to be rude, to brush past him to seek tranquility in an empty aisle of handcrafted cheese and imported wine, I turn to look at him. He's watching my face.

"I'm a Freegan." For the first time, I notice his dark-brown hair, which is curly and a little too long like the hair on an ancient Greek sculpture or that painting by Da Vinci, *St. John the Baptist*. The one with the disturbing Mona Lisa smile. This *Freegan* , whatever that is, is the oddest-looking guy I've seen since my days on BU's campus.

"Freegan?" I'm too confused to even understand the word I'm repeating back to him. I move toward the mushrooms, grabbing a handful of the closest.

He laughs. "It's a bit hard to explain, but I don't mind rescuing worthwhile items other people throw away."

"Like the wok?" I realize at that moment that I'm having a conversation, awkward and confused as it is. Marcie would be so proud, but I don't know his name. "Excuse me," I say before he can answer my question. "It's a little weird talking to you. I don't know you." I start to walk around him. Maybe he'll leave me alone now. Go back to work.

He doesn't. Instead, he falls into step at my side. "I'm Tom Paul." He says nothing else and I wonder if he's waiting for me to share my name. That feels too risky. My breath flutters, but I keep it quiet, deep in my chest. I've learned never to let anyone else hear my fear. He doesn't seem to notice and stays at my side as I pace down the bulk aisle in search of Arborio rice. In my bemused state, I can't decide if it's dangerous that he doesn't sense my fear. Can't decide if I should feel more fear because he's still at my side.

"So, you must live around here." It isn't a question. Icy heat burns through the center of my chest. *Will he find me*? And then another question follows so rapidly on the heels of the first that I'm stunned when I understand it. *Do I want him to*?

I lurch to a stop in front of the rice bin and grip the scoop in my hand so tightly I know there will be marks later. "Yes."

"Good. I'll see you around then." Is that a threat? A treacherous promise? Why can't I tell? "I only work here on the weekends, though. I spend most of my time in my studio."

That makes me look at him again. The afternoon sun streaming in the Co-op's window turns the gold flecks in his eyes opaque and mysterious. Inhuman as a mythical Greek god. I suppress a shudder.

"Studio? Are you a photographer?" It's the first thing that comes to mind, but I know before I ask that it's wrong.

He smiles and the image of him as aloof divinity wavers and dissolves. He's just another twenty-something wearing baggy chinos and a white t-shirt smeared with green plant juice.

"No, though I *am* fascinated with manipulating light. I'm a glass artist." He says this as though it should be clear what that means.

I frown. I remember a sidewalk kiosk at an arts festival with hand-blown glass chimes. I think of glass paperweights and glass figurines in mall jewelry stores. "What kind of art do you make?" My voice sounds a little breathless to me.

I frown again. I need to escape, to put some distance between this stranger and me. I edge half a foot back, calculating the distance to the end of the aisle out of the corner of my eye.

"Come and see." He hands me a postcard, which I accept against my instincts. On its black background, a luminous male torso hangs suspended. "My first gallery opening in six weeks. There'll be food."

"Um," I say. I can't say yes, but I don't want to say no. "I'll have to see how my schedule shapes up."

He smiles and shrugs. "No pressure. I'm sure I'll see you again before then."

I duck my head in what I hope comes across as an uncertain nod and swivel around to my right, hurrying away. I chant *cheese, wine, chicken* to keep myself focused. To keep from flying off into a mist of panic. When I finally emerge from my surreal shopping trip into the filtered sunshine of a city block, the air redolent with the scent of car exhaust and heated brick, I almost glimpse the edge of the looking glass I've just tumbled back through.

* * *

Lauren and I became friends one morning on the playground, during the fall of fifth grade. I'd had her in class once or twice before, so I knew her name, but we'd never even managed to stand in the bathroom line together. I don't even remember what she looked like before that fall, but everyone noticed her as soon as she walked in on the first day of school.

Like me, Lauren towered over the shortest boys in the class. Unlike me, she'd developed a woman's figure over the course of the summer. In her thin blouse, the visible white straps of her bra intrigued and tormented most of the class. From my seat in the back, I heard Karen Morgan tell Lauren not to think she was something special for looking like Dolly Parton. Lauren never looked at her, but I saw the way her shoulders hunched and her long hair slid forward to hide her face. She sat that way all morning. I could tell from the whispers around me that the boys too speculated about Lauren's miraculous transformation. She was going to get it from all sides. I found myself trailing behind her as we filed out to recess.

A few boys ran for the jungle gym and the kickball field, but many huddled together near the swings. Lauren wandered past them, alone. Two girls, Lisa and Debbie, stopped at the swings and looked her way, but they didn't join her. I must've had other friends from previous years in this new class, but that day, I too

52

was alone. I continued walking, hanging behind her. I had some sense, even then, about predators. But then, I'd spent all summer with Tim.

Lauren had just reached the one tree allowed to border the vast expanse of asphalt that we played on when one of the boys detached from the huddle and began to follow her. I hurried a little to catch whatever he had to say.

"Lauren, Lauren!" Pat called. He had a sullen, dense face. Sloppy, his hair needed a cut and his shoes needed tying.

She slowed and looked at him. Wrong reaction.

"Hey, Lauren." His voice badgered her. "Do you stuff? Is that Charmin in there?" He shot a glance over his shoulder to the waiting group of boys. They jeered and clapped.

Lauren's head jerked as if she'd been slapped and her shoulders hunched so fiercely that the back of her thin shirt pulled away from the telltale bra strap. She shuffled away from Pat, who continued to follow her into the open part of the field where no equipment or playing children could shield her from his nasty taunts. I picked up my pace, determined to put myself between them before he had time to twist his words into a clumsy variant.

"Leave her alone, dipweed!" I made my voice as mean as I could. Being taller than Pat helped my confidence. His eyes opened wide, taking in my bunched fists. "Go on, scram!"

Muttering, he turned and fled to the boys, who'd watched this confrontation silently. I waited until he'd joined their ranks before turning to face Lauren. She'd halted next to the tree, but her shoulders remained hunched and her face hidden in her dark-blond hair. I moved closer so that I could lower my voice and shield her from the other kids. I thought she might be crying.

"He's an idiot."

"I know that," she said without looking at me. Her voice sounded strangled, but I decided that she wasn't crying after all.

53

"Why would I stuff? Just so everyone can make fun of me? *I'm* not an idiot, so *he* must be."

"They *all* are."

That's when she looked at me. I met her gaze and didn't look away. After several breaths, she smiled a shy smile that hardly showed her crooked teeth. Her shoulders unbent and her head returned to a normal position. She was pretty, if you didn't see her teeth.

"Thanks for sticking up for me."

I shrugged. "I got a jerkface for a stepbrother. Anytime I see someone actin' like him, somethin' comes over me."

We didn't say much more that first recess. Lauren stayed by the tree and I waited with her. I'd stolen some gum from Mona's purse before school and I gave her a piece. We chewed it, blowing thin bubbles in an ecstasy of snapping and popping, but Lauren spit hers through the chain-link fence when the bell rang. We trudged back into class side-by-side, returning to our seats without making any overt plans to continue our friendship. I watched her, though, for the rest of the day. There was something different about her beyond her startling and ludicrous figure. Something in her alert posture while Mr. Grace questioned the class, in her confident hand when no one else knew the answer, in the way she patiently explained math to Jeannie, who'd already been held back a year and missed school a lot for illness. Lauren, I realized, was really smart. And friendless. That's when I decided that I would be her friend.

The next day, I waited by the outside door for her at morning recess. She blinked her surprise when I fell into step next to her but didn't flinch or pick up her pace. We didn't talk until it was almost time to go back inside. Instead, she kicked at the dusty grass under the tree while I kept watch for rowdy boys. Once or twice, I caught Pat's glower, but he always looked away first.

"Wanna sit with me at lunch?" She asked this diffidently, over her shoulder.

"Sure." I hoped she didn't notice my reduced-lunch voucher.

After a few days, no one paid any attention to Lauren any more. The mornings turned cooler, scented with wood smoke and filled with the sound of drums from the high school's marching band. Frost coated Mona's windshield and crisped the golden-brown leaves cluttering the sidewalks. Lauren's figure disappeared beneath cowl-necked sweaters and blouses. Free to talk, we spent weeks discussing our favorites, from TV shows and Saturday morning cartoons to foods and toys, games and dreams. We both liked to watch *Three's Company* and *The Love Boat*, but Lauren also liked *M*A*S*H* and *Cheers*, two shows that I didn't understand and knew it. I'd rather watch *Spiderman and His Amazing Friends* or just about any superhero cartoon. Foods beyond the fare offered in the cafeteria proved harder. Mona had never found a packaged meal she didn't like—Hamburger Helper was her favorite—but Lauren's grandmother fixed farm food. Beef brisket and pot roast, chicken and dumplings, biscuits and gravy. They sounded old fashioned and impossibly satisfying.

We'd mostly given up on toys and games, Lauren because she didn't have any siblings to play with and me because Mona and Frank had little money to spend on them. What we both did, and did incessantly, was read. Lauren's grandma took her to the Carnegie Library while I had to settle for the school's library and stealing Mona's paperback romance novels, the thick mass-market editions found in every grocery store. Lauren, tired of reading *Nancy Drew* and *The Hardy Boys*, had forayed into the young adult section over the summer. Here she discovered *I, Robot* and *Alice in Wonderland*. I read *Shogun* and *The Thorn Birds*. We did have one title in common, however, that of *Flowers in the Attic*.

Lauren found the story of abuse and incest fascinating and repulsive. I just found it too close to home to enjoy.

"Can you imagine?" she asked on the playground one afternoon, the chill October air at odds with the robin's-egg-blue sky. "Being shut in an attic for years? I can't believe how evil Olivia is." She shuddered. "My grandma's nothing like her."

I shrugged. I didn't want to admit I didn't have to imagine such a horrific scenario, but I didn't like to lie. "Plenty of evil people around. What I don't get is why they stayed there so long."

"Because," Lauren said and dangled her feet down from the monkey bars, "they didn't know what evil was. Their whole life, no one had been mean to them. You'd stay if your mom stuck you in the attic."

I thought about this. Maybe I would. After all, I knew what evil was and I certainly hadn't left home yet. What would it take to get me to run? I sighed. "I guess I'd wait until she killed one of us, too."

Lauren looked at me. Her strange expression made me wonder if I'd let something out I hadn't meant to. "We're not even as old as Cathy. It would be really scary to run away. Not like *The Boxcar Children*, Weeble."

"I'm not scared." When her expression changed to disbelief, I went on, "I'm not! I could make it okay. My cousin Missy showed me how to shoplift. She's fifteen and hitchhikes all the time. She told me what to do. I could run away if I had to." The idea appealed to me. I wish I'd thought of it before.

"Good thing you don't." Lauren looked away before jumping down. "Then I'd not have any friends."

Just as quickly as the thought of running away had surged in me, it left. She'd sounded rather forlorn. I squared my shoulders and pretended I hadn't heard her tone. "We can run away together, when we're older. Save up some money first." I jumped down beside her.

Lauren's eyes shone. She touched my hand. "Really?" At my nod, she grew excited. "That's a great idea. Let's go somewhere far away!"

"Where? Like Japan? New Zealand? India?" My supermarket novels had introduced me to these places. India fascinated me the most. That's where widows burned as *suttee* on their husbands' funeral pyres. In Japan, it was the male samurai who committed *seppuku* when they lost something called "face"— whatever that was. Mr. Grace certainly didn't teach us about these practices in social studies.

"Not at first. We have to get plane tickets." I'd never seen her so animated. "That won't be too hard for us, though."

"Why?" I found myself caught up. It had been a while since I'd played pretend. This version had more potential.

"That's easy, Weeble. We'll get jobs. We'll go wherever we want."

Something like hunger filled me. Was it possible? Could I really make my own future this way? I decided to try. "We'll have our own cars. And an apartment. Together."

"Yes, yes!" She laughed now. I'd never seen her skip. She'd always been so hunched and careful as she walked through the halls or on the playground. "A big-enough apartment for each of us to have our own bedroom. We'll go shopping and do our hair."

"We'll have our own library."

Lauren rolled her eyes. "Not until we get our mansion, silly. In the apartment, we'll have bookshelves. Filled with books."

Playing *Independent Women* as we called our pretend game took on a life of its own after that day. What an exhilarating adventure, a heady concoction of hope and self-determination! With Lauren, I began to consider the future, formerly an abstract concept, as something a little more substantial and knowable. I

57

began to consider that my life didn't always have to look or feel like the one I'd always lived in.

"Come sleep over at my house," Lauren said at the end of October. "Tomorrow is Friday. Grandma always makes pork chops with applesauce. And chocolate cake. Then, for breakfast, we have eggs and bacon. It's Saturday, so we'll watch cartoons in our pajamas all morning if we want."

My throat clenched a little. I didn't know what Mona would say. I'd never been invited to sleep over before. "Um, I don't know. I'll have to ask my mom."

"I've got some pink nail polish we can use. And some lipstick. Grandma doesn't know I have it. I saved my lunch money and then asked Debbie to buy it for me. Her mom lets her wear makeup."

"Missy gave me some old eye shadow," I couldn't stop myself from offering. I *really* wanted to stay over.

"We can listen to K-Jo and practice getting made up." Lauren had a faraway look on her face. "We have to practice for when we're older." The magic words. When we were older, we'd be independent and self-sufficient. Safe. But not alone. We'd have each other.

I needn't have worried about Mona. She took one look at me, dragged on her cigarette so strongly the end blazed orange, and let the hot smoke out with a faint pop. "'Bout time, Weeble, you gotta friend. Gotta ride the bus home with her?"

"No," I said, relief and tension wavering in my voice, "her grandma picks her up. You gotta write me a note, though."

Mona waved the cigarette around her face. "Sure, sure. I'll leave it out on the table. Don't go wakin' me up if it's not there." At this reminder of her unreliability, my hopes sank a little. "Call me Saturday morning and I'll come get you. Just not before ten."

I nodded, grateful for my good fortune. "Thanks, Mom."

She smiled and waved me away. I took the cue and ran to pack a paper bag with a change of clothes and something to sleep in. On impulse, I tucked in my favorite paperback, *The Far Pavilions*, and my Magic 8 Ball.

Although afraid it wouldn't be there, I found Mona's scrawled note on the table in the morning but not my milk money. Tim had stolen it again.

Neither Lauren nor I could concentrate all morning. I managed to sneak the Magic 8 Ball out for recess so that we could ask questions about our future. Unwrapping the toy from the edge of my sweater where I'd hidden it, I showed Lauren what I had with a grin and then headed for the far side of the tree.

"Let's ask about the future," I said and squatted down.

Lauren looked excited. "I want one of those." She touched the black plastic ball with a fingertip. "Grandma won't let me. She says it puts silly ideas in your head. But I've got something better, something she doesn't know I have."

I'd started to shake the ball. The white die rose sluggishly through the murky purple liquid to clack against the clear plastic window. "What's better than the Magic 8 Ball?" Belligerence fought curiosity in my voice. I'd pleaded for weeks to get this toy.

"A Ouija board." She delivered this statement in a tone of mystery and high drama.

I looked at her and frowned. "What's that?" It sounded much more exotic than 'Magic 8 Ball.'

"It's a message board for communicating with spirits." Her eyes must have been as wide as mine felt. "I found one at a garage sale. Grandma refused to buy it. She said it's a tool of the devil, but I went back later and the woman gave it to me because no one had bought it."

"My mom won't let me have one either," said Debbie. While we'd been talking, she and Lisa had joined us. I pulled my sweater over the Magic 8 Ball. I could feel my frown tighten into a glare. Who'd asked them to spy on us? "My cousin Angie has one, though. My aunt says it's just a game."

But Lauren didn't seem to mind. "Have you used it?" Her voice was slightly breathless.

"Yeah. It was pretty cool. I asked if I was getting a tape player for my birthday and it said yes. Then I got one."

"Awesome." Lauren quivered. "Weeble, let's ask the Magic 8 Ball if we should use the Ouija board tonight."

I scowled, my gaze darting from Lisa to Debbie and back to Lauren, who waited. I wanted to stomp off in a huff, but something made me shrug and give in. Maybe it wouldn't be so bad to include Debbie and Lisa in our game. "Okay." I extricated the ball and closed my eyes while asking, "Should we use the Ouija board?"

Yes. Definitely.

Lauren squealed and clapped her hands. "That's settled then. Ask it if the Ouija board communicates with spirits."

Without a doubt came the answer.

Lauren put cold fingertips on the wrist of my hand that held the Magic 8 Ball. Her gaze traveled around our little circle. "Ask," she whispered, "if they're demons."

My heart stuttered and began to race.

You may rely on it.

A collective shiver ran down our backs. For a moment, no one spoke. Then I felt defiant. I wanted to test the predictive ability of this toy. If it said yes to both questions, then I'd toss it over the fence.

"Are they angels?" I turned the Magic 8 Ball over once and then back.

Most likely.

"What's that supposed to mean?" Lisa asked. "Are they demons or are they angels?"

Lauren looked thoughtful. Before I could offer the opinion that the ball couldn't be trusted, she said, "Angels and demons are the same. I mean, Satan is a fallen angel, right?" I didn't know this, but Lisa and Debbie nodded. I decided to consider Lauren's argument before throwing away my beloved toy. "Maybe the spirits are both. Maybe you can't know if you've summoned an angel or a demon."

Lisa and Debbie looked scared, but I knew which question to ask.

"Will we get an angel tonight?"

Cannot predict now.

Lauren and I stared at each other. Before either of us could think of a follow-up question, the bell rang. After that, the excitement of my first sleepover paled against the rather delicious dread conjured up by the risk we'd talk to an evil spirit that night, never mind the risk we'd get caught by Lauren's grandmother. I went back to the classroom sure that nothing would distract me from that bone-chilling eventuality, sure that the afternoon would drag by.

It didn't. Instead, I forgot about the Ouija board in the midst of converting fractions to decimals and percents. We learned about political geography and had a spelling test. Before I could find myself watching the clock, the principal had come over the PA system to make the afternoon announcement and then the first bus riders lined up. Lauren waited while I grabbed my paper bag from under my desk and then we scurried down to the east doors and out to the street where parents sat in parked cars.

Lauren's grandmother drove a dull-red Buick, which she'd parked near the steps. When Lauren and I got into the backseat, she swiveled halfway and smiled at me, the skin around her friendly brown eyes curling up until they were lost in its folds. Although her plump cheeks sagged gently, her chocolate-brown hair didn't have any gray. She just didn't look like my idea of a grandmother, gray-haired and shrunken-sour. A cigarette smoldered in her right fingers against the steering wheel, which she had to sit on a cushion to see over.

"You must be Weeble. Lauren told me all about you. Except why you're called Weeble."

I mumbled something and looked away. No adult had ever looked at me before with such friendly interest. As if I was a person whose thoughts mattered and not an entity somewhat more intelligent than a dog but not worth paying attention to. Whatever I said must have been adequate because she nodded once, looked back over her left shoulder and eased the Buick away from the curb.

"You can call me Grandma Nan," she said. I caught Lauren's gaze and she smiled.

Grandma Nan had baked oatmeal raisin cookies and brownies for us. They didn't taste like the prepared dough that Mona got from the store. They were much, much better. She let us grab one of each to have with a glass of milk and then shooed us off to Lauren's room so she could watch another soap opera before making dinner.

Once in her room, Lauren shut the door, turned on the local radio station, and pulled out the nail polish. I sat down on the end of her double bed, mute at the delicate pink furnishings and white furniture. The frilly curtains framed the last of the golden October afternoon and for one disconcerting moment, I felt as though I'd entered the private chamber of a fairy-tale princess. Magic dusted the air. I could almost smell it. It smelled like Love's Baby Soft, ripe apples, and crisp fallen leaves.

"I'll paint your nails and you paint mine," Lauren said, oblivious to my bemused wonder. "We'll have to wait to put on the lipstick and eye shadow. I don't want Grandma to catch us. She'll blow up."

I shook my head, trying to clear it. I couldn't imagine such a sweet, mild-mannered woman whom I could look in the eye getting as angry as six-foot Mona. "She doesn't seem like she can get too mad." I sounded a little dazed still.

Lauren bent over to study the nails of my left hand. "She can, trust me."

While Lauren clipped and filed my nails, I read to her from *The Far Pavilions*, switching hands as necessary. I'd fallen again under the spell of the story so completely that I didn't realize that Lauren sat listening, only three nails painted, until I'd finished the first chapter.

"Where does that story take place?"

"India."

"What kind of story is it? Adventure? Science fiction?"

I frowned. "It's a love story, mainly. Between Ash and Juli. But it takes place a long time ago, like more than a hundred years ago."

"Can I read it?"

"Yeah, I brought it to loan to you."

"Good. Keep reading while I finish." She grinned at me. "Don't worry about painting my nails."

I'd read through only four pages of the second chapter when Grandma Nan interrupted us with a knock. Lauren grabbed the paperback from me, shoved it behind a pillow on her bed, and skipped to open the door before I could react. From the open door drifted the smells of pork chops and apples with cinnamon. My stomach growled. Grandma Nan stood there holding a cup of coffee. She laughed and put her hand on my shoulder.

"Hungry, Weeble? Good thing dinner's on the table. You two go wash your hands first."

We ate at a table on one side of the large, white kitchen that was wallpapered with blue-and-white stripes and roosters. Grandma Nan served us pork chops from the skillet, but the mashed potatoes and green beans sat steaming in bowls on the table along with cooked apples swimming in cinnamon and butter. I'd never seen a table laid out with empty plates and silverware let alone napkins and tall glasses of milk. Mona expected us to serve ourselves from the stove and pour our own Kool-aid from the plastic pitcher in the fridge. I hesitated until Grandma Nan waved me to the seat closest to the wall and handed me my plate.

I started to cut my pork chop as Lauren sat down, but Grandma Nan stopped me.

"We say grace here, Weeble."

Confused, I looked at Lauren, who'd reached for her napkin and unfolded it into her lap. She shrugged and left her silverware beside her plate. I set my knife and fork down on the edge of mine and mimicked her by laying my napkin in my lap. The fleeting sensation of being in a foreign place unsettled me again.

Grandma Nan sat down, picked up and arranged her napkin, and then took Lauren's extended hand. Lauren reached for my right hand where it lay limp in my lap.

"Dear Lord, we come to you tonight to give thanks for what we are about to receive into our bodies," Grandma Nan said. Her soft voice sounded odd to me. I had no way to recognize reverence then. "Thank you, Lord, too for the gift of Weeble's friendship. May we share Your Light with her. In Jesus' name, Amen."

"Amen," Lauren echoed.

I mumbled "amen" half a second later, but neither of them seemed to notice.

After dinner—which tasted so good I ate seconds of everything—Lauren got up and cleared the table. I helped her, conscious that for the first time I hadn't run away from the kitchen as soon as I'd swallowed the last bite. Grandma Nan filled the sink with water and washed the dishes while Lauren dried. I stood, shifting from foot to foot, feeling as though I should help but not sure how even to offer. They worked quickly, Grandma Nan asking me questions about school and my family. My lips grew stiff, trying to prevent me from answering and betraying my shameful origins, but I managed to tell her that Mona worked in the office of the local Harley dealership while Frank repaired motorcycles there.

"Hmm," she said. I recognized the expected disapproval.

Afterwards, we sat in the living room with her and watched TV, but when *Dallas* came on, she told us to go to bed. This surprised me, but I wasn't about to protest. Lauren pulled me eagerly into her room and shut the door.

"We've got an hour 'til she goes to bed. Let's get out the Ouija board." She scampered to her closet and began moving items on its floor. "Turn out the light. I've got a flashlight."

All the dread and excitement from earlier returned to clench my gut as I switched off the overhead light and waited for my eyes to adjust. As I sat down on the end of her bed, I heard a click. In the dark room, the bright circle of light shining from her flashlight increased the eerie tension already enveloping me. The circle danced across the air and hovered while the bed shifted as she climbed onto its head. I saw a shadowy figure with the faint outlines of a face looming above the glow.

"Here," she whispered. I felt something move on the bed between us. Lauren aimed the light onto the wooden Ouija board that now lay there. Its antique black alphabet and simple graphics stirred strange emotions in me. Without understanding why, I knew that this board held great power for prophecy. And danger.

"We put our fingers on this *planchette*." Lauren continued to whisper. She placed a triangular piece of wood onto the board and then laid two delicate fingertips on it. I copied her. "We'll warm up first by pushing it around in circles. Then we'll take turns asking questions."

"Okay." I whispered too. A frisson of mingled terror and excitement raced down my spine.

We slid the *planchette* in tentative circles around the board, swirling it over the words YES, NO, GOOD BYE before touching each of the alphabet letters followed by the numbers. As we reached the 0, Lauren spoke.

"You first."

I gulped and nodded. "Do you feel someone here with us?" My whisper hissed in the dark.

I felt, rather than saw, her shake her head. "No," she said, her voice a little louder and firm. "Just ask a question."

But already the *planchette* was moving. I watched, silent, as it spelled out I AM.

My palms began to sweat. Lauren stifled a squeal.

"Are you an angel?" I asked.

The *planchette* zipped to the word YES.

"Are you lying?" Lauren asked.

NO.

I could feel her eyes on mine in the shadows above the flashlight.

"How do we know you're not lying?" Lauren asked. She was persistent, but some shift in temperature or air pressure made me trust the presence. I just *knew* it wasn't lying.

We waited while the *planchette* spelled out YOU DONT.

"What do we do?" I directed this question to Lauren, but the presence answered.

TRUST ME.

I bit my lip. Lauren sighed.

"Okay," she said. "Let's see what you know. I'll ask something Weeble knows but I don't. She'll take her fingers off so she doesn't give the answer."

I lifted my fingers from the *planchette*.

"Why is Weeble called 'Weeble'?"

Startled, I let out a gasp. What would the presence say? Would it give away my awful secret?

BECAUSE SHE WONT FALL DOWN.

I blinked. It had only told part of the story.

Lauren expelled her breath. I heard a tinge of exasperation. "That's pretty obvious."

NOT TO HER.

Neither of us had asked a question.

It was my turn. I put my fingers back on the *planchette*. Lauren kept hers there. "Will we go to India someday?"

YOU WILL.

"Both of us?" Lauren asked.

WEEBLE ONLY.

Lauren snorted and pulled her fingers away. "Stop playing games, Weeble!" She sounded angry.

"I'm not." I could hear the shock and upset in my own voice.

DONT LET TIM NEAR ANNIE. Again, we hadn't asked a question.

"Isn't that your brother and sister?"

"Half brother," I said. Foreboding filled me.

"This is stupid," Lauren said and knocked the board off her bed. She got up and the flashlight beam wobbled around her.

I reached out to grab her arm. "Lauren, come back. Try again."

But she ignored me and turned on the overhead light. In the warm incandescence, her ordinary pink-and-white room banished the presence. When I looked at Lauren, I saw her annoyance dissolve into tears. I stood up and put my hands on her shoulders.

"It wasn't me," I said.

"Promise?" she asked. She looked fierce, but I knew she wasn't.

"Cross my heart and hope to die." I traced an X over my chest, a cold thrill pulling goose bumps up my arms and down my back. There was, I knew, no reason to utter those words. After all, the angel had said *trust me*.

Four

Just as Marcie promised, Evan disappears into the spare bedroom they use as an office once he's helped me herd Flat Stanley and Hero into their Somerville house. Hero circles the living room, sniffing to ensure that no dog has claimed his space since his last visit, while Flat Stanley accepts his usual perch on top of Marcie's crowded bookshelf. Marcie has cleared a space on her cluttered dining table for the glass of iced tea she always makes just for me. Another of my odd Midwestern habits she indulges.

"Weeble!" She comes through the door from the kitchen, her arms outstretched, and grabs my shoulders before planting a kiss on both cheeks. Even after eight years and close friendship, I still find this ritual kissing discomfiting.

I hold up the canvas bag with my food purchase. "The chicken and cheese need to go in the refrigerator. I'd love a glass of the *Chianti*, too." I've wanted some wine since I left the Bread of Life Co-op but I keep that to myself.

She accepts the bags, but I see the speculation in her eyes. I've forsworn bars and nightclubs and rarely drink these days, so perhaps she wonders why I'm so eager for a glass of wine now. "I'll join you," she says before returning to the kitchen.

I sit down at the table. It's an old maple one, its surface scarred and water stained. In the center is a sloppy stack of reading material: *Journal of Social and Clinical Psychology*, *Journal of Family Psychology*, *Journal of Contemporary Psychotherapy*, and *Psychopathology*. In front of these sits a bulging manila folder with the words "Bea's Haven" scrawled in black marker across the outside next to the words "case studies." Next to a glass half full of orange juice and an open bag of M&M's, lies a notebook missing its cover and a mug filled with an assortment of pens, pencils, and a letter opener with the Boston University logo on the handle. Next to these a glass Torah paperweight sits on a stack of invitations for her grandparents' 50th wedding anniversary.

Even though Marcie has cleared a space in this mess, I pick up tickets to a Klezmer Conservatory Band performance and a bottle of ibuprofen and move them on top of a scrapbook Marcie has been putting together for the past six months for her sister Jill.

Marcie comes back with two glasses of *Chianti* and hands me one. She watches me sip before she sits down. I can see the concern in the sharp crease between her brows and I tense.

"You've got bags under your eyes. Not sleeping well." It's a statement. Marcie shared a dorm room and an apartment with me, so she's heard the moans and shrieks. It's one reason I live alone now. "Why don't you ask Julius to prescribe you something? Better yet, tell me why you're really doing this. Don't keep it in."

I sigh and swallow more wine. Marcie and I've discussed this over and over. "Marce, do you have some hidden reason for volunteering at a women's shelter? Isn't it enough to care about remembering children who died violent, horrible deaths?" I glare at her, but the threat of sudden tears isn't dissipated through this medium. I bring out my final argument, the one I made after we'd visited the Holocaust Museum in D.C. the summer it opened. "No one's built a museum to the thousands of women and children targeted by serial killers. No one's built a memorial. It's the right thing to do. Why do I have to have another reason?"

She looks at me for a long moment. I think I see a tinge of sadness among other emotions I don't want to recognize. "You don't." Her soft voice surprises me. I look away and shift in my seat, angry and confused, and play with the stem of my glass. I sigh again.

"Her name's Leslie Ann Bishop." Now my voice is low. It trembles a little. "The one I'm going to write about first. She's British. I might have to fly to London, stay a week or so. That is, if she's got any relatives still living."

I stop, but Marcie doesn't say anything. In the silence, her even breathing soothes me, urges me on. I keep my eyes from hers.

"Leslie Ann was 12 in 1952. Looked a lot like Shirley Temple, big blue eyes and curly blond hair. She lived in a flat with her parents and a little sister. Rose. Her parents hired a teenage neighbor, Maura Haines, to baby sit Leslie Ann and Rose from time to time. Maura had a boyfriend, Sean Brady. Sean was a bit older, maybe 24. He was a petty fascist, spent time reading old Nazi propaganda and wearing thigh-high black boots. Sadistic little shit. Caught pigeons on the sidewalk outside Maura's flat and kept them in a cage to torture. He'd cut off a foot and laugh while the mangled bird struggled around his yard."

I know I'm in danger of rambling. I've got to finish this off, finish off my wine. Drink another glass and get into the kitchen so I can chop and mix and sauté and forget.

"Maura apparently had a little sadistic streak, too. Seems she talked Sean into taking Leslie Ann out to a lonely moor. They taped their session with Leslie Ann, dumped her body where no one ever found it. It was the day after Christmas."

I look up now, aware that hot tears are streaking down my cheeks. Hero, who'd been lying at my feet, nudges and nudges my free hand but I ignore him.

Marcie is looking somberly at her empty glass. When I don't go on, she looks up and cries out. Her glass plunks on the table, tottering and almost falling, but she's got her arms around me before I can reach for it. She's soft and warm and smells of vanilla and musk. Almost as soon as she's put her hands up to my hair, I stop crying. A silent sob convulses me, but then I am still. I stand, stiff and awkward, as she croons to me. I want another glass of wine. I want to forget.

Marcie steps back, puts her hand on my face and sighs. "Weeble, I'm always here for you."

"I know," I say and turn to go to the kitchen where the *Chianti* waits. Marcie and Hero both follow me. I suppress my sudden irritation, my regret for coming here this weekend. I pour myself more *Chianti* but force myself to sip it. To regain control.

"I ran into my own stalker," I try to joke.

"What?" Marcie's sharp voice slices the air between us. "What happened?"

"Nothing much. Last week, when I was running one morning, I startled this guy in a dumpster." I laugh, remembering his face as he peered over its side and my reaction. "He said he was dumpster diving. Ever heard of that?"

"No." Marcie watches me with an odd expression. "So he's stalking you?" Her voice sounds as though stalking is right up there with delivering babies and open-heart surgery.

It's easier to ignore her tone than to answer her in complete honesty. "Not really. I ran into him at the Bread of Life Co-op today. He works there. Recognized me even with my celebrity ball-cap disguise."

"Did he confront you?"

Now I regret my joke altogether. "No, Marcie, he didn't. Actually, he apologized for scaring me. Gave me a card to his gallery opening."

"Ah. He's an artist then." She turns away from me and heads for the refrigerator. Something tells me she's feigning casual, but I don't have proof. "Did he tell you what 'dumpster diving' is, by the way?"

I feel I've dodged some sort of bullet. "Yeah, I guess. He's not so different from you. He rescues stuff other people throw out. You rescue people other people throw out. Only he calls himself a 'Freegan,' not a psychologist."

She pulls out the buffalo mozzarella, basil, and tomatoes. "*Insalata caprese*?" She's grinning. "Chicken *piccata*, too?"

"Yup." I grin back. It feels good, natural.

Marcie heads to the dining room to retrieve her wineglass while I pull out the cutting board and a knife. She pours herself another glass and watches while I pull down a bowl.

"Get your stalker's name?"

Ah, the subject's not over. Now it's my turn to stay casual. "Tom Paul. Says he's a glass artist."

"Tom Paul Theophilus?" Marcie's voice rises in excitement. I look at her, surprised enough to miss the tomato I'm slicing and almost cut my thumb. "The gallery opening—is it *The Soul Illuminated*?"

I recall the luminous figure suspended on the card. "Yes. How'd you know?"

Marcie doesn't answer. Instead, she scurries back to the dining room only to return holding the Torah. I look at it, confused.

"This," she says, holding it up between us, "is Tom Paul's work. It's called *pâte de verre*, paste of glass. It's an ancient technique."

She lays the paperweight in my hand, where its cool weight glows mysteriously. I look at it more closely. Two blue scrolls lay side-by-side, each appearing to wrap around a rough metal spool. I touch it with a fingertip, tracing the fine details of the gold Hebrew lettering trapped inside the scrolls. I've never seen anything like this anywhere. It had lain on Marcie's table for months. How had I never really looked at it before? *He'd* made this exquisite piece?

"Where'd you get this?" I hear the wonder in my voice, but I don't look at her. I can't take my eyes off his work. "How do you know him?"

Marcie wraps her hands around mine, the warm texture of her palms contrasting with the smooth glass. "My friend Sharon is a glass artist who specializes in kiln-casting. Tom Paul apprenticed with her a couple of years ago, but he taught himself how to do *pâte de verre*. Not many glass artists do it these days. Sharon rents her studio and kiln to him. He made some of these for her and some of her friends. You like it?"

I shrug and hand the paperweight back to her and turn to wash the basil. It's hard to keep my voice neutral. "It's nice, I guess." I want to ask if she's met Tom Paul, if she's talked to him. What kind of man is he?

"I met him once," Marcie offers, but I say nothing. "He and his girlfriend"—I twitch at the word and then go still except for my fingers, which tear, tear, *tear* the basil—"came to a show Sharon held last year. Knows a lot about mythology and ancient history. Got a degree in classics at Hellenic College and spent the night describing Greek sculpture, Roman glassmaking, and Byzantine mosaics to some adoring groupies. He was really funny and sweet." I hear admiration in her voice. "You going to his gallery opening?"

"Doubtful," I say almost before her question is asked. "He kinda gave me the creeps, if you want to know the truth." And that's the last I speak of Tom Paul that weekend, even if I see his eyes all the time now, waking and dreaming.

* * *

Lauren and I very nearly stopped being friends after Grandma Nan discovered the lusty paperback romance I loaned her just before Thanksgiving break. We'd already quit being friends and reconciled once as it was. As fall had cooled toward winter, we'd continued to fantasize aloud about our future, our plans growing ever more elaborate and intertwined. And dictated by Lauren. I began to discover what it meant to have a best friend who had no siblings and usually found a way to get what she wanted. I let her take charge but only so far. I resisted including Lisa and Debbie in our scheming because I half-believed that only by keeping it a secret would it ever come true. Lauren begged and pleaded, and when I still refused to admit them to our secret world, she dumped me. This hurt more than I ever admitted. I'd always been her friend even when Lisa and Debbie had held back those first few weeks and now I sat alone while they chatted together on the playground.

Almost as if they'd been waiting for their chance to harass Lauren, the rowdiest boys swarmed her at recess on the second afternoon. I'd been sitting, listless and glum, on a swing when I heard a shriek and babbling followed by wild boyish laughter. I glanced toward the old tree to see Pat, Zack, and Victor darting around Lauren's huddled form while Debbie patted her back and Lisa shrilled at them.

I sprang from the swing and ran, pell-mell, into the chaotic mass of boys, knocking Victor down. Pat and Zack glanced over their shoulders, saw me, and ran in two directions. I had my fists clenched before me.

"Get out of here, dipshits!"

Victor, sitting propped on his palms, looked at me, his eyes wide.

"Go on!" I screamed at him and raised my fist.

He scampered away, darting glances over his shoulder. I didn't follow although I wanted more than anything to punch one of them.

"What happened?" I said through clenched teeth. Lisa cowered near Debbie, her shoulders hunched. Debbie looked up from where she bent next to Lauren, who hadn't looked at me yet.

"Pat snapped her bra strap," Debbie said, her round face incongruously grim. "Then Zack dared him to touch her boob and he did."

My stomach flipped. I'd just started to feel tender around my nipples and noticed that the skin was swollen like a bee sting—a monstrous bee sting. I held a forearm across my chest, my fist still clenched. The first boy who touched me there would get a knee to the balls *before* I punched him hard.

Lauren raised her teary eyes to me now. Her face looked sunburned and had a fine red rash like chicken pox in patches along her forehead and cheeks. "He–he said, 'Nope, it ain't Charmin' and laughed." She hiccoughed and started crying again.

"Fuck 'im," I said. The three other girls looked at me with round eyes and frozen faces. "You heard me right. I said it. I said fuck." My voice had grown husky and fierce. I'd done it. I'd used

76

words I heard every day at home and it felt powerful. "I'll kick their asses if they come near Lauren again."

I turned and shouted at the three boys who watched us from the fence between our school's playground and the high school's parking lot below. "Don't touch Lauren again or I'll kick your ass. You got that?"

I got in trouble for that. Ms. McKinney, a second-grade teacher, overheard and reported me to Mr. Grace. I stood not looking at him, my lips pressed together so I wouldn't say anything I regretted, as he lectured me about my language. It didn't matter what he said. It only mattered that Lauren wouldn't be harassed again.

She called me that night.

"I'm sorry, Weeble." She sounded contrite. "I shouldn't have ignored you. It was mean."

This surprised me. I'd expected her to pretend she hadn't done anything wrong. She'd done it before.

"It's okay," I said.

"Please, can we be friends again? I won't hang out with Debbie and Lisa anymore."

I sighed. It was too late for that. I didn't want to cut them off as I'd been.

"No, it's okay for them to play with us. Lisa's good at screaming. She'll warn us if Pat comes around again."

"Sure?"

"Yeah."

And that's how we resolved our differences in time for me to loan Mona's copy of *Ashes in the Wind* to Lauren before Thanksgiving. I'd identified with the feisty Alaina from the very start and now toyed with the idea of running away disguised as a boy. We hadn't learned about the Civil War yet at school, but some details from the romance disturbed me. What would it be like to live with enemy soldiers all around? To find your home

77

burned to the ground, lost forever? Frankly, I envied Alaina for even having a home she cared about. Mine could burn down any time and I'd rejoice. I couldn't wait to see what Lauren thought about the love story.

But we never really discussed it.

Monday after Thanksgiving Lauren brought the book back to me wrapped in brown paper. She couldn't look at me as she handed it back.

"Grandma caught me reading it."

"So?" Mona knew I read her romances. At least, I thought she did.

"She threw it out the window before I could tell her it was yours. She said it was trash and if that's what your mother let you read then we couldn't have any more sleepovers or go home together." She sounded miserable.

"Did you read any of it?"

Now she did look up at me. She grinned and all the misery on her face disappeared. "Yeah. I stayed up really late and finished it. I was just rereading some of the juicy parts."

I grinned back. I knew which parts she meant. Then my grin faded and I held the book up. "But this book isn't nearly as bad as *Flowers in the Attic*. And what about all those books her friend loaned you? The Barbara Cartland ones?"

She shrugged and looked away. "She doesn't know I read those. I took the books from Marge's shelf when she wasn't looking. *Flowers in the Attic* I got from Debbie's older sister."

I could see where this was going. "So she doesn't know you read 'trash'?"

"No."

"We can still be friends at school," I said. Secretly, I was relieved. I hadn't yet had her come to my house, but Mona had started to complain that I'd never had Lauren over. It wasn't Mona or the dumpy house that smelled of cat urine that worried me. It was Tim. He'd take one look at Lauren, sense her vulnerability, and target her. It was one thing for me to stand up to the wimpy little shrimps on the playground, another altogether to stand up to my older stepbrother. At 16, he'd beat me to a pulp and make me watch while he got Lauren to do things to him.

Lauren looked disappointed. And sad.

"Don't you like me anymore?" It came out as a whisper.

I sighed. For all her high-handed stances, Lauren needed a lot of reminding.

"Don't look like that, Lauren. Please. I want to be your friend. It's just that Grandma Nan scares me." This was true, too. Grandma Nan had figured out that I wasn't good enough to be Lauren's friend, no matter how hard I tried. Grandma Nan didn't just talk in my direction or around me. When she spoke to me, her gaze was direct. She really *saw* me.

Lauren looked thoughtful. At lunch she pulled me to the end of the table closest to the wall so most of the other children in Mr. Grace's class wouldn't be able to hear us.

"I know Grandma scares you, but she's not so bad, Weeble, really. Just give me time to work on her. I'll be on my best behavior and read only little girl books. I won't talk about you though. Grandma's stubborn and if she hears your name she'll get upset. If I don't say anything, she'll change her mind. I know she will."

I shrugged. "It's okay, Lauren. I don't mind. Maybe Mr. Grace will let us sit next to each other."

"That's a great idea. I'll ask."

Mona wasn't so easy to placate later. After school, I found Annie on the sidewalk and we waited for the bus together, her hand in mine. She smelled like glue and poster paint. I hated those smells, but I always asked her about her drawings, which consisted of pink and green lines tangled in a nest like her hair.

That day, she held a drawing that showed more recognizable figures.

"That's you," she said and pointed at a horizontal figure with orange lines around its face. It had a slash for a mouth and two black dots for eyes. "That's Tim." The other figure, hairless and twice as big, appeared to stand on mine. She'd scribbled over him in black.

"Why'd you color over him?"

"He's bad. I wanna get rid of him." Her matter-of-fact tone shocked me.

"He ain't goin' anywhere, Annie." I heard the warning in my voice, but I hoped she didn't also hear the fear.

The house was empty when we got there. Tim didn't come home right after high school, but I suspected he often didn't even make it there. Not that I cared what he did as long as he stayed away. The two hours Annie and I had alone every afternoon were peaceful. I'd started baking Betty Crocker cakes and Jell-O cheesecakes in the past few months. Annie liked to lick the beaters after I'd put the cakes in the oven. That afternoon she had a cold and kept wiping her snotty nose on her right sleeve.

"Stop that, Annie. Get some toilet paper and blow your nose," I told her. Ever since the night of the Ouija board, I'd been more aware of Annie, who'd been nothing but a large pink larva when she came home from the hospital. Instead of a butterfly, she'd changed into a spindly, tangled-headed weed while I wasn't paying attention.

Annie obeyed me while I pulled out the cake mix and turned on the oven. I didn't know why that Ouija warning had bothered me, but it had. Tim took as much notice of Annie as he did Miller. Then again, so had I. Now I worried about her. She seemed so little to me, so trusting and breakable. As I thought again about the eerie words, she came back carrying a nubby stuffed rabbit, her face flushed as if she'd been running outside in the cold.

"Can I he'p?" she asked.

"Sure." I let her crack the eggs and add them to the mix. If Mona was here, she'd shoo Annie out of the kitchen. She didn't have much patience for little girls under foot while she baked. "I'll pour the oil in. You hold the mixer."

"'kay," she said. She loudly sucked the snot back into her head. I rolled my eyes. Small, breakable, and irritating. She watched me assemble the beaters, otherwise quiet even in her excitement.

I held the mixer with one hand while she grasped the handle with both of hers, the tip of her tongue between her teeth. Her hot breath smelled bad, like old dirty snot. I shifted my grip on the mixer and as my hand brushed hers, I felt heat radiating from her skin. Frowning, I put my hand over her smaller ones. They were hot. I put a palm on her forehead.

"Hey," she said and pulled away from my hand. She sounded irritated. "I can't see, Weeble."

I studied her face. Her eyes shone like wet glass against her reddened skin. I switched off the beater. "That's enough. You feel okay, Annie?"

Her tongue disappeared into her mouth and she sucked at the snot again. "My head hurts." She coughed a little. "My throat hurts."

It was more than a cold, but I didn't know what to do for sure. Mona drank Alka Seltzer sometimes when her stomach was upset. I wondered if I should have given Annie some.

"Go lie down on the sofa, Annie. I'll bring you some medicine." Again, she obeyed. She was really sick to go without arguing about the beaters.

I pulled the Alka Seltzer down and peered at the dosage instructions. She wasn't old enough. And her stomach was fine. I rummaged around in the bathroom cabinet, reading labels on bottles and tins until I found the baby aspirin and throat lozenges.

When I brought a cup of 7-Up and the medicine, Annie lay on the sofa, still except for her eyes, which followed me. "Here, take these, squirt."

She choked on the aspirin but managed to get it down after sipping the 7-Up. "I'm cold, Weeble." As if to prove her point, she shuddered and her teeth clicked together.

I went to our room and grabbed her Strawberry Shortcake blanket. After tucking it around her, I turned on the after-school TV special and returned to the kitchen to finish mixing the batter. I'd slid the second cake pan into the oven when Mona came in carrying a paper shopping bag, a cigarette dangling from her lips. Chill autumn air clung to her jean jacket and cut through the sweet scent of vanilla. She dropped the bag in front of the refrigerator and pulled the cigarette free and further degraded the scent by exhaling ashy smoke.

She looked at me. "Damn, that smells good."

"Annie's sick, Mom." I watched her as she bent over to pull out a package of hamburger, a box of spaghetti, and a jar of sauce. "She's really hot and says her head hurts. I gave her an aspirin."

She paused in getting out a pot to boil water. "Regular Hot Lips Houlihan, aren't ya?"

I shrugged and looked away. Was this a good thing or not?

"Brown the meat. I'll check on her." She left and came back a few minutes later. "She's burnin' up. If she's sick tomorrow, I can't stay home from work."

She pulled a can of beer from the refrigerator and popped it open. I said nothing, just continued poking at the lump of hamburger in the pan with the spatula. I felt her gaze on me.

"You'll have to stay home with her."

I looked up, surprised. "Me? Why me?" I heard the whining in my voice. Two hours after school was one thing. A whole day with a sick six-year-old was another.

"Tim sure in the hell ain't gonna do it," she said, tipping her can at me. "And your daddy can't do it, neither. Speaking of the little dipshit, where *is* Tim?"

"How should I know?" I asked. Resentment edged my voice. "I'm just glad he wasn't here when we got home."

"Don't give me no lip, Weeble." But she said this without any real sharpness as if she was thinking about something else.

Mona left the kitchen while I continued to stir at the clumps of hamburger. After a few minutes, I went to the doorway to see if she'd gone to sit with Annie, but she wasn't in the front room. The door to her bedroom was shut. Sighing, I went back to the stove where the pot of water had started to boil and added the box of spaghetti. No point in complaining about getting stuck making dinner. Miller came in and jumped on the counter and started licking the Styrofoam meat tray I'd left on it. I heard the screen door bang and then Tim walked into the kitchen. I stiffened but didn't move.

He stood for a minute next to the table. I smelled him, a sickening mixture of body odor, cigarette smoke, motorcycle oil, and the sweet herbal scent of reefer. He grinned at me, and I could see by his enlarged pupils that he was trashed. I gripped the spatula tighter. Would Tim be too far gone to look for trouble or just enough wasted to forget where he was?

"If it ain't the Weeble who falls down?" He laughed at his own joke. "Get me a Pepsi, cunt."

My anger flared. Tim's unsteady balance emboldened me. "Get your own Pepsi, dipshit."

"What'd you say to me?" His wide pupils contracted as his eyes squinted. His mouth narrowed into a tight slit. "Better not've said what I think you said."

I recalled the power I'd felt on the playground a few days before. "Fuck off, Tim." I shifted my shoulders and lifted my chin. He was taller than me but not so tall.

He growled and lunged for me. I stepped out of his way, swinging the spatula and catching him just above the elbow. The loud slap reverberated in our small kitchen. "Fuck!" he yelled and grabbed for my hand. His steely fingers wrapped around my wrist and he began to pry open my fist with his other hand. I fought him, wild now that I found myself trapped. He pulled his free hand back and slapped me. My ears rang and my cheek stung, drawing unwilling tears from my eyes.

"Stop it!" Annie stood in the doorway, her voice shrill and her eyes wide in her flushed face. "Stop hurting Weeble!"

"Get the fuck outta here!" Tim's hand gripped my wrist in a vise.

"No!" She flung herself at him, her arms around his waist and her head butting his abdomen.

"Well, now." He held my hand high and looked down at Annie. His dilated eyes gleamed with a strange light that made me shudder.

Without knowing quite why, I stopped struggling and let myself sink into deadweight. This took him by surprise and I fell free. I wriggled around before he could react and grabbed Annie, shoving her behind me and shuffling us toward the refrigerator where we'd be cornered if Tim didn't give up. His eyes narrowed; I could almost smell the anger fusing his rank odors into an overpowering assault on my thoughts.

It took half a second for me to realize that the anger was mine.

He'd taken no more than two steps when Mona materialized in the doorway, trailing the fresh scent of the joint she'd snuck off to toke. She took in the scene before her: me defiant and

84

brandishing a greasy spatula, holding my ground, and Tim looming over me, his fists clenched.

"What the fuck's goin' on?"

She didn't wait for anyone to answer. Even as I started to rattle off a description of the motivating event, even as Tim whirled to face this new threat, she stepped forward and grabbed his arm to pull him a safe distance away. Tim might be taller than me, but Mona towered over him still.

She glared at him. "I said what the fuck's goin on? You'd better have a good reason for what I just saw, you little twerp."

Tim yanked his arm free. "Weeble's startin' trouble, that's all. I ain't gonna take none of her mouth."

"You ain't her dad, you ain't in charge of her mouth nor nothin' else of hers. I don't give a flyin' fuck what she said to you, you gonna let it go or answer to me, hear?"

Tim stared at Mona, his gray eyes under his wild bangs hard as concrete and about as yielding. The air vibrated with the power of their locked gaze. Annie, standing behind me, hugged my waist and buried her face into my shirt. I couldn't stop looking at them, wondering whether Mona would back down, desperate for her to stand her ground.

It took maybe another thirty seconds and then Tim looked away. Stuffing his hands into his front pockets, a gesture that raised his shoulders around his ears, he shuffled his feet and said nothing.

"That's what I thought." Mona's hazel eyes, though dilated, still had a steely edge. "Get out. Go to your room. You, Frankie and I are all gonna have a little chat after dinner. I got a call from the vice principal at work today. You know damn well what about, don't you, you little jerk."

Tim's swift gaze slid toward me as he loped through the doorway. As brief as the look was, I'd had no trouble identifying the poison it held. I didn't relax my stance until I heard his bedroom door bang shut.

"So what the fuck was that all about?"

I turned to find Mona staring hard at me. "He ain't bossin' me around." I heard the sullen edge to my words and regretted it, if only because I didn't want Mona to blame me for anything.

Before Mona could respond, Annie wormed her head under my elbow and looked out. "He hit her, Mommy!"

"That true, Weeble? That little prick hit you?"

I didn't answer, just lifted my chin higher. If Tim thought I said something about him to Mona, he'd make me pay.

Her eyes narrowed. "Don't have to answer that. I can see the fingerprints on your cheek. That little fuck. You do somethin' to provoke him?"

This time I did answer. "If tellin' him to get his own Pepsi provokes him, I did."

Mona started to speak and then looked over at the stove where the hamburger sizzled and smoked and the pasta boiled over, hissing and steaming. "Shit!"

It took the next fifteen minutes to recover from the interruption, fifteen minutes in which to throw out the near-gelatinous clump of pasta and to scrape the stuck and burned hamburger from the skillet bottom. While Mona started a fresh pot of water, I pulled Annie back to the sofa and tucked her blanket back around her until she looked again like a plump larva. With her reddish-gold hair, she might have been Strawberry Shortcake's younger cousin.

"Thanks for sticking up for me, squirt." I leaned over and kissed her forehead.

She looked up at me. Her eyes had lost their wet glassy sheen, but they drooped as if she was about to go to sleep. "I hate Tim."

"Shh. Take a nap."

As if all she'd needed was permission, her eyes closed and her breathing evened out.

I returned to the kitchen to see Mona, arms crossed and beer can held next to her face, staring out the back window with unseeing eyes. I walked behind her to get a Pepsi from the refrigerator and she turned at the sound of the door clicking shut.

"What am I gonna do with you, Weeble?" She watched me. I could see no trace of the marijuana's earlier effects in her gaze. "You gotta stay out of Tim's way. He's nothin' but trouble. You can't give him no reason to get angry at you."

The patent unfairness of this stung my eyes with angry tears.

"How can I stay outta his way?" I heard the outraged demand in my voice. "I'm in here cookin' dinner. He's gotta stay away from *me*." What I didn't say, what I shoved down so hard I felt it lodge in the base of my spine as indestructible as cold steel, is how little it mattered if I provoked him. I was a bug pinned to a saggy mattress and wriggling its futile legs, a moth trapped in a jar beating weak wings against glass. I had no escape.

"Go to Lauren's house tomorrow. Better yet, have her here so you don't get on Tim's nerves."

I blinked my eyes and looked away. What could I say to her? I had a sudden urge to cry. I wanted to race outside and hide, in the garage maybe or down the street behind the huge trunk of an old tree. Instead, I grabbed the jar of spaghetti sauce and twisted its lid off.

"You got a problem with invitin' your friend here?" Mona's voice didn't hold any accusation. Yet. Just curiosity. But I saw my way out without letting Mona think that Grandma Nan disapproved of us.

"Yeah, I do." I snarled this so she wouldn't hear the tears roughening my voice. "I'm not inviting anyone to this house. It stinks like cat piss." I said nothing about my cramped room, its shaggy carpet, or the rickety shelves where I displayed my few books and treasures. I didn't talk about the difference between Lauren's home and ours because I didn't know why ours felt so dirty, broken down, and tense.

"Gettin' a few airs, are you?" Mona still didn't sound angry and I didn't know why.

I whirled to face her, my eyes burning but dry. "What's that mean?"

"C'mon, Weeble. You read those romance novels lying all over this place. You damn well know some people don't belong with the fancy lords and ladies. If the scullery maid puts on her lady's dress, she's puttin' on airs. Pretendin' she's somethin' she's not." She watched me while she said this.

"What's that got to do with the way our house smells?" I still couldn't figure out why she wasn't angry.

"We are what we are, Weeble. Lauren's either your friend, or she's not."

"She's my friend, but I ain't invitin' her here." I raised my chin and squared my shoulders. "Maybe there's nothin' wrong with this house, but there's somethin' wrong with Tim." And that's all I'd say about him.

Mona sighed, shrugged, and tipped her beer up for a long draw. "Whatever, Weeble. If you ain't gonna be smart, what can I do to keep him from pesterin' you?"

"I can take care of myself." I thought, *but what about Annie?*

The next late night Tim slunk into our room, I waited for him with the spatula. He pulled me from bed just as he always did, but this time I didn't stumble and fall to my knees. I swung the spatula toward his looming shadow, not caring where my blow struck. It whistled for half a second and then a soul-satisfying thwack! split the dark.

That was the last time Tim came for me.

Yet I'd seen his eyes when Annie came to defend me, and I knew the monster hadn't been destroyed, just deflected. I'd never much played with Annie, but now I kept her close. I pushed my bed next to hers and told her stories after the lights went out, clutching the spatula while she snuggled her dirty rabbit. Annie never asked why I did these things. She just lay there in the dark, gentle sucking noises interrupting her mouth breathing, as I called up some of my favorite fairy tales. Mona never read to either of us, but I'd spent all of second grade going through the shelf in the school library, so I knew *The Matchstick Girl* and *Thumbelina* as well as the familiar *Cinderella* and *Beauty and the Beast.*

Annie's ratty hair and stained clothing made me aware of my own lackadaisical hygiene. Smelling her hot, pungent breath made me seek out toothpaste on my own. I began to pay attention to the clothes I wore, and how often I'd worn them. I noticed that my underwear smelled funky, so I began washing them out by hand in the bathroom sink. I started bathing to scrub my underarms and dirty soles more than to soak while listening to the radio. My scalp started to itch so that only shampoo and conditioner kept me from scratching.

At night, as I read to Annie, the scent of her along with my overpowering sheets distracted me. I began to dread lying next to her. I imagined she smelled as wild and feral as a raccoon or fox. I coaxed her away from the TV after my own bath, setting her tatty rabbit on the sink's edge to watch over us. Wet and with her fine hair slicked onto her scalp, Annie gave a splendid impression of a scrawny rat terrier.

I shouldn't have done it. I shouldn't have soaked and soaped Annie, combed the tangles from her hair and clipped her toenails smooth. I shouldn't have brushed her teeth and dipped a Q-tip into her ear canals. I shouldn't have washed her nightgown or dressed her in clean play clothes. I should have encouraged her to continue morphing into a foul-breathed troll with sharp eyes and sharper claws. Then Annie would have been safe from Tim.

Five

TELLING MARCIE ABOUT LESLIE ANN BISHOP chips a tiny, if crucial, hole in the numbness that has frozen my higher-order thinking for as long as I can remember. I begin to thaw, ever so slightly. The rest of the weekend flows by in a pleasant atmosphere of camaraderie, fueled in no small amount by *Chianti* and, later, single-malt whisky. I ignore the image fragments and increasingly coherent babble that float at the back of my thoughts and wonder if this is what it feels like to be a schizophrenic in bare control, if there is such a thing. I watch Marcie and Evan, who have been together since our freshman year at BU. An unfamiliar, aching hunger fills me. They've never been overt in their affection, but I see how Evan orbits Marcie as Earth orbits the sun.

I'm not the sun. I'm a black hole who swallows moons and planets. On Monday, when I return to my sprint training, I alter my route to keep my distance. To throw off anyone who tries to anticipate my movements. Especially an artist who resembles a Greek god with an intent, generous gaze.

During my run, the tingling awareness sets in. The images I've held at bay for days return and coalesce. The babble focuses and takes on the clarity of meaning. At first, as I run, I hear *trash, throw away, rescue, Freegan*, but then I see Leslie Ann's face, Annie's face, Lauren's face. They're black-and-white photos in an exhibit, architectural track lighting shining down on their childish faces. Their wide-eyed stares castigate me. They whisper that I haven't been honest. I've tried to keep my past from tainting my present research.

But my past is the reason for my research.

I have Tim to thank for my need to remember the other children, the ones who didn't survive rape and torture. Who didn't survive the lusts of the monsters that lurk in the black seams of society's fabric. If Tim hadn't molested me for all those years, would I too have paid scant notice to these victims, who'd been used and tossed aside like Big Mac wrappers in tall grass on a berm?

As I ask myself this question, I see how like Marcie I'm becoming. How like the mysterious and disturbing Tom Paul. I don't have the fortitude or the compassion to rescue broken people, nor the pragmatism needed to rescue used but useful items from a dumpster, but I do have the tenacity and eyesight to spot the bits of shredded story lying forgotten in the wasteland of old news. What I don't know is whether I have the courage to face the bitter sorrow that must still line the hearts of the people who loved these children, their parents, their brothers and sisters, their grandparents. The courage I must have if I'm to talk to them so that I may honor their murdered loved ones.

The rest of the week I work on my courage. I've done this before, after I'd decided to leave St. Joe and come to Boston University, which resided somewhere over the rainbow, in Oz. I'd pretended that I was moving to a new apartment across town. After that, packing everything I owned into the backseat of my

Ford Fairmont quit daunting me. Driving over the horizon, into the U.S. heartland and the misty reaches of my imagination, became manageable when I focused on driving first to St. Louis, and then Indianapolis, followed by Columbus, Pittsburgh, Philadelphia, and Hartford. Arriving in Boston, though intimidating, held a trace of inevitability.

So now I pick up the phone and call one person at a time, tracing Leslie Ann's family. In the end, I find Rose Bishop in the village of Ashford-in-the-Water. She's middle-aged and reluctant, but I'm pitiless now that I've found her. When I suggest that I fly to meet her, Rose grows agitated and angry before settling into a dull voice. I let her veer among all of these emotions, waiting until she agrees before I hang up and phone a travel agent. I've wanted to travel overseas ever since the days when Lauren filled my ears with tales of our future together, but I arrange only a lightning visit. It's as though I'm on some spiritual tether, one that will sicken and shrivel me if I'm stray too long or too far from my sanctuary.

Thinking about my trip excites the sharp prickles that wake my memory. New images and sounds percolate through me, pressuring the fissures in my defensive numbness. I can't stand it, so I run more even though it isn't on my schedule. I run until sticky sweat burns my eyes and the band around my ponytail slips off. Wisps of pale mousy hair flutter about my face, blinding me, but I keep running. I've been running blind for so long that I prefer not seeing where I'm going.

I don't stop until I'm exhausted, something that has become harder and harder to achieve now that I've reached the peak training levels that will get me through the final thirteen weeks. I want to give up. To abandon the course I've set for myself and admit defeat before I waste any more time. The simultaneous urge to keep on running into the setting sun, to run until I'm nothing but the pistons of my legs and the velocity of my stride, hits me with equal force. *Newton's Third Law of Motion*, I think. *For every action, there is an equal and opposite reaction.* A tiny voice tells me I'm lying: they are the same reaction.

I'm bent over, breathing and trying to wrestle my thinking back into manual mode when movement catches my attention. I look up and see a display of glass sculptures behind a storefront. I look around and realize I don't know where I am. Fear races through me. How could I have been so careless? The redbrick buildings and clean sidewalks hold no threat on a late Saturday morning, but a premonition fills me. I've stepped into the future, but I'm not ready.

My eyes focus on the flyer displayed on the glass door. I recognize the luminous figure against its black background. I'm squinting, trying to figure out where I know the figure from, but my hand opens the door before I remember.

"Hey." The happy voice that greets me sends a quiver down my spine. I think of smooth chocolate truffles and warm caramel sauce. "You found me." Tom Paul stands in front of a plinth where he has just set an exquisite sculpture.

I start to protest, but then I know it's true. I step forward to look at it. It's the Madonna. Her holy face glows in the late morning light. I feel drawn to her. Something in her serene expression assures me that she knows and understands my sorrow. She holds my gaze long enough for my heart to quit fluttering, for an unfamiliar ease to settle around my shoulders. Tom Paul says nothing, but I feel his gaze as I look around the gallery. More statues glow on a multitude of bare plinths, their colors as incandescent and vivid as liquid gems. On each of the walls is a large saintly figure in mosaic, radiant and pure. There is such a profound presence here, such a feeling of majesty and mystery that I fear to speak and bring the space down to my size. If I were religious, I might kneel. Or cross myself.

My eyes rise to the ceiling where an unmistakable image of Christ watches over us in gentle melancholy. His right hand beseeches me to listen; his left hand holds a richly decorated book with a jeweled cross on the cover. He floats on a field of gold. As I study him, I see the sheen of glass.

"Christ Pantocrator," Tom Paul says as I continue to stare. "Christ Who Sustains All."

I bring my eyes to look into Tom Paul's. He doesn't look like a Bible-thumper. A fire breathing, hell-and-damnation, joy-eater. Instead, his eyes resemble Christ Pantocrator's, minus the sorrow.

"Why is He so sad?" I ask, but I know the answer to that, surely better than Tom Paul.

"Let's sit." Tom Paul takes my elbow and leads me to a red couch along one wall under a wildly bearded man. As I sink onto the stiff cushions, my gaze drifts upwards again.

"I don't know. Christ Pantocrator is often perceived as judging humanity. Perhaps that saddens Him." His warmth radiates out to me with the strength of conviction. In the potent atmosphere of light and grace that envelopes us, it hits me like a bottle of wine on an empty stomach. "But I see Him as Christ the Teacher."

"Are you Catholic?" I have only a vague idea of what it means to be Catholic. His art resembles pieces I learned about in art history, lending them an air of ancient authority.

He shakes his head. "Eastern Orthodox." At my puzzled expression, he goes on. "During the Middle Ages the Christian Church split into two, the western Roman Catholic and the Eastern Orthodox. We've got a lot in common, but there are many subtle theological differences."

"Oh." I don't know what to say. I have no church, no theology. I know believers exist, but they're as exotic and removed from me as natives who shrink the heads of enemies or men who walk on smoldering coals. "That's beyond me."

95

"Me too." He smiles, that beautiful lifting of his full lips that half shuts his eyes. I catch my breath, hoping he doesn't hear.

"I'm Weeble." A silly urge to shake his hand makes me wedge mine between my thighs. I don't know why I've told him my childhood nickname, a name I should have left behind in St. Joe years ago. "You know, like the toy."

"I had a Weebles tree house." He grows grave. He holds out his hand. "Nice to meet you, Weeble."

Thinking of my own silly urge, I giggle and take his hand. It's warm and slightly calloused. I like the way my fingers fit inside his. They linger for a moment and then his hand drops back to his lap.

"I fell in love with Byzantine art in college. I'd always seen it at Mass, but learning more about the history of my faith inspired me to look more closely."

"They're beautiful," I whisper. It's disconcerting to admit that religious images affect me.

"You think so?" He seems pleased. "When I visited Italy, I made a kind of pilgrimage to all the churches with Byzantine mosaics and icons. The way the light hits them, it's like it reflected something inside me. That's when I knew I wanted to work with glass. The way it captures and holds light is the best visual metaphor for the divine that I know about."

I ponder this. The divine. What is that? Nothing in my life to this point has been divine. Everything has pointed to the nasty, brutish, and short. But in the stillness inside this gallery, I catch a glimmer, a sinuous presence that flows between and among the pieces that Tom Paul has fashioned, like spilled quicksilver. Too fast for human eyes. Impossible to hold onto.

I find my chest growing heavy, breathless. What am I doing here? I don't belong here with this man who wears the face of an angel, whose heat draws me like a moth to flame. I can't get close or I'll burn. Burn like the unworthy chaff I am. Dross left behind when gold is purified. I've certainly been through a crucible. *Crucify* pops into my head and my gaze darts to Christ Pantocrator. He judges. He must.

"I have to go," I say and rise, stepping back and away from Tom Paul as if he's contagious. Or maybe I'm the contagious one. I've certainly brought the Black Death into his gallery with me. "I have to finish my run. Maybe I'll see you at your opening."

He nods and doesn't take his eyes from mine. "I hope so, Weeble."

As on the occasion of our first meeting, I feel those wonderful eyes watching me as I escape from the overpowering intimacy of his modern sanctuary.

* * *

By February of fifth grade, Lauren's grandmother had relented about our friendship. I chose the mortification of inviting Lauren to my house over the fear of leaving Annie home alone, although I couldn't have her there every time. We were very careful about what we read around Lauren's grandmother, so much so that Lauren wanted to read Mona's paperback novels as soon as she got to my house. We'd grab Pepsis and Cheetos from the kitchen, Annie tagging behind with a cup of her favorite Hawaiian Punch, and head to my room. Lauren didn't seem to notice the mess that was Annie's bed or the clumps of cat hair sticking to the shaggy carpet. She sighed at the unrestricted access to both junk food and pulpy adult novels.

"Read to us," she commanded, including Annie in our little secret society. Annie sat, patient and unmoving, as Lauren brushed her thin hair and practiced braiding it.

So I read aloud from *The Far Pavilions* or *Shanna* or even *Shogun*, skipping over the parts that I found myself too shy to read aloud, never mind that I didn't want Annie to hear them. In the quiet winter afternoons before the brusque noise of Mona or

Frank or Tim, the only sounds beyond my voice were the soft hissing of the radiator and the comb in Annie's tangles.

Lauren made me read her favorite scenes with Ruark the hero in *Shanna* over and over.

"You didn't read that right," she complained once. "You left out the juicy parts."

My eyes slid toward Annie, who sat between Lauren's legs. "Not everyone is ready to hear the juicy parts."

"What? Yes, I am." Lauren looked up at me, a handful of Annie's hair clutched between her fingers. She took in my wide eyes and nod in my sister's direction. I hoped she wouldn't insist I read them anyway. "Oh, right. I'll just have to remember them."

"I don't know. I really don't like Shanna much, Lauren. She's so mean to Ruark. He keeps saving her, you know, from all those guys, but she doesn't want to be his wife for real just because he's a slave. She's kinda snobby."

Lauren sighed and rolled her eyes. "She just doesn't recognize she's in love. It takes time, you know."

I didn't respond to this, but what I was thinking was: *what does that matter? If a guy saved me from rape, I sure in hell wouldn't be mean to him.*

One day, after I'd finished *Shanna*, we talked about falling in love. Annie had wandered into the front room to watch an after-school special, so for once we didn't have to watch what we said.

"What do you want him to look like? You know," Lauren's voice dropped to a whisper, "your lover, the man you marry?"

I shrugged and frowned. I'd never thought about it before.

"I know what I want," she said, confident and assured. "He'll have an aquiline nose, emerald-green eyes, and a cleft chin. He'll be tall, with broad shoulders and big hands."

"He sounds like most of the heroes in the romance novels. But I've never seen any guys around like that."

"Of course not, Weeble. That's why we're going to travel to faraway places, like India. Don't you think Ash sounds really handsome? Dark and mysterious."

She had a point. Ashton Pelham-Martyn certainly sounded exotic.

"How will we know if they're good guys?" I asked, skeptical. After all, some of the villains in the romance novels were dark and mysterious, too.

"Their eyes," Lauren said. "Villains always have something wrong with their eyes. They always have something wrong with them, too. Like a scar. Or missing finger."

"Then we're surrounded by villains." My words tasted sour.

Lauren giggled. "Oh, heroes aren't easy to find, Weeble. That's why they're heroes. They're like buried treasure. Or gemstones hidden underground. Not everyone can see them, only women who are worthy to win their true love."

"How do you become good enough to get a hero?" I held my breath. Lauren appeared to have figured this all out and I realized I'd been slow to do the same. She'd find a hero for sure.

Lauren sighed. "It's not easy. Just think about it. All the heroines have to suffer first. They have to lose all their money and be taken away from their families. Other women have to want the hero, too."

Her description reminded me of some of the fairy tales I'd been rereading to Annie. "Cinderella has no money. Her stepmother and stepsisters treat her bad. And all the women want Prince Charming."

"Exactly. Except that's a fairy tale. There isn't any magic, Weeble. And no one's going to throw a ball where the hero dances with all the girls until he finds his true love."

I frowned hard. "Then how do we find him?"

"We have to wait for him. We have to believe in him."

"Whadya mean, wait for him? Are we looking for him or not?"

"I mean," here Lauren lowered her voice, "we can't give ourselves to another man first."

"Give ourselves?" I studied her face. She wiggled her eyebrows, but I still didn't get it.

She rolled her eyes. "Do I have to spell it out for you? We can't, you know, have another man in our bed."

My eyes snapped wide. "Why would we?" Just the thought of *any* man in my bed, hero or no hero, made me shudder.

"We wouldn't. Not on purpose. But remember, we have to suffer first. How are we going to suffer if we don't have any money to lose?"

She waited while I thought about this. She'd pointed out the main ways heroines had to get ready for the hero. Besides being taken from their families and having all their money stolen, the women in romance novels were often beaten, even raped. I shuddered again.

"So we have to be hurt before a hero appears?" I could find no argument against her logic.

"Yes."

"Then I'll pass."

"What? Are you crazy? Don't you wanna hero?"

"Not if I have to get beaten or raped first."

"But he'll save you. He'll protect and love you forever. He'll hold you in his strong arms and kiss you. It'll be worth it. Besides," now she whispered, "he'll do all those things to you, you know, like in the juicy parts. Don't you wanna feel a man inside you?"

"No!" I almost shouted this. Lauren sat up, looking shocked. "No, I don't wanna man inside me. Anywhere," I added without thinking.

Lauren didn't catch what my last word implied. "Don't you want to be loved?"

I squeezed my eyes shut and wrapped my arms around my chest. "Yes. Why can't I be loved without suffering first? Why can't I be loved without the kissing? Without him in my bed?"

"I don't think you can, Weeble. None of the love stories work that way, do they?"

"So what? Most of the heroines are stupid, Lauren. Look at Shanna. Who cares if she gets Ruark or not? She should suffer. I'll just be good so when my hero shows up, I'll be ready for him."

"He won't." She sounded sad. "He won't know how to find you unless you've been hurt. You won't know who he is unless he comes to save you."

I gritted my teeth and huffed. "It doesn't have to work that way." I heard the sullen stubbornness in my voice. "What about *Beauty and the Beast*, huh? She saved *him*. And he wasn't just ugly, he was a beast. He was the one who had to control his temper. He had to be nice. He had to suffer when she left him."

Lauren thought about this, but then she had an answer that I couldn't refute. "That was a fairy tale, Weeble. Didn't I tell you there's no magic? Where are you going to find a beast anyway?"

I slouched, deflated. Lauren was right. Not about finding a beast, of course. No matter how much I wanted to be safe and loved, I couldn't escape the fact that a beast lived just across the hall from me. A beast who would never transform into a handsome, sweet-natured prince. She'd been wrong about the hurt part, too. No hero had shown up to rescue me from the beast.

After that conversation, I pushed aside thoughts about falling in love, what makes a hero, and the most disturbing topic of all: a man in my bed. I refused to discuss or reread any 'juicy parts' with Lauren, who grew sulky and huddled in the corner of my bedroom to read them to herself whenever she visited my house. But at night, after I read fairy tales to Annie, I found myself arguing with Lauren in my head. I'd figured out the flaw in her logic, but I didn't have the nerve to tell her. Fairy tales might require magic, which didn't exist, but her ideal romance required a lifestyle that didn't exist either. Elegant mansions, servants, balls—even adventurous treks across the vast reaches of the Indian subcontinent—none of these things existed in the real world. I'd seen enough TV to know that modern life looked just like what I saw around me.

So what could be the harm in wishing fairy tales were true? During the daylight, when I saw Tim's scruffy hair and sneering mouth, I knew there wasn't any magic left in the world anywhere. But at night, when it was dark and pleasantly warm and I was on the verge of sleeping, I thought about the magic in the fairy tales. About a handsome young man who didn't need me to hurt, who would be horrified if anything bad happened to me. A gentle young man who wanted nothing more than to whirl me around a dazzling dance floor, his eyes only for me. We'd laugh and tell stories and plan to ride horses until the wind stole the words from us.

Sometimes while I lay there, lulling myself with these vague images of sunlight and smiling eyes, I'd hear Frank and Mona's voices raised in drunken anger from the front room. Annie whimpered when this happened and rolled closer to me, making it harder to maintain the imagined beauty I'd worked so hard to create. I'd squeeze my eyes tighter until the red-orange pressure behind my eyelids hypnotized me, took me away.

One Friday night, Mona sent us to our room early when Ricky showed up. I knew the three of them would sit around smoking pot and laughing until late at night. Tim had just gotten his driver's license. Usually Mona told him to quit bothering her about driving, but that night she'd laughed and tossed him the keys. I knew she'd been drinking beer since four, when she'd gotten off work early.

"Just don't stay out past one," she said as he caught them. "Or you'll fuckin' wish you'd never been born. Right, Frankie?"

Frank, who'd been watching TV, ignored her until she kicked his foot. Then he turned bleary eyes on Tim. "Right, boy. Do as your stepmother tells you or you'll answer to me, hear?"

Tim just nodded and grabbed his fraying jean jacket. He didn't even look back when the screen door slammed behind him.

I breathed a sigh of relief. "Can Annie and I take some Pepsi to our room and read for a while?"

Mona squinted at me. "Why the hell do you read so much, Weeble?"

"I like it." I didn't know what else to say.

"Ah, what the fuck, Moan. Let 'em read. What does it matter as long as they ain't out here botherin' us?" Frankie asked.

"She's always got her damn nose stuck in a book. It ain't natural. She'll get screwy ideas."

"What am I supposed to do then? It's only eight o'clock," I said, defiant.

"Watch your tongue, girl." Mona's voice was sharp, but she didn't look like she really cared. "Okay, whatever. Just stay out of our hair. When I bang on your door, you'd better turn out your lights and go to sleep."

Annie and I sat on our beds, leaning against the wall with our pop sitting on the rickety nightstand near my hand. I'd brought home a large anthology of fairy tales and flipped through the pages trying to decide what to read. While she waited, Annie ate candy hearts, which she chewed with an open mouth because her nose was clogged with perpetual snot.

"That'un." She pointed a sticky finger at the image of a goblin holding a mirror. "Read that'un."

It was *The Snow Queen* by Hans Christian Andersen. Not one of my favorites. It made me shiver. "Let's read something else." I flipped the book over to look towards the back and less familiar

103

tales. "How about *The Marsh King's Daughter*? Or *The Golden Treasure*?"

"No." Stubbornness hardened Annie's voice. "The other'un. The one with the ugly little man." Outside, the early March wind picked up in howling support.

All right, I thought. *It's Snow-Queen weather anyway.* I turned to the story and began reading with what I thought was a dramatic voice.

"*You must attend to the commencement of this story, for when we get to the end we shall know more than we do now about a very wicked hobgoblin; he was one of the very worst, for he was a real demon.*"

"What's com'cement?" Annie asked. I wondered why she didn't ask what hobgoblins or demons were. Or why they didn't scare her.

"The beginning. It doesn't start with 'once upon a time.' Can I go on now?" I let impatience roughen my voice.

Annie snorted, sucking in wet snot, and nodded as she snuggled into my side.

"*One day,*" I read, "*when he was in a merry mood, he made a looking-glass which had the power of making everything good or beautiful that was reflected in it almost shrink to nothing, while everything that was worthless and bad looked increased in size and worse than ever. The most lovely landscapes appeared like boiled spinach, and the people became hideous, and looked as if they stood on their heads and had no bodies. Their countenances were so distorted that no one could recognize them, and even one freckle on the face appeared to spread over the whole of the nose and mouth. The demon said this was very amusing. When a good or pious thought passed through the mind of any one it was misrepresented in the glass; and then how the demon laughed at his cunning invention.*

"*All who went to the demon's school—for he kept a school—talked everywhere of the wonders they had seen, and declared that people could now, for the first time, see what the world and mankind were really like. They carried the glass about everywhere, till at last there was not a land nor a people who had not been looked at through this distorted mirror. They wanted even to fly with it up to heaven to see the angels, but the higher they flew the more slippery the glass became, and they could scarcely hold it, till at last it slipped from their hands, fell to the earth, and was broken into millions of pieces.*"

I stopped reading, a cold thrill dancing down my back.

"Go on."

"You're not really listening to this, are you?" I looked down onto Annie's head. I'd talked Mona into taking her for a haircut and now many of the ear-length strands stood up in a static-electricity halo.

"Yes I am. What happens to the pieces of the mirror?" she asked to show she was listening.

I sighed and began reading again. "*But now the looking-glass caused more unhappiness than ever, for some of the fragments were not so large as a grain of sand, and they flew about the world into every country. When one of these tiny atoms flew into a person's eye, it stuck there unknown to him, and from that moment he saw everything through a distorted medium, or could see only the worst side of what he looked at, for even the smallest fragment retained the same power which had belonged to the whole mirror.*

"*Some few persons even got a fragment of the looking-glass in their hearts, and this was very terrible, for their hearts became cold like a lump of ice. A few of the pieces were so large that they could be used as window-panes; it would have been a sad thing to look at our friends through them. Other pieces were made into spectacles; this was dreadful for those who wore them, for they could see nothing either rightly or justly. At all this the wicked*

105

demon laughed till his sides shook—*it tickled him so to see the mischief he had done. There were still a number of these little fragments of glass floating about in the air, and now you shall hear what happened with one of them."*

I read on then about the girl Gerda and her friend Kay, mesmerized despite myself with the story. I read about their innocent love for one another. I read about Kay's foolish boast to melt the Snow Queen and about the tiny grains of the goblin's broken mirror that entered his eye and his heart. Even though I trembled at Kay's icy fate, I read how the Snow Queen came in her sleigh and took him away from Gerda. I kept reading while Gerda went out into the warm spring sunshine to ask the river if it had drowned Kay. I read about the old woman and the enchanted garden, about Gerda's lapse into forgetfulness in the midst of such blooming beauty. I didn't stop reading until Gerda had escaped this garden only to find her feet bare and autumn well advanced.

"But her little feet were wounded and sore," I read even though I heard Annie's soft snore next to my shoulder, *"and everything around her looked so cold and bleak. The long willow-leaves were quite yellow. The dew-drops fell like water, leaf after leaf dropped from the trees, the sloe-thorn alone still bore fruit, but the sloes were sour, and set the teeth on edge. Oh, how dark and weary the whole world appeared!"*

I clapped the anthology shut and let it slide onto the floor disregarded. I slid Annie onto her side on her own bed and tucked her stuffed rabbit under her arm before pulling her blanket up to her neck. I sat thinking about the demon and the mirror. Something about this fairy tale felt so *real* it chilled my bones. Almost as though the author spoke in code about things he couldn't say directly. Things that not everyone wanted to know about, that not everyone could understand. Like Gerda, who didn't understand the stories the flowers told her or got impatient because Kay wasn't in them. And the flowers, they didn't care about Gerda's search. They just sang their own strange stories whether anyone listened or not. I didn't understand what the author spoke about either, nor did I want to, but the contrast between the ever-blooming garden and the sad decay of late autumn haunted me.

I tiptoed to the door. Mona hadn't knocked yet, but I suspected that she'd forgotten. I needed to pee and brush my teeth. I cracked the door and stared out into the front room, which was dark except for the flickering light of the TV. Voices filtered through Frank and Mona's closed bedroom door. I figured Ricky had gone home.

I snuck down the hall to the bathroom and brushed my teeth as quietly as I could. After I peed, I stood for a while, trying to decide if I should flush the toilet or not. Our house was so small Mona often said she could hear us *thinking* about farting. I knew that wasn't true, but I worried the flushing sound would be unmistakable in the stillness. It had been a long time since Mona had clobbered me, but I hadn't forgotten the sting her large palm left after it struck my buttocks.

As I stood there debating with myself, an odd sound interrupted me.

I inched toward the bathroom door and listened, holding my breath. There was a rhythmic squeaking interwoven by a throaty grunting. Images of wolves nuzzling at the flesh of deer, of boars snorting in the underbrush, of ogres ripping the limbs from little girls filled my thoughts. When a high-pitched, thin keening joined the first two noises, the last seemed most likely. Someone tortured a little girl down the hall. I felt faint.

Frank's drunken voice cut through my confused dizziness. "Givit to her, Ricky. That's it, let'er have it!"

Puzzled, I listened as if my life depended upon his next words. If Frank encouraged Ricky to mutilate and murder someone, I'd

107

rush to my bedroom, wake Annie, and escape barefoot into the snow.

Frank did urge Ricky on toward depravity, but it took me a long moment to understand him when he spoke. "Fuck'er, fuck'er hard!" His words sounded torn from his throat, breathless and desperate.

When I realized what he'd said, I groaned, pressing my lips together and pushing the sound down inside where it wouldn't give me away. Not murder. Sex. Until now, I'd had no idea they sounded anything alike.

I'd returned to my room and put my icy feet next to Annie, whose sweaty body radiated heat, before the implication of Frank's words blossomed inside me. He meant Mona. My mother. I could still hear the muffled sounds of their excitement through both closed doors and down the short hall. I lay there, as stunned as a half-dead fly under a swatter, while Mona's keening rose as the squeaking got faster and the grunting got deeper, wilder. Snarled words interrupted the grunting. Whatever Ricky said, I couldn't understand him in my dazed state.

I cried then. For the first time I could remember since Annie was born, I cried. Somewhere inside me, something broke open and hot tears flooded my eyes and washed down the sides of my face and into my hair. I gasped, but I couldn't take air into my lungs. I thought I might drown in my own weeping. Annie lay as hot and still as burning charcoal along my side, dead to my grief and shame. I wept until my insides were hollow and hard and my sore eyes stung from the salt. I felt dizzy and a fierce ache clamped my temples. After that night, I no longer wished for magic. After that night, I no longer read fairy tales. An icy grain had entered my eye and everything looked as bleak and barren as the Snow Queen's eternally frozen northern palace.

TOM PAUL

LOVE HIT TOM PAUL WITH THE FORCE OF EPIPHANY one cool morning in April as he climbed, distracted and grimy, from the second dumpster in whose contents he'd scrabbled around for more than twenty minutes. It wasn't the first time he'd seen her, just the first time they'd come face-to-face. He'd seen her before at the Co-op. He'd even seen her running once early in the morning when the foggy air rolling off the Charles River dulled the sound of sneakers on damp pavement. That morning the cloudy ambiguity of the light had blurred the boundaries between heaven and earth. In the expectant hush, Tom Paul heard God breathing.

As he sat on a bench outside his studio, she'd floated, wraithlike, past him. Only her determined panting and clenched fists belied the easy rhythm of her stride. Instead of shattering his serenity, her exhalations sharpened his acute sense of union with the divine. He remained, awestruck, long after she'd disappeared into the fog. The dazzling sun, which burned away the ephemeral spiritual connection, only bemused him.

Even though he'd seen only the outline of her face that misty morning, Tom Paul recognized the wraith on the sidewalk next to the dumpster. She looked terrified. In that instant, he wanted to comfort her, to take her into his arms and keep her safe.

His sister Callista, who shared his fascination for the mystery and unpredictable beauty of life, nodded and shrugged a little when he told her how he'd lost his heart.

"That sounds about right. I've heard love shows up when you're not really looking for it. Or in places you'd never look."

"Meeting her was a bolt of lightning. It shocked me alive." He heard the wonder in his voice and reveled in it. He'd thought love at first sight was a trope from another era, a golden age that never was. Camelot and the Holy Grail. "Even the light's brighter."

"You sound like Frankenstein. Take a few old body parts from here, a few from there. Apply some electricity and *voilà*! You're a monster looking for love." Callista, her expression dreamy, often said things at odds with her mild manner. Odd, true things. "Is that good or bad for her, do you think?"

Tom Paul, although used to Callista's bizarre mental wanderings, was taken aback at the analogy. And then he laughed when he realized that she teased him. "Only if I follow her all over the place, killing her loved ones until she agrees to be my mate."

"If she's like most women, you wouldn't be her first stalker." She smiled to soften the comparison, a smile that lit her ethereal features from inside, turning her into a living luminaria.

He slipped his arm around her shoulders and squeezed. "She's not like most women, but I'm sure I'm not the only guy who can see that." He frowned a moment. "I don't want to scare her again. I'm definitely not following her around."

He remembered how his lady of the mists had trembled after he got out of the dumpster, how wide her eyes had been as she took in his bag. When he'd smiled and tried to reassure her that he wasn't a mugger, she'd stilled and gone as soft and vulnerable as a doe under a predator's gaze. Even though he knew he'd talked about the wok he'd salvaged from the dumpster, he couldn't remember his exact words. He only recalled the bitterness with which she'd answered him. He'd looked up and seen the translucent darkness that hovered around her like a smothering mantle and lifted an instinctive hand toward it. She'd flinched and bolted.

"Did you see it, her aura?" Callista, intuitive as always, had guessed the source of his frown. Only she knew his secret: ever since he'd devoted himself to mastering *pâte de verre*, his innate sensitivity to the emotional states of others had heightened until he often saw the distinctive glow that limned them.

Beneath the woman's darkening shroud, he'd sensed a spirit so beautiful its jewel colors defied coherent description. A spirit, though strong, still poisoned and sick.

"Yes." He shuddered. "Someone's hurt her, really wounded her soul."

She studied his expression and then put a light hand on his forearm. "Don't worry, love heals. Wait for her. She'll find you, I know it."

His sister Zandra, more prosaic and blunt, just snorted when he told her he'd fallen in love with a stranger who ran from him at their first meeting.

"Why do you keep sorting through garbage and muck? No wonder you scared the hell out of her. You probably stank unbelievably." She pressed her lips together and tilted her head. "Still, you're not bad looking. Or scary. Even if the women you usually date seriously lack judgment about either one."

Tom Paul thought of his last girlfriend, Renee, and grinned. She'd had a little-girl voice around him, but Zandra swore it was put on. He'd been taken with Renee's high cheekbones and knowledge about medieval Italian madrigals. He hadn't seen her aura at first, but her face and manner had been so sweet he'd been sure it was as light and golden as a butterfly wing.

He'd been wrong about that, though. His grin faded. Renee had gotten tired of waiting for him to make love to her. She'd crawled into his lap one night while they watched *Before the Rain* by Macedonian director Milcho Manchevski—not even a particularly romantic movie at that. He wasn't a snob. It didn't bother him that she didn't really like watching foreign films, that she'd only done it out of an obvious desire to please him. In fact, her initial willingness to watch a movie about political chaos in the Balkans had meant a lot to him. What *had* bothered him was that she'd gotten petulant and hissy when he'd extricated his torso from her enwrapping legs.

He'd turned the movie off and laid a hand along her cheek. "Renee, don't. Do you really want to be with someone who isn't ready to experience that kind of intimacy with you?"

"Why not?" she'd sobbed and flung herself into the corner of the sofa away from him. "Why don't you want to make love to me? Is there something wrong with me?"

He'd sighed and switched on the lamp next to him on the end table. When he'd turned to look at her, he caught her aura at last: fractured and veined with sickly greens and browns, the impure yellow had a deep red-orange at its heart. A red-orange of selfish lust and neediness. He hadn't known why he'd held back from growing closer to Renee, but in the forgiving light of the incandescent bulb, he saw what his heart had suspected.

"When I give myself, it'll be forever, Renee." He'd told her that before, but until tonight, he hadn't realized that she hadn't understood. "I want to be sure. Now I know I must still wait."

It took her a moment to digest what he'd said. He saw acidic comprehension wash down her features, etching disappointment and pain. Even though he'd been honest from the start, his affection and respect hadn't prevented her hurt. He'd regretted it, regretted adding more pain to a world filled with darkness when all he wanted to do was spread light. If he'd hurt Renee, who'd set herself up, how much more would he hurt a woman that he'd allowed himself to be prematurely intimate with? Was it worth it to quench his body's lusts? Did it really matter that he held back when most other men wouldn't? It did. It mattered to him, and that's who he had to live with. He wouldn't die of need. It wasn't air and water and food. It was a gift of his spirit that he didn't want to degrade through casual use.

Renee had stormed out, but six months later he saw her laughing and dangling from the arm of another artist, one known to enjoy women as one enjoys a glass of exquisite wine or handmade truffles. When their gazes met, sharp light glanced off Renee's eyes. She tossed her head and looked away. Her turned shoulder and the way she huddled against the other man's side warned Tom Paul against speaking to her.

After that, Tom Paul, who'd never dated much, withdrew into his studio and didn't think once of love and romance. Until he'd looked into the mysterious runner's face, he hadn't realized that he'd shut himself off. That he'd decided to forego dating altogether. Now that he'd fallen in love, as quickly and unreservedly as Lucentio in *The Taming of the Shrew*, he understood what he'd done. To see her, to really see the right woman, he'd had to clear his inner eye. He didn't understand how he could help her draw out the venom that darkened her aura, but he prayed for her during his early morning meditations.

His friend Jonah came to the studio the day the printer delivered the postcards and flyers for his first gallery opening. He whistled when he saw the illuminated torso of St. Sebastian hanging disembodied on the black background.

"These are stunning! The image just pops out at you. You're done with the main sculpture then?" He turned the postcard he

113

held over. "June twentieth. Fredda's beside herself with excitement."

Tom Paul sighed. "Not quite done, Jonah. Mostly done. I'm just not happy with the heads. Every mold I make looks like it's got the right expression, and then when I cast it, it's all wrong. Didn't have any problems with the arrows projecting from the torso, though."

Jonah, a folk musician, sometimes saw the answer to Tom Paul's creative dilemmas much more clearly than he did. "Forget the head, then. Put a mirror where the head goes and let the viewer imagine she's the one who's been martyred."

The profound rightness of Jonah's advice stunned Tom Paul for about fifteen seconds, and then relief blew through him as welcome as fresh air through a dusty glass studio.

Laughing, he threw his arm around Jonah's bulky shoulder and clapped his back. "That'll get you dinner in a heartbeat. Bring Fredda and some *pinot grigio*. After my shift at the Co-op, I'll splurge on fish or meat to go with the bounty they send home with me. You certainly deserve it."

Jonah, used to Tom Paul's impromptu menus based on the discarded foodstuff from markets, coffee shops, and restaurants, grinned. "I'll go all out and get some coffee beans and cream, too. I anticipate a mouthwatering dessert, y'see."

"Too early for local fruit, but there's some pears and blackberries due to hit the bin. I've saved a jar of lemon curd from the teashop. I'll bake a tart. That's all I promise." Tom Paul spread his hands, shrugged, grinned back at Jonah. How could he not feel so upbeat?

The problem of St. Sebastian's facial expression had tormented him since he'd first conceived the installation, and yet he'd plunged into the work, confident that his *genius*, that 'guiding spirit' of the ancients, would produce an answer when he required one. He'd never faltered, not once, since he'd apprenticed with a master glass artist, nor when he'd struck out on his own to discover how to recreate *pâte de verre*. None of his early setbacks, not the pieces that crumbled as he tapped their molds off of them, nor the wobbly, uneven texture that ruined many of the later surviving pieces, shook him. He'd expected early failure until his expertise developed. Only once he'd achieved consistent glass quality among pieces that ranged from paper-thin to massive, had he allowed that sprite living alongside him loose to imagine something as ambitious as *The Soul Illuminated*.

Sometimes his *genius* either dozed or made Tom Paul wait for some outside spur to deliver the answer to his creative dilemmas. Aware of this, Tom Paul had long ago named it Puck after Shakespeare's mischievous, unpredictable fairy. They'd grown comfortable with each other, the artist and his muse, so that when Puck led him astray or let him down, Tom Paul felt affection mixed with his annoyance.

So for now Tom Paul didn't worry—he still had time. Instead, he whistled along with Jonah's jaunty *Tripping Up Stairs* until Jonah segued into the more wildly haunting *King of the Fairies* as easily as spreading butter on a hot griddle. Tom Paul grinned. He and Jonah had talked once about their creative impulses, and Jonah, a Celt himself, had no trouble describing the irrationality and uncontrollability that drove his music as a magic imp.

"I've got a fae spirit livin' on me shoulder, too," he'd said in a mock brogue. "I call me spirit 'Oberon.'" Oberon, of course, was the King of the Fairies. And therefore lord over Puck.

What he didn't share with Jonah, now tuning his fiddle for a daylight *seisun*, was his other trouble solving the lighting. He'd relied on his innate feel for light, a feel that allowed him to manipulate light waves as easily as he might adjust a blanket around a loved one. Once he'd learned to mold glass, a medium that both contained and magnified light's properties, his ability to compose with light had grown breathtaking—until he tried choosing bulbs, arranging fixtures, and wiring rooms. Something in the rigidity, the density of metal, of plastic, of technology in general, frustrated his organic control. Even Puck had no power to solve this riddle beyond prodding Tom Paul to read treatises on optics, descriptions that defied his artist's logic. Puck hadn't given up, however. Tom Paul sensed his *genius's* latent resolve. When the answer to his lighting challenge appeared, Puck would be ready.

The pleasant morning passed as all Tom Paul's creative mornings passed: in a lucid dream directed by supernatural senses. Although he focused on the mold he sculpted, he'd entered into the imagined world of his installation and it held him as strongly as the mundane world of frit, kiln, grinding, and polishing. For him, the familiar work served as incantation, as ritual, as chant, as meditation, as prayer: he lost all sense of self and saw more clearly the truth of his spirit. Almost as soon as he touched the first jar of glass powder or the mallet or the clay, Tom Paul fell into this heightened state as easily as one bending over to study his reflection falls into a still pool. Early in his career, he'd expected to have to chase Puck through swamps as well as fairy meadows. He thought he'd have to trap the obstinate, mercurial spirit and force him to do his bidding, but Tom Paul had discovered that he could tempt Puck instead with his artistic trance. Today he hadn't been disappointed; indeed, he'd finished the mold for St. Irene's bust when he'd feared it would take another week to perfect.

After Jonah left to meet Fredda, Tom Paul put away his tools and cleaned up his workbench. He checked the annealing oven where a bust of the Theotokos—the Greek Orthodox title for Christ's mother Mary, literally God-Bearer—cooled to room temperature. He removed the mold and set it onto open wire shelves until tomorrow, just to be sure that the glass inside had

116

cooled enough to handle. When he returned to his studio, he'd break the mold off and let it cool for several more hours while he layered glass paste over St. Irene's mold and fired the casting. It would take several castings to finish the saint's bust, and when he'd moved her to the annealing oven, the Theotokos would be ready for cleaning and polishing.

He'd packed lunch, so he grabbed a Mexican blanket and biked to the Riverside Press Park to eat and enjoy the warmth of the early spring sun. Yesterday, he'd taken home half a dozen artichokes from the Co-op and then steamed and marinated them in balsamic vinegar. To this delicacy, he'd added gourmet fresh linguine, not far past the sell-by date, with a *fra diavolo* sauce made from crushed canned tomatoes, wilted fresh parsley, and chopped garlic from a jar that had almost expired. He'd spiced up the sauce with red pepper flakes from a half-empty jar he'd found in a dormitory dumpster (that had been a fine haul, given how wasteful and lazy college students were, including a microwave still in its box). The tiny canned shrimp, although not typical for the recipe, worked rather well. The stainless-steel thermos, only a little dented, that he pulled from his canvas knapsack, kept the pasta hot, too. A couple of oranges, damaged on one side and therefore inedible to most shoppers, completed his meal. He'd even gotten a few bottles of iced tea yesterday at the chain bagel place near his apartment.

Tom Paul finished eating and lifted his face to the sun. As productive as winter had been, he needed the rest and relaxation that summer meant. He still worked in his studio then, but not nearly for so many focused hours. Puck craved a hiatus and Tom Paul gladly gave it to him so that he could play Ultimate Frisbee, hike with Jonah and a few other friends in the White Mountains of New Hampshire, and camp at the beach. Once *The Soul Illuminated* opened in six weeks, he could let Sharon handle the show. She'd be sure to drum up orders for more *tchotchkes*, something he had to do to survive but hated nevertheless.

One day, his work would win a grant, perhaps tour museums. He knew this, just as he knew that God had brought his lady of the mists into his life once he was ready for her.

He biked to the Co-op for the afternoon shift, filled with sunlight and expectancy. He wasn't let down. When she walked in, her presence electrified the dusty air in the produce section, but she seemed oblivious to him until, reaching for some cluster tomatoes, her fingers grazed his. The jolt that ran between them brought her gaze, hidden beneath the bill of a baseball cap, to his.

Stupidly, he said the first thing that came to mind. "Hey. It's you." He saw white and orange hairs clinging to her fleece jacket and understood she had pets. He saw the blankness in her green eyes replaced with fear and then confusion. A frown creased the gap between her eyebrows. She hardly spoke while he followed her around the produce section, a puppy or an annoying baby brother, rambling and eager to please. He found himself trying to explain what he'd been doing in the dumpster when he'd never felt the need to explain before. At his confession that Zandra thought he was crazy, this beautiful, haunted woman teased him despite her fear.

"That's not a good thing. You know that, don't you?"

After the teasing, she'd pulled away but, despite not wanting to frighten her, he'd followed her to the bulk-foods aisle. When he asked whether she lived close by, he could have bitten his tongue off at the look of sheer terror that froze her features.

She firmed her mouth, straightened her neck and answered anyway. He loved her even more for it. "Yes."

"Good," he said, his pleasure suffusing his voice before he could stifle it. "I'll see you around then."

She didn't flinch at his words even though he suspected that it cost a great deal of effort for her to stand firm. He told her he only worked at the Co-op on weekends to give her the choice to avoid him, hoping even as he said it that she wouldn't take it. When she heard that he had a studio, light came into her eyes. He fell into their gaze, seeing the jeweled colors of her spirit, shadow free and brilliant. The intensity overwhelmed him, sent his heart beating a staccato and his breath to quicken. Bemused, he smiled to diffuse the feeling gripping him.

She asked about his art and took the postcard for his opening that he'd slid into the pocket of his chinos and now thanked God he'd done so. The shadow dropped over her gaze again, and she answered vaguely about coming—but it wasn't no, he kept reminding himself afterwards—and scurried away, her basket gripped so tightly her knuckles shone white through the skin covering them.

He still didn't know her name. But he knew what she was eating for dinner and he hummed as he selected his own cluster tomatoes, basil, Portobello mushrooms, Arborio rice and buffalo mozzarella. It didn't even matter that they hadn't expired and he'd have to pay full price for them.

Tom Paul wasn't surprised when she showed up early Monday morning at his studio, her face glowing from a hard run. He'd eschewed his usual meditation outside, moved by Puck to head straight to his workbench to model St. Sebastian's head yet again. Puck, who didn't have a clue about how to stage this new face, whispered that the installation needed both the mirror and the model. When the viewer first gazed at the scene, St. Sebastian should be complete. Only when the lights dimmed and the spotlight highlighted his figure should the viewer see herself in the mirror that replaced the head.

He tried over and over to capture the mixed expression of shock, sorrow, and pain that he knew suffused St. Sebastian. Over and over, he had to discard his efforts. His fingertips had lost their sensitivity. His inner eyesight had fled. Frustration seeped into him. He felt like a blind man whose hands fumbled inside a closed box. Just as he threw the clay knife down, he heard the bell on the gallery door. He'd known. Somehow, he'd known that she'd come to him this time, that their third meeting would be no fortunate accident. Wiping the clay from his fingers, he stepped out to greet her.

She stood, breathless and wide-eyed in the radiant light of the front gallery. When he spoke, she turned confused eyes to him and then took a step toward the Theotokos. She stretched out a tentative hand and studied the Mother of God, a fearful frown marring her features. After a long moment, her breathing quieted and he saw her shoulders relax, as if she'd been reassured by that most loving mother. As she looked around her, her face melted into serenity and her eyes radiated awe. His heart skipped a beat. The dark shadow hovering over her aura had vanished as so much clinging smoke in a brisk wind. When she brought her gaze to his, he recognized the purity of spirit he'd caught glimpses of before.

"Why is He so sad?" she asked, her head back to gaze at Christ Pantocrator and Tom Paul heard pain and understanding in her voice. She knew why. Perhaps even better than he did.

He led her to the couch under John the Baptist, taking her elbow as delicately as if he held a thin-walled glass sculpture. She didn't pull away, but he felt a tremor waver through her. He sat at the far end of the couch to give her a safe distance. Even so, her body heat cushioned the space between them. He longed to brush away the wispy hairs freed from her ponytail by her run, to care for her as he knew she didn't care for herself.

"Are you Catholic?" The word sounded clumsy in her mouth.

"Eastern Orthodox." Her puzzled expression was familiar to him, but this was the first time he really cared to explain the difference. He wanted her to know and understand him, just as he wanted to know and understand her. "During the Middle Ages the Christian Church split into two, the western Roman Catholic and the Eastern Orthodox. We've got a lot in common, but there are many subtle theological differences."

"Oh. That's beyond me."

She looked so worried that he wanted to reassure her. "Me too." He smiled and was rewarded with a tentative curl of her lips. What would it take to coax it to bloom into a full smile?

"I'm Weeble. You know, like the toy." The fact that she slipped her hands between her thighs didn't escape him.

He must open himself up first.

"I had a Weebles tree house." He held out his hand. "Nice to meet you, Weeble."

She giggled; it was a sound surprisingly young and carefree, as if it had been bottled up inside her for a long time. She took his hand, the soft skin of her fingers making him all too aware of his own heat-abused and calloused ones. Still, she didn't pull away at once, letting her hand rest inside of his. He wanted to keep it there, to tuck her arm up under his own and draw her close to his side, but he sensed that she'd gone as far as she could for now. He let her hand go and dropped his, bereft of its warm softness, to his side.

"I fell in love with Byzantine art in college," he said, holding her gaze with his. He might as well have said *I fell in love with you*. "I'd always seen it at Mass, but learning more about the history of my faith inspired me to look more closely."

She didn't look away. "They're beautiful." Her whisper told Tom Paul that she didn't speak about his art. But he also understood that she didn't recognize what she'd just revealed so he talked about how glass represented the spiritual for him. Sharing this belief meant little danger for him. He'd long ago exposed his inner life when he'd let Puck take charge and created St. Sebastian's final agony and apotheosis.

121

As he spoke, Weeble looked around the gallery, her head moving a little from side to side. He thought she strained to glimpse something that darted, elusive and hidden, around her. She frowned, tilting her head, and again considered Christ Pantocrator on his Byzantine ceiling.

Without warning, she rose. "I have to go. I have to finish my run." She reached the door before her next words. "Maybe I'll see you at your opening."

He nodded, holding her gaze for as long as she'd look at him. "I hope so, Weeble."

He watched her, a woman who must have earned her nickname by keeping her feet through any number of blows, as she raced away with demons nipping at her heels.

Six

▼

BOOKS NO LONGER MEAN MUCH, if anything, to me. Where once I devoured supermarket novels, I never buy them anymore. Just glimpsing a wire rack filled with pulp draws bile into my mouth. Each story printed in small type on cheap, yellowing paper promises to supply the reader with an exciting yet safe adventure, but it's all bullshit. Romances especially fill me with angry horror—not at all the reaction their housewives-turned-authors intended. I don't believe in the whole scenario, hero and heroine and happy endings. Legal and spy thrillers caught my attention for a short time, at least until I figured out that they were just more contrived fantasy for couch-bound executives who wished they'd signed up when the CIA recruited on campus. Contrived and ultimately boring. Most science fiction and fantasy is just plain ridiculous. Preposterous. For people who can't live with their feet on the ground in the real world. The worst of all the supermarket escapism is horror. White-hot fury blinds me when I think about the benign evil of suburban horror, cats returning from the dead and nightmare-assassins. People who read and write those books indulge their darker sides because they're immured to the horror extant in the world. I can't read any of these self-centered genres.

There's no escape for those who've seen the absolute worst that human nature can produce.

I did try more upscale fiction in college. Hardcover titles from the bookstore in the mall whose covers relied on cerebral type and a classy line illustration. Here I found beautiful language, more realistic settings, ordinary events, and quirky characters like the oddball outsider. For a time, I read these books until I realized they are another form of escapism cloaked in respectable shades of literary. An inverted escapism to be sure where the reader loses the scales from her eyes, gets dragged through the muck of the human condition, and is finally left stranded asking, "Is that it? That's what life's all about?"

It wasn't until I complained to Marcie that I understood what was going on. She herself stuck to nonfiction, either practical texts to refine her already prodigious insight into the human psyche or straightforward histories and biographies. Her favorite is a two-volume biography of Eleanor Roosevelt, a woman who held her own against the larger-than-life man she'd married. I'd finished Cormac McCarthy's *All the Pretty Horses* and flung it against the apartment wall in angry frustration. Marcie, who'd been studying at the dining table, put down her pen and made us some coffee before explaining the difference between supermarket fiction and modern literary novels.

"They're two sides of the same coin. That's what happens when the high brow gets separated from the low brow. Mom"— her mother teaches literature at a state college—"says that somewhere along the line, people decided that Art is Serious and that means you can't use it for escape or pleasure. It has to show sophisticated readers what the world really looks like, you know, ugly, broken, and mean. And pointless."

She scanned my bookshelves, pulling off a recent title and waving it around her head, her dark brown eyes wide and emphatic. "When you finish a serious novel, you're older, wiser, and sadder. Naturally, most people don't read to be edified. They want a little hope and some conviction that there's meaning in what they're going through. Adventure and romance and comedy all depend on hope and conviction. So of course more people buy their books at the supermarket than the high-end bookstore. I suspect more buy self-help books than fiction, too."

Marcie turned and replaced the book on my shelf. I watched her, my thoughts tumultuous and sharply unhappy.

"So what you get when you separate the two are Santa Claus and Bogeyman stories. Santa Claus stories sugarcoat and downplay and make you feel good for a little while. And Bogeyman stories warn you about the grim realities of the wide world so you're scared, maybe depressed."

"What am I supposed to read then? Or don't I get to read?"

She pressed her lips together and stuck her hands on her hips. "I'll ask Mom, but I suspect she'd say read the classics. Shakespeare for sure. There's a reason he's never been toppled as the best writer in the English language. He kept the bawdy with the poetry. How about historical fiction? And you know I like biographies. Other non-fiction, the kind told as a narrative. There is more written than you can ever read. Just don't give up. Stories and poetry feed our souls, Weeble."

I often think about that conversation. Why are stories and poetry soul food? There's no soul in most of what I read. To paraphrase the Bard, just sound and fury signifying nothing.

I contemplate what the ancients would think of modern storytelling. The gods were omnipresent in their tales. What would they think of stories that had no gods? Are we really wiser than they are?

I lean back against the cushioned airplane seat and close my eyes, my hand holding a history of the Byzantine Empire open on the tray in front of me. The man wedged into the middle seat looms into my space, his aggressive elbow planted on the armrest between us. He doesn't read anything, just types a frantic staccato on his laptop. I will myself to ignore the claustrophobic terror he inspires in me or the seven hours I sit here will leave me raving.

I return to my reading. The exotic and mystic Byzantines unexpectedly fascinate me. History never meant much before, although I did fixate on ancient Roman engineering for a couple of years during college. The pragmatic and skilled Romans, who obsessed over roads and aqueducts, public baths, and fountains, still impress me. Roman stoicism appeals to my nature too, but the intrigues and battles that comprise the rest of history remind me too much of violent soap operas. I don't really know what made me buy this book. Do I really need to learn that most Byzantine emperors died violent deaths, that eye-gouging ranked high on the list of torture used by emperor and usurper alike? Human nature never changes. I don't have to dwell on the countless ugly details.

Still, the author's claim that Byzantine artists succeeded in triumphantly reflecting the image of God—their paintings and mosaics suffused with a degree of spirituality not accomplished anywhere else in the history of Christianity or by any other major religion—snags my attention. Over and over again, the Byzantine Empire reached for and grabbed the sublime even as its emperors, acting as God's regents on Earth, wallowed in utter depravity. What's the point in reaching for more if it means nothing? I fidget, sigh, and fidget some more. I want to toss this book against a wall, too.

Instead, I return to reading. It's either that or turning over my visit with Rose Bishop in the duly quaint English village of

Ashford-in-the-Water. Her voice plays a second track in my thoughts, at times overriding my own voice, at other times murmuring beneath it. Either way, her tone grates, high-pitched and irritated, no matter the volume. In my memory, I sound coolly pragmatic. Of course Rose can't understand why a damn nosy Yank traveled over hill and dell to badger her about a 45-year-old murder. I understand she doesn't care about her dead elder sister. I understand why she sees no point in digging up history. She was a young child, for God's sake. I don't argue with her. Now, on the plane back to Boston with type swimming in front of my eyes, I wish I'd never gone to ask for photos and family stories about a Shirley Temple lookalike tortured and killed by demons in human guise. God knows Annie would deny we were even sisters.

In my backpack, shoved under the seat in front of me, are black-and-white photos of Leslie Ann's London flat and a road sign near the moor where Maura led police and waved a vague hand to indicate Leslie Ann's final resting place. If I don't bring them out, Leslie Ann won't exist. It's up to me. I can leave her death in the shadows or illuminate her life.

I return to an echoing apartment. Hero and Flat Stanley have gone to board with Marcie and Evan, and I won't see them until tomorrow. As I shoulder my door open a severe ache hits me between the shoulder blades. Weight precipitates into my carry-on bag, dragging it down until it slips with a thunk to the floor. Without my two loyal companions underfoot, I'm free to start laundry, shower, and run to the Co-op for fresh produce, milk, and eggs. Free to think only of me. It's not until I'm strolling toward the Co-op's entrance, my hair damp and twisted into a messy knot on my nape, that I remember that it's Sunday. My chin rises and my shoulders press back. No matter. I can shop whenever I want.

I see Tom Paul immediately. He's pushing a large mop under a long display of New England greens, his dusty white t-shirt and tan cargo pants at home among their vivid leaves and crisp stems. I have only about thirty seconds to watch the muscles dance along his upper back before he turns gleaming eyes on me and a hollow feeling opens up inside my gut. I swallow, aware that I've not eaten since breakfast on the plane, and nod once. Without a word I pivot, squashing the hungry tremble in my thighs and ignore the lightheadedness lifting my crown from my neck. I keep my stride controlled and read each price placard attached to the front of the display, considering what I will eat for lunch and dinner. All at once, a strange craving hits me. I don't recognize it. I barely understand that the strong feeling washing over me is indeed craving. It's like nothing I've ever felt before.

Irritated sadness fills me. Am I really so hard to figure out? I'm hungry, I'm tired, and I've eaten strange foods for almost a week. It must be that. I focus on identifying what my body lacks as though my life depended on it. The phantom taste of chocolate truffles and warm caramel sauce coats my tongue, sweet and soothing. Well, I can't have them. I won't have them. Instead, I evaluate an artichoke and a bunch of asparagus. My renegade body struggles against my will and my craving deepens into an ache as fierce as a rotten tooth, no matter how I clamp down on it. Before I give in, I trot down the aisle and snatch spicy arugula and crisp radishes, pungent chives and tart rhubarb. They'll overwhelm my rebellious taste buds, much as capsaicin lotions burn and numb arthritic joints. Fire fights fire. Pain cancels out pain.

Almost as quickly as it flares, the insane craving dies away. It was only a flash in the pan, producing no long-lasting burn. Even this saddens me. I don't have the fuel to sustain an internal fire. On the far side of the produce section, I catch a glimpse of Tom

Paul, who appears to concentrate on reaching the furthest edge of floor under the displays, his overlong hair obscuring his profile. My lips start to form words, but I stifle their sounds before they reach the hollow of my mouth. He never looks my way, though, and I trace a meandering path toward the dairy section, exhausted from the lack of sleep on the overnight flight and unable to think now that the hollowness has left me. I hurry through my shopping and scurry home as fast as my tired legs can carry me.

Inside my apartment, the echoes swell to fill the space, the pressure of the lifeless rooms bearing down on me while I unpack my groceries. I only get as far as putting the milk and eggs into the refrigerator before I collapse and crawl to the sofa. My weighted lids descend almost before I lay my head against the armrest. My last coherent thought whispers that maybe this time I won't wake up. Relief carries me to sleep.

To sleep and to nightmares.

Nightmares populated with fire-breathing demons, their grotesque puce bellies distended over obscene erections and their flat black eyes scraping my inner thighs. They rake vicious claws down my side, pry into the tender flesh between my legs, the whole time breathing sulfurous, ashy breath so that my screams are choked in my throat. I'm impaled on the bitter adamantine of their sex; they won't stop until I'm crucified, raw and bleeding my life out on a sooty plain of lust and pain.

Eternity passes before a brilliant point of light punches a hole in the obsidian sky above my head, followed by radiant hair cracks zigzagging across the black night in a destructive web. My eyes are dazzled, my wounded heart stutters and races near death, but sweet air blows away the foul demon stench and my grateful lungs gulp. The demons chitter, twisting claws and sinking fangs into my breast, the iron rod between my legs threatening to tear me asunder. I am expiring. I am disintegrating

129

on a river of agony when the heat and light invading the dark dome combust in a silent explosion, ripping away hell.

Particles of my being fly outward on light waves, escaping to infinite oblivion. Even as I lose myself into eternity, I recognize the incandescent figure next to me, his face lost in blinding white but his calloused hand extended toward me.

* * *

The first and only time Easter promised more than chocolate bunnies, jelly beans, and hard-boiled eggs dyed outlandish and unnatural colors was that fifth grade after I met Lauren. When Grandma Nan invited me to stay for a sunrise service at her Methodist church, my curiosity overcame my reticence and I left Annie unguarded at home. To this day, I can recall the glow creeping up the stained-glass window depicting Jesus as the Good Shepherd at the front of the sanctuary. Reverence and awe still wash over me as I envision His gleaming, slightly smiling face. Sometimes the scent of institutional carpet, dusty and tinged with cleaner, transports me to that dawn in early April. And for that instant, I stand again on the cusp of direct knowledge of good and evil, still capable of turning back into innocent forgetfulness. Still hopeful and free.

Lauren and I slept over at the church along with a group of other children, our blankets and pillows laid out on the carpeted sanctuary floor so that we'd awaken to the sunlight transforming the image of Christ above us after falling asleep anticipating His Resurrection. Nearly nothing of the story the pastor told us the night before stayed with me, its significance lost on my ignorant paganism. Even so, Lauren's excitement and the strangeness of sleeping in a church embedded itself into my psyche.

After a solemn dawn service that included a dance we'd learned the evening before, we trudged, hungry and happy, to the church basement where cheerful mothers greeted us with endless stacks of blueberry pancakes, sausages, and scrambled eggs. Grandma Nan wandered among the tables of children pouring milk and delivering coffee cake, her smile turning her eyes up and lifting her whole face. The chatter and the camaraderie hit me in between frantic bites of pancakes, and I sighed, never wanting to leave the fluorescent basement cave, so odd and yet so comforting in its oddness.

By now, I'd joined Lauren in the ranks of the changed. My breasts, appearing in the fall as swollen as stings from alien mosquitoes, had filled out enough that I wore a real bra, a torturous sling designed to rub my chest raw and pinch the soft skin of my back. But that was better than *not* wearing one and letting my shirts rub my newly sensitive nipples. I felt ugly and uncomfortable in my ill-fitting skin and imagined myself a snake or lobster or beetle, just after molting. No one seemed to notice my resemblance to awkward insects and reptiles. Except Tim. Tim cornered me in the kitchen often to whisper crude and cruel things about my body. He said no man would want me unless he wanted to rub up against a brick shithouse with hard nubbins for titties. He said my budding breasts were a joke of nature but my full-grown breasts resembled monster teats, not big but grotesque.

"More'n a mouthful's too much." His mocking voice insinuated into my ear, but he always turned before I could retort. It took me weeks to respond, but nothing I said ever insulted or angered him. He just laughed and sidled away out of reach of my hand, which began gripping a spatula as a matter of course after he tweaked a nipple. He didn't dare do it again.

He hissed that I stank, that my crotch reeked, that my funk clouded the air in the kitchen. If he caught sight of used sanitary products in the bathroom trash, whether they were mine or not, he'd badger me about being on the rag and mutter (when Mona wasn't in the room) about bleeding bitches. I wanted to hide, to turn back the clock, to disappear into thin air. I began wearing baggy adult t-shirts and let my hair grow shaggy to cover my face. I locked and re-locked the bathroom door, afraid that Tim would break in on me while I studied my changing genitals, tugged on growing underarm hair, or shaved my legs.

Boys at school weren't much different. Pat led Zack and Victor on bra-snapping raids once the weather grew nice enough for us to doff our coats on the playground—at least until I knocked him down and punched him hard, once in the gut and once in the nuts. He squirmed and moaned, his pinched and pale features pleasing me no end.

"I warned you, you little prick. Keep your hands to yourself."

Victor, braver than Zack, defied me. "You're a bitch. Wait'il I tell a teacher."

I turned fierce eyes on him. "You do and I'll find you after school and beat the crap out of you, you little turd."

This time, Ms. McKinney didn't catch me. My scowl and a brandished fist sent the boys scurrying away. I waited until they'd reached the fence on the far side of the playground before sucking on my bruised knuckles.

Debbie, Lisa, and Lauren all stood in a silent knot behind me.

"Doubt they'll bother us again," Lauren said as I stood to join them.

"God, Weeble, you're like Wonder Woman," Debbie said, her eyes shining. No one but Annie had ever looked at me like that before.

"Yeah," Lisa said. She hardly spoke, her soft, high voice easy to ignore when she did. She tossed her long, thin blonde hair. "I wish I was as tall and big as you. They wouldn't dare snap your bra."

I'd just looked at her. Until that moment, I hadn't considered Lisa or Debbie a friend, just girls to tolerate around Lauren. It occurred to me that day that perhaps it wouldn't hurt to be nicer to Lisa and Debbie, just in case. Lisa, a skinny girl who wore blue jeans and western shirts, daydreamed about owning a horse and drew one every art class. Debbie, cherub-faced and bubbly, struggled with spelling but always shared smuggled jolly ranchers at recess. She had an older sister, the only one of us who did, and her knowledge of pop music, make-up, and dating struck the rest of us as prodigious.

Lauren and I split the leadership duties of our little group. Or rather, Lauren led us in most things, but I accepted the familiar role of protector. For a few glorious weeks after Easter sunrise service, the sun shone, lending a hopeful tint to the world and thawing the icy splinter in my eye a bit. I decided to risk my happiness on a birthday slumber party. Even before I sidled up to Mona to see if she'd let me have one, I tested the idea out on my friends. No point in asking if no one wanted to come.

"My birthday's coming up." I hung from the monkey bars, which we'd co-opted during afternoon recess, and let my bodyweight drag my toes along the pavement.

"Ooh!" Debbie squealed. "When?"

"May 26th."

"That's the last day of school," Lauren said. "It's on Wednesday."

My armpits had started to burn, but I refused to let go until I'd finished my piece. "Yeah."

"Are you having a party?" Debbie asked. Lisa just watched me.

I swung on the pivots of my shoulders. The simple mechanics of my body soothed me. "I was thinkin' about a slumber party." I said this with my face turned from them as if the statement endangered me. It did.

"Ooh!" Debbie squealed again. A smile emphasized the cherubic in her features. "Can I come?"

That had been almost too easy.

Lauren, who leaned against the uprights of the monkey bars, grabbed one and swung out at an angle. Her dirty-blond hair dangled limp as wet laundry at her side. "We could use the Ouija board," she said and I knew the slumber party had passed the test. Mona couldn't say no.

I looked at Lauren to see how serious she was about the Ouija board. We hadn't used it since that disastrous sleepover in October. She grinned at me. I grinned back. "I gotta ask my mom first if I can have a slumber party."

"You can come to my house," Debbie said, "if she won't let you."

"Or mine," Lisa said, her soft voice interjecting. Her shy smile made me let go of the monkey bars and straighten up tall.

"There. We'll have a slumber party no matter what," Lauren said. She'd tilted her head all the way back to bare her throat to the sun. "Summer. We're almost sixth graders. Can you believe it?"

Joy rose up in me at their obvious warm friendship, but like mercury it couldn't remain expansive when cold reality returned. I'd forgotten about the eerie interaction with the Ouija angel and I'd ignored the very real demon in my own home.

Mona, who'd been wandering around the family room searching for her current paperback romance, stopped and stood up to blink at me when I asked her if my three friends could come over after school for my birthday.

"About time, Weeble." Her raspy voice chided me. "I figured that little Miss Lauren was too good for the likes of us."

I squirmed under her gaze even though I refused to meet it. I couldn't let her blame Lauren. "I never asked her to come before."

Mona snorted and returned to pawing the sofa cushions, but she'd agreed to my birthday sleepover and I ignored her criticism of Lauren.

My birthday brought summer with it, hot and promising the unending delights awaiting our vacation. I can still recall the smell of cut grass drying its dew under the powder-blue sky, the rough grumble of lawn mowers down the block, and the rhythmic click-and-shoosh of sprinklers. Anticipation sounds like birds twittering in leafy maples and tastes like sweet lemonade mixed from tap water and powdered mix.

For the first time all year, Annie and I didn't have to ride the bus home. Instead, we waited outside school on the sidewalk with Lauren, Debbie, and Lisa for Mona to pick us up. Mona was late and the crossing guards had already gone inside to return their orange belts when I glanced across the street and saw an angular man leaning against a parked car watching us. At first he reminded me of the Scarecrow from *The Wizard of Oz*, all elbows and bony knees, but when my gaze traveled to his eyes, the benign image faded. Their flat black stare gave me the creeps. For all their burning life, they called to mind the empty sockets of skulls. I'd turned to tell the others that we should go inside to wait when Mona's dented Chevy turned the corner. By the time we'd all piled in, the stranger had disappeared.

I sat next to Annie in the front seat but turned and knelt to talk to the others on the ride home. Lauren sat in between Debbie and Lisa, her eagerness apparent in her chattiness. Mona, who'd greeted my friends, watched them in the rearview mirror while driving, a cigarette dangling from her mouth. When we got home, I was stunned to see that she'd cleaned the house so that I almost didn't recognize it. It certainly smelled better.

"Made your favorite Jell-o cheesecake," she said as I stood gap-mouthed in the living room. "Girls, just put your pillows and blankets on the floor. You'll camp out here." I saw the telltale signs of the vacuum in the shaggy carpet and blinked back tears.

We left our pillows and blankets in the living room and ran into the kitchen for Doritos and Pepsi, giggling in sheer giddiness. Annie, snuggling her rabbit under her arm, tucked herself against the wall next to the refrigerator and watched, aware that she could be in the group as long as she said little. Mona left us alone except to tell us she'd make Hamburger Helper around six. We snacked and then they each gave me a birthday gift, which surprised me even though it was my birthday. I'd never gotten a gift from anyone outside Frank and Mona and my Aunt Susie. Lisa gave me a sketchbook and charcoal drawing pencils. Debbie gave me a set of cosmetics with a purple vinyl cover. When I opened it, I saw eye shadows in Easter egg colors, blush in a variety of mauves, peaches, and pinks, and a row of lip gloss. Lauren gave me a set of stories by a man named C.S. Lewis and a tablet of Mad Libs. I ran my fingers over the black sketchbook cover, feeling choked and not knowing what to say.

"Thanks," I finally whispered to them.

"Let's go outside and do the Mad Libs," Lauren said. "They're super funny."

I'd seen Mad Libs in the Scholastic book catalog at school, but I never had any money to order from it. We grabbed our pop and headed to the picnic table out back, Annie following. We stayed outside laughing at the inane stories we created by filling in random verbs, adverbs, nouns, numbers and adjectives. Any time a proper name was needed, Lauren declared that my name had to be filled in. After a while, Debbie put make-up on all of us, although she sighed a lot over not having mascara or perfume to complete our makeovers. Even Annie got to pick out her favorite eye shadow and blush. Afterwards, we wandered my street, talking about sixth grade and which teacher we wanted. For the first time since my body molted, I felt at home in my new skin. Perhaps not entirely graceful and grown-up but on my way.

"I know what to ask the Ouija tonight," Lauren said as we shuffled back to my house.

"What?" Debbie asked.

"I'm going to ask about Tucker."

"Tucker?" I felt my face screwing up in puzzlement. "Why?"

Lauren shrugged and a funny smile curled the corner of her mouth.

Debbie laughed. "You like Tucker?"

Lauren nodded and ducked her head. Her reaction stunned me. I hadn't given the new boy a second thought after he showed up in March.

"Why?" I heard myself ask.

Lauren shrugged again, her gaze sliding over me. "His eyes."

My puzzlement deepened. "What's so special about his eyes?"

Before Lauren could respond, Lisa spoke, her soft voice conveying undeniable enthusiasm. "They're blue-green."

"You can't miss them, Weeble. They're really bright." Now Debbie looked at me and something in her expression made me feel like an oddity. "You really didn't notice?"

"No." I mumbled while my earlier sense of fitting in evaporated in the early-evening sun. Somehow the world had shifted again and I hadn't kept up. I'd never noticed anything beyond Tucker's shaggy hair. Next to me, Annie reached for my hand as if she knew about my sudden confusion.

Tim, his long hair half obscuring his face, slouched outside the front door smoking as we returned. Something in his stance sent a thrill of terror up the back of my neck. I refused to look at him as we went into the house, but I could feel his gaze on us. On my friends. He stayed outside while we ate dinner, but my senses had gone on alert and when I heard voices I knew his friends Joey and Pete had arrived. Unease permeated me, but I ignored it. What could I do about it anyway?

We went to my room after we ate, shutting the door to play Monopoly while we waited for it to get dark enough to justify flashlights once I shut off the overhead light. Lauren and I grew quiet at the end of our exuberant game and I wondered if she remembered the last time we'd consulted the Ouija. For my part, I remembered the previous sinister movement of the *planchette* under our fingertips and the answers to questions that we hadn't asked. Had we in fact called forth a spirit from another world? Already I felt something lurking in the corners of my room, waiting for Debbie and Lisa to stop talking before joining us around the board. I squinted at the edges of the room, half-afraid that I'd catch something in the shadows softening the lines of wall and ceiling, but I saw nothing before switching the light off.

Debbie and Lisa both gave a little shriek before stifled giggling. I waited until they'd stopped before turning my flashlight on. The sharp click startled me and when I pulled the wavering beam across the other girls' faces, I saw that they'd been startled too. I hurried to sit next to Annie before she fussed. It was just a damn game. As I sat down each girl snapped on her own flashlight and we set them at our sides to illuminate the board. The room was dim but not dark.

Lauren sat cross-legged, her fingertips already resting on the *planchette*.

"You begin," I said as I placed my own fingers on the small wooden triangle.

"Okay." She wiggled herself upright and cleared her throat. "Angel, are you here?"

YES. I AM ALWAYS WITH YOU.

Lisa gasped and Debbie giggled, high-pitched and nervous. Lauren glanced at them, frowning until silence returned. Annie snuggled closer to my side.

"Angel, why are you here?"

TO TELL YOU THE TRUTH.

"Does Tucker like me?"

YES.

Lauren's eyes met mine over the board. She looked excited, but before she could ask another question, the *planchette* spelled out more.

HE WILL KISS YOU BEFORE EVIL TAKES YOU.

138

Now Lauren shrieked, but it was a happy sound. Something about the way the shadows caressed her face afterwards made me quake. Premonition filled me. She hadn't paid attention to the whole message.

"What does that mean? 'Before evil takes you'?"

HE IS COMING.YOU HAVE SEEN HIS FACE.

Icy blood trickled through my veins. Debbie began to cry softly.

"What does he look like?" I heard my strained defiance as I forced myself to ask. Lauren just sat stunned, her fingers fallen to the side of the *planchette*.

DEAD EYES.

Lisa began keening, but I ignored her. There had to be more. I had to learn more.

"What else? How will we know him?"

HE IS A SCARECROW.

I started trembling. I had seen a scarecrow with dead eyes that afternoon. No one else had seen him. Was he the one?

"Is he coming for me too?" Panic threaded my voice.

YOU WILL CHOOSE.

What did that mean? "What do I do?" I whispered, oblivious to everyone else in the room.

WEEBLE STAND UP. YOU WONT FALL DOWN.

A sudden thwack on my window startled us from our trance and the *planchette* went skittering across the board to land in Lisa's lap. Five seconds later we'd all jumped up and jostled one another on the way to the bedroom door. Another thirty seconds passed before Lauren scrabbled through us and then she'd pulled the door open and we all fell into the lit hall. Twenty feet away the TV sat flickering in the corner of the living room. Frank sat hunched in his recliner, a Miller in his hand. He raised his eyes as we tumbled around him. I'd never realized before how ordinary the living room was.

139

"What's wrong?" Even Frank's growl comforted me.

"N-nothin'." Breathless, I didn't convince myself.

Frank ignored me to ask the one person sure to tell him the truth. "Annie, what the hell's goin' on in your room?"

Annie hugged her rabbit to her chest and pressed her lips together, twisting in place. She darted a glance at me and then answered Frank. "An angel spoke to us."

Frank rolled his eyes and sipped his beer, astonishing me with his restraint. "That so? I guess that'd scare the shit out of me, too."

"Can we put out our blankets now?" I asked, my shoulders tensing for his answer.

Frank lowered his beer can and looked around my group of friends. For the first time I wondered if Mona had told him I was having a slumber party.

Just then Mona walked in from the kitchen. "Weeble, ready for your cheesecake?"

"Cheesecake?" Now Frank looked perplexed. I watched his face as his gaze circled my friends again and then his forehead smoothed. "It's your birthday, ain't it?" At my nod, he raised his beer can. "Happy birthday, Weeble. Get me some cheesecake, Moan."

By the time we'd all grabbed some cheesecake and settled on the floor of the living room to eat, the crushing terror that had sent us tearing out of my room had evaporated. We began to snicker and joke about the message, but when I tried to suggest that I'd made up the answers to scare everyone, Annie piped in.

"No, you didn't. The angel talked to us." As she spoke, Lauren said, "You didn't, Weeble! How could you?"

"Yeah, right," I said to Annie, ignoring Lauren's angry interjection. "You're just sayin' that because I made the *planchette* say it."

"No, I'm not." Annie's stubborn refusal irked me. "I saw him."

140

We all stopped eating and looked at my little sister, her hair sticking up on the back of her head and her face serene.

"If that's so, what'd he look like?" Demand made my voice harsh.

"He's beautiful and white. He hurt my eyes."

My unease dissolved, to be replaced by a strange feeling in my chest. I believed her. Why hadn't I seen him? I looked at Lauren, who watched me with an angry light in her eyes.

"I didn't do it," I said. "I didn't push the *planchette*, Lauren."

She didn't answer, just nodded once, but she avoided speaking to me until later, when we'd already turned out the light and lay stretched out on the floor. We'd all whispered together for a while, but the excitement of the evening had been replaced by a heavy sleepiness and my eyes closed during one of Debbie's stories.

"Did you?" Lauren whispered next to me in the dark. No one else spoke and the quiet felt old as though I'd been asleep for some time.

"What?" My voice, thick in my throat, sounded strange.

"Did you move the *planchette*, Weeble?"

"No."

"Then why did you say you did?"

I sighed and rolled onto my side away from her. "I don't know. Maybe I thought it would sound less scary."

She didn't say anything for so long I thought she'd gone to sleep. I'd started to drift away when she spoke again. "Less wonderful, too." Her voice grew softer still as though she spoke to herself. "I want Tucker to kiss me."

I didn't know what to say to that, so I let myself go before the insistent heaviness pushing against me. Sometime later I awoke again, confused and unhappy. A hush lay over the room around me broken only by soft murmuring from either Debbie or Lisa across from me and the slight whistle of Lauren's breathing at my side. I'd rolled back to face her and now lay curled toward her, so close that I felt her hair brush my forehead. It smelled like baby powder. Beneath me, the floor felt hard under the shag rug and the scent of dust, cigarette smoke, and faded cat urine weighed on me like melancholy. Something had awakened me. Something was wrong. I lay there probing my thoughts for remnants of a nightmare, but emptiness responded to my query. I looked around, but in the darkened room my sand-filled eyes saw nothing to confirm my alarm. After a long moment, a sharp burning in my bladder invaded my awareness along with relief. That's what had disturbed my sleep: I had to go to the bathroom.

I pushed myself to my feet and staggered to the bathroom, barely sitting on the toilet in time. I hadn't switched the light on, afraid to dazzle myself. As the burning in my lower gut faded and sleepiness made me yawn, I heard it. A low, desperate sobbing. I didn't recognize it at first, listening hard while I pulled up my pants. A soft click extinguished the sobbing for a second, but my oversensitive ears heard it, muffled and vague.

All at once I knew.

Running the handful of feet from the bathroom to my bedroom door, I twisted the knob and stumbled inside as if I had any chance of saving Annie from him. But even as I pushed the door shut behind me, I knew I was too late, that he'd already come and gone.

Why had I left Annie alone? I hadn't needed an angel to warn me. I'd seen the evil in Tim's eyes and I'd chosen to abandon her.

Seven

WHEN SOMEONE KNOCKS ON MY APARTMENT DOOR, the sharp sound punctures my reverie as I sit staring at the blinking cursor, drawing me from the past. I don't move. How like me to procrastinate, thinking about myself instead of Leslie Ann. *Self-pity looks good on you, dahling.* The knock comes again, insistent and unyielding. Whoever stands there has either come on a fool's errand or has just pulled me from running away—again. Now the knocking beats on my door, hooves hastening me to the present. I blink and swallow. The blank screen mocks me.

I stand, stiff from sitting still so long. Hero sits in front of the door, panting. Flat Stanley waits, inscrutable and wise, on my breakfast bar. I wish I could face the future as calmly as they do.

"I'm coming," I call to halt the knuckles on wood.

The rhythm stops. A muffled voice that sounds like Marcie responds. Of course. Who else would come to beard the lion in its den? I sigh and open the door. Hero barks once, happy and wagging his tail. He sniffs at Marcie's crotch and nudges her hand.

"About time, Weeble." Her chiding voice warms me despite myself. She stands, her arms crossed over her thick chest, wearing a black, long-sleeved t-shirt, a pair of gray carpenter pants, and Doc Marten Mary Janes. Her black eyes crackle and energy dances off her skin. I've always been attracted to Marcie's warmth and vitality, her hue and depth. When she walks into a room, everyone's eyes turn toward her, their ears strain to hear. She doesn't fade into the walls, colorless and wan. She doesn't have to. I who have the coloring of an indistinct gray moth, who should blend against pale bark, flutter toward her light, too stunned to fear burning.

I run my hand through my hair, pulling short strands from my ponytail and gesture for her to come in. "Sorry. Just lost in thinking." I wave toward the glowing screen on my desk in the corner.

Marcie leans against a chair near my small table, crosses her ankles and her arms. Her posture is decidedly frowning. "Yeah, about that. You look like shit, Weeble. Why are you doing this? You can't go on like this. Not alone."

I ignore her question. Her assertion. And walk into my tiny kitchen to pull out a box of Lipton teabags. I stall instead. "Tea? I have orange spice and mint, too."

"Sure. Orange spice." There's a pause, but I know what's coming. "Don't think I'm letting you off the hook this time."

I sigh again. "Of course not." I set the kettle on to boil but avoid turning to her. I pull out cups, spoons, a plate for the shortbread that I'd hand carried back from England, and my sugar bowl. I feel Marcie watching me, concern girding her irritation. *She can't help it*, I remind myself. The shortbread is for her. I expected her to come.

We sit down and I stir my tea to cool it. "English shortbread?" Her soft voice draws my gaze to her face. "Thank you, Weeble."

She's leaning toward me and her hand reaches for mine. "Your nightmares are back." It wasn't a question.

I nod and lose her gaze. Something stabs through me, down my shoulder and across my chest to land in the tender part of belly just above my thigh. I'm pinned by it to my seat.

"God, Weeble, you've gotta stop this."

"I can't." My voice, instead of firm and defiant as I'd intended, sounds mumbling and uncertain. "I spoke to the grant coordinator yesterday. I told her about my research and my trip. She put a *Boston Globe* reporter in touch with me about my project. I have an interview next week."

Marcie's grip tightens. "Then not alone."

I pull my hand from hers but regret for drawing away forces me to grip my teacup and take a sip. When I look into her sharp eyes, I know she's not fooled. I turn the conversation to my recent findings. "Leslie Ann wanted to be Ginger Rogers when she grew up. Just like Anne Frank, she had photos of her favorite stars plastered all over her bedroom, but Ginger was the one she most liked. Her favorite book was *Ginger Rogers and the Riddle of the Scarlet Cloak*. Kind've a Nancy Drew story. She studied tap and ballroom dance to get ready."

My voice has shaded into husky and my eyes burn, but I stop before I'm carried away.

"Oh, honey." Marcie's concern has lost all trace of irritation. It nearly undoes me, but I gulp my tea, its searing heat distracting me. Marcie takes both my hands now. "She's not the only little girl who needs remembering."

I sidestep her comment. "Her sister Rose told me to bugger off. She gave me photos and a journal and told me she was damn glad to be rid of them—and me. She doesn't see any reason to revisit something that happened so long ago to one little girl."

Marcie's thumbs rub the back of my hand. "She's wrong."

Now I look at Marcie. I hold her gaze with the sticky heat of my own. "I know." I clear my throat, swallow some more tea to fortify my crumbling demeanor, and change the topic. "How was your grandparents' anniversary?"

Marcie doesn't stop rubbing my hands, but she answers me. "Beautiful, just beautiful. Zeidy looked at Bubbe with such love on his face. He was so choked up, he couldn't speak. She just patted his cheek." She pauses and takes a sip of her own tea. Her gaze drops as she continues. "Did I ever tell you how they met? It was after World War II. She'd been in a concentration camp, Bergen-Belsen. The same one as Anne Frank."

Marcie's eyes get a faraway look as she stares across my apartment toward the window.

"Bubbe came to Bergen-Belsen from Thessaloniki in Greece. The Jewish community there was nearly annihilated. Ninety-six percent killed by the Nazis. The Greek Orthodox Church, it tried to protect the Jews. Some of them, including Bubbe's ancestors, had lived in Thessaloniki for almost two thousand years." Her voice breaks and she stops. In the quiet, I hear Hero shift and sigh on the floor. When she speaks again, her voice holds a trace of liquid grief. "The *Romaniotes*, that's what they're called. They speak their own Greek dialect, have their own Jewish traditions. Bubbe's family went into hiding with their Greek neighbors. Because Romaniotes had lived in Greece so long, they spoke Greek without the same inflection the Sephardic Jews had. It fooled the Nazis for a long time but not long enough."

Now Marcie laughs; it's a rough sound without humor. "The thing is, Bubbe didn't know what anti-Semitism was, not like the Jews from northern Europe anyway. Greece treated them so well, they thought of themselves as equally Greek and Jew. In fact, the Eastern Orthodox Archbishop wrote a letter to the Nazis to protest the deportation of Jews, reminding the Germans that in Christianity, there is neither Greek nor Jew. So when she got sent

146

to the labor camp, she almost died of shock when the Nazis shot a woman right in front of her."

I whimper and Marcie's eyes come back to mine. She squeezes my hands, hard. "She had to stay at a refugee camp for more than two years after the Allies liberated Bergen-Belsen. She was sick for months, severely malnourished actually. When she got better, she taught in a high school for the refugee kids. Taught Greek literature and philosophy. By the time she got to New York, she didn't look like she'd gone to hell and survived. She was twenty-one. She met and married Zeidy the next year."

Silence dominates the space between us, a silence filled with more than our breath and the fluttering pulse at her neck. I'm fascinated by that slight dance, that sign of life.

"She almost didn't. Marry Zeidy. She thought she was too damaged, too broken to deserve love. Zeidy grew up in Brookline. He'd served in the Pacific and didn't even see the horror of the Holocaust as a liberator. It didn't matter to him though. All he saw when he looked at her was the beauty of her soul. He thought she was the strongest woman he knew. It was his vision of her that healed her, Weeble. Zeidy knew we're not the sum of our experiences. Or at least not *only* our experiences."

I should've known that Marcie would find a way to bring us back to the topic at hand. She's a master at keeping conversation on track. "She's so lucky to have found him, then. Your Zeidy." I speak softly because I fear that my longing will sound like a clarion in the close confines of my apartment.

"More than lucky, Weeble. Thank God she didn't shut Zeidy out when they found each other." She doesn't say anything more for several moments, leaving me to my thoughts. What would've happened if her grandmother hadn't allowed herself to fall in love? To open up to a beautiful man without scars on his heart? I shift in my seat, aware of what I owe to Marcie's grandmother.

Now it's Marcie who changes topics. Or so I think at first.

147

"Hey, Evan and I went to a klezmer concert last weekend. My friend Sharon—you know, the glass artist—had an opening the same night." I stiffen and then nod, aiming for nonchalance. "We stopped by on the way to the concert. Beautiful stuff. She uses something called *dichroic* glass, along with other kinds of transparent or iridescent glass. She melts fragments and ribbons into these textured sculptures and panels."

Images of Tom Paul's studio fill my thoughts with clarity and luminous color. Intense longing cuts through me. I don't say anything because I don't know what to say about Sharon's art. Because I'm afraid of what I might say instead.

As if she can read my thoughts, Marcie speaks of him. "We ran into Tom Paul, who was there with his sister Callista. Sharon asked him why he didn't have a date. He just shrugged. When he didn't say anything, Callista answered for him. Said he'd stopped dating after breaking up with his girlfriend last year and now he only has eyes for some mystery woman he met one morning while he was dumpster diving." Her eyes slide sideways, but she doesn't say anything about the identity of the mystery woman. My heart thunders in my chest and I can hardly breathe.

Still, I take the bull by the horns. "Must've been some chance encounter." My voice sounds strained even to my ears.

"I imagine so." Marcie picks up her teacup and tilts her head back to finish its contents. "That's what Sharon said when Tom Paul told her it was love at first sight."

I shudder at her words. He can't mean me. He doesn't know me. He *can't* mean me, the woman who betrayed her best friend to a killer.

"That's crazy. No one falls in love at first sight." Right then, I know I must stay away from Tom Paul and his prescient gaze.

* * *

Denying the existence of evil doesn't make it go away, but then an eleven-year-old girl can't know that.

For more than a week after my slumber party, I ignored the memory of Annie's sobbing even though it kept me awake at night, at least until the day I got my first period. Perhaps it was the sight of blood darkening my panties with its metallic scent and stickiness that terrified me out of my numb passivity. Perhaps I recognized that my body had its own timeline, its own agenda, and that again, I had no control over what I was or what happened to me. Whatever the reason, I'd gone to my room after dinner feeling out of sorts, anxious and achy, ready to lash out at everyone. Annie wandered in while a fiery orange glow from the setting sun suffused our room and found me pushing the *planchette* around the Ouija board, which Lauren had discarded. I refused to look at her while she stood at my shoulder.

"Read to me."

"No."

"Yes. Read *The Snow Queen*."

"No. Go away."

Annie changed tack. "Play Monopoly."

"No." Irritation welled in me. I looked at her, scowling as I'd seen Mona do. "Get lost, twerp."

Annie, who clutched her stuffed rabbit under one arm, pulled her thumb from her mouth and tugged on my shirt. "C'mon, Weeble. Let's play hide and seek with Robbie and Mary."

I sighed, feeling the exhalation all the way to my toes, and flicked the *planchette* across the foot of the bed to the floor. "Okay. I'm coming." I stood and a sharp twinge knifed my lower groin. I groaned and cursed.

Annie, waiting for me at the door, widened her eyes. "What's wrong? Are you sick?"

"My stomach hurts."

"Oh. You gonna tell Mom?"

The thought of telling Mona angered me somehow. After the shock of seeing bright blood in the toilet bowl, I'd clenched my jaw and stolen one of her pads. She didn't need to know yet. "No, let's just go outside."

Outside in the cooling evening, I forgot about the achy crankiness which gripped me. Our quiet neighborhood had little traffic and kids accumulated along the edges of front yards, screaming and babbling before darting across street and lawn. I smelled grass and somebody's charcoal grill and heard traffic a quarter of a mile away south on Mason Road. When I looked overhead into the soft purple sky where faint stars waited for full darkness, I glimpsed dark winged shapes.

I let Robbie order me into the role of seeker, only too willing to drag out the counting to a hundred. Leaning against my house, I looked out of the corner of my eye at the chipped white siding and its mottled green mold. For the first time, I noted the familiar herby scent of tall grass and weeds in their shaggy fringe against the foundation and the uneven and rocky ground leading to the broken-down shed in the corner of the yard. Lauren's house had a flat yard with trim green grass and red and yellow tulips bordering the porch. My house smelled of dust, ashy smoke, and cooking odors. Hers smelled of lemon furniture polish and vanilla-scented candles in the living room, a myriad of Sunday pot roasts in the kitchen, and Grandma Nan's faint vanilla-rose perfume. No wonder Lauren hadn't spoken to me all week.

While I counted, the sound of swift feet and overloud whispers filled the air as the three younger kids flitted around me. I heard giggles and a muffled grunt as someone stumbled. Rolling my eyes and shaking my head, I slowed through the eighties, but as I got to the last ten numbers, I sped up. By the time I bellowed out my warning, the deepening gloom hushed our ragged yard.

I stomped off toward the back, loudly muttering. Six and seven year olds had little ability to stay quiet or hide well. I could just end the search in thirty seconds by looking under the picnic table or behind the shed, probably in the backseat of the tireless clunker at the side of the driveway. Dragging my feet, I questioned the evening at large about the possible whereabouts of the hiders, aware that crickets chirped in hidden pockets and fireflies winked gold in the deepening twilight. Behind me, the sunset blazed a final fiery glory at the edge of the world and before me darkness transformed my backyard into a mystery. The gentle cool only added a sharper edge to the unfamiliar pain in my abdomen, making me want to lie down, tuck my knees to my chest, and moan.

Scowling, I decided to end the game. I bent to peer under the rickety picnic table that had mutely guarded our play over the years, but no one shrieked in delighted submission. I straightened and stalked toward the dilapidated shed leaning toward the rustling maple in the back corner of the yard. Here the weeds were taller than Annie: a perfect place for hiding if you didn't mind the scratchy tickling of the stems or the sting of mosquitoes. But though I slunk among the tough clumps, I found no one either crouching against the rough weathered wood of the shed or leaning behind the tree trunk.

I trotted around the side of the house and to the front, certain the three younger children had crawled into Frank's old Ford, but when I pulled open the stiff back door, I saw nothing but the cracked vinyl seat. No one crouched on the floorboards in front either. I would have opened the trunk to check is cavernous space, but Frank had tied it shut last summer after the lock had grown rusty and Annie had gotten trapped in it one morning. If I hadn't heard her muffled whimpers, she might have passed out in the increasingly heated air and suffocated. Frank's thunderous rage at Annie's close call had only terrified her. Even now, she wouldn't hide inside any closet. That thought made me frown. Where could they be, all three of them? Were they together?

I hurried inside, but only Frank sat in front of the TV while Mona talked to Aunt Susie on the phone. Tim, as usual, had left with his friends. He wouldn't return until the middle of the night, probably after his midnight curfew, smelling of pot and cigarettes and cheap beer, which lingered on his clothes since he often slept in them and wore them to breakfast. Once or twice I'd smelled other things, sharper, saltier, wilder, *dangerous* scents. Sweat and body odor, but more than that I couldn't identify.

Giving up, I went outside and circled the house again, calling out in a voice choked with angry frustration. "Where are you twerps? I'm done. Come out."

The only sounds that met me were the distant rush of traffic, the nearby gabble of neighborhood kids, the sound of our TV through an open window, and the less intrusive chirrup of crickets.

As I stood scanning the back yard, some slight sound made my gaze pause on the old shed. Frank stored parts and an old lawnmower in there, but we'd been told to stay out of it. Glass from its broken windows littered the ground outside and the rough concrete floor inside. More than that, jars and cans and random bits of machinery lined the walls, rusty and oddly threatening in their mechanical dissolution, forgotten and neglected pieces left behind by who knows whom from long before Frank and Mona moved into our house. The door, always ajar due to its swollen, jagged state, seemed a little more ajar than usual. When I squinted in the growing dark, I saw that the latch had been peeled back and I knew where my quarry had hidden itself. Clamping my hands on my hips, gripped by a vicious abdominal cramp, and righteously angry, I stomped to the shed. At the last second, I halted at the sound of murmuring. An instinct warned me not to throw the door open. I would surprise them. The door, no longer stuck against its frame, slid out across the bumpy bald spot so that I could look around its

152

edge. It took a dozen startled breaths to interpret what I saw in front of me. When I did, my shock rooted me, made me a wraith caught on the threshold between the living and hell.

Annie leaned against a table along the back wall of the shed, her stuffed rabbit under one arm and her other hand on Robbie's head where he knelt in front of her. Her closed eyes and open mouth lent her a cryptic expression, either pained or blissful. Her shorts and underwear drooped around her ankles, but Robbie's head covered her nakedness. Mary stood watching, a strange look on her face.

Shaking as violent emotion washed down me, I yanked the door open, shouting, "Get the fuck away from her!" The next thirty seconds disintegrated into a chaotic jumble. Annie opened her eyes, Robbie looked up, and Mary backed toward the door as I lunged the five feet to knock him out of the way. My gaze locked on Annie, who just stood there, eyes wide, while Robbie and Mary scrambled to leave.

"Get the fuck outta here! Don't come back!" I didn't take my eyes from Annie as the other two dashed out of the shed, their harsh breathing and skittering footsteps tearing across the calm evening. When the noise had faded, I bent and yanked up Annie's panties and shorts.

"Don't tell." Annie's eyes shone in the shed's dim light.

I stood and glared at her, ignoring her plea. "Get inside." I had no intention of telling Mona. Not yet.

The fist in my gut clenched and unclenched, nauseating me. I shoved at the back of her head until she stumbled, and she scurried forward, sniffling. At the house, she waited, head bent, until I pulled the screen door open and stepped in first. She stepped on my ankles twice on our way to our bedroom, but neither Frank nor Mona caught the twisted pain on my face or Annie's tears. In our darkened room my fury and horror thickened the air. Still, I swallowed and forced myself to sit next to her while she choked on her snotty sobs.

I put my arm around her shoulders and drew her into my side. "It's not your fault." My harsh voice sliced through my anger and my own tears scalded my throat. "It's my fault. I didn't keep you safe." I stroked her hair to keep myself from rocking on the mattress and banging my head on the wall. I wished I could sink into the floor or fly into the sky, losing all conscious thought in the process. I never wanted to close my eyes and see Annie and Robbie frozen in that hideous posture again.

Annie sagged against me and her torrential crying faded like thunder rolling away on the horizon. We sat there as the darkness deepened to night, not speaking against the warmth that bound us. After only a handful of minutes, I heard her soft snoring and realized that she'd fallen asleep. I wanted to sleep too, to forget what I'd seen and to pretend that the ice sliver in my eye hadn't grown so large it threatened to blind me, but I couldn't. I waited until her heat had dampened our sides, gluing us together in sweaty complicity before slipping my arm away from her shoulders and guiding her down to her mattress. I made sure her rabbit snuggled under her arm and then turned on the box fan in the window. The cool night air soothed my feverish cheeks and lulled me. I didn't sleep but passed into a trance where my heart banked its fury. I waited.

Through the closed bedroom door I heard Frank's booming voice as he went to the bathroom, followed by Mona's razor tones. After they shut their bedroom door, silence reigned. I studied the night sky as the starlight sharpened against the blacker heavens. Above and behind the roof brightness attested to the shy moon, lurking but companionable.

"Star light, star bright, first star I see tonight," I intoned softly. I kept the rest of the incantation to myself: *Wish I may, wish I might, have my wish tonight.* I didn't know what to wish for, my

154

mute yearning tugging at me and diluting the virulence of my anger. The rhythmic soughing of the fan blades and the twittering of the crickets wove a spell around me. In my dazzled state, I sensed another presence.

"Angel?" My excited whisper trembled across the air drawn from outside. "Angel, help me take care of my sister. Help me stop Tim."

A breeze caressed my cheek. I leaned against the windowsill, my forehead on the frame, and concentrated on the angel sitting at my side. For this short time and in this place, I knew that divinity shared the fractured and bitter world with me. I closed my eyes, grateful.

I must have dozed because when I opened them the light had changed. The moon no longer radiated overhead and the mystery had fled. I was alone in the expectant night.

A kitchen cabinet slammed shut, followed after a few seconds by the refrigerator clanking closed. Tim had come home. At the sounds, my fury flared like a grease fire doused with water. I jumped up and stormed down the hall, fists pumping. Tim heard me as I crossed the threshold into the kitchen and looked over his shoulder, his sneer sliding into a startled, wide-eyed expression. That's the last thing I saw before I launched myself. I knocked him into the cabinets behind him, cracking his head against the counter as I landed on his chest.

I followed him to the floor, punching and punching and punching. For whatever reason—the surprise ferocity of my attack, the blow to his head, or the beer that so heavily laced his breath—Tim offered no more resistance to the vicious blows I rained on him than his upturned palms over his face. For the next five minutes only harsh breathing, the thunk of hardened fists meeting cheekbone and torso, and heavy grunting filled my ears.

A shrill scream pierced my reverie. Silence followed. I sat over Tim, my hands clenched in mid-air, as the kitchen held its breath and time returned. A hot seed of sweat slid from my forehead and trailed down my nose. I noted its feel there in detached curiosity, waiting for it to slip free and splash onto Tim's bruised and bleeding face. His wide gray eyes watched me, their glazed and pained stare fiercely comforting.

"Weeble, what the fuck's goin' on?" Mona's tired voice freed me from my fury's spell. I craned my neck over my shoulder in time to see shock transform her features. Annie, her face hidden, clung to her leg.

That's when I noticed my chest heaving and the stinging ache of my split knuckles. The scent of sweat and body odor mingled with beer and cigarette fumes. On the scuffed gray-and-white linoleum, a bright red bead of blood drew my gaze. I blinked and said nothing.

"God Almighty, Weeble! What've you done?" Mona pulled Annie away and stumbled across the kitchen to fall next to me. I followed her gaze down to Tim, whose swollen eyes had closed. "He looks like he's been in a bar fight. Get off 'im."

When I didn't move, she shoved me to the side and bent over him, running her fingers over his face and down his torso. He moaned. "Christ! I think he needs a doctor."

Still I said nothing. Keeping my eyes on Mona as she jumped up to get ice and aspirin, I sucked on my knuckles. While Mona faced the sink, Annie prodded Tim's chest with her foot, gazing at me out of the corner of her eye as a sly grin curled the corner of her mouth. Although I'd just attacked her abuser, that grin turned my stomach. Annie drew her toe back and kicked, hard. Tim grimaced, but the rush of the tap water concealed his pain. When she brought her face up, her fine hair tangled into a messy halo, the wicked satisfaction I saw in her features transformed her into a hobgoblin. I closed my eyes and turned away.

"Frank!" Five minutes later, Mona stood in the doorway and called down the hall. "Frankie! Get your ass in here. Weeble just beat the crap outta Tim."

A creak followed by a deep thump presaged Frank's lumbering, sleepy presence. He shuffled, yawning, into the bright yellow kitchen light, his eyes fluttering as he tried to open them. He stretched his joined hands over his head, cracked his knuckles, and yawned again.

"What the fuck's wrong, Moan?" Frank's hoarse voice abraded my raw nerves further. I began to shake even though I huddled around my bent knees. "Why in hell are y'all in here at fucking two a.m.?"

"Look at Tim." Mona crossed her arms over her chest. "That's why we're in here."

Tim no longer lay on the floor. Instead, he sat propped against the base cabinets holding ice wrapped in a kitchen towel against his face. Frank's head turned toward his son and he blinked and squinted until his eyes appeared to focus. Then he took a step toward Tim with his hand outraised.

"What the fuck happened to you?" I heard awe mingled with concern that shifted into quick anger. "You get into a fight somewhere? I warned you not to go sniffin' around those girls from Gower."

"This ain't from no fight over cunts from Gower." The icepack muffled Tim's sullen voice. "Ask the cunt sittin' over there what happened."

I'd started to shake so bad my teeth rattled and gooseflesh tightened the skin of my arms and legs. When I looked up at Frank, my wide eyes ached.

"Forget about Weeble," Mona said, not looking at me. She glared at Tim and then turned to Annie. "Annie, why did Weeble do it?"

I jumped up before Annie could speak, but the look of terror on her thin face suggested she wasn't going to say anything anyway. "I smashed that asshole's face in because he won't leave me alone." I squinted a warning at him, daring him to deny my reason.

Frank growled and stepped toward me, his outraised hand fisting, but Mona slipped a palm onto his hairy chest. He stopped and looked at her, his confused frustration written along his forehead and around his bearded lips. Mona's narrowed eyes studied me. Even though I could hear Annie's frightened breathing, stillness settled between us. For once, we knew Frank and Mona focused on us, really paid attention to what happened and what we said.

"Weeble, Tim won't ever leave you alone. *What* did he do this time?" Her rough patient voice stunned me. What more would I have to tell her?

I opened my mouth, but I couldn't force any air over my vocal chords. I couldn't pronounce my fury and my shame.

"He touches us." Annie's voice quavered, but she looked at Mona without dropping her chin. "At night, when you're asleep. He comes in our room and makes us do things."

Mona's gaze swiveled to Annie. She stiffened. "What things?" I'd never heard the emotion in her voice before. "What does he make you do, Annie?"

Annie darted a look at me. I blinked. My hot eyes stung, but still no words came out.

"I don't have to listen to this shit," Tim announced and started to push past me, but Frank's hand clamped onto his shoulder.

"You ain't fuckin' goin' anywhere." Frank's mean eyes glinted.

Annie shifted and hugged her rabbit to her chin. "Do I have to tell you?" Her muffled whimper sent chills down my spine, unleashing my tongue.

From a distance, I heard myself say, "He pushed me to my knees. Then he pulled down his underwear and made me suck him." Almost as soon as I said it, I started gagging.

"Holy fuck!" Mona shouted at the same time that Frank jerked Tim to face him. Tim dropped the towel-wrapped ice, scattering chunks along the linoleum, Mona lunged at him, and Annie darted next to me. I wrapped an arm around her, pulling her away from the adults and into the corner next to the refrigerator. As I watched the mayhem unfold, queasy spasms rolled through me.

The heaving mass of Frank's biker bulk, Tim's scrawny torso, and Mona's sturdy frame threatened the cramped kitchen. In my exhausted terror, their macabre dance mimed the ripping and tearing of claw and fang. Annie and I cowered together, me with my eyes screwed tight and wishing the world would disappear, her crying. Curses and panting, grunts and shuffling thickened the air.

"Stand up, you little pervert. Stand up before I knock you all the way down." Mona's hoarse shriek serrated me. I flinched.

"Do it." Frank's growl deepened. "Stand still, dammit."

The shuffling halted, leaving only harsh breathing. Drawing Annie closer, I peeked through slit lids. Tim stood leaning against his father with his arms pinned back. Mona faced him, trembling, her fist cocked. I saw only the back of her head, but Tim's features had turned to stone at what he saw on her face. I looked up and saw the tiny glitter of tears in Frank's eyes, but he didn't speak. Seconds dragged by and still Mona said nothing. Did nothing except tremble and waver as if an icy winter wind buffeted her.

Then Mona lifted her face to the ceiling and howled.

"How could you? How could you, you fuckin' animal?" She dropped her chin and by Frank's expression I knew she'd shifted her gaze to him. "What are we gonna do with him, Frank? Huh?

159

What do you do with a piece of shit like him? He's your son. Get him outta here before I get a knife and carve his heart outta his chest." Her last words seemed to strangle her.

Frank hustled Tim, pale and strained looking, around Mona, who jerked away as if she'd been burned. As her face twisted toward her shoulder, I saw the tears sheeting across her cheeks. She hunched there, sobs rocking her, and something shifted in the kitchen, the temperature or time or reality. The stench of sorrow drifted as an invisible mist around us. Guilt twisted my guts. I'd done this. I'd shattered Mona's innocence. I shrunk back against the wall, shielding myself with Annie. Her clear eyes gazed at me and then she stepped away toward Mona, leaving me exposed.

Mona drew Annie into her side, appearing to struggle to control her weeping. She hiccoughed and moaned. Closed her eye. Sighed. Then she raised her head and focused red-rimmed eyes on me.

"I shouldna stopped you. I shoulda let you beat him into the floor."

Eight

⌄

I HAVEN'T SLEPT IN THREE DAYS, not since the brutal and surreal nightmares, dormant for years, resurrected after my visit to Rose Bishop. Running, my old cure and constant prevention, no longer works. I'm at the mercy of vicious incubi that threaten to suck the marrow of my soul. They're the price I must pay to expose the truth.

If Marcie could see me now, she'd shut off my computer, call Ethan, and drag me and mine to her house. She wouldn't grill me. She knows better. She'd wrap me in a warm blanket, make me hot soup and tea, and snuggle me on her sofa with my feet elevated. She'd put on soothing music and massage my cold hands. But there's no external injury to treat, no blood to staunch, no bone to set, no laceration to stitch. No bruises, no concussions—nothing but internal bleeding of the spirit. No x-ray, no CT-scan, no MRI can find it.

Marcie would wait until I'd settled into an exhausted slumber and then she'd set Ethan in the wing-back chair to guard me while she broke into my apartment and destroyed my files. I can't let her do that. It's a canker, this need in me to remember the dead. Maybe it's a kind of emotional rubbernecking, a diversion from the ugliness of my childhood. A pity party for one, complete with identifying with innocent victims of serial killers. But maybe Marcie has it right. All my photocopies, newspaper clippings, scribbles and outlines, even the electronic documents should be tossed on a bonfire—a term from the Middle Ages for the conflagration of fake saints' bones—where all such superstitious and self-deceptive relics should burn.

Or maybe, in reality, I identify with depravity and the need to kill. Maybe *I'm* the incubus, feeding off the bones of the blameless. That's what I'm most afraid Marcie, student of psychology, will diagnose, if she knows what shatters my sleep every night.

I leave my chair and the flat glare of the computer to sit next to the window. Hero joins me on the sofa, laying his head consolingly in my lap. I finger the ragged fringe of his mangled ear and he noses my inner thigh. There's something soothing about the cold wetness. I stroke his head and stare out into the robin's egg blue of the May morning. That color of blue, so bright and true, haunts me. It's trusting and sincere. It promises hope and new beginnings. It hurts my bloodshot eyes just to look at it.

But I'm procrastinating.

I'm not writing the short history of serial killing I've decided needs to be included in my memorial Web site. I don't want to write a single word about the unquenchable bloodlust that leads human monsters to murder, over and over again. I don't want to give the dark impulse that power. That precedence. Even if all I do is skim over the past, I've given the monsters more than their worth. Yet I have to give them their due. I have to acknowledge their predatory nature and contrast it against the lives they've taken, especially those of children. It's a delicate balance and I don't know if I've got the writing chops to achieve it. I'm an engineer. I calculate loads and force and angles and rates of acceleration. I don't have the skill to compose an elegy for the dead or a screed against the men and women who took what they had no right to take.

See how I procrastinate, how I devote time to the unworthy when I should be girding my loins and researching another victim? I'm delaying the time I must delve into the last effects of Joseph Holiday, a fifteen-year-old boy from Ohio, who disappeared one summer in the company of a smooth-talking, eagle-eyed salesman named Avery Francis Easton. Police never recovered Joseph's body, but Easton confessed to bludgeoning the teen in a field "twenty miles from the south of nowhere." I can still see his thin-lipped grin in the grainy 1960s photo, the crazy tilt to his eyes. The colors are off in that photo, but my gut feels the rightness of the alien-green tint to Easton's skin.

Serial killing is an ancient evil. Likely the seeds germinated when Cain led Abel to the fields, but for multiple murders over time, people had to live in a stable, organized society. Although many men must have killed for pleasure on the battlefield in the cradle of civilization, the true birth of serial killing in the western world came later. It came with the *Pax Romana*, that peace that Augustus Caesar brought. A peace whose rich soil nurtured and spread the love and hope of Christianity even as the worst impulses of humanity also blossomed.

Her name was Locusta. And she destroyed as a swarm of locusts destroys. She is the first recorded serial killer, darling of Roman aristocrats and assassin for Nero, who allowed her to experiment on condemned criminals. She even opened a school to teach others her dark arts. Her method of killing? One that most women serial killers favor: poison. She poisoned Emperor Claudius and his son Britannicus. When the Senate condemned Nero to death, Locusta lost her imperial protector and his successor had her publicly ripped apart—after rape by a specially trained wild beast. Serial killing had gotten off to a glorious start at the highest echelons of the ancient world.

The phone rings, bringing me back to the modern world. I lunge for it as if it were a rope ladder flung from a hovering helicopter. It's Grandma.

"What's wrong?" Concern sharpens her husky voice. I want to put my arms around her and lay my head on her shoulder. To smell the coffee on her breath and the musty scent of her favorite afghan mixed with the vanilla-rose of Shalimar, her favorite perfume.

I laugh and it sounds shaky. "How can you tell?"

"It's been more than two weeks since your last call. You don't call me when there's something wrong."

I sigh and rub my forehead. Flat Stanley, sitting on the top of my bookshelf, squints at me. He isn't fooled any more than Grandma is. "That's because you'll grill me. I don't want to be grilled."

"Save your whining for that friend of yours. She's training for the couch, I'm not." She pauses and I suspect that she takes a drag on a cigarette, even though I'd begged her for years to quit. "The nightmares, they're back, aren't they? You can't wade through the nasty muck without it clinging to you."

I get stubborn. Grandma, of all people, should understand. "I have to do this, Gran. For her."

Silence fills the connection between us. When she speaks, her voice is older than I've heard it in a long time. I've dragged her to the past with me. Before I can apologize, her words stop me. "I know. You have to do it for yourself too, Weeble. Don't forget that."

"I don't matter."

Now she sounds angry. "Yes, you do! Don't ever say that again. You matter to God. You matter to *me*." A catch, so tiny I'm not sure it's there, hitches her voice.

"More than her?" I ask the age-old question, the question I asked her once, when I was old enough to understand what had happened. When she says nothing, I press on. "Do I, Gran? Because I sure as hell don't think so."

At that, she answers, and her voice is breathless as the words tumble out, as if I might interrupt her before she can say what she wants to say. "Not more than her, Weeble, but not less. I never had to make that choice and you know it, so don't make me do it now. I still have you and I thank God every day for that. *Every day.* Just don't lose yourself again doing this. She wouldn't want that for you. You've got to get on with your life, be happy. You deserve that."

The age-old argument, one I took on as a teen. One I won't have now.

I sigh. "I can't control the nightmares, Gran."

"The ones with the demons?" Her voice is soft now. "Lord, child, I'll pray for you. I'll pray that the Good Lord takes this affliction from you."

I don't retort that the Good Lord likely sent them to me. "It's different now."

"How?" Sharpness replaces the brief soft tone.

I sit down. Hero, prescient just when I need him, sinks his head onto my thigh. Flat Stanley jumps down into my lap. My loyal bodyguards are closing ranks. I stroke Flat Stanley, who purrs in loud reassurance.

"There's a blinding light, and I swear I can smell new grass. Sometimes it's sweet, like those teacup roses you used to grow. The ones—" my voice chokes and it's some moments before I can calm myself enough to go on—"and then this figure steps into the nightmare as if he's shattering it. That doesn't make any sense, but when I'm with the demons, I'm breathless and it's so claustrophobic and hot. Then the world cracks into a million pieces and he steps in."

"What does he look like? Like him?" Grandma doesn't have to say who "him" is. We'll never use his name. That would make him into a person.

"No. *God no*. He's lit up like a light bulb. I can't see his features at all, but the demons go crazy when he shows up. They tear at me as if they've run out of time for torture. He always takes my hand and then I wake up."

"Hmm." A small pop bursts the end of Grandma's thinking—she's taking another drag on the forbidden cigarette. "Does he hurt you?"

"No." I hear the reluctance in my voice. How can I make her understand how he frightens me?

She figures it out anyway. "He scares you."

"Yes."

"Because he's not part of the familiar nightmare, is that it?"

"Now you sound like Marcie."

"Don't get cranky with me. I have no idea what it means." She pauses to let that sink in. "When did the nightmares start?"

"After I traveled to England to research a victim."

"The first?" When I don't answer, she sighs. "Maybe you'd better see a doctor, get a prescription for something to help you sleep. You can't go a year without sleep."

"I did before." My voice is so quiet, I'm not sure she'll understand.

But she does. "That was then, this is now. There has to be some other way." She sounds frantic.

We're circling around the same worn bone and I'm exhausted in more than body. "I can't do it any other way. I've tried to deny the truth for fifteen years, but the truth didn't disappear just because you and I want it to. I'm not eleven any more, Gran, living in my own fantasy world by blotting out what happened. The cold light of day has taken that away from me."

166

"But you *do* keep denying the truth, Weeble! When are you going to accept that it wasn't your fault that Lauren died and you didn't?"

I flinch and drop the phone. All through our conversation, we've kept up the old tacit agreement not to say her name. Flat Stanley doesn't move as I bend over to pick it up.

"That's what you don't understand," I say as the phone touches my ear. "I *did* die that day. I died when Richard Lee Grady slit her throat."

* * *

The saying goes the truth will set you free. I learned the summer after I turned eleven that it doesn't—at least not without shredding the fragile cocoon you've wrapped around yourself. Even if that cocoon was ugly and suffocating and dark. Because what's inside is raw, tender, and blind. When you've spent more than thirty years shellacking yourself in as Mona and Frank had done, well it's damn painful when you're left exposed and quivering.

For the better part of two weeks, no one spoke during the day, not even Annie, who used to babble from the moment she opened her eyes. Instead, she spent long hours rubbing Miller as he lay on the back of the sofa, bringing him bowls of milk and bits of cheese, and snuggling him alongside her stuffed rabbit as she napped in the living room. If I came into the room, she'd gravitate to me, orbiting my position without touching, whether I stood looking out the window estimating how far away I could run in a day or sat in Frank's easy chair calculating the distance to the Kansas City airport. Most of the time, I knew she waited next to me, but I didn't know what to say. At least not until the afternoon she started to cry. I didn't know she was crying until a hot tear splashed on my forearm, jolting me from my reverie.

I looked up from my seat on the sofa, but I couldn't see through the messy tendrils surrounding her face. "Annie."

She said nothing, just kept her head bent while more tears and a saliva string pooled on my skin.

"Annie, it ain't your fault I had to tell about Tim. Don't cry."

When she didn't say anything, I pulled her into my lap. I'd grown three inches since the start of the year and her head fit under my chin if I curled her up into my side. She was sweaty and her breath smelled bad, like it always did after she'd slept with her mouth open. I squeezed her, hard.

"I shoulda told them before." I felt my throat clot up, but I pressed on. "Before Tim hurt you. It's my fault he hurt you."

She pulled away and looked at me. She looked awful. Snot coagulated under her nose and her watery eyes were red-rimmed and swollen. "No, it's not. You didn't let Tim hurt me. He just did all on his own."

I closed my eyes and squeezed her again. We sat that way for a long time, not talking. I felt Annie relaxing against me and her breathing deepening. I dozed until something woke me. When I looked around, I saw Tim standing in the doorway to the hall watching us. He looked beaten in spirit as well as flesh and wary as a lone wolf. His split lip had returned to normal size, but grayish-green tinged with yellow mottled his cheeks from the bruises I'd given him. He held my gaze, but I knew he'd never bother me or Annie again.

I don't know how long we might have stayed there, acknowledging our new relationship, if Mona hadn't come from the kitchen. For a heartbeat, the powder keg waited. And then, Mona's fuse sizzled and it exploded.

"What the hell are you doin' outta your room?" Her eyes slid to take me and the still-dozing Annie in. "I don't want to see you anywhere near my girls, you hear?"

Tim shrugged and turned away. "Just wanted a snack." His dull voice sounded muffled.

"Don't come out unless I say so." Mona shouted at him, but he didn't turn.

After that, the nightly hell broke loose. The front door opened and Frank came in, fatigue etched in motor oil on his face, his dark hair greasy with sweat and his coveralls stained with grime. He hadn't even shut the door behind him when Mona lunged and began shouting at him in the latest of their many heated arguments about Tim's fate. Mona wanted to send Tim to live with his mother's parents, but Frank insisted his sister Joanie would take Tim in, once her oldest moved into her own apartment in a few weeks. He pushed past Mona into the kitchen, clanking his metal thermos onto the counter and getting into the refrigerator for a beer, but she followed him, buzzing until he roared at her to get off his back. Then he retreated to the living room and turned on the TV, but Mona didn't give up, not then and not later. She stayed right with him, looming over his recliner, confident and angry in her faded cut-offs and tube top. Annie and I, fascinated, watched this unfamiliar, yet familiar, drama.

When Ricky showed up that evening, scruffy and carrying a can of Schlitz malt liquor, Mona ignored his knock on the screen door and continued screeching at Frank, who held his middle finger up where she could see it but said nothing. Ricky opened the door and sauntered in, a grin smeared across his gaunt, hard-used face.

"Frankie, rippin' you a new one, eh? What'd you do this time? Piss on her stash?" He laughed. He tipped up the beer can and slurped.

"Stay the hell out of this, Ricky." A flush colored Mona's cheeks, but her eyes stayed cold. "Go home."

Frank growled. "Leave 'im be, woman! Enough! Nothin's happenin' tonight, so get your ass in the kitchen and make dinner."

"Fuck you, Frankie! Girls, we're leavin'." Mona's swift glance brought Annie and me off the sofa to follow her. "We're eatin' at the diner."

Frank grumbled but didn't stop us. When we got to the diner, Mona left us in a booth after she'd ordered and went to use the pay phone. Twenty minutes later, Aunt Susie arrived with the tuna melts. She grabbed Mona hard and then they were both sobbing, something that made me want to hit them and tell them they didn't have any goddamn right to slobber over each other. Disbelieving, I watched their faces turn blotchy, their voices turn soggy, and the cigarettes dangle from their trembling fingers. Annie ignored the indulgent display, calmly eating all her French fries and then devouring mine. When I realized what she'd done, I snapped.

"Get your damn fingers off my fries." My snarl interrupted the pity fest across from me. Aunt Susie and Mona stopped babbling and looked at me. I thought for a moment Mona was going to snarl back by the looks of her tight lips and the thin lines etched around the corners of her mouth, but she just closed her eyes and shook her head.

"Junie!" She called over to our waitress. "Can we get some more fries here? Thanks."

Aunt Susie said nothing. She watched us.

Mona dragged on her cigarette and then let the hot smoke out on a loud sigh. "Weeble, you're not gonna stay in the same house with that perverted little fuck any longer. You and Annie are goin' to Susie's until Frank gets it through his thick skull that Tim's gotta go."

"What if he don't?" I kept my eyes down and played with the wrapper from my straw, twisting and twisting until it tore. "What if he don't want us back?"

As I looked up, Mona leaned forward and grabbed my wrist, hard. "It's me or that boy, Weeble. Frankie ain't gonna have us both. He's got two weeks."

Aunt Susie nodded and drank from her coffee. "Don't you worry 'bout nothin', Weeble. You girls and your mom can stay with us if need be."

I didn't answer. Instead, I looked out the diner's window toward the cornfields that lined the other side of the highway. Red and gold from the setting sun set the horizon on fire, leaving the green stalks as tall as my thighs in deep shadow. I thought I had no delusions about the life that awaited us for the next two weeks, but I had. No sooner had Mona dropped us off while she went back home to get some clothes than Missy descended on Annie and me. She wore heavy eye liner like her idol Pat Benatar and her jeans were so tight my own body hurt just thinking about such an invasion in my soft flesh.

"If it isn't Timmy's duo." She stood blocking the hallway, a cigarette in her hand. I knew Aunt Susie let her smoke openly now. "What's he taste like?"

"Same he did for you," I said, my shoulders jammed up around my ears and my fists clenched. I wanted to knock her down, but she stood as tall as Susie now and was a lot heavier than me. I didn't have fury to give me an edge like I'd had when I'd attacked Tim. She'd pound me black and blue if I tried to lash out at her. Instead, I moved to step past her.

Her hand clamped down on my shoulder, yanking me to a standstill.

"Whatever that prick told you, it ain't true."

I looked up at her. Her eyes narrowed at my glance, and she brought her cigarette up to her mouth. She looked old already. I could see what she'd look like when she was thirty, all the bitter lines etched in smoke on her freckled cheeks.

"Not much of what comes outta his mouth *is*," I muttered.

Something in her eyes held me still. I hardly breathed. Then she pushed me and I stumbled. "Get outta my sight."

"No problem." I mumbled my defiance as I shuffled down the hall with Annie clinging to my hand. I felt Missy's gaze on my back and a shudder shook me.

Missy had always made it clear to me that I belonged with Annie and Joey, that she'd only ever included me in activities because Tim did. Now that Tim had lost his authority over us, she no longer even tolerated me. She refused to have me in her room, insisting before Susie returned that I had to sleep with Annie in Joey's room. I didn't mind sleeping on the floor among Joey's toys and smelly sneakers. Missy's room smelled of pot and echoed with the whispered secrets of her high-school friends. I didn't like the rock she played or the posters of Metallica and Iron Maiden papering her walls. All the musicians looked like Tim, only older and even meaner. I knew I'd have nightmares if I slept under their brooding glares.

During the day, I stayed out of Missy's way. Annie appeared to forget why we were living with our cousins and left her rabbit in Joey's room to follow him around, chattering non-stop. Until Aunt Susie brought me a novel from the supermarket, I hid in Joey's room, staring at the ceiling and wondering if the cold lump in my chest meant that a sliver from the demon's looking glass had lodged in my heart.

On the third afternoon after we left home, I sat reading out back, my legs exposed to the hot sun while I leaned against the huge maple tree in the corner of the yard. While I read, Joey and Annie played a game based on the TV show *Fame*. They sashayed and sang for more than half an hour before disappearing around the side of the house when several neighbor children arrived. Soon familiar shrieks and babble drifted back from the front to compete with the grumble and buzz of horseflies hovering over the pile of weathered wood, glass, and tires not far from where I sat. I smelled hot overgrown grass, the musty decay of evergreen bushes, and damp maple bark. The soothing drone and smells contained powerful magic, one I no longer believed in. I was Alice who'd tumbled through the rabbit hole. I was Lucy who'd gone through the wardrobe and into Narnia. It didn't last long.

I don't know when I realized I was no longer alone, but I looked up at harsh laughter. Missy and her friends stood outside the kitchen door, smoking and talking. Still in the grip of my childish fantasy, I had the unshakeable impression that they were twisted fairies in their torn t-shirts, faded Levi's, and lank hair come to warp the fabric of fairy land. Some instinct warned me against being seen, so I pulled my legs out of the sun and scooted further into the shadows under the maple. I strained to hear what they said, holding my breath until I heard my name.

"Weeble's a nasty piece of shit." Missy tossed her cigarette into the grass. "Wouldn't leave my cousin Tim alone."

"I remember him." This was the girl closest to me, but all I saw was her skinny back. "He brought some good shit to Dave Henderson's party last month."

"Whad she do?" The third girl, her hair inky and bitten, looked away toward where I shrank back into the shadows. I wondered if she could see me there. "Pester him for some of his Mary Jane?"

"Nah." Missy scoffed. "That ain't nasty. It'd show she has some brains insteada the snot clogging up the space between her ears."

"What then?" Skinny Back asked.

Missy shifted back onto her heels, hooking her thumbs inside her belt loops. "Kept getting' inta bed with him, sayin' she had nightmares and all. Then she'd rub up against him. You know," here her voice took on the sound of a whisper yet it grew perversely louder, "get his leg between her thighs and move up and down." She demonstrated by bending and straightening her legs. "She'd climb into his lap when he was watching TV and rub her butt on his dick."

Something hot stung my eyes and then splattered the open book in my hands.

"He told you?" Inky Hair asked. She looked over her shoulder again, but my sight had blurred and I couldn't make out the expression on her face.

Missy laughed. "No. I caught her crawlin' in his lap. Saw her with my own two eyes. So I asked him and he told me. Didn't want to. 'Fraid he'd get in trouble with my Aunt Mona."

"Isn't she stayin' with you?" Skinny Back tossed her cigarette butt like a dart into the yard. "Aren't you creeped out by her?"

"Are you kiddin'? Who wouldn't be? Aunt Mona caught her with Tim, so she made it sound like it was all his fault. Now I gotta put up with the little shit until Tim finds someplace else to live."

"He can come live with me." Inky Hair looked like she was in pain the way she pursed her lips and squeezed her eyes shut. "I'll make him forget his nasty little sister."

They laughed and headed back into the kitchen, Missy going inside last. When she got to the screen door, she held it open and looked over her shoulder right at me. Her heavily lined eyes gleamed. Then she smiled a thin, flat and utterly cold smile. Until that moment, I hadn't understood just how wicked this fairy was. Fairy land receded completely, never to return.

By the time Mona got home from work, I'd already packed my clothes into a brown paper grocery bag and sat sullen at the table in the kitchen. Aunt Susie, after trying to draw me out once or twice, had given up and put a glass of iced tea in front of me before turning to the hamburger she was browning on the stove. Even though the box fan barely stirred the hot, heavy air in the kitchen, I'd felt cold all afternoon.

Mona came into the kitchen and dropped into a chair. Aunt Susie handed her a can of Miller.

"What's up, Weeble?" Mona asked. Her gaze dropped to the paper bag I clutched in front of me. "What's in the bag?"

"Her clothes." Aunt Susie ripped open the box of Hamburger Helper. "Damn Missy said some shitty things about her to her friends."

"What things?" Mona asked me.

I refused to answer.

"Missy stood right out back with her bitchy friends telling 'em Weeble was the one who bothered Tim, climbing in his lap and his bed." Aunt Susie sounded tired and angry. "If that stupid little Tina Updike hadn't been high and started giggling about Missy's lies, I never woulda found out. Weeble sure wouldna told me." Here she gave me a frown that wasn't entirely sympathetic. I squared my shoulders.

"I'll string that little cunt up." Mona's low, intense declaration brought my gaze around to hers. She didn't look away. "Why didn't you beat the crap out of her, Weeble? Sounds like she deserved it."

I shrugged and looked away.

"She's already called her friend Lauren and asked to stay overnight." Out of the corner of my eye, I could see Aunt Susie nodding toward me. "That's why she's got her clothes with her. I told her we'd talk to you first."

I waited, the cold from the afternoon melting into an instant heat of desire, shame, and pain. I didn't understand why the hot tears that had been dammed up behind an ice wall all afternoon threatened until Mona spoke.

"All right, Weeble. Go to your friend's house. She's a nice girl. So's her grandmother."

That's when the relief broke through along with the tears. I'd been terrified she wouldn't let me go, that my bravado would crack and leave me shaking and defenseless.

She drove me over without saying a word, but when I put my hand on the car's door handle, she stopped me. "You're not as tough as you look, Weeble." She nodded toward Lauren's house. "You belong in a house like hers with a grandmother who watches what you read and cooks you dinner every night." Her voice sounded oddly muffled.

I couldn't look at her. "I don't belong anywhere."

Mona snorted but said nothing so I pulled the latch and swung the passenger door open. Before climbing out, I said over my shoulder, "Watch out for Annie." I don't know why I said it. I shuddered and slammed the door shut.

Mona sat at the curb while I came up to the front door. Grandma Nan met me, swinging the screen wide and waving at Mona. I heard the Impala screech to life and rumble away down the street, but I'd already stepped inside before she got to the corner.

"Lauren's out back, Weeble. We're playing a game of Scrabble before dinner. I've got some fresh-squeezed lemonade. Would you like some?"

I nodded, unable to speak around the lump in my throat.

"Just drop your things in Lauren's room and head out the back door. I'll bring out a glass."

I set the bag down next to her desk, careful to let it rest against the side so the clothes wouldn't spill out. The brown paper didn't belong in the pink-and-white princess room. It belonged to the princess's shabby servant girl, who slept by the fireplace all covered in soot. Hearing voices, I crossed over to the window and peered into the back yard. I might have been looking through a magic mirror into another world. Lauren and Grandma Nan sat at a picnic table covered in cherries on a white background. My response to Mona came back to me. No, I didn't belong here.

Lauren looked over just then and saw me. She stood up and started waving.

"Weeble, Weeble! Come out! Come out!"

When I opened the screen door, she stood waiting for me, holding a flower the color of a baby's cheek. In her hair she wore more, like a crown.

"Smell that. Go on. Put your nose up close and take a good sniff."

I did as she instructed. A sharp, sweet scent pierced me. It was the scent of all my longings.

"It's a tea rose," Lauren said. "Grandma Nan said these were my mom's favorites. Whenever I smell one, I remember her, just a little. It's almost like she's here with me." There was a slight catch in her voice and she paused. "Here, you take this one." Before I could raise my hand, however, she'd leaned forward and slid it behind my ear. "You look so pretty, Weeble. I know, let's make you a garland like mine."

She turned around and ran over to the table where a short glass vase stood holding a dozen more of the blushing, delicate blooms. I followed more slowly and watched as she pulled them out.

Grandma Nan patted the bench next to her. "Here's your lemonade, Weeble. Why don't you enjoy it before the ice melts?" She glanced over at Lauren. "Do you want me to get some ribbon from my sewing box? I think I still have some of that satin kind."

Lauren didn't look up from her task of weaving rose stems. "Yes, that would be perfect, Grandma."

Curious in spite of myself, I sat down next to her. "Aren't you worried about thorns?"

She laughed. "No, silly, we stripped them off earlier." That possibility had never occurred to me. I laughed with her, as much in wonder as at my own ignorance.

After a few moments, Grandma Nan returned and handed her a length of gleaming ribbon the rich color of cranberry sauce. It made me think of rubies and ball gowns. Lauren finished and held the garland up where we could all admire it.

"There, let me put this on." She set it on my head. My nose filled with the scent, making me dizzy. Hunger flared in the pit of my stomach. I felt hollow. "Perfect. Now we match. We're rose sisters, Weeble. That's even better than blood brothers."

I thought of Gerda and Kay from *The Snow Queen*. I remembered that the summer before Kay had been wounded by shards from the hobgoblin's mirror the roses in their garden had flowered in unusual beauty. Gerda had learned a hymn which she taught to Kay, one in which an angel descended. They'd held each other by the hand, kissed the blossoms, and looked up at the sunshine as if they really saw angels there. It had been a lovely summer filled with roses that seemed as if they would never stop blooming.

Lauren stood watching me, her head tilted, a slight smile on her face, and the last rays of the sun turning her hair into a halo. For a moment, I imagined that Gerda had looked just like this.

"Rose sisters," I repeated. "I like that." But I didn't for a moment believe in fairy tales or angels. Just icy shards from the hobgoblin's mirror.

Nine

MARCIE GIVES ME A WEEK before she calls and practically orders me to go out with her and Evan. "It's your birthday, woman. I know you hate to celebrate, but you've gotta go out. Jana and Julius will be there. It's about time you two kiss and make up."

"What took you so long? I thought you'd call days ago." I try to joke, but I'm so exhausted, I feel strung out. The stray thought that Julius the ER doctor would know how I feel enters and exits my mind before I realize I'm answering Marcie. I don't have the energy to resist her or worry about Jana's offended haughtiness. "Sure. Where're you going?"

"Oh, no place special. Just that club with the bowling alley on the second floor. Not far from Fenway."

Now I know Marcie's desperate. Every time I took her bowling in college, her average had been about the same as the number of balls she'd thrown each game. Sour as I feel, I smile anyway. "Doing everything you can to lure this Midwestern girl out, huh?"

"This has everything to do with you," she says, laughing. "I've secretly been bowling so I can take you on. My balls go in the gutter only a third of the time."

I squeeze my eyes closed, pinch the bridge of my nose, and laugh. It sounds hoarse to me. "What time do you want to meet there?"

"No you don't," she says, sounding like the Marcie I know and love. And fear. "You aren't going to promise to be there and then not show up. Someone will be by at seven to get you. Don't even think about backing out. I've reserved a lane for us. There'll be food. You *will* eat. Or I'm coming back to your apartment and throwing your PC out your window."

I groan, but inside I'm relieved. Someday I'm going to make it up to Marcie for not giving up on me. I don't deserve her love or her persistence. Without her, I might have succumbed to the nightmares long ago.

I can't work after Marcie's interruption even though it's only two. I shut my computer off and grab Hero's leash. He butts up against me when I bend over to snap it on his collar and for a moment I let him hold me up. Our run—the second of the day—passes in a blur. Although I'm tired, my muscles are warm and now, after weeks of hard training, conditioned for far more than the five miles I ask of them. I come home afterwards and fall face down onto my bed still wearing my sweaty t-shirt and Lycra shorts to sleep the sleep of the innocent for the first time in weeks.

When I wake up, I'm more rested and alert than I should be for sleeping two hours in the afternoon. An unfamiliar sense of well-being washes over me and I realize just how much my fatigue has colored my outlook. Nothing else has changed in the world. Or in me. Yet the power of my nightmares has faded, leaving a vaguely unpleasant memory that retreats the more I try to recall it. Humming, I pour a glass of iced tea before popping in a Mary Black CD and turning up the volume so I can hear while I shower. The spray rinses away the sweat from my run. On impulse, I twist the dial for a momentary blast of frigid water and when I come out of the stall, panting and invigorated, the lyrics to *Summer Sent You* grab my attention.

> *Done with time and patience*
> *I moved with the crowd*
> *Lonely in my silence*
> *and being without*
> *Then all in one instance*
> *straight out of the blue*
> *Out of all its goodness*
> *The Summer sent you*
> *All in one sweet instant*
> *straight out of the blue*
> *Out of all its goodness*
> *The Summer sent you*

I grab a towel, and instead of the brisk rub I usually give myself, I sit down on the edge of my bed to listen to the song again. Flat Stanley lies on my dresser, blinking against the ray of late afternoon sun filtering through the blinds. He begins to purr. Something in the song weaves a seductive spell, making me think of summer moonlight through an open window and compelling me to slide to the floor to rummage under the bed. My knees ache and the towel slips down to pool around them before I feel the broken corner of the Ouija game box. I haven't played since the night of my slumber party that summer. As I pull it out, a queer exhilaration fills me.

I set the board on my bed and stare at the antique letters. A shiver pimples my bare skin. I don't feel alone, but whatever is here with me feels comforting, not threatening. I palm the *planchette*, turning it over and over, pressing its corners into my flesh. It's ridiculous to believe that an angel waits for me, but I can't call up any anger to deny it.

I set the *planchette* onto the board and place gentle fingertips along its edges.

"Angel?" Why am I whispering? "Are you there?"

YES.

"Did you leave me?" Where did *that* question come from?

I AM ALWAYS BESIDE YOU.

A flicker of anger sparks in me, but I ignore it. "Will he be there?" I'm still whispering. So much for staying away from Tom Paul.

YES.

"Do you know him?"

ABSOLUTELY.

"How?"

HE SEES THE LIGHT.

"Will he hurt me?" Tom Paul's eyes glow in my memory. Is that pain mixed with the compassion I see in them?

HE WILL HEAL YOU.

I snort. "That's not likely." My voice grows firmer, louder. I try to raise my fingertips from the *planchette*, but they refuse to move.

YOU HAVE SEEN IT.

"What have I seen?"

HIS POWER.

"Power?" Again my voice emerges in a hush. My head feels light from lack of oxygen.

DO NOT DENY HIM.

I fling the *planchette* away from me. It strikes the corner of the wall and disappears. Hero, who lies at the foot of my bed, lifts his head and whines. I ignore him. The sense of well-being flees, to be replaced with jitters. I stand up, grabbing the towel at the same time and dropping it into the laundry basket. What's gotten into me? What do I think I'm looking for? Why in the world would I, grounded in the practicalities of physics and engineering, seduce myself with techniques for probing my own psyche? Do I need to play a child's game when I know what's been bothering me for weeks now? I close my eyes and shake my head, hard. There's no point in denying I hope Tom Paul wants me—no matter how irrational and dangerous hope is. Best to admit it in the harsh light of day so I can exorcise him. Then perhaps the nightmares will cease.

The next two hours pass in a restless funk. Now that I've come clean to myself, I'm anxious to get over him. To be done with my obsession. If Marcie hadn't promised to send someone for me, I'd grab a baseball bat to handle any potential attackers before running to Tom Paul's studio. I know he's not likely to be there, but I'd seek him out anyway. I'd turn into the stalker to set myself free. I shrug and pace my apartment, feeling Hero's eyes on me. Flat Stanley begs for caresses as I pass him on the kitchen counter, but I don't dare touch him, to let him soothe me. If not tonight, then tomorrow. Or the next day. I refuse to think about what I'd say or do when I find him.

A knock halts my pacing. I sigh, relieved. A little bowling and some beer is good medicine.

After I open the door, I forget to breathe. I can't hear anything.

Tom Paul's gaze captures mine and the rest of the world disappears. Only the two of us stand there, floating in a silent vacuum. All the light in the world rests on his features.

"Hey." His voice detonates something between us and my breath returns with an indrawn whoosh. Concern suffuses his face and he steps forward, wrapping his fingers around my upper arm. They sear me. "Are you all right? Let's sit down."

He leads me to the sofa, shutting the door behind him. The walls contract around me. I'm burning up. I start shaking. He sinks down next to me, his hands holding mine. He doesn't say anything for what seems like hours, just looks at me. I can't look away.

"Weeble." His breath drifts across my cheeks. I shake once, violently, and go still. Still as a rabbit waiting for the piercing fangs to sink into my side. Tom Paul raises a hand and brushes hair from my eyes with calloused fingertips. I quiver and feel icy-heat arc along synapses all the way to my toes. "Do you want me to leave?"

Something wild and broken cries out in me. "No." I don't recognize the thin sound of my voice. "Please stay."

His fingers find their way to my hands again. I look down. How small my hands look in his. I shiver again and look away, but I feel him threading his fingers through mine. Their roughness calms me. When his warm palm meets mine, the intimacy soothes even as it frightens. A small tic tattoos these joined planes, echoed by a stronger twin. After a moment, I realize with a shock that his heart beats in time with mine. Vivid images of veins and capillaries, tiny corpuscles scurrying along them to our hearts, imprint upon my mind's eye. I fancy that our blood mingles now, that our permeable skin waited only for this moment to establish a portal between us.

"I'm not going anywhere." At his words, my heart stutters. A dazed part of me wonders if he notices.

"I don't want to go bowling." Again, I don't recognize my voice. I don't recognize the sentiments. Who is this speaking? Even as I ask myself, I understand the truth. I don't want to leave this sudden sanctuary, to let his hands go for even a moment.

"Then we won't go." He eases himself back against the sofa and slides me into his side, his arm circling around my shoulders and his hand returning to mine. Instead of terror, I feel safety envelope me. I relax against him. The scent of basil, cilantro, and thyme threaded with his musk hits my nostrils. He smells like life and living. Now images of rioting greenery, thick clumps of herbs and flowers, invade my thoughts. I want to turn and bury my nose in his armpit, to burrow within his arms, but I don't. "Did you eat, Weeble? You look like you haven't eaten in days."

"I haven't," I mumble, avoiding his gaze.

"Then let me fix you something to eat." His thumb, its pad thick and rough, rubs the back of my hand. I watch, transfixed.

I don't want him to let me go, but I'm desperate now that he's touched me. Perhaps there's still time to sever this connection, to cover my vulnerability. When I say nothing, he disengages himself, leaving me bereft. I grieve as he leaves, savoring the pain. I want to wake up from this beautiful dream that has more power to shatter me than the nightmares ever did.

I watch Tom Paul as he moves around the kitchen. Hero, who has come to lie at my feet, swivels his ears, listening, but he shows no signs of alarm. So much for my guard dog.

Tom Paul. Who is he? Who is this familiar stranger opening my refrigerator, searching my cupboards, humming—flashing me a smile? I can't make sense of what he's doing, but after fifteen minutes the smell of sautéed butter and onion ignite hunger in me so strong I feel as though I'm going to pass out. I close my eyes and clench my fists. The memory of Tom Paul's thumb rubbing my hand plays upon the back of my eyelids and squeezes my heart until I'm almost panting.

"Drink this."

I blink and sip from the cup he holds under my chin. Even as the sweet, spicy heat of whatever it is glides across my tongue, I take in every line and pore of his hands. His fingers, though calloused, are neither narrow nor thick. Fine dark hairs cover the olive skin. The thought washes over me unbidden that he is Perseus resurrected to slay my demons. The hunger flares into gut-wrenching nausea, but the drink soothes it to a dull ache and trembling. I close my eyes and focus on the scent of vanilla and ginger rising on the steam.

When he lowers the cup, I rest light fingers on his wrist. "What is it?" The creamy sweetness still coats my tongue, lingering with promise.

"*Masala chai.*" At my puzzled look, he adds, "Indian tea. It's got milk, honey, and some spices like allspice and clove— whatever I could find in your cupboard." I hear apology in his low voice. "Like it?"

"A lot."

He nods and my fingers slip from his wrist. They tingle as though, having been asleep or numb, they are now brutally awake.

Tom Paul brings me an omelet and toast with butter and honey and more *masala chai.* I let him feed me like an invalid. When he's done, fatigue descends, pushing me into the sofa and lowering my eyelids against all my efforts to keep them open. In a far corner of my mind, panic flares. Has he drugged me? But that thought disappears as I slide into the bottomless chasm of sleep.

When I wake, it's morning and I'm in my bed, alone and still dressed though my shoes have been removed. For an instant, grief so strong it impales me against the mattress takes my breath away. And then I hear him. I turn toward the door, knowing that something blazes from my face, to see him standing there.

"You're still here." Tears prick my eyes but don't fall.

"I said I'm not going anywhere." He sits next to me on the bed, his hands seeking until they find mine. "I won't leave you unless you send me away."

* * *

I spent two blissful weeks at Lauren's house, going to the pool, reading books, and staying up late with her dreaming aloud about the future. Neither of us had any sense of impending doom despite the Ouija angel's warning. When I recall those two weeks, they are drenched in sunlight, filled with birdsong, scented with grass and chlorine, and vanilla-sweet as the ice cream favors we bought from the truck every day. Most mornings Grandma Nan stood under the ceiling fan flipping buttery pancakes or frying eggs and bacon while we packed tote bags with towels, books, chips and spare change. Nearby, an AM station droned out tinny-sounding news about pork-belly futures and shares of International Harvester. After we ate, she drove us to the branch library, its dusty shelves beckoning with hundreds and hundreds of books. I'd always gotten my books at the supermarket or school library where fluorescent lighting bounced off covers and dulled my imagination, but the old stone building under the leafy shade trees contained mysteries of the deepest kind, begging for exploration. We never left without a dozen books each.

Then Grandma Nan drove us to the pool around one and let us off with instructions to be waiting on the sidewalk at six. Lauren and I scarcely agreed before we'd slammed the car door and dashed to the admissions window. Through the open doorways to the showers we heard squeals and running water; beyond the pool building screams and splashes wove themselves around the intermittent rattle-thunk of the diving board and the occasional shrill of a lifeguard's whistle. We'd duck our heads under the spray in the girls' shower room while cradling our dry tote bags against our chests, and then we'd scamper and slip on the slick tile and out into the brilliant afternoon.

Men, women, and children darkened the menthol-blue water and concrete deck like giant debris from a shipwreck. Mothers and their teenage daughters lay on large towels, one arm flung over their eyes or with both arms along their sides. Their bodies glistened, held together by nylon shreds of tangerine, lime, and flamingo pink; coconut and baby oil fumes hovered over them. Around these sun worshippers, boys and girls too young to lie still picked out careless paths to the water's edge or the stairs to the diving board at the deep end. Reckless teenage boys sprinted to the end of the board where they pulled their knees to their chins and plummeted into the water. One or two fathers clung to the sides of the pool, talking; occasionally, a young child would clamber onto a broad, freckled back and clutch at a father's neck. Then he'd erupt from the wall, dunking his child, or perhaps he'd push off into a lazy breaststroke around the shallow end, his child a willing barnacle.

Lauren and I always spotted a space large enough on deck for two towels smoothed side-by-side. We'd spend the next few hours slipping seal-like into the water and push ourselves downward along the wall, grinning at each other while bubbles escaped from the corners of our mouths. When our lungs burned and our eyes stung, we'd let go of the pool and pop up to the surface, elated and breathless.

On the second Monday after I'd entered into my fairy tale, the fairy tale ended forever.

"Let's get some pop and popcorn," Lauren said as we sat on our towels after Grandma Nan dropped us off, her normal enthusiasm missing.

I didn't respond for a minute. Overhead, sudden massive clouds, shadowed in deep blue-gray and glowing along their top edge, blocked the sun. The eerie light made everything clearer and the colors more vivid, as if I hadn't really seen the world before then. The air smelled hot, dusty, and slightly metallic and an almost visible tingle wavered, like diluted lightning, around us. Something more than rain threatened. I shivered despite the heat smothering me. Even the usual cheerful shrieking and splashing sounded muffled and far away. For the first time since we'd started coming to the pool, I wished we'd stayed home. Though Lauren seemed more disappointed than uneasy, she'd called Grandma Nan to come get us. But her grandmother didn't answer, adding to the heavy feeling in my gut.

We made our way back through the showers to the concession stand at the entrance. No one else seemed bothered by the coming storm so I said nothing and ordered popcorn and a Slushie. While we stood on the sidewalk licking fluffy kernels from our palms, Lauren's school crush and a friend left the boys' shower. The tingle in the air got stronger. Seeing us, the two boys strolled over, towels draped around shoulders and trunks sticking to legs. I caught the look in Tucker's eyes and a shudder rolled down my back, but I didn't know what it meant.

Lauren stroked her tongue over the salty butter that coated her palm; small flecks of white popcorn clung to her lips. She said nothing to Tucker but turned to face him.

"Hey, Lauren." I realized Tucker's eyes were the same brilliant shade as the pool we'd just left. For the first time, I understood their magnetic pull. The sky darkened behind his blond head and the lines of his cheekbones and chin sharpened as though I'd been looking at him from underwater until just this moment. "Done swimming for today?"

Lauren sipped her Pepsi and shrugged. "Dunno." She looked up and wrinkled her nose. "Looks like a thunderstorm. They'll close the pool when it starts."

Tucker kept his gaze on her. "Maybe it won't."

Lauren glanced out of the corner of her eye at me and the electric feeling jumped. I wondered if sparks would crackle around us when we moved.

"Want some popcorn?" She held her bag toward Tucker. There was something odd with the way she stuck her hip out. And the way she blinked while talking.

"I'm Jamie." The other boy pointed to my bag of popcorn. "Can I have some?"

I shrugged and held it out. "I'm Weeble."

"Let's go sit at that picnic table." Without waiting for anyone to agree, Lauren slung her towel onto her shoulder and walked around the building.

The four of us sat near the fence surrounding the pool, Lauren and Tucker chatting while Jamie and I said little.

After she'd eaten every last kernel, one at a time, I'd had enough. "Can we get back in the pool now?" I asked. "It's so hot and humid I gotta jump in before I die."

"Yeah." Lauren didn't look at me. She spoke to Tucker instead. "Let's go."

They walked together toward the showers, his hand slipping down and taking hers. The heavy feeling moved up my torso and into my lungs. I didn't wait for Jamie before tiptoeing through the grass, its blades like a bed of splinters. Hot dust powdered my toes. The contrast between light and dark increased as the clouds, menacing and alive, rolled and bunched above us. I imagined them swallowing the sun whole and the world going dark.

"Wait! You forgot your towel," Jamie called after me.

I stopped and turned toward him, surprised when he wrapped the towel around my neck. For the first time since we'd met, I looked directly at him. Unlike Tucker, there wasn't anything particularly outstanding about Jamie, but he had freckles and an easy smile. The squeezing feeling around my chest loosened a bit. We fell into step, and just before we reached the sidewalk, he slipped his hand around mine. I didn't say anything, but I didn't pull away. After we returned to the pool, we spread our towels next to Lauren and Tucker, who sat talking, and headed for the diving board.

I don't know when the wind picked up or the clouds got more threatening. I lost myself in diving, over and over. I couldn't swim well, but I loved studying the board, anticipating where to place my feet in a running jump or experimenting with bending my knees or launching off my toes. I imagined my body in space, how it would twist and turn or fall straight down. Whether I could arch my back and keep my stomach from slapping the surface. How far out into the pool, or how far down, I could go. Every dive was different. Every dive was glorious. For a heartbeat I hung suspended in air, somewhere between heaven and the water. I sensed Jamie behind me in line, but beyond a few quick grins and one or two exclamations, we said nothing.

I'd just climbed out of the pool, hair dripping and ears filled, when the first ominous rumble of thunder sounded behind the chattering and shrieks. Everything happened at once then. Jamie came off the board, the lifeguards blew their whistles, and I glanced over to see Lauren and Tucker holding hands. Something in their posture or perhaps the look on their faces held my attention. While I watched, Tucker leaned forward and kissed Lauren.

Jamie, hanging off the side of the pool, must have followed my frozen gaze. He whooped and lifted himself out. I stood, rooted to the concrete, exposed and trembling. Something besides the storm threatened indeed.

"Lauren and Tucker, sittin' in a tree, k-i-s-s-i-n-g!" sang Jamie.

"Out of the pool! Everyone, out of the pool!" yelled the lifeguards, their whistles shrilling.

Lauren pulled away from Tucker and darted a glance at me. I looked away. Lightning flashed. That's when I saw him. The scarecrow with the dead eyes.

All around us was frenzied chaos, but in that small triangle formed with Lauren, me, and the scarecrow, there was absolute stillness. In the silence of our geometry, I read the force of his stare on her. She saw nothing but Tucker. And I watched them both.

Then thunder rumbled again and Jamie tugged my hand, drawing my gaze away and breaking the connection. When I looked back at the spot where I'd seen the scarecrow grasping the chain-link fence with his long fingers, he'd disappeared. I swiveled my head in time to catch Lauren and Tucker holding hands as they ran up the steps toward the exit. The heaviness moved up my spine and lodged in my head, leaving a fierce ache. The peculiar brightness of the daylight trapped under the evil-looking clouds hurt my eyes.

When Jamie and I reached the sidewalk in front of the concession stand, Lauren and Tucker stood under a tree, oblivious to the mothers and fathers urging their children to race for their cars before the rain hit. Thunder boomed right above us and an echoing boom rolled away towards the lake. I watched them as the crowd brushed past me, the hot, damp wind whipping through the trees and sending dust swirling to stick to my sweaty skin. The metallic scent of unshed rain and hot cement clogged my nostrils. I struggled to breathe. I struggled to understand what was happening. The crowd thinned and I saw Tucker doing something to Lauren's hand before he leaned in to kiss her again. Under the tree, they looked like shadows, indistinct and unreal. A premonition stopped my heart.

"Tucker Murphy! Tucker! Where are you?" A worried-looking woman stood on the sidewalk, craning her neck and shouting.

Tucker pulled away from Lauren, leaving her in darkness as he came out into the unnatural light. He looked over his shoulder once, waved, and then trotted towards his mother. I watched as they passed me, but when I looked back to find Lauren, I couldn't see her under the tree anymore. A thrill of terror zigzagged through me and sent my heart racing. I lurched forward before Jamie, who still held my hand, squeezed it.

192

"'Bye, Weeble."

In that moment, the image of his smiling face, freckled and honest, imprinted on my memory as a kind of bookend to my life before and after.

* * *

The cops found Lauren's ring, the one that Tucker Murphy gave her that afternoon, under the tree where Tucker kissed her good-bye. They almost didn't find it, they told Grandma Nan, because the mud after the thunderstorm had been thick and deep. But the detectives, careful as they searched for footprints near her abandoned tote bag and discarded towel, spied it half buried near a small rock—and the flip-flop she'd lost. Tucker, whose mother brought him to the station to identify the ring, told me in high school that he wore it on a chain even though he dreamt about kissing Lauren over and over. We'd both ditched the Friday afternoon pep rally, he because he'd turned out to be a stoner and me because crowds always made me nervous. We crouched outside the open gym door, listening to the catcalls while the pep band played for the flag corps, a rather sad group of uncoordinated girls who didn't have a prayer to be a cheerleader let alone the more gifted pompon dancer.

He reached into the open collar of his plaid shirt and yanked something out. "Here. Not even real fuckin' gold. I got it from my grandma's yard sale. Just costume jewelry she said. Lauren loved it though."

I leaned over and politely looked at it. The peculiar odor of burnt grass invaded my nostrils. I ignored the scent to study the filigreed oval on the top of the ring. It looked like an antique. "You sure it's not real?"

Tucker lifted the joint to his mouth for a deep drag before offering it to me. I started to shake my head and then reconsidered. I accepted it with careful fingers before taking a toke. The hot smoke seared my throat, but it kept the tears out of my eyes.

"Pretty sure." He leaned back against the brick wall which radiated heat from the late-afternoon sun. I kept scanning the parking lot, certain that a predator darted from car to car while the glare off the windshields blinded me. I swiveled my head to look over my shoulder, making sure that I hadn't gone more than five feet from the open doorway. Gripping a large rock in my hand, I wondered if I'd be given enough time to push Tucker in the way.

We sat silent until the joint had been consumed and then Tucker spoke as if I'd been waiting for him to continue.

"It was too big. She squealed when I put it on her finger." He closed his eyes and raised his face to the sun, catlike. "I keep dreaming about it. I always wake up when she squeals."

"But you said you dream about kissing her. I saw you kiss her after you gave her the ring."

He squinted at me from the corners of his eyes. "I always wondered if you saw that." His voice didn't rise above a murmur.

Irrational black anger surged in me. I jumped up and ran, too panicked and furious to fear the phantom killer in the lot. I always remember that conversation with Tucker when I think about his suicide. Remember it and wonder if I hadn't run away if we'd have started hanging out together. Wonder if I'd have spent high school in a pot haze, dulling the pain and failing classes but too stoned to care. Maybe Tucker and I would've gotten it on. But I always stop when I get to this part of my "what-if" narrative because I remember Lauren's crush and Tucker's surreal blue-green eyes, the ones that had grown cloudy and faded by freshman year. No matter how much I wish it'd been me who'd died that summer, I couldn't make Lauren's dream come true by fucking her first real love. I couldn't resurrect Lauren either—even though a dark little voice pointed out I only remembered what she looked like around Tucker. For years after he stuck the gun in his mouth, I hated and admired him. Why didn't I have his courage? Why did I cling so stubbornly to something so worthless? Why did I think I could ever take Lauren's place and live for her? And then I realized four years ago at the Holocaust Museum I could never be as selfish as Tucker. To kill myself would be to make it all about *me*, to focus attention on *me*. Who the hell cares that I have nightmares? I'm alive. I need to make sure no one forgets Lauren. I need to make sure *I* don't forget Lauren.

And so, here are the facts of Lauren's abduction and murder.

On June 28, 1982, Richard Lee Grady abducted Lauren Case, 11, of St. Joseph, Missouri, from the Hyde Park swimming pool at approximately 4:30 p.m. Although there were over two dozen people in the vicinity, no one saw Grady snatch Lauren. Grady, who'd been on a six-state killing spree over a fifteen-year period, took Lauren to the mobile home he'd rented next to Sugar Lake, Missouri, where he raped and tortured her for two weeks. In addition to sixteen confessed murders, including one while in prison, Grady repeatedly raped or sodomized children and teens, for which crimes he spent little time in mental health facilities, and committed auto theft, burglary, and forgery. During this time, numerous psychiatrists and psychologists diagnosed and treated him for insanity, manipulative institutionalized sociopathy, and paranoid schizophrenia. Eventually, after good behavior and credit for time served, he was released. Within two months, he began assaulting children again, finally snatching Lauren. Police captured Grady after a witness tipped them off about his whereabouts. He was convicted of two child murders in Missouri in 1983, but he hung himself after the jury refused to give him the death penalty.

Ten

∨

Some few persons even got a fragment of the looking-glass in their hearts, and this was very terrible, for their hearts became cold like a lump of ice. A few of the pieces were so large that they could be used as window-panes; it would have been a sad thing to look at our friends through them. Other pieces were made into spectacles; this was dreadful for those who wore them, for they could see nothing either rightly or justly. At all this the wicked demon laughed till his sides shook—it tickled him so to see the mischief he had done.

LAUREN'S MURDER STABBED ME IN THE HEART, transforming it from a seat of passion to an arctic wasteland. All my finer feelings—affection and empathy, grief and rage—all evaporated in the bitter, dry air where moist heat used to flow. That's the secret of the arctic: its aridity. Most people think of the broiling Sahara or Mojave when they picture a desert. They don't imagine the icy realm near the poles. But the chill white landscape where my heart used to be has desiccated my very soul.

So why does it feel as though a thousand violent pinpricks beat an uneven tattoo along the surface of my dead heart, here jolting a section to life, there stabbing through scarred muscle?

When I leave my apartment in the morning to run, I don't bother to warm up. I just sprint down the stairs and toward the river, denying the density of my bones and scarcely letting my soles touch the ground. I'm so swift nothing can catch me or tear my stunned heart from its icy chamber. I can't feel my legs pumping or my lungs inhaling and exhaling. I feel only the sun's heat on my forearms and the sports bra binding my chest. I run until my legs threaten to collapse. I run until sweat blinds me and my throat swells from dehydration. My thoughts have flown from the bony cage of my head and soar, mindless, into the brilliant blue morning.

Clouds drift over the sun and a cool breath caresses the back of my neck. Gentle pressure tugs on my center, urging me to stop. I'm not alone. I blink and falter, but when the world comes into focus around me, I see no one. Instead, bone-melting exhaustion sinks through me like a flash flood and I'm drawn up short, bent over, panting and nauseous, unable to take another step. That's when I see the bloody paw prints. Hero's paws are rubbed raw and bleeding. I start to retch, but there's nothing except bitter bile on my tongue. Even the swallow of water I took before leaving has evaporated on my suddenly clammy skin. Dizziness overwhelms me and I stagger to the bench on the sidewalk.

For long moments, I can't think or move. I concentrate on counting breaths. When I've reached twenty, I concentrate on slowing them down. As I do, I remember a yoga class I took in college. The teacher, a young dark-haired woman whose sincere eyes almost convinced me that purity and goodness existed, told the class that our lives are measured by the number of breaths we take. We can't add to that number, so we should concentrate on slowing them as much as possible. My head pounds, but I focus on breathing until I'm calm. That's when I feel it. The fresh pain in my reanimated heart.

Desperate, I look around, for what I don't know. The silvered window behind me mirrors my anguish, but beneath the surface, I see vague objects. Curious, I stand up and approach, my hand outstretched. As I come closer, I slip beneath the opacity and into this silent world. Before me is the most serene and beautiful face I've ever seen, its eyes sad and the corners downturned. In her arms she holds a child, her cheek pressed against his. Her gaze holds mine while the window superimposes my image onto her. I am her. She is me. Stunned, I realize who she is. At that instant, I see the compassionate understanding in her sad eyes. Fear flashes like lightning through me and I step back, stumbling over Hero and falling on my ass to the sidewalk.

"Weeble, are you all right?"

Before I can process the sound of his voice, its velvet an instant balm for the pain in my chest, Tom Paul wraps his arms around my shoulders and helps me to my feet. He leads me and Hero to the same old sagging sofa I sat on during my last visit. Shock reverberates in me when I realize the glass sculpture above me is a decapitated head on a silver platter. I stare in horror at the closed eyes and Medusa-like hair, my bruised buttocks throbbing.

"John the Baptist," Tom Paul says next to me. I realize he's making slow circles around my palms with his thumbs and tugging gently on my fingers. I nod, but I don't know why John the Baptist had his head cut off. The nasty thought *why does it matter* flits through me. I shudder.

"Hero's paws are bleeding," I blurt, not looking at Tom Paul.

He lets my hands go and kneels on the floor before examining Hero. "Poor boy." His low voice trickles into the cracked earth of my heart, easing its parched terrain. I lean towards him. I need to keep him talking.

"Your gallery opening is in a few weeks."

He looks up at me, his eyes warm and intense. "June twentieth." He levers himself to his feet. "I've got some salve in the back. You wouldn't believe how often I burn and cut myself." He waggles his fingers at me and then leaves. I watch him go. Under his dusty gray t-shirt, the back muscles slide and bunch. For the first time in my life, I want to run my hands along a man's shoulders and down his sides. For the first time, I want to press my heated flesh against his, to trace the ridges and hollows that define him. I shake my head, confused. What's happening to me? I draw my knees into my chest and look away, measuring the distance to the door before I realize what I'm doing and stop.

Tom Paul returns carrying what looks like an artist caddy. Instead of brushes and palette knives, however, he has a tube of strong-smelling ointment, antiseptic wipes, and what turns out to be a package of Swiss chocolate.

"That's for you," he says when he sees me eyeing it. "You need to eat, Weeble, after such a hard run. I've got tea steeping in the back for us. Just let me take care of your pooch first."

I hadn't realized I was hungry until he opens the chocolate and, breaking off a piece, feeds me some. While he ministers to Hero, I force myself to eat slowly, savoring the rich sweetness on my tongue. The sharp electrical storm within my ribcage subsides, leaving only a dull ache.

Tom Paul sighs and stands up again. Hero watches him leave to get the tea, his expressive eyes adoring and anxious. The fringed banner of his tail thumps when Tom Paul returns carrying two glass mugs. As he sits beside me, he hands me a brilliant orange confection filled with steaming *chai*. I study it. The mug has two layers fused together. Tiny bubbles in the translucent outer layer give it a textured appearance, like moist, glowing sugar. On top of that layer whimsical shapes frolic.

"It's beautiful."

"Thank you." He sips his tea, his eyes never leaving me. The heat from his thigh where it touches mine distracts me. "You coming?"

I blink, bewildered. Everything about him, *this*, bewilders me. "What?"

"My opening. You're coming, right?" His free hand takes mine, anchoring me here with him. My heartbeat stutters and speeds up. "I'd really like you to be there."

I gulp too much *chai*, burning my tongue. My throat remains dry, however. I clear it and look away. "I don't know."

His fingers squeeze mine a little. "Come to dinner tomorrow. My friend Jonah and his girlfriend Fredda come over every week, along with a few other people. You can't keep training if you don't eat right. Bring Hero, too."

Hearing his name, Hero lifts his head to Tom Paul's knee and looks at me. The message is clear. My heart thuds and I wish I'd never told him about the triathlon. "Okay. What time?"

"Six. You can help me cook."

I sip the spicy tea while looking out toward the studio. A strange restlessness fills me. "I should go." I can hear the plaintive note in my voice.

"No, stay."

"You've got work to do."

"Not much and nothing I can do before inspiration strikes."

I look at him again. I can't help it. His eyes are a searing, potent magnet. I remember the pity and sorrow in them yesterday when I told him about Lauren. Without thinking, I draw my hand from his, my fingers rising to touch the side of his face. He's as still as a fawn that senses the lurking wolf; his eyes never lose contact with mine. After half a dozen heartbeats, I let my hand drop.

"Talk to me then. Tell me about *pâte de verre*."

Tom Paul's gaze searches my face for an instant before he pulls my mug from me with gentle fingers. Setting both our mugs on the floor, he draws me into his side. His scent fills my nose. Cilantro and basil, sunshine and cinnamon. Mysterious musk. Dizzy, I feel his heartbeat through my shirt and the shifting of his chest as he breathes. My own erratic heartbeat calms. I think about the yoga teacher and begin to slow my breathing, to extend this moment. I imagine that Tom Paul does likewise.

"I discovered *pâte de verre* quite by accident." The easy cadence of his voice mesmerizes. My eyes grow heavy—I'm too exhausted to fight its seduction. "After college, I spent a year in Florence studying sculpture at the *Accademia Europea di Firenze*." His rolling, lilting Italian stirs something in me. "Then I traveled around Europe for a while."

"That must've been wonderful." My voice slurs as though I've had too much wine. I can hardly think straight. "Never been to Italy. Never been anywhere."

"Ah. I'll do my best to describe it to you then."

As he describes the beauty of Florence, I watch the living light shifting among his glass sculptures in the studio around us, luring my mind's eye to the Tuscan landscape. Just as I'd slipped beneath the mirrored surface of the studio window, my imagination slips free from reality. In this ethereal place, old white stone buildings mellowed under a Mediterranean sun loom before me, their arched entrances leading to domed ceilings and fabulous frescoes peopled with Greek and Roman gods. Bronze and marble statues keep stoic vigil along cobbled streets and frolic in fountains in the ubiquitous plazas. Beyond the city limits, rolling hills and lush vineyards embrace a sky so cyan blue no artist can capture it—the pure blue of an atmosphere penetrated by the most undiluted sunlight. The fragrant flavors of olive and tomato, basil and bread haunt my tongue. I'm dazzled and hollow, sleepy and bemused.

We sit together through most of the morning while Tom Paul describes his days mastering modeling and molds, carving and welding, and bronze casting. As he talks, he rubs a light palm along my bare upper arm, squeezing my elbow with his fingertips. Learning those few square inches of me with infinite gentleness, shaping me little by little. Electricity thrills down my spine as I imagine those long elegant fingers molding the flesh of my back, my hip, my inner thigh.

Tom Paul notices my tremor and hands me my mug before snuggling me closer, never stopping his story about his time in Europe. He takes me with him as he visits each museum, studying painting and architecture as if he's starved. In a hushed voice, he tells of his first view of Michelangelo's David, its innate beauty that pierces his chest. Although I know the statue, something shifts in the cool white image I hold in memory at Tom Paul's awe-filled tone. My stomach clenches and irrational longing fills me, whether to see David or to have Tom Paul speak about *me* that way, I don't know.

"But I got frustrated with the clumsy stiffness of wood and stone. I hate the coldness, the impersonality, of metal—the hard edges. Glass, glass is a different medium altogether. When strong light hits glass, it draws out fire. It doesn't sharpen the boundaries." Here he pulls a smooth piece of glass from his pocket, something not quite big enough to be a paperweight but polished and heavy. He hefts it in his palm and then holds it up where its fiery radiance sends orange-gold spots onto the wall above us. It's a fairy stone, full of magic and delight. It's a knife full of truth that burns. I shudder at my bizarre thoughts. I almost don't notice Tom Paul's hand as it strokes my arm again.

"I also fell in love with *chiaroscuro* and tenebrism."

"Tenebrism? *Chiaroscuro*?" The words are clumsy on my tongue.

"Painting techniques for dealing with light and dark. That's what *chiaroscuro* means. 'Light-dark.' Tenebrism is extreme contrast between light and dark. The background is so dark details are lost. Instead, the most important subject in the painting is spotlighted." He shifts and I look up to see him gazing at me. "Do you know Caravaggio?"

I half shrug. "I recognize the name. I must've learned about him in art history."

He nods, unsurprised. "Before Caravaggio, painting was something you just looked at. It had nothing to do with you. After him, painting was something you experienced. He caught you up in a dramatic moment—you were right there, right in the middle of something vivid and stirring."

He falls silent, remembering, I suppose, his own experience looking at a Caravaggio. I wonder if I'll ever feel that way about anything but my own sad life. My own stirring drama. I envy him the freedom to care about something bigger than himself.

"When I saw his painting *The Martyrdom of St. Matthew*, I felt guilty. I felt like a murderer."

I startle at his words and pull away from him, keeping my eyes angled to the floor. I can feel him looking at me, certain he knows my secret. Hadn't I seen him wielding a burning knife full of truth?

"But I'm not a painter. I'm a sculptor. And while I was in Florence, I learned to love Byzantine glass mosaics."

"Are they made from *pâte de verre*?" I hear the uneasy edge in my voice. I want to stand up and pace, but I hold myself still. All traces of sleepiness have fled and I'm stone-cold awake.

"No." He laughs. "It's really not easy to explain how I came to this place, making sculptures using glass paste. Sometimes I think Puck moves around my imagination at the speed of light. I can feel where he gets his material from, but I don't know how he puts it all together."

"Puck?" The name sounds familiar, but I'm too wary to try to remember. He's not making sense anyway. I remember him telling me his sister thought he was crazy. Maybe it's true. It certainly explains why he's here with me.

Tom Paul laughs again, a rich belly laugh. The hollowness in my stomach flares, fierce and bitter. I'm starved for that sound. "Puck is the name I gave my muse, my creative genius. I got his name from Shakespeare—you know, *A Midsummer's Night's Dream*? The ancients thought inspiration came from a divine creature separate from the artist. It helps me to think of it that way."

I squeeze my eyes shut, and my fingers clasping the mug ache from my grip. Images of light and dark, of mad imps darting through dappled forests, whirl in my thoughts and make my head throb. My stomach feels queasy. The earlier tastes—olive and tomato, basil and bread—sour on my tongue.

Without looking at him, I ask, "What do you want from me, Tom Paul?" Although I say this as calmly as I can, I still hear the hope and pain. I wonder if he can hear them too.

Something touches my cheek and I open my eyes to look at him. Now it's his turn to trace the line of my cheek, my jaw. My heart patters against my ribs and my breath quickens.

"I don't want anything from you, Weeble." Another pair of dark eyes, flat and deadly, rises like a specter between us, but the heat in Tom Paul's own burns the image away. This close, I'm snared by the gold flecks in the brown irises. Flying or drowning. I don't know what I feel, but it isn't fear.

"What if I want something from you?" I try to tease, but my voice croaks, turning the levity into heart-thumping earnestness. I can't hold his gaze and look away.

Light fingers pull my face around, drawing my gaze back to his. "Do you?" His quiet question waits in the charged space between us.

"I-I don't know." The restlessness invades again. I want to squirm away, jump up, pace. "Maybe."

His steady gaze stills me. "What? What do you want from me?"

Now I *am* frightened. My mouth opens and closes, but nothing makes it past the ice crystals still in my heart. Flashes of longing, of imagined back and buttocks, of pressure and sweat, and a thousand nameless things fill me, but I have no words to describe them.

"Shh," he says and I realize I'm letting out little sounds of distress. He takes the mug from my aching fingers and sets it down. "You don't have to tell me now. Remember, I'm not going anywhere."

I nod, blinking and dumb. A rush of air from the studio door caresses the side of my neck. We both look and the spell holding me here dissipates and disperses out the door as a stranger walks in. I burst to my feet. "I've gotta go. I'm late for the pool."

Tom Paul stands, but he doesn't touch me. "I'll see you tomorrow then. 6?"

I turn, ignoring the ethereal woman who floats over to us. Without looking at him, without giving him a chance to respond, I say, "I want you to know me. I want you to know the truth."

I try to tell myself that it's nothing but relief I feel as I escape back through the looking-glass and into the harsh reality of sunlight and concrete, but I'm too familiar with grief to succeed.

TOM PAUL

TOM PAUL WATCHED WEEBLE SPRINT OUT the studio door, Hero limping at her side, before he turned to Callista, who slouched on the sofa. She studied him for a moment before speaking.

"That your lady of the mists?" Her soft voice drew blood from his battered heart. He sat down next to her and looked toward the door where Weeble had been only moments before.

"She's hurting, Cally. So much it hurts *me*." He let out a shaky breath. "The darkness blotting her aura has gotten thicker, like an eclipse. I see only the absence of light now."

Callista's hand found his and she gave it a squeeze. "They say it's always darkest before the dawn. Maybe whatever's got her doesn't want to let go. Doesn't want to let you see her."

Tom Paul frowned down at his sister. From anyone else, this would have been the epitome of platitude. But not from Callista.

"It's grief. I know that much. I went to her apartment Saturday night after her friend Marcie called me—you know, the construction boss masquerading as a therapist, the one who knows Sharon? She knows I met Weeble a couple of months ago outside a dumpster. Said flat out she thinks I've fallen in love with her, that Weeble feels something for me in return."

He laughed. "I told her yeah, she feels something for me. Fear. Marcie said yeah, she's afraid. Afraid of what she feels. Marcie told me Weeble needs me to draw her out among people again, away from the dead. When I asked her what that meant, she said I'd have to trust her and get the details later. I wanted to believe her so much I took the chance and knocked on Weeble's door."

He let go of Callista's hand and let his gaze wander to the head of St. John the Baptist. Every time he looked at the downcast eyes and solemn mouth, he wondered how far he himself would go to tell the truth.

Callista waited until he met her gaze. "What happened? Clearly she didn't kick you out or she wouldn't've come here today."

"I thought she was going to pass out when she opened the door. She had no idea Marcie had called me. Between the shock of seeing me and the lack of eating and sleeping for days, she looked awful. There were these shiny dark patches under her eyes," here he pointed to his own face, "bruises almost, and her skin had lost its healthy glow. She looked seriously ill."

Callista made a clucking sound but didn't say anything.

"I asked her if she wanted me to leave. She said no." He stopped, remembering the raw emotion in Weeble's eyes and the sound of her voice when she'd asked him to stay. "So I stayed, made her some tea and fed her." Again he paused, remembering how she'd fallen asleep while clinging to his hand, her weight in his arms when he'd carried her to bed. The memory of her body curled alongside him all night long, her hands twined with his, filled him with a yearning he'd never known before. But it was the thunderstorm of grief and hope on her face the next morning that had haunted him for the past two days.

"She told me she's been having nightmares about her childhood best friend Lauren. Lauren was murdered a few weeks after Weeble turned eleven by a serial killer."

An image of Weeble speaking through stony lips, her eyes dull and lightless, flashed through him. He'd cried then, hot tears sliding down his cheeks before he'd realized that they'd slipped out. Something like wonder dissolved the awful dead mask on Weeble's face when she saw his tears and she traced their path down his cheek with trembling fingers.

Callista shuddered, drawing him from his reverie. She laid her hand on his upper arm and shuddered again. "That's what Marcie meant when she said 'away from the dead.'" Her whisper should have clued him in that she'd gleaned something in that brief touch.

"Yeah. Marcie won't say why, but she thinks Weeble blames herself."

Callista let her hand drop from his arm. She shifted on the sofa, once, twice, before looking down and away to hide her old habit of pulling at her lower lip. When she raised her eyes, he saw worry darkening her gaze. A premonition thrilled the pit of his stomach.

"There's evil here, Tom Paul. Old evil." She took his hand. Hers were cool and clammy, a sure sign that she'd had some insight. "When I said it's darkest before dawn, I just meant the garden-variety type. You know, a young woman who's had a really bad boyfriend. Maybe some abuse, even hitting."

Tom Paul started and nearly stood up, but Callista kept a surprisingly strong grip on him. "Don't act so shocked," she said, her soft voice slicing him. "It's not that uncommon, you know."

"Have you—?" He couldn't even formulate the question. "'Garden variety'?"

"Four in ten women, Tom Paul. What do you think my chances are?"

"No." He groaned. "Why didn't you tell me?"

"It's not about me." An unfamiliar emotion sharpened her voice, but he caught the bitter turmoil she tried to disguise. "It's about you. You're not like other guys, okay? I know Zandra gives you grief, makes fun of your quirks, but she's no different from me. We worry about you."

Now he was dumbfounded. Slight, fragile Callista and no-nonsense, tough-as-nails Zandra united in their concern for him? Sure, he and Callista were close, but he'd always felt protective of *her*. And Zandra? Well, Zandra could take care of herself without breaking a sweat, but she rarely extended much compassion to anyone beyond their mother. They couldn't be worried about him.

"Me? Why?"

"You don't know?" When she smiled, he glimpsed sorrow and understanding as old as humanity. "For all your special sight, the beauty of these—" she waved an encompassing gesture around her—"you don't really see the world as it is. Remember when I joked about stalking Weeble? You looked horrified. But I wasn't entirely joking, Tom Paul."

She took his hand again and when she spoke her voice had an urgency he'd never heard before. "I fear you're going into this blindly. And unprotected. I don't want you to get sucked into a spiritual vortex."

"You said love heals, Cally." He heard reproof in his voice. And, for the first time ever toward Callista, anger. "Was that just a platitude—just like it gets darkest before the dawn?"

"No! No, I don't want it to be." Her hoarse voice sawed at him. She looked away. "I guess I just never wanted your faith to be tested." She brought her gaze back to his. "I can still see the light through your eyes. I'm in Plato's cave, Tom Paul, but you, you're on the mountaintop."

His anger died away as he understood. He squeezed her hand. "You're afraid."

"Terrified."

"Don't be." He hugged her. Even as he tried to console her, he felt awed that Callista remembered their philosophy discussions. No one else in his family had shown the slightest interest in his classical studies. "I'm right in the cave with you. I just peek now and then out of the cave mouth, so I've seen a sliver of real light."

Callista studied him for a moment, testing his words before responding. Her doubt won out. "Maybe you shouldn't look. The brighter the sliver, the less you can see to move around the cave."

"Or the darker the cave, the brighter that sliver will be. At least I know there *is* an outside that's lit up. Would you be happier if I told you I'd felt all around the inside of the cave and that's all there is?"

A sheepish look descended over her features. She shrugged. "Maybe I'd like it better if you told me there's no way to know if we're really in a cave. It could all be a figment of our imagination."

He laughed. "Forget about reality. You can put on a shadow-puppet show with the other people chained up in front of the fire." At the cross look that swept away her brief embarrassment, he got serious. "Don't worry about me, Cally. I'm grateful for your warning. You know I take your insight seriously. I'm not so dazzled by the light I've lost my mind."

"You'll be careful then? I hope Weeble figures out what a gift you are, Tom Paul."

During the next twenty-four hours, Tom Paul turned their conversation over so often that his stomach got queasy. A queer dread permeated him. When Weeble, eyes wary and legs stiff, strode into his studio trailing shadows, his heart jolted. Who was she anyway? He still didn't know her real name. Just the childish nickname.

He wiped his hands on his apron and turned to look at her standing at the temporary wall hiding his sculptures for *The Soul Illuminated*. He'd spent all morning trying to stage them, hoping that the simple act of setting the grouping up would spur the elusive answer to his lighting problem. No such luck. Puck had taken an extended holiday after he'd finished molding St. Irene's head, and nothing had cajoled him to return. Tom Paul still didn't know how he'd solve his problem before the opening. For the first time, he doubted Puck's numinous skill. He doubted himself.

Weeble didn't speak at first, instead drawing her gaze around the haphazard staging area and giving Tom Paul plenty of time to study her. He'd found her unusual green eyes and dark-blond hair attractive before, but today she was heartbreakingly beautiful. Her coloring and features had a clarity and depth found only at twilight, that magical portal at day's end. The disturbing thought flitted through him that she'd grown more vibrant because the darkness had seeped deeper into her aura.

When she turned to look at him, the daylight outside his window dimmed as a cloud passed across the sun.

"I can't come tonight." No preamble. No apology.

Instinct told him to accept it, not to question. "Okay."

She blinked and drew back a little, hesitating. Perhaps she'd expected him to resist. She'd shifted as she spoke, her shoulders and one foot turned as she started to flee. Against reason, he wanted to pull her to him, hard. He wanted to slide his palms down her flanks and grip her hips against his groin. The sudden unfamiliar hunger stunned him, left him dizzy and shaking.

"It's just ... I don't know what I'm doing right now, okay?" She took another tiny step backwards, her mouth opening and distress clouding her eyes.

He looked away. What was happening to him? Had he taken Callista's fears too seriously? He squeezed his eyes shut in response to that thought. When he opened them, he had a fleeting glimpse of luminous nature before a thin skin spread like black oil across his vision. He blinked again and again, but his sight remained dull. Whatever the cause, he now saw the world as through a glass, darkly. *Perhaps*, he thought, *just as everyone else does.*

"Are you all right?"

Tom Paul brought his gaze back to Weeble's face. Concern had replaced her distress. She took several steps forward, laying her hand on his forearm. A spark jumped from her cool palm to his bare skin, causing the short hairs to prickle, and zigzagged to his chest. His breathing accelerated as his heart began a rapid tattoo.

"Yes." It came out rougher than he meant. He sighed. "I'm sorry, Weeble. I guess your visit came at a bad time." He waved his hand around the staging area. "I can't seem to get the lighting right for my sculptures. The sculptures are nothing without the light."

Weeble looked toward the staging area again, this time a small frown pinching her brows together.

"What're you trying to do?" She stepped into the space.

"*That's* part of what I'm trying to do." He stepped past her to stand next to St. Sebastian's arrow-studded torso before drawing a figure in the air to encompass them. "I'm trying to bring the viewer into the installation so she becomes part of the crowd. Some of the people—" here he gestured to a cluster on the far wall—"are curious, avid and otherwise. Others are horrified or anguished. Some are complicit."

She swiveled around to look at the figures as he pointed to them, swallowing visibly at the last one, whose greedy eyes gleamed above a ravenous mouth. Her face held a mix of fascination and dismay. "I don't know the story. Tell me the story." Her wide eyes focused on Tom Paul, locking her gaze to his. He wondered at the small tremor that shook her.

"Of St. Sebastian's martyrdom?" At her dumb nod, he went on. "He lived at the end of the third century, probably born in Gaul—

present-day France. He became a captain of the Praetorian Guard. Do you know who they were?

"No." Her hushed voice hung in the air between them.

"They were imperial bodyguards. They'd been around in some form for hundreds of years, but Augustus formally named and organized them. They played a crucial role in the *Pax Romana*, keeping good emperors in power and getting rid of weak ones. Just before Sebastian joined them, though, they'd become a ruthless bunch of mercenaries. The Emperor Diocletian took away their political power by taking most of them out of Rome and using them in imperial field armies that defended the frontier." He paused to see if she understood. She did, so far.

"The stories about Sebastian say Diocletian made him captain and that he was a favorite of the old emperor. Diocletian had no love for Christians, however. They'd never been popular in the Empire, but the average Roman had come to tolerate them." Again he paused, letting her absorb that. "Diocletian was a traditionalist. He wanted to return Rome to its golden age and that meant making sure all Romans worshipped the old gods. When he came to power in 284, he purged the army of Christians."

"I take it he didn't know his favorite captain had converted?"

"No, but when Sebastian made a nuisance of himself, converting other soldiers and even a governor, Diocletian eventually heard about it. He had Sebastian tied to a post and shot with arrows." He smoothed a fingertip over the fletched end of an arrow in Sebastian's torso, watching as Weeble flinched and threw out her hand.

"That's horrible." Her choked whisper moved him. She looked toward the torso, her mouth working. Strong emotions eddied across her features, washing the darkness away. For the space of a heartbeat, she was a child again, vulnerable and speechless.

"He didn't die." Something choked him too, pity or empathy mixed with the hunger to hold her. "A widow named Irene found him and nursed him to health. Sebastian used his second chance to publicly rebuke Diocletian for his cruel treatment of Christians."

She whirled to face him. "Why?" From her expression, he knew that she understood that Sebastian had sacrificed himself.

"Why didn't he save himself? Be grateful for recovering and live quietly?" He watched her as he spoke. She flinched again and ducked her head. In that moment, she lost her vulnerability. Her sideways gaze matched the angle of the last sculpture. Her terrible beauty deepened. Without being aware of what he did, he stepped forward and pulled her into his arms. They said nothing.

Outside the gallery window, the day darkened further.

Eleven

AS I STEP THROUGH THE DOOR FROM THE STAIRS onto my floor, I see the figure slouched against the wall ahead. For an excruciating heartbeat, I know that Richard Lee Grady has returned for me.

And then the figure rises and turns and even through my terror I recognize Jana. Her surly expression flees as her gaze locks on my face. She strides over to me, her arms outstretched, and I'm pulled into an embrace scented with soap, lemon, and cherry blossoms. Despite myself, my eyes close and I inhale. I tremble against her solid warmth as if I've just stepped in from a frigid afternoon.

"Good God, Weeble! It's just me."

My weak laugh catches in my throat, ending almost in a sob. "Why are you here?" I ask, but I know.

She pulls back and looks at me. At this distance, I'm forced to consider the variegated green and brown in her hazel eyes, the powdery black of her mascara, the uneven shimmer of pale pink lip gloss. A surge of blunt envy broadsides me between my shoulder blades. The familiar sourness sharpens my palate. I shove them aside. It's an old battle, my conflicting admiration and jealousy. I'm past letting the jealousy goad me into proving it takes more than beauty-queen looks to get a man into bed.

"Are you going to ask me in?" she asks.

I step away and unlock my door. Over my shoulder, I ask, "Where's Jacob and Juliana?"

"With Julius. He took them to see his parents. I didn't feel up to dealing with his mother today." She follows me into the apartment, accepting Hero's enthusiastic welcome while I drop my keys on the counter and my gym bag on the floor. "It's been six weeks, Weeble. What happened to last Friday night?"

I feel a headache coming on. Hunger, thirst, and spiritual weariness beat at me. "Let me grab food first, Jana."

"Okay." She slides onto a barstool. "But we're gonna talk, so don't try your usual duck-and-slide routine, huh?"

I dart a glance at her. Her somber expression warns me. It warms me, too.

I put a glass of iced tea in front of her before pulling out the *hummus*, *baba ganoush*, and roasted red pepper spread that Tom Paul had made and brought me. I wish I could eat them alone. Instead, I dip a defiant finger in the creamy roasted eggplant. A different heat spreads through me as I lick it off.

Jana ignores my eating and dives into her interrogation. "Marcie says she's called and left half a dozen messages since last Friday. I know you and I have our little snits, but you always talk to Marcie."

"She tell you she sent a man over to seduce me?" My shoulder blocks my rough voice, but she hears me anyway.

"What?" She sounds incredulous. "The same Marcie who volunteers at the women's shelter? He must be some guy."

"He is." The words claw their way from my reluctant throat. We look at each other a long moment.

"Did he?" she asks, her voice soft.

I look away. "In a manner of speaking."

She bites her upper lip and drills her nails on the counter. It's her most unattractive habit. She looks like a troll. I love her for it. A wave of longing for our old friendship, hers and Marcie's and mine, floods me, and I blink back tears. That's gone now. They've moved on. Marriage and kids and careers while I struggle to push the demons of my childhood back into the shadows just so I can cling to the painstaking illusion of sanity I've built.

"When do I get to meet him? Are you bringing him to the Cape next month?"

A bolt of fear almost as strong as the terror that had gripped me in the hallway smites me. My breath stops and I spin on my heel, blind and deafened by my heartbeat. Somehow I manage to pour a glass of iced tea and sip it, restarting my breathing afterwards.

"I don't know if that's such a good idea."

"Hm." She continues to chew on her lip a moment. "You won't return Marcie's call because you don't want to tell her she was right about you. What's his name?" she asks before I can protest.

"Tom Paul."

She blinks hard. "The glass artist? I met him last year at her friend Sharon's gallery opening, the one you missed because you had that Big Dig deadline." She pauses as if measuring her words and I go on alert.

"What's the matter?" I suspect Marcie's been holding back on me. She's always reluctant to share anything negative about someone—she believes in the power of positive expectations. "Is he some kind of pervert?" I, of all people, know that's not true. I struggle to come up with other problems, but nothing occurs to me. Outrageous suggestions fly out of me anyway. "Bipolar? Schizophrenic?" Then I remember our first meeting when he described my aura. "Delusional? Filled with New Age religiosity?"

Jana listens, wide-eyed, to my laundry list of perversity. When I finish, she laughs. "Desperate, Weeble, to find some reason to ditch and run? Sorry, old friend. I found him fascinating. Otherworldly. He's an enigma wrapped in something pure and hopeful."

"You make him sound like a flake." Doubt fills my voice.

"Hardly." She leans forward and places her fingers on my wrist. "You know me. I'm nothing if not pragmatic. I don't see the world in shades of gray so much as I don't have any illusions about how things work, how people are. That's why I like Marcie so much. She sees the world the same way, she just draws different conclusions."

She looks away as I absorb her self-description. When she speaks again, her voice sounds wondering and surprised as if she'd just discovered a living member of a species previously believed extinct. "Tom Paul sees the world as it should be, Weeble."

"So he's idealistic," I mutter. I feel the sullen set of my features. "Naïve and inexperienced."

She brings her gaze back to me and the wonder fades. "Perhaps. But he didn't seem young to me. I would've said he seemed timeless, somehow."

"That's the Greek god resemblance." I don't recognize the bitterness in my voice.

Jana laughs again. "Got it bad, huh, Weeble? Marcie thinks Tom Paul's a mystic."

"I thought you said he wasn't filled with New Age religiosity?"

"He's not. Shit. I don't know how to describe him. It's just he's such a wise innocent. He's the kind of person who makes us cynical modern types deeply uneasy."

"Too good to be true?"

Jana eyes me. I see the speculation in her gaze. "Or too good for you?"

I busy myself putting away my lunch. My appetite has evaporated.

"He may be too good for you." When I spin to look at her, her eyes have hardened. We both know why she's agreeing with me. Until Julius, I'd had a habit of luring the guys she wanted to date into my bed. Even though she came to joke about it later, calling me her frog filter, Jana hadn't been so pragmatic she let me get by without a few cutting remarks.

A defiant surge of stubbornness grips me, but I don't meet her gaze. "There's no *may be* about it. He is."

"But it doesn't change anything?" Her soft voice catches me off guard. When I look at her, she surprises me by smiling. "Good for you, Weeble. It's about time you're with someone who sees more in you than a chance to get laid."

My defiance fades and my earlier weariness returns, magnified by a factor of a hundred. "What does it matter, Jana? I can't seem to stay away from him and he's either too idealistic or too inexperienced to know what I am." Frustration seeps into me, and I want to weep. "I feel like I'm strapped into a speeding train on a collision course, and I can't do anything to escape or avert it. I don't want to hurt him."

"Then don't." Her matter-of-fact tone slices into my wallow, stopping it cold. "You have power. You always have, Weeble. Use it."

* * *

Jana's words torture me over and over. I can't hide from their blunt truth. They weave their way into the rhythm of my run, they propel my strokes in the pool, and they power my pedaling as I tackle hills on my bike. I ponder their meaning as I turn them over and over like strange artifacts from an archaeological dig. Or mysterious alien technology discovered in a fallen meteorite. They distract me from researching and writing my tribute to victims of serial killers. They whisper to me that I'm nothing like those women and children. They seduce me with hope.

On Saturday, my rest day from training, Tom Paul arrives at my apartment bringing the sunrise with him. He carries groceries scavenged from Bread of Life, pastries from *Notre Pain Quotidien*, fruit and vegetables from the Cambridge Green Grocer, cheese and olives from the Greek market not far from Kendall Square, and coffee from Beans & Leaves Importers. I watch him unload it all in my kitchen as I stand bleary-eyed and foul-mouthed, my hair a rat's nest of snarls, my t-shirt holey, and my shorts threadbare. His presence fills my apartment until sharp tingles course up and down my spine. I fear what will happen when I get close to him.

"What're you doing?" I hear the incredulity threaded with hope in my voice.

"I've taken on the task of feeding you," he says and stops to grin at me. A reluctant smile curves my own mouth. "I know you just started your final thirteen weeks. I'm going to do my part to get you through them."

I ignore this. "I look like shit, Tom Paul."

"You do? Hadn't noticed." He grins again and the pressure in the room increases. "Course, I'm pretty sure I can recover something useful from that mess you call your hair. Hey, don't leave! I didn't mean anything by that."

I glance over my shoulder as I go back into my room. "I know. Let me wash the crust from my eyes and brush my teeth, so I don't fell my Good Samaritan before he's even had a chance to fulfill his mission."

When I return, Tom Paul stands at the stove holding the long handle of a small copper pot. Flat Stanley sits before a plate on the counter picking delicate bites from finely diced meat. Hero lies in the walkway between kitchen and living room, his patient eyes adoring the man who's doing his damndest to insinuate himself into my life. His fringed tail thumps the floor once or twice when he sees me slide onto a stool, but he doesn't move.

Tom Paul glances at me and smiles, the same eye-curling smile he gave me the morning we met. "I guess you were right. You did look like shit before."

I laugh and it feels good. For an instant, it feels right for Tom Paul to be here. I look down at Hero, who raises his head as if he knows what I'm thinking.

"So what's on the menu this morning? And should I trust Greeks bearing gifts?"

"Not a chance." He picks up the copper pot and tips its contents into two tiny, espresso-sized cups. "This is *glykos*, sweet Greek coffee. Drink it slowly and leave some or you'll get a mouthful of sludge from the bottom."

I sip the aromatic coffee, its rich foam surprising me. While I watch, Tom Paul grates an unfamiliar white cheese into a bowl before cracking eggs and adding honey, sugar, and lemon peel. "What're you making?"

"*Melopita*—Greek honey pie. I'm being rather lazy today and using a pre-made crust." He smiles at me before pulling out a package from the refrigerator and a pie plate from a bag. I watch him lay crust on the plate bottom and pinch its edges.

As he sprinkles chopped nuts on the crust, I ask, "How'd you get all this stuff here anyway? I didn't think you had a car."

"Fredda has a car. She has a real job, too. Good thing one of my friends lives a rather conventional life or I wouldn't have been able to bring all this food over to sustain you."

"Did you really scavenge all of this?"

"No. I couldn't wait for it to be thrown out. I had plans for feeding you. Eggs and cheese are best fresh anyway."

Watching him fill the crust with the egg-cheese mixture, I think over what he's said about feeding me during my training, buying food, and borrowing cars. I scowl, but when I catch Tom Paul looking at me, I let it slide into a weak smile.

"I'll have to help you scavenge then. Maybe even dumpster dive with you." I try to say this last lightly, but my voice hitches a little. My chest tightens.

Tom Paul doesn't look at me as he answers. Instead he slides the *melopita* into the oven. "I can always use the help."

He sets the timer and then joins me on a stool. "Would you like to learn how to make *pâte de verre*?

His question startles me. "Can I? I mean, is it possible for me? I don't know anything about making glass."

"That's not a problem. I'm an excellent teacher." When he grins at me, the sun from the kitchen window catches the gold flecks in his eyes. I become aware of his upper arm brushing against mine, the fine hairs on his forearm, and his hand on the counter clasping the saucer under his cup. Through the sweet, rich scent of honey, cheese, and egg permeating the air, I catch his subtle musk. I grow dizzy and hot. My stomach grumbles. He laughs. "I'd better feed you first."

I know he'd better run from me.

I look down at my cup, trying to ignore the heat of his skin against mine. I wish I'd changed my t-shirt and shorts. They seem so thin now. "Does this mean you've figured out how to light your pieces?"

It's his turn to play with his cup. From the corner of my eye, I study his fingertips on its rim. "No. Puck seems to have taken a vacation to parts unknown."

He sounds so forlorn that I reach for him. My fingers twine through his. An image of me twining around him flashes through my thoughts like heat lightning.

"It's just that this is my first major show and I'd rather blithely assumed everything would work out. What do I know? Sharon says sometimes she has no idea how everything's going to come together until the last minute and even then she's so filled with doubt she wants to run and hide."

"I have faith in you." Even as I say it, I know beyond doubt that I do. This faith in someone is so new, so complete, that I lose myself in wonder.

The calloused pad of Tom Paul's thumb rubs the base of my own, soothing and binding. His strokes bring me back to myself. We sit there, unspeaking, for several minutes, our hands clasped in the most intimate embrace I've ever experienced. Something shifts between us, takes substance, grows. It's as if our joined hands promise more than mere comfort. They are a lifeline, a flexible filament to light my dark path. The atmosphere thickens around us.

"Do you have faith in yourself?"

"No." I shake my head, trying not to look him in the eyes.

"Then we'll have faith in each other."

I turn to confront him, to question his motives. But when I swivel my face towards his, he kisses me. The air around us crackles and sparks, but he doesn't appear to notice. When he leans back, he places a fingertip on my chin and holds my gaze with his. "Thank you."

I ignore him. "If you're going to feed me, I'm going to figure out how to light your show."

He tilts his head and studies me. "Are you serious?"

"Damn straight."

"How? I thought you were a writer of some sort."

At his reminder, I shrug. "Not really. I'm a civil engineer, actually. I got a grant for creating an Internet memorial that let me take a sabbatical this year."

"What kind of memorial?"

I look down as I pull our hands closer. With the fingers of my free hand, I trace the back of his. The thought *I could do this for hours* flits through me. "For victims of serial killers. I'm writing biographies and compiling statistics and photos. For a few victims, I try to visit their family and any other places related to them like their schools." My voice trails into a whisper with the next detail. "I even have an appointment to visit a killer in prison to ask about his victim's last moments."

"Good grief." Shocked air explodes from Tom Paul. I refuse to look up at him. We sit there in silence until he says, "I'm sorry."

I shrug again and pull my hands from his to take my cup. They are bereft. "It's something I have to do."

He accepts this, sipping his coffee while I rub my fingertip around the rim of my cup. When he speaks again, his voice is matter-of-fact. "So how can a civil engineer help me?"

Now I do look at him. "Well, I know a thing or two about optics, angles of reflection and refraction, that sort of thing. Would you mind taking me back to your studio, so I can study the pieces for your show? I have an idea niggling in the back of my head, but it would help me envision the set up better if it were in front of me."

I see speculation in his eyes. "You sound like an artist. I had no idea engineers used so much imagination."

"Of course," I laugh, strangely pleased at his indirect compliment. "Just like artists master various techniques and media, engineers master building techniques and materials. We're not much different once you think about it."

"Okay, I accept. But on one condition: let me teach you at the same time."

"Deal." I grin.

Over the next three hours at my apartment, we devour Greek honey pie and talk about music, books, art, traveling—anything and everything. After his surprise kiss, Tom Paul makes no other effort to kiss or touch me beyond holding my hands. When he gets up to clean my kitchen, I insist on helping him even though our careful choreography around the tiny tiled floor brings me within his magnetic sphere. As soon as I imagine particles limning his body, creating an invisible if powerful buffer around him, I can't let the image go. Or it won't let me go.

After Tom Paul leaves, I head to my shelves looking for my physics textbook, but what I'm looking for isn't there. I'll have to go to the library to get what I need or maybe visit BU, talk to my old physics professor. It feels good, this other problem to tackle. Marcie would roll her eyes and snort at my epiphany. I look at Hero lying next to my feet watching me.

"Do you think she's really as confident and together as she puts on?" His tail thumps. "Right. She can't be."

That night I dream about Lauren for the first time since high school.

We're in her backyard. It's early summer and she wears a rose garland in her hair, which is backlit by the sun. She sits on the picnic table, leaning back on her palms, and frowns at me. I finger my head, frantic to confirm that my own garland still encircles it. Over and over I rake through my hair, but I can't feel anything. Lauren watches me, her eyes shadowed and her lips pressed into a disapproving line. I give up at last, sobbing from my failure. Then she reaches behind her where the most gorgeous garland I've ever seen has lain hidden. My chest aches. I feel I will die if she doesn't let me have those sweetly scented blooms whose silky petals I long to caress. I know without being told that wearing the garland will keep me here with Lauren forever. I hold my breath while Lauren studies me. I fear I don't measure up. I've never measured up. Everything begins to grow hazy and indistinct.

Just as I begin to lose consciousness, Lauren hands me the garland. As the roses come toward me through the fog of forgetting, they sharpen and clarify. I can see the velvet texture and wavering edges of the translucent pink and peach petals. They glow as if lit from within. They remind me of something else, but I can't remember what until my palms touch the fragile flowers. At that instant, they rust and wither. I wake up clammy and shaking.

I think about this dream as I bike along the Minuteman Bikeway early the next morning. Unlike running through Cambridge, biking along the ten wooded miles of former railway requires little vigilance, freeing me to replay the vivid details. The cloying scent of roses fills my nostrils until I'm nauseous and have to stop near Spy Pond. Of course, I know why I dreamt about Lauren last night. I've brought her into my world. By talking about her with Tom Paul, I've broken the hermetic seals on my past and let its dark poison flood into my present. I feel unstable, as though I've mixed two reactants together and it's only a matter of moments before I explode—unless I can control the reaction. I should never have told him. I should've doled out the volatile information online as though laying out a fuse while I waited in the safety of my apartment.

I manage to bike back through Arlington without getting sick, but the knowledge of what I've done dogs my every move. My feet are bricks; my calves have lead in them. My hips ache in growing moral decrepitude. I'm supposed to meet Tom Paul for lunch at Riverside Press Park. I grind to a halt in North Cambridge, unable to continue against the opposing forces of my desire and my anxiety. I want to be with Tom Paul. I can't be with Tom Paul. For a full five minutes, I hesitate at the side of the street, so paralyzed I can't monitor my surroundings for predatory danger. It's Marcie's fault that I'm in this predicament. Latching onto this thought, I dismount and lock my bike to the nearest street sign and go into a nearby convenience store where I call Marcie.

"Come and get me. I'm at the corner of Harvey and Mass Ave."

When Marcie pulls up to the sidewalk, I'm standing next to my bike shivering even though it's eighty degrees and sunny. She leans over and pushes the passenger door open. "Get in. I'll send Evan back for your bike."

I slide in and slam the door. "He's waiting for me. I can't do it. I'm going to leave him in the park waiting."

Marcie speaks as she looks over her shoulder to merge back into traffic. "He deserves better." She looks back. "I'm sorry I didn't tell you I was sending him over, but I knew you'd never go for it."

I say nothing.

"Is it your friend Lauren?"

I look at her. She's asked me before and I've refused to tell. I didn't want to get into it with her. I still don't. But maybe I can talk to her, so I won't have to talk to him. I shift my gaze out the window, but I don't see stores and pedestrians and trees held hostage in a sea of concrete. I see Lauren and the mythical rose garland.

"Yes."

Marcie waits. Damn her. Where does she get her patience from?

"She died a long time ago."

"That must've been hard." I hear the therapist's smooth sympathy. I almost don't go on. I find myself clearing my throat and squirming. A tic starts behind my left eye. We drive in silence until she parks near my apartment. It's just like Marcie to find a spot on the street when she needs one.

"She was murdered by a serial killer named Richard Lee Grady."

Marcie's hand finds mine, which I realize are clutching one another. I want to push it away, but I don't. The tic intensifies.

"For a whole year after, I couldn't accept it, you know?" Tears sting my eyes, tears I couldn't cry back then. I'm embarrassed and swipe at them. "Mona used to tell me how I sat talking to Lauren like she was right next to me. The only way she could get me to finish my homework was to pretend Lauren was coming over afterwards to see me. I really thought she would come."

"That's magical thinking."

"Wha–?"

"The belief that hoping for something enough will make it happen."

Magical thinking.

Magicalthinkingmagicalthinkingmagicalthinking. That's all it was.

"You're doing it now." Her dark brown eyes watch me to see if I'm going to jump out of the car. "You believe Tom Paul will go away if you pretend nothing's happened. The problem is," now she leans close enough to me that I smell coffee on her breath, "he will."

I close my eyes. "I'm going to hurt him."

"Maybe. Or you won't. Either way, he's a big boy. And you're a big girl." She touches my cheek so I'll turn to look at her. "Is there something more, Weeble? Something you're not telling me? This isn't just about Lauren, is it?"

I ignore the familiar question in her eyes. "What if what I want to happen is really magical thinking?" I whisper.

"Just because you want something badly doesn't make it a fantasy, Weeble."

I remember Jana's words. I have power. Magical thinking and power. Maybe I can turn my fantasy into reality. "You really think I can make this happen?"

"I think you should try."

"Riverside Press Park. Don't tell him I tried to bail."

"Never." She mimes locking her lips and throwing away the key.

She drops me off at the Shell station next to the park. Across Mem Drive, the Charles winks at me in the late morning sun. I wait until she's gone before heading inside. As soon as I see Tom

228

Paul leaning on a blanket, his head dropped back to lift his face to the sun, he's all I see. Everything else falls away. As I walk towards him, it occurs to me that his faith in me has been tested without him knowing it. And for one brief, shining moment I understand what faith is. I understand its power.

Twelve

▼

DIORAMA. THAT'S WHAT I'VE GOT IN MIND for Tom Paul's *The Soul Illuminated* show—the pinnacle of the pre-cinema era that began with the *camera obscura* invented in the Middle Ages and ended with George Eastman's invention of film in 1889. Along the way, any number of optical toys amused and entertained people. Peepshows, kaleidoscopes, stereoscopes, and magic lanterns are just a few. It was only a matter of time before these handheld devices morphed into larger attractions. Louis Daguerre, the French artist and chemist who invented the first modern photo, thought big. He was a real showman, a lot like Walt Disney in fact. In 1822, Daguerre brought optical amusements to audiences with his Diorama, a forerunner to Disney's Carousel of Progress at the 1964 World's Fair. In the Diorama, Daguerre moved an audience around a transparent, cylindrical canvas much like Disney moved audiences around his animatronic scenes. Using transmitted and reflected light and composite imaging, Daguerre created transitions between day and night settings.

Another Frenchman, Pierre Seguin, adapted the popular Diorama into a simpler, handheld version using a box and painted or printed cards. It's this smaller *polyrama panoptique* that became our modern museum and grade-school diorama. Somewhere along the way, the meaning of "through" in the Greek preposition "dia" got lost—along with the use of light to affect the scene. I think it's time to bring it back for Tom Paul's show. I just don't know how yet.

Even though I prefer to solve problems on my own, I tell Tom Paul about the Diorama when we go out dumpster diving before his next Freegan dinner. After all, it's his problem.

"Right—the space is just a big box." Tom Paul looks back over his shoulder from the corner of the dumpster where he's been sifting through someone's moving-day trash. He holds up a mangled toaster oven, shakes it so that crumbs fly everywhere, including his hair, and then grins. "There's better stuff at the end of the spring semester outside dorms. College kids would rather dump stuff than take it home. That's how I got my blender. KitchenAid. Top-notch."

I look down at the garbage bag I've managed to untie with gloved hands. I'd been moving pieces of slimy watermelon rind off of paper and packaging covered in eggshells and coffee grinds. "I really don't think there's much worth saving in here."

Tom Paul bends his head over the open bag. Under the hot June sun, his hair smells like musk and the warm, woody scent of his shampoo. Unable to resist, I lean over a bit and inhale.

"How about this?" He pulls out a bound collection of reeds or some other flat, woody stems. They look like somebody's craft project. "Don't know what it is, do you? Hey, Jonah. Tell Weeble what she's got here."

His friend Jonah, big as a linebacker but as delicate with the bow of a fiddle as a clockmaker with his tools, turns from the garbage pile he's rummaging through. His face is as open and honest as a proverbial Midwestern farmhand. "Aye! Faith and begorra!"

231

Fredda, Jonah's freckled and apple-cheeked girlfriend, pops up at his thick brogue and slaps his shoulder. "Stop it, you Irish ham! Just tell her what the damn thing is."

I laugh, as much from the contrast of her rough tone and fresh countenance as Jonah's exaggerated air of hurt. "It's some preschool craft project, isn't it?" I tease.

Jonah sucks in his breath and mimes shocked outrage. "Why no, me colleen. 'Tis not a child's plaything." He takes the woven object, which reminds me of a swastika without the bent arms. "'Tis a cross of the right saintly Brigid, she who explained the Passion of the Christ to a dying pagan by weaving it from the rushes on his floor."

"Really?" I take the cross and turn it over. At its center, the rushes form a box and each arm is tied off with a thin rush strip. "It looks pagan."

"Bite your tongue, me girl!"

Tom Paul laughs. "Caught you there, Jonah." He looks at me. "No one can say for sure there ever was a St. Brigid, but there *is* a Celtic goddess named Brigid. It seems pretty likely the Irish snuck her into the canon."

"It wouldn't be the first bit o'blarney outta an Irishman's mouth," Fredda says.

Jonah scowls, but even I can see he's not angry. "It's the likes o' disbelievers such as yourselves that got St. Brigid dropped by the Church, Tommy me boy." He points at the cross. "That's a great omen, that is. Brigid is the muse of poets and musicians."

Tom Paul shifts nearer in the muck of the dumpster, his arm going around me while he traces the woven pattern at the cross's heart. "Brigid's a conundrum. She's the sun goddess, the goddess of forge and hearth. The goddess of fire. Yet she's also associated with water and wells, which lead to the Otherworld. Both the sun and water mean healing and wisdom."

Fredda, who'd returned to picking out aluminum cans from the garbage, adds without looking up, "Didn't you Irish throw good bob in wells to Brigid?"

"Why would anyone throw this away?" I ask.

"Because you needed to find it," Tom Paul says in my ear. "Keep it."

I think about St. Brigid's Cross all the way back to the gallery where Tom Paul plans to initiate me into the delicate art of *pâte de verre*. The cross and magical thinking. The year after Lauren's death doesn't exist in my memory. I don't remember much of middle school or my freshman year of high school, but only the sixth grade has disappeared into oblivion as if aliens had abducted me. Or fairies. This thought startles me. Where did I go when I was 11? Where was that part of me that makes me who I am? Did fairies take me away? Did all of me come back? My unease grows. I shove thoughts of faith and power, healing and inspiration aside, ignoring the cross now weighing down my backpack.

But the cross returns when Tom Paul begins his lesson in glassmaking,

"What do you think about using the St. Brigid's Cross to make a mold?"

I stare at him. "What in the world for? I want to make a mug."

"We can do both." He tilts his head and squints at me. I wonder what he's thinking about my reluctance. "I can't help it. I see a glass St. Brigid's Cross, something you can hang in a window. Glass is the perfect medium for expressing the healing power of the sun." Here he looks toward the windows lining the back two walls of his workroom. "I'm sure your friend Marcie would tell you that sometimes you need to shine light on your problems before you can solve them."

"And some things are best left in the dark and forgotten," I mutter.

Tom Paul doesn't answer me and when I sneak a glance at him, he's busy lining the table in front of us with bags of clay, bowls, measuring cups, brushes, rubber gloves, and face masks. Above us glass jars line shelves filled with what looks like colored powder, organized by color. I'm intrigued and excited despite myself. I sidle closer to him and watch his fingers. Flashes of remembering them on my skin intrude on me.

"What're we doing first?"

"Making the molds. In the case of your teacup, we'll use models I made, but we'll use the St. Brigid's Cross itself as our model for the other one. We'll coat it with some oil or soap to make sure we can release it from the plaster mold."

I strain to look. Beneath my chin, his shoulder is firm and solid. I'm aware of the movement of his muscles as he works and his heat. The entire studio has grown intensely stuffy. I wonder if the AC is working or if we can open the windows. I step away and lean against the table's edge, folding my arms across my middle.

"How soon do I get to take my mug home with me?"

He laughs. "Patience! You might have some trouble making the plaster molds. After we get a plaster mold you like, it'll take a few days for it to dry. We won't get to layering in the frit until the weekend at the earliest. The firing and annealing takes several days. So depending on your schedule, it could be a couple of weeks before you get to take it home with you. If all goes well, that is."

I swallow my disappointment. "What's frit?"

He looks toward the shelves and nods, his hands busy pulling slabs of clay onto the table. "Those jars contain frit. It's ground glass. Most of the frit I use is a very fine powder. But I often use frit that has larger grains for my bigger sculptures. It's tricky to use, so we'll stick to the powder for your pieces. Here, we'll use this to make negative forms for the plaster." He hands me a block of clay and a mug made from some kind of plastic. "Watch me."

I watch as he slices a layer from the block and lays a second plastic mug sideways onto it, describing his steps as he goes. "Anchor the model in the clay like this. We'll bring the clay halfway up the side. When we pour the mix, we'll fill the inside too." He pauses and I listen to the soft sounds of his exhalations as he builds the clay around the model. "We'll let the mix set, then flip it over, remove the clay, and pour the rest on the other side." His graceful hands demonstrate before he turns to me. "Your turn."

Gamely I pick up the wire he'd used and try to slice a layer that looks like his. I pull it through the resisting material, the tip of my tongue between my teeth, but the layer comes out uneven anyway. Feeling like a preschooler creating a Mother's Day present, I slice off clay and build it around the model. When I'm done, it looks like a child did it.

"Don't worry. I've had a lot of practice. Here take this and trim the edges to make a square." Tom Paul hands me a clay tool. "Now we'll create a casting box."

As he reaches for a stack of thin plywood boards beneath the table, I watch his shoulder muscles slide under his thin t-shirt. Without warning, the image of his shirt sliding over his head invades my thoughts. My imagination—that surprisingly nimble faculty—follows with a vivid portrait of his torso. I close my eyes and try to keep my sigh inaudible. When I open them, my gaze hones in on Tom Paul's hands, which appear to caress the boards as he smoothes a thin coat of oil over them. My stomach grumbles, low. I press a palm there, willing it to quiet with all the fervency of my soul.

Seemingly unaware of my actions, he continues talking as he guides me through the steps to build a box around his model. Sighing, I follow his lead. I've built models for work dozens of times. C clamps and boards I can handle. We pull on face masks and gloves and then he shows me how to mix plaster with silica to create a mold that can withstand the high heat of the kiln. After spraying the models with a releasing agent, Tom Paul pours the plaster mix—the investment as it's called—slowly into the corner of one casting box before gently shaking it to release trapped air. I follow with my model. After the plaster sets up, we remove the clay and pour more investment over the exposed plastic.

"We'll let the plaster air dry before we release the models. I usually slip this"—here he holds up a thin strip of metal— "around the cup and kinda pry it out. But I'll show you how to slice the mold in half to release it. Then we'll put the molds in the kiln to heat off any remaining water. If everything works out, there won't be any cracks and we can move on to layering the frit. Got it?" He pauses to examine my face. "Good. I'll get us something to eat while you work on the St. Brigid's Cross."

"By myself?" My voice squeaks in harmony with the lurch in my heartbeat.

He grins at me. "Sure? Why not? Just remember to coat the cross with soap first so the clay doesn't stick to it. You've got the basic steps down. As long as you remember to wear a mask and gloves while mixing the silica into the plaster, you'll be fine."

I grumble to myself after he leaves, but I'm pleased that he trusts me enough to try this on my own. In the comfortable silence of the empty room, I sink into my work. My silica-plaster mix looks less smooth than Tom Paul's, but I give it a final stir and wait for it to slake, to absorb every bit of water, before filling my casting box until the plaster covers the St. Brigid's Cross to twice its depth.

Tom Paul nods when I find him outside the workroom arranging sandwiches on the low table in front of his sofa. As we eat, he tells me about the steps in filling and firing, annealing and cold working the finished glass—cutting, grinding, polishing, and gluing of handles, bases, and decorative glass or metal. As he describes the process, my gaze rolls around his studio, multiplying hours and days and multiplying again by a factor of two to account for his time creating models. Even though I've seen how deftly he works, I suspect my estimates are too conservative.

"No wonder you scrounge your food from dumpsters," I say when he finishes.

"What?" He sounds perplexed, but the corners of his mouth curl, encouraging me.

"You can't possibly earn enough money from selling your work to live on."

"No, I guess not. But I don't need as much as some people do and I like being resourceful. I sometimes think I have Native American or pioneer blood in me. Now what do you say we talk about your idea for turning my gallery into a Diorama?"

For the first time in months, perhaps years, I'm totally absorbed in the challenge of helping Tom Paul manipulate light to achieve an artistic goal. The engineer in me dominates as I sketch angles of reflection and refraction on a diagram, explaining how to place lamps, the various kinds of bulbs and their output, and how we can reveal or conceal light to affect his audience. I won't let him refuse my help in building props and wire fixtures, shoving his protests and my own project out of my thoughts. When he glances at his watch and grins, I'm shocked to learn we have to hurry to his apartment for dinner. A brief surge of panic flickers through me, but it doesn't find any purchase and fades. An unfamiliar feeling replaces it, but I don't have time to puzzle over it as I hustle to follow Tom Paul home.

His apartment—a single large room on the top floor of an old warehouse—has exposed bricks and pipes and large, cloudy glass windows making me think of industrial-era sweatshops. Long stainless tables and shelves salvaged from restaurants that've gone out of business and a jungle of hanging racks define

237

the kitchen area. Fredda and Jonah are already there, drinking red wine and laughing while she slices eggplant, tomato, and zucchini for *vegetale al forno*. I watch Fredda's flushed face and Jonah's antics, his expressive hands and puppyish head rolls. They remind me of sitcom lovers.

We've barely pulled the out-of-date linguini from the fridge and started sorting through a large bunch of wilted basil when other Freegans filter in. I've never dined with more than a handful of friends and after the tenth person arrives, my breathing clogs in my chest. Before I can escape or faint, Fredda's fingers close around my upper arm and she guides me to the stairs leading to the rooftop where tables wait.

"Why don't you light the candles and turn on the light strings?" Her voice is casual, but I know she's seen my discomfort. "I'll bring you some wine and the antipasto."

"Thanks."

I'm still moving around the rooftop lighting candles when a couple arrives carrying a large salad bowl. Behind them stream more people carrying *bruschetta*, olives, and a large pot of Italian wedding soup. After that, the theme breaks down and a corner of the long table holds cinnamon rolls, a fruit tart, brownies, iced cookies, and an angel-food cake with a lemon-honey-yogurt sauce. In the golden light of early evening, open red and white wine bottles appear on the tables as if by magic. I grin. It's good to know that even Freegans recognize the value of splurging on *Chianti* and *pinot grigio*. Fredda and Jonah set out a tray of marinated vegetables, cheeses, and a variety of salami and prosciutto.

My glass of wine has gone to my head. I feel transported, giddy with the sounds of talk and laughter. Fredda and Jonah have introduced me to an intense young man named Kurt, who's wearing 50s-style eyeglasses and a white button-down shirt. He's a Harvard grad student studying art history. Kurt quizzes me on my work and refills my wine, his dark eyes sharp as he watches my mouth. Its heat rises along the flesh of my throat and over my cheekbones. A blond woman wearing a wrap dress dominated with vivid blocks of color and her scruffy, bearded boyfriend wander over.

Even though I'm having the best time I've ever had among a large group of strangers, I miss Tom Paul. In fact, I realize I miss him because I'm so happy. I want his solid warmth at my side while I chat with Kurt and Angela and Yan. Guilt at not helping him with the pesto rides on my intoxicated flush. I'm about to stumble down the stairs to see if he's waiting on the linguini when I catch sight of him emerging from the stairwell carrying a huge bowl. In the gloaming, his thick curls gleam and his light t-shirt glows against his olive skin. Sweet Lord, he's handsome. Something rises in my throat, but I catch it before it can escape and leave my newfound friends without a murmur. I've just slid eel-like between a massive bald-headed man and a woman wearing heavy mascara when I see Tom Paul stop and look over his shoulder at someone ascending behind him.

Candlelight illuminates his features. For an instant I'm transfixed, waiting.

And then a tiny woman, her hair as fine and pale as a snow angel, rises from the dark depths. Where Tom Paul is honey and earth, she's ethereal. I don't have to see her eyes to know they are deep blue and large. I imagine I smell roses and lilacs. I hear harp strings.

"Don't worry about Renee." It's Fredda. She holds a wineglass toward me. "That ship sailed a year ago."

"Then why does he look like he's blinded by the sun?"

"Darlin', you should see the way he looks at you." I lift my hot gaze to Jonah's. "I don't think he's ever really *seen* a woman before you. He just hasn't learned how to control his new eyesight."

"And that makes me feel better how?"

Fredda ignores me and grabs my elbow, propelling me toward the table where Tom Paul and Renee stand chatting. "Go flirt with him. Remind him where the sun really rises and sets."

The lovely sense of well being has fled along with the last of the sunlight. I gulp half my wine, hoping to deaden my awareness, and trudge over to the buffet.

Tom Paul doesn't notice me as I come up behind him. He continues to talk to Renee. In the brighter light from the floor lamps placed around the table, I see her face clearly. Delicate pink transfuses the translucent skin over her cheeks, emphasizing her likeness to a Precious Moments figurine. When she speaks, I almost laugh at the childishly high pitch of her voice. Instead, I listen to the tone of Tom Paul's response. He sounds smitten.

"Hey. I'm sorry I didn't return to help with the linguini." I lay my hand along his upper back and feel him flinch. "Fredda gave me a job up here." I turn and look at Renee with what I hope is a welcoming smile. "Hi. I'm Weeble."

What looks like annoyance flashes across her serenity and then she smiles a doll smile with perfect little teeth. I'm pretty sure my fist will shatter them if I don't master my black impulses.

"I'm Renee, an old friend of Tom Paul's." Her slight, lisping emphasis on *friend* makes it clear they are much more.

I link my arm through his, feeling the tension in the hard planes of his side. When I look up, I see confusion and worry. He has no idea why animosity sizzles around us. Instead of warm sympathy, acidic anger burns my heart. I drain my wineglass and hold it out to him. "More *pinot grigio*, please? Renee? Do you need anything?"

She tilts her snub nose. "Please, just half a glass. Do you have any sparkling water? I'd prefer a spritzer. Otherwise, it goes to my head." She smiles again.

"Not a problem. I've got some in the pantry." The frown flees as his fingers brush mine when he takes my glass. "I'll be right back."

We watch him head toward the stairs. Then Renee turns to me. "'Weeble'? What kind of name is that?"

"The kind a drunken biker gives his daughter after she's had a few beers." Even I don't believe the movement of my lips qualifies as a smile.

"Does that mean you don't hold your liquor well?"

"Just the opposite. It takes a lot to knock me off my feet."

"I see." She pauses, crosses her arms over her chest. "How do you know Tom Paul?"

"I met him while running past a dumpster he was diving in."

She laughs; it's a tinkling sound that makes me think of fairies. "That doesn't sound like a promising encounter. Tom Paul and I met at a Cambridge Madrigal Singers concert."

I can't look at her. Instead, my eyes scan the rooftop until they latch onto Kurt, who watches us. Her gaze follows mine. She preens a bit. Something clicks and I ask, "So you're not a Freegan?"

She laughs again. "Not hardly. I don't climb into nasty dumpsters to scavenge."

Someone steps behind me. I look over my shoulder thinking it's Tom Paul, but it's Kurt. He has a glass of *pinot grigio* for me. I accept it, sipping. From the corner of my eye, I see Renee's eyes narrow. "What say you, Kurt? Is dumpster diving nasty?"

Kurt stands so close his overpowering cologne fills my nose. He shrugs and smiles at me. "It's not for the faint of heart, that's for sure. I've found some pretty amazing things, though. Once I came across a handmade Syrian chessboard with all the pieces. Someone threw *that* away by mistake, trust me."

"So if you're not a Freegan, why're you at a Freegan dinner eating food that's been thrown away?"

"Not thrown away," Kurt corrects, sounding amused. I suspect he's delivered this lecture a few times and I appreciate his tolerance. "Deemed expired based on the tastes and biases of most American consumers. None of it's spoiled. Just not as pretty or fresh."

Renee slides her gaze to Kurt, who doesn't seem to notice. She stares until his eyes shift towards her. "I don't mind eating good food others would throw away." She smiles, a cat-whose-gotten-cream kind of smile. I'm sure she bats her eyes, too. "I've rescued lots of furniture from the sidewalk on trash day. I just draw the line at climbing into a dumpster." Then she looks at me although her torso still tilts toward Kurt. "To answer your question: Tom Paul invited me."

Before I can think of anything to say, he's back among us. He appears surprised to see the glass in my hand, but I take the one he brought me and combine them without a word. It doesn't escape my notice that he stands next to Renee. I turn to Kurt.

"I'd love to see that Syrian chessboard some time. I went to a gallery opening at the Boston Center for the Arts last winter featuring Syrian artist Abal Haddad. Have you seen any of her works? They're amazing."

"No, I haven't. I did look into Syrian handicrafts when I found the board, but my research is in medieval Russian art. That's what Tom Paul and I have in common beyond our outrageous Freeganism." He laughs, drawing a smile from me.

"Medieval Russian art?"

"The Russians adopted their faith from the Byzantines." Tom Paul's voice sounds odd. Strained? "The story goes that they were shopping for a religious faith and when their emissaries visited the Hagia Sophia in Constantinople, they were bowled over by the magnificence. Kurt and I talk iconography from time to time." Something dark crosses his brow.

"Weeble, Tom Paul told me you've been helping him figure out some lighting issues for his upcoming show," Renee says, laying a hand on his arm. "I told him I'd love to take a look at what you've been discussing, give him some professional input."

"Really?" I look at Tom Paul, who shuffles his feet and glances away. "What profession are you then?"

"I work as an admin at a law firm by day, but I'm a trained lighting designer. I just don't make enough on shows to pay the rent."

A twitch starts in my armpit. "I'm rather surprised he didn't pick your brain right away." I nod and catch Tom Paul's gaze. "You don't have much time to get it all sorted out. Better consult someone who knows what she's doing before it's too late."

Jonah's beefy form sidles in between Kurt and Tom Paul. "What's so engrossing over here that none of you are eating? If I have to reheat the soup, there ain't gonna be any fiddle music after dinner."

I address Kurt, careful to enunciate my words. "I *have* had too much wine on an empty stomach. Why don't we grab some food and you can tell me more about medieval Russian art." I look over my shoulder as I grab a plate. Tom Paul's face is half in shadow, his eyes dark and his expression obscure. An electric bolt rends the air between us. "I'm sure Renee and Tom Paul have lots to discuss."

By now my head is swimming. I pile a plate full of anything I can reach, ignoring the soup, which I'm sure I'll spill. I pick my way through bodies and tables, but I stumble and nearly fall until Kurt catches me, his arms going about my waist. I laugh and let his hands take my weight. It's been years since I've had more than a glass of wine for good reason. I swivel my bottom into the nearest chair, feeling his hand slide across me, and plop my plate and glass onto the table, sloshing wine.

"Oops." I grin at Kurt. When he grins back, I notice that his lower lip is fuller than his upper. He sits in the chair to my right, which is wedged into a dark corner. The heavy denim of his thigh presses against my bare skin.

I barely taste my food, shoveling in bites of meat, cheese, and olives to try to slow down some of the wine but knowing it's too late, far too late, to clear my head before I've done something to regret. As in the past, I find I don't care. In fact, I'm astonished I don't drink more often. I'm not so far gone to forget there are consequences, of course, but on this side of inebriation it seems plain they're much preferable to the pain of sobriety. While I eat, Kurt describes his latest visit to Moscow to see the reconstruction of the Cathedral of Christ the Savior, originally built by Alexander the First to celebrate Napoleon's retreat and later dynamited at Stalin's orders. I try to pay attention, but I can't.

"So tell me, Kurt. Why is Tom Paul scowling at us?" My nod in Tom Paul's direction transforms into a wild dip.

His gaze transfixes me as his hand slides across mine when he reaches for his glass. "Because he knows all too well what a degenerate cynic I am. Do you know he's never left me alone with his sisters? He fears what kind of mischief I'll get them into."

In the candlelight, I watch his mouth, the lazy grin following his words. A delayed tremor rolls down my spine ending with a strange pang in my lower back as I realize what he's just said. I dart a glance at Tom Paul, but he's talking to Renee, whose eerie complexion glows under the string lights over their table.

"What kind of degenerate cynic are you?" Despite my care, 'cynic' slurs off my tongue. I stop eating to wait for his answer.

"Oh, the best kind." The candle sputters and goes out. His voice, velvety and low, twines around my now-thumping heart. His palm rests on my knee, searing the skin. "I don't believe in

God or evil or sin—only pleasure and pain. I never worry about the consequences to my immortal soul of anything I do."

Drunk as I am, intimidated as I am, his last words coming on my own earlier thoughts make me laugh. "You're a fool, then."

"How so?" A sharp edge has crept into his tone.

I raise my wineglass in mock toast, squinting in his direction. "Evil is very real, my friend." I swallow the rest of my wine. "I've seen it. I've touched it. If I could open up my chest and show you my heart, I'd show you the claw marks."

His silence speaks volumes and I think I'm scot free. And then he chuckles. The sound of it overwhelms me. "Ah, then, lovely Weeble, you've nothing to fear from me. I'm better suited for you than Tom Paul, ever hopeful in his quest for the *lux aeterna*. I knew as soon as I saw you we are two of a kind. Leave him to the fragile embrace of that washed-out creature." His fingertips caress my inner thigh.

I close my eyes, sickened. *Please, angel*, my anguished soul whispers. *Please bring Tom Paul back to me. Don't leave me alone with Kurt.*

"Weeble, are you all right?"

I look up to see Tom Paul standing at my side. Kurt's hand slips from my knee.

"No, I—" My stomach clenches. I've got to get away before I vomit. "I drank too much. Can you show me where the bathroom is?"

"Of course." He slips his arm around my back and lifts me from my chair. After I stand, his hand finds mine and he leads me toward the stairs, guiding me down them. I cling to him.

"I'm sorry. I'm sorry. I'm sorry."

He stops at the bottom. I feel his fingers on my wet cheeks. "There's nothing to be sorry for, Weeble." H e looks up at footsteps on the stairs. It's Fredda.

"Take her home. Here're my keys." I hear a jangle, but Tom Paul doesn't take his eyes or his hand from my face as he reaches for them. "I'll stay and clean up with Jonah."

"I'll help, too." It's Renee, sweet, sweet Renee, standing halfway down the stairs. When I turn my blurry eyes upward, a halo surrounds her.

"That's not necessary," Fredda says.

"It's no problem. Tom Paul and I haven't finished our conversation about his show. I'll wait for him to get back."

I focus on Tom Paul, willing him to tell her not to bother.

He shifts his gaze to Renee. "It might be late."

"I'm used to late nights, remember? I'll grab some paper and sketch my ideas for the lighting design. Take your time."

"Thanks."

His hand takes mine. In the close, stale elevator my mouth begins to water. I swallow and swallow. The ache in my stomach increases, but I clamp my lips tight and clutch Tom Paul's fingers as if I'm drowning. He says nothing, thankfully, even when I run from the elevator through the main door and head for the nearest bushes. I miss, splattering the sidewalk. My throat burns almost as much as my eyes.

"Here, sweetheart. Get in the car. I'll clean that up later."

As soon as Tom Paul realizes I'm crying again, he steers to the curb and draws me against his chest where sobs shudder and roll through me.

"Weeble, what's the matter? Did Kurt proposition you? I shouldn't have left you alone with him." His voice sounds grim. I've never heard anything more beautiful in my life.

"No, no." I gasp and wipe my eyes. "No one's ever called me 'sweetheart' before. I guess it just took me by surprise."

He brushes hair from my face. "I promise to call you sweetheart until you can't stand the word any more, okay?" He waits until I nod before pulling away to drive. "Then I'll find some other endearment for you."

After he escorts me to my apartment, he leads me to my bed where he strips my clothes and shoes off and presses me back onto the mattress. I want to kiss him, to hold him there with me, but the foul taste of partially fermented food coats the inside of my mouth, reminding me how rotten I am. His warm lips caress my forehead.

"I'll get you some water and an ibuprofen, and then you should go to sleep. Don't worry. I'll walk Hero before I leave."

I grab his hand as he turns away. "Tom Paul."

"Yes, sweetheart?" I hear the grin in his voice.

"Come bike with me in the morning."

"Sure thing."

I struggle to keep my eyes open as he leaves, his body silhouetted against the weak light from my living room. I can't help but see that he's left me in darkness.

Thirteen

A DAY BEFORE THE GALLERY OPENING, I call Jana and Marcie to see if they want to get their nails done. I've never had my nails done. Ever.

When I ask Jana, she laughs for a full minute before responding. She sounds crazed. "He's perfect for you."

"What?" Even I can hear the defensive tone. "You've been trying to get me to have a spa day with you for six months. Can't I take you up on it without the smart-ass comments?"

"I'm clearing my schedule. We're going to get that mess you call hair cut, too. And your eyebrows waxed."

"Excuse me? What the hell?"

Now she's gasping so hard I have to fume until she gets her breath back. "Okay, Weeble, I know you think I'm either mocking you or pushing you, but honey, I've got a feeling you'll be drop-dead gorgeous after a few choice treatments."

"'A few'? 'Choice'? What the hell does 'eyebrows waxed' mean?"

"The beautician shapes up your brows by removing some with wax. No, no," she says as I try to interrupt indignantly, "it's not a big deal. Just something to emphasize your eyes."

248

"I won't look like a freak, will I?"

"Weeble, I do it once a month. Do I look like a freak to you?"

"No, I guess not." I'm still grumbling, but we both know I've given in.

"Is Marcie coming too?"

"Yup. She sounded nearly as ecstatic as you as a matter of fact. And I think the only time she's had her nails done was for her grandparents' big anniversary bash."

"That's because she knows one way to tinker with the inside of your head is to spruce up the outside. It's documented, trust me."

I sigh. "I'm sure you've got sources to cite, Jana." I pause but plunge on after only a breath. "Would you like to come to the opening too?"

"Oh, absolutely, love. I want to kiss Tom Paul. He's a miracle worker, he is."

They're both waiting for me when I return from walking Hero the next morning, Jana slouching against my building holding a paper coffee cup while Marcie scans a newspaper. Jana looks as fresh and groomed as ever, but Marcie wears a headband around curls that don't look brushed. When she looks up, I see pouches under her eyes and stains on her t-shirt. In the dull light of an overcast sky, she looks so wan, so unlike herself that I quake.

"A two-fer, huh, Jana?" I laugh. "It's not enough to torture me. You've got to drag Miss Slug-A-Bed out, too? Don't you know she'll die if direct sunlight touches her?"

"Har-har." Marcie snaps the paper and folds it shut. "Can we just cut the small talk until after I've had some tea or coffee? The Wicked Witch of the North here has been tormenting me with the smell of hers for the past ten minutes. It never occurred to her to bring one for me."

Jana smirks. "Oh, it occurred to me all right. Just thought it served you right to do without since I had to literally go into your room and wake you. Evan wasn't about to risk his own neck to do it."

Marcie scowls. "Of course not. I've got him trained."

"Just wait 'til you have kids, Marce. They recognize no boundaries. They think half-asleep adults who growl and curse are playing. Worse, they're notoriously hard to train."

"Speak for your own brats." Marcie blows by Jana through the door I'm holding open. I raise my brows at Jana, who grins and follows her inside.

While I feed Flat Stanley and put water on for tea, I listen to their good-natured sniping and long for our old communal life. They are the sisters I never had. At that thought an image of Annie the last time I saw her ambushes me. It had been late autumn, my first Thanksgiving home from college, and I'd come across her during a walk through Hyde Park on the other side of the bathrooms. She stood among a thick carpet of coppery leaves, her faded Levi's and darker-blue denim jacket vivid against the ashy-brown tree trunks. Eyes closed and arms raised, her fine hair falling around her face like a silky sheet, she made me think of a white-trash Madonna. At the slithery sound of my steps, she looked at me and smiled. It didn't reach her eyes.

For a moment we sized each other up. It was the first time we'd been alone since she'd screamed at me for interrupting her lovemaking six months before.

"If it isn't the East Coast intellectual."

"And the South End whore."

She'd shrugged and reached into her pocket for a joint. "At least I'm honest."

"Really? And what exactly did you tell Mona you're doing right now?"

The otherworldly serenity had evaporated as she squinted back at me, but a second later it returned as she dragged on the joint. Turning her head, she screwed her lips to shoot hot smoke away from us. "Listen, Weeble, I'm sorry. I was drunk, okay?"

"I'll keep that in mind next time I think you're being raped."

She'd scowled. "I meant what I said about you being damaged goods and no one wanting you."

"And not the part about having a normal sex life? You're not sorry about saying that, right?" I hadn't waited for her to answer but plowed on. "You think getting so trashed you can't stand up and losing your virginity in your mother's bed is normal? Huh, Annie?"

I'd noticed the rims of her eyes reddening, but I'd gone for the attack anyway. "Who's being honest? *I* know I'm damaged goods. When are you going to admit you are too?"

She'd started crying then, bawling actually, but I'd walked on by her. I didn't even stop when she said, "I chose to do it. You of all people should understand, Weeble. It was *my* choice. Not his."

Would Annie be glad to know I'd adopted her idea of a normal sex life in college?

"Weeble? Hey, Weeble! You okay?" It's Marcie. She's standing in front of me holding my right hand, which I've seared when I missed the handle on the kettle. "Let's run some cold water on that."

"You look like you've walked through a battlefield," Jana says.

"Shell shocked?" I laugh, but it sounds shaky. Ignoring their shared glances, I search for antiseptic spray and tend to the burn in silence. I suspect a whole eyeball conversation takes place behind my back. "Hey, what do you think of my mugs?"

"I've never seen anything so amazing."

"Did Tom Paul make these for you? They're incredible."

"He made one, I made the other. Can you tell which one?"

Jana and Marcie examine the two mugs with forensic eyesight, but both proclaim an inability to discern whose handiwork is whose. Jana takes the yellow-orange mug that Tom

Paul made according to my color choice and Marcie accepts the blue-green one that I'd crafted. As they listen, I pour hot water and describe how we'd mixed glass as fine as Caribbean sand with glue and then painted a thin coat on the inside of our molds. They sip strong breakfast tea as I step them through multiple coats and firings.

"Why so many coats and firings?" asks Jana. "This is so delicate it seems you could have done it all in one shot."

"I'm sure Tom Paul could've gotten by with fewer coats and firings, but he said he wanted me to get a feel for how long it takes for even one-sixteen of an inch of glass paste to fuse. Plus, I think he just wanted to teach me some patience."

"Oh?" Marcie's cheeks have taken on a nice pink hue and her rumpled hair looks fetching now.

I grin, feeling sheepish. "I kept trying to rush him. He let me talk him into using the molds before they were dry, so of course they cracked. And I had to start over. Then I tried to use my engineering brain to deduce how thick to layer the paste and then how fast to heat the kiln to get it to casting temperature. That didn't work so well. I cracked Tom Paul's mold and my mug.

"The toughest part, though, was the time for annealing and cooling. First, you 'crash cool' the cast glass to about 1100 degrees. Then you reduce any internal stresses in your glass so that it won't be so brittle it shatters or cracks or even explodes when you take it out of the mold. That's annealing. Apparently this is more an art than a science and experience really matters."

"You asked Tom Paul how long to anneal, didn't you?" Jana smirks.

"Absolutely. I'm not stubborn *and* stupid. At least, not usually at the same time."

Marcie and Jana laugh. It feels good to hear them laugh at something I've said.

"He said every piece of glass has its own annealing temperature, but in some ways it doesn't matter—you can't over-anneal glass. So to be safe rather than sorry, we had to let the kiln cool down slowly to room temperature."

"How long does that take?"

"Again, it depends on the type of glass and the object you cast." Here I picked up Marcie's mug. "A mug isn't very big or thick, so Tom Paul anneals it for about five or six hours. But once the kiln's cooled to room temperature, it takes another couple of days for the mold and the mug to cool to the touch."

"Ah, so you had to keep your greedy little hands off of it while it sat on a shelf somewhere?" asks Jana.

"Yes."

Marcie has that look on her face she gets when she's analyzing the results of a psychology study. "Steady high heat strengthens the glass rather than stresses it. That only works if the glass has no major flaws to begin with, right?"

"Well, yes."

"Your mug didn't have any major flaws. You just needed help with the annealing and cooling."

"Right." I'm puzzled, but Marcie seems satisfied.

"That's what I thought."

* * *

While our trio makes its way to Newbury Street, the gloom intensifies until we step out of the T stop under massive blue-gray clouds that glow along their upper rim. It's as though a giant yellow photo filter has been slipped between the earth and sky. Eerie daylight lends a lurid cast to brick and concrete, iron and steel. In the heavy air, the poisonous scent of exhaust mingles with dusty asphalt and cement. The sounds of engines, tires and brakes, even the voices of passersby, are all deadened. Something more than rain shimmers around us. Premonition shudders down my backbone even though the heat smothers me. A slight ache pierces my right temple and heaviness settles into my gut. I ignore them.

"Follow me, neophytes!" sings Jana and we fall into step behind her. Two blocks away, she leads us down steps to a nail salon promising a manicure and pedicure for twenty-five dollars.

At the delta of the doorway, the odors of polish and remover, perfume and lotion meet the outside air, creating turbulent eddies around us. The roiling stink ratchets up my nausea, but Jana and Marcie say nothing. Clinching my jaw, I follow them to a row of dark recliners where basins of warm water wait like ritual objects for our pedicures. Novices in dark tunics kneel before us, cleaning and scrubbing our soles.

Two hours later, purified and polished, we leave in search of lunch where I plan to drink enough cocktails to drown the lingering stench in my nostrils. The earlier electric feeling has grown along with my unease.

"Let's get inside ASAP. I don't want to be caught if it decides to pour."

Marcie, who'd been speaking to Jana about child psychology, frowns and glances at the sky. "Crap! When did it get so oppressive? Pick it up, Jayjay. I don't want to sit sopping while I eat."

While they bicker about restaurants and my future hairstyle, I keep looking over my shoulder. I can't shake the sense that I'm being stalked.

The afternoon passes with the weight of inevitability even though I have no idea what the gallery opening holds for me. Jana and Marcie herd me back to my apartment to apply cosmetics before I feed and walk Hero. His tattered ear flutters in the wind that picks up under the ominous clouds clustering and writhing above us. It's a forlorn flag in the face of an insubstantial enemy, one who flits among the deepening shadows. Their contrast against the vivid saffron light of the open street scares me. I hurry Hero home where I hope he'll be safe.

By the time we arrive at the opening, the evening sky has grown into an oily seething mass of blue-black clouds swallowing the sunset. The luminous figures glowing in the window promise sanctuary. I sigh when we enter, soaking up the energy from the other guests already milling about with wineglasses and canapés. I come to a standstill two feet from the doorway, my exposed heart thundering above the plunging neckline of my little black dress.

There's a tug on my hand. "Over there." Marcie's low voice cuts through the clamor. "His eyes were glued on you as soon as you stepped inside."

I turn my eyes toward Tom Paul. Electricity jumps between us, drawing me. As I walk through the crowd, sparks crackle and pop. Through the open door, thunder rumbles in counterpoint to the guests' murmurs.

"My God, you're beautiful." I've never had such awe directed at me. I've only seen it in movies or I wouldn't know how to recognize it.

I've been with more men than I can count and this is the first time I've ever felt vulnerable.

"Jana insisted I wear this." I pluck at the front of my dress.

"I'm glad she did." His palm runs up the back of my arm, raising goose bumps. "You deserve a much grander event, but I'm ever so happy to have you on my arm for mine." He slips an arm around my waist and draws me closer. For an instant I'm soaring as I've never soared before. I want to throw my head back and laugh.

Behind us I hear a little girl's giggle. My giddiness dies, choked off at my throat. I plummet below earth.

Slowly I turn to face Renee, frost-blond avatar with *manga* eyes. She's so close I can smell her powdery perfume. Beside her stands her gothic twin, a tall black-haired woman wearing heavy mascara, a black turtleneck and black leather skirt, black tights, and Doc Marten work boots. Goth girl glares at me through slitted eyes. I shrink into Tom Paul's side.

"Oh, good, Weeble. We can send people through now." Renee's sugar-and-spice voice plays a bitter tune on my spine. "Tom Paul wouldn't let us start viewing until you got here."

"Oh, I'm sorry," I stutter. "I didn't know."

Tom Paul squeezes me. "Hey, don't worry about it. Everyone's eating and chatting anyway." When I look up at him, he winks. "Besides, I find it's always best if my audience has at least a glass of wine in them beforehand."

"Speaking of, where can I get mine?" Even though I turn from the disturbing duo, I can feel their sharp eyes on me. "I want to be properly prepared so I get the full effect."

"Go ahead, Renee, take Micheline through the exhibit. I'll announce it to everyone else." He turns and raises his free arm and his voice. "Listen up! The time has come to unveil *The Soul Illuminated*. Renee's in charge of traffic. It's rather an intimate space and we want everyone to be able to see."

I don't like his use of "we."

As the group shifts toward the dividers surrounding the installation, Tom Paul leans down to whisper. His lips are warm against my ear. "Do you mind waiting to see it? I have my heart set on you going through after the madding crowd has left."

I start to shake my head. Out of the corner of my eye, I catch sight of Kurt, his dark eyes gleaming. He's wearing a pale-mauve silk shirt and loose gray trousers. Pheromones mist the air around him. His wolfish grin snags at my breath. I resolve to stay close to Tom Paul and watch how much I drink tonight.

We wait by the food table as people filter in and out of the exhibit. As they circulate back into the main space, they are subdued. Some look puzzled, others disturbed. One young woman leaves weeping. Tom Paul chats with any who want to talk to him, but I half-listen. I'm waiting for something else. Something I can't name, but it's old and familiar to me. Outside the gallery's large windows, red taillights compete with flashing white headlights. Exhaust rides the humid air as the wind picks up.

"Clever, old man." At Kurt's voice, I snap out of my reverie. He slides a sharp, knowing glance at me that continues from my face down my front. "You and Renee have staged it exceedingly well. If I weren't such an unrepentant sinner, I'd be moved to examine my conscience. As it is, I can only appreciate your talent without appreciating the meaning you wish to give to your art."

As before at the Freegan dinner, Tom Paul stiffens at Kurt's words. "Not every message is for everyone." He draws me closer, but I can't tell if he's aware of what he does. Is he protecting me or himself? "In fact, I'm surprised you came at all."

When Kurt smiles, I notice his large, square teeth and a dent near the corner of his mouth. "Wouldn't have missed it for the world. Appreciating the history of art requires an understanding of contemporary work."

"Ah." Tom Paul turns and calls to others who are saying good bye, dismissing Kurt.

Kurt aims his hungry expression at me. "You're looking delectable." Before I can speak, he nods, hands me a piece of paper, and pivots to leave.

Renee fills his spot. Her friend Micheline smirks when I catch her eye. Suddenly the gallery has grown hot and the air tastes metallic. Heat lightning crackles in the black night.

Standing on tiptoe, I lean in so only Tom Paul can hear me. "Meet me in the exhibit when everyone's gone."

He nods and I hurry away before I can lash out at Renee. Almost without thinking, I tuck Kurt's note into my bra.

When I arrive at the exhibit, I realize that whatever I've been waiting for is here. The temporary walls have been painted an ocher color, increasing the intimacy. Light pools on various groupings, leaving shadowy corners. As soon as I step among the dozen or so figures, I am one of them. Most have their backs to me, facing something or someone beyond my immediate line of sight. Near me, a woman hunches away from them, horror clear in her eyes.

I take a tentative step through this ominous host. I should recognize them from my previous visit, but they are strangers to me, their features vivid and clear. It's as though my vision has focused for the first time in my life. That's when my nightmare demons begin chittering and wheezing. I scan the room, my heart pounding, but I glimpse only their rapid malignant energy in the play of light on glass, in the leering expression of the man to my left. Panicking, I search the room for allies, but all I see are squatting women, their faces bewildered and shocked. One has a hand over her open mouth, another pointing toward my destination.

Ahead of me are three men in black cloaks, their dark faces lit from below. They stand in judgment or perhaps to prevent whatever waits in the darkened niche beyond from escaping. I'm shaking now, wondering when Tom Paul will join me, but I continue forward as if compelled. As I pass by the glowering henchmen, I swear I feel their eyes on me, but I can't take my own eyes from the niche. A palpable stench thickens the air. My palms grow sweaty.

To my right stands another man wearing somber clothes. He frowns, his thumb hooked in his belt and his other hand on a dagger hilt. Is he the leader who has condemned whomever huddles before me?

Trembling, I step forward. A spotlight snaps on, blinding me. Blinking, I see only a glittering kaleidoscope behind the huddled figure. Then my vision clears and the demons abruptly still. In the mirror beyond St. Sebastian's headless figure, I see the man's face beside me. A scarecrow with dead eyes. The palpable hatred of his stare transfixes me, forces me to recognize myself as well.

I've been pierced. I'm bleeding from mortal wounds. I'm dying. And no one will come forward to protest. Or save me. I'm alone.

"Weeble?" A hot palm grips my shoulder.

I scream as I whirl. I dash from the scarecrow. I shy from knowing leers and wicked smiles. I hunch from disapproving frowns and crossed arms. Memories of a sweltering June afternoon in 1982 when I was eleven cascade through me, suffocating and relentless. I halt and fling my arms over my head, squeezing my eyes as though I can keep the images of Lauren and Richard Lee Grady from invading my thoughts.

"No! Christ, no!"

Someone's moaning. Someone's arms are around me. Someone's hand soothes my back. Among the jumble of voices and sounds, a crack of lightning brings me to myself. When I open my eyes, I see myself reflected in the imperfect mirror of the gallery's window. Tom Paul's muscular back in a white shirt stands out in stark relief against the ghostly images of cars and streetlamps.

"Sweet Jesus, what happened in there?" He's panting and his wild gaze searches my face as though I've come back from the dead. I haven't.

I wind my arms around his neck and press up against him, shoving memories of pain and torture into the background. My breasts ache as my nipples harden against his chest. The heat of my groin melds to his, my thighs strain in the tight dress. I want to lose myself in him. Right now. I kiss him roughly, forcing his lips open and thrusting my tongue into his mouth. He tastes of wine and pâté, rich and savory. Heady. Already the memories are dimming. Losing power.

I reach down and caress him. He's hard and ready. I whimper.

"Take me. Take me here, now."

"Hm?" He sounds dazed. He dips his mouth and kisses me, a searching and deep kiss, unlike the sweet and careful ones he's always gifted me before.

I pull back and hold his head still until his dilated eyes focus on mine. "Fuck me."

Bewilderment washes down his face, but when understanding dawns it clears. Brilliant veins of lightning crack the obsidian heavens, illuminating fury on his features. He disengages my arms and steps back from me, holding my wrists.

"What did you say?" I had no idea his voice could hold such ice. "Did you just demand that I fuck you?" Thunder booms just outside the studio.

I'm rooted to the spot, cold terror chilling my formerly heated skin. I struggle to breathe. I struggle to understand what I've done. When he speaks, his words are foreign.

"No, Weeble. I don't know what's wrong with you. I don't know what you're reliving. But I'm not going to take you like some animal on the floor just because you don't think you're good enough for real intimacy."

"You don't want me?"

He growls. "That's the stupidest thing I've ever heard." His hands slip from my wrists and up to my shoulders. I think he should shake me, but he doesn't. "I want you as you damn well know. I've never wanted anyone else, only you. I fell in love with you that morning you came running out of the mist." His gaze wanders and his voice grows wistful. "My lady of the mists."

He pauses, letting me absorb that. Then his eyes focus on me again and when he speaks, his voice has turned sharp as broken glass. "But I'm not going to be with you like this. You're using me.

Pushing me away. I'm not going to let you. When you're ready to be intimate with me, *really* intimate, come find me."

He steps away, letting his hands fall. I'm alone again. Alone. There's nothing between me and the memory of following after Lauren fifteen years ago.

I turn and plunge into the black night, losing one of the strappy heels that Jana had shoved onto my feet.

Fourteen

▼

I TRIP, FALL, AND SMASH MY KNEES against the sidewalk in front of Tom Paul's gallery. As pain rips through my kneecaps, I twist to grab for the other heel.

"Weeble, wait! Let me take you home." Tom Paul stands like Prince Charming holding my lost shoe.

I'm not Cinderella. This is a horror story.

I lurch to my feet and fling the heel, hard. It hits his chest and bounces to the ground.

"Umph!"

I scarcely see him double over as I turn to sprint away. Overhead, heat lightning flickers and shimmers, its light eerie among the massed clouds. The tight skirt catches at me, threatens to keep me here, so I grip and tear until it splits up to my crotch. And then I run.

I run through rising wind and growing heat. I run along the corridors of hell, but I can't outrun *him*. I'm running toward him instead.

* * *

The metallic scent of unshed rain and hot cement clogged my nostrils. I struggled to breathe. I struggled to understand what was happening. The crowd thinned and I saw Tucker doing something to Lauren's hand before he leaned in to kiss her again. Under the tree, they looked like shadows, indistinct and unreal. A premonition stopped my heart.

"Tucker Murphy! Tucker! Where are you?" A worried-looking woman stood on the sidewalk, craning her neck and shouting.

Tucker pulled away from Lauren, leaving her in darkness as he came out into the unnatural light. He looked over his shoulder once, waved, and then trotted towards his mother. I watched as they passed me, but when I looked back to find Lauren, I couldn't see her under the tree anymore. A thrill of terror zigzagged through me and sent my heart racing. I lurched forward before Jamie, who still held my hand, squeezed it.

"'Bye, Weeble."

I waved and took off for the spot where I'd last seen Lauren. Beneath the tree, her tote bag and a single flip flop marked the speed of her disappearance. "Lauren! Lauren! Where are you?"

The only answer was the whipping wind. But as I dashed around the trunk, movement fifty yards away caught my attention. I put my head down and pumped my arms and legs as fast as they'd go, knowing from my previous calculations I'd catch up to whoever it was in less than thirty seconds.

I'd covered two thirds of the distance when the ground dipped and I tumbled, knocking the wind from my lungs.

"Weeble! Help me, Weeble!" Lauren's shriek drew my gaze and caused the scarecrow who toted her like a sack of potatoes over his shoulder to halt.

He pivoted and came back. I lay there with a heavy chest, terrified I'd never draw air in again. A shallow heaving roared in my ears. When I looked up, everything but his black eyes faded into nothing. He nudged me with the toe of his cowboy boot.

"Two for one." The twang in his voice reminded me of *Hee Haw*, the country variety show I'd seen a few times when Frank and Mona were gone. He set Lauren down and slowly stood upright. At that instant, I saw the wicked long blade jutting from his fist. He motioned toward the direction they'd been headed. "You, walk. I'll carry your friend here. No funny stuff, girlie. Got it?"

A visible tremor moved down Lauren's back, but she nodded her head. Before I could react, the stranger tossed me onto his shoulder, grunting and cursing.

"What the fuck are you made of?" Then his hand slid up my thigh and onto my buttocks which he pinched, hard. "I'm gonna love finding out, sweetness."

Overhead the black clouds swirled, filling my thoughts. I must've passed out because the next thing I knew he'd tossed me onto a torn vinyl car seat. My chest ached and I felt lightheaded, but I'd started breathing again. A car door slammed, followed by Lauren's shaky murmur and two more doors slamming. Then a rough engine rumbled to life and we were moving.

As soon as I'd recovered enough to realize what was happening, I sat up. From the looks of the leafy street we drove on, we hadn't left Hyde Park yet. Although we were in a pickup, we weren't going fast. Images from TV of men jumping out of trains and cars flashed through my mind. I'd grabbed the door handle and pulled before I'd finished calculating distances and impact using my limited experience from bailing off my bike. The passenger door ripped free of my grasp and swung wide.

Tires screeched, Lauren screamed, and I banged my face against the back of the front seat, biting my lip and tongue so hard they bled. The door clanked back into the frame.

As the stars faded from my vision, I saw the stranger watching me. It took another second before I realized he waited for me to see what he'd done. When I looked, the sour taste of vomit joined the metallic taste of blood in my mouth.

He'd cut Lauren's earlobe off.

She sat there, her mouth open and her hand to the side of her face, just below the oozing ear. I stared at the bright red streaking her fingers and matting her dirty-blond hair. *So much from such a little wound*, I thought dumbly.

"Now, now. Sweetness. No opening doors 'til I tell you." The stranger's voice slithered over my scalp, tightening it until it hurt. He touched the knifepoint to my cheek. "Next time, I cut *you*, got it?"

I swallowed and nodded.

"Now shut that door."

I obeyed.

I sat back against the seat, afraid to look at Lauren, who never moved or made a sound. Instead, I watched as the familiar intersection of King Hill Avenue passed by. I saw cars and people, but no one looked at us. An idle wonder flitted through my numb thoughts: how many other cars carried terrible secrets?

We turned onto 59 Highway and drove past Hawkins Café, where my Aunt Susie waitressed. Her black Ford sat parked in front, and I thought I saw her behind the counter holding a coffee pot. A sharp pain skewered my heart. Was this the last time I'd ever see her? Where were we going and what would he do to us? My gaze flitted to Lauren huddled against the passenger door as far from the stranger as she could get. I suspected she was crying by the regular movement of her shoulders.

The stranger turned on the radio and sang along with *Coca-Cola Cowboy*. He sounded just like Mel Tillis. His voice, the rumble of the engine, and the flat farmland sliding by my window lulled me into a kind of stupor. I scarcely noticed when he opened a can, but the bitter stink of cheap beer filled my nose. A longing for Frank bit into me.

Time passed. The sky opened up and let loose a fury of rain. A sign announcing Horseshoe Lake materialized and then one for Bluffwoods. We were so far from St. Joe, I knew we'd have to hitch a ride to get home again. Yet there were fewer and fewer farm houses, separated by endless cornfields and no signs of life. At least we'd stayed on 59. We could get home if we had to walk the whole way. Finally a sign for Sugar Lake appeared out of the downpour. The stranger slowed and turned onto 138 and then again onto the road that followed the edge of the lake, skirting the scattering of houses there.

We turned into a gravel drive just before the road swung away towards open fields. The car halted, tires crunching.

Without a word, the stranger got out of the car and came around to the passenger side. Yanking open Lauren's door, he let her fall to the ground. She yelped. He bent over and looked in, his flat eyes pinning me to the seat.

"Wait here or I'll cut off her other earlobe. Got it?"

I nodded.

He picked Lauren up, who whimpered. Rain plastered the stranger's plaid shirt to his back and Lauren's hair to her face before he'd managed to open the screen door to the mobile home we'd parked in front of. I waited in the growing darkness, wind lashing rain against the windshield. Against this background, I became aware of a faint odor of spoiled meat. A muffled scream followed by a bark reached me.

I closed my eyes and prayed. *Dear angel, don't leave me. Please don't leave me.*

Nothing but the indifferent sound of rain answered.

Darkness settled over my steel prison. I scrunched down in my seat and let my mind wander. I have no idea how long I sat there, only that the rain stopped, leaving behind an exhausted hush. When the door next to me creaked, I jumped.

"Your turn, Sweetness." The stranger wrapped fingers as strong as steel cable around my wrist and yanked me from the seat before I could react. Stumbling behind, I followed him up two steps and into a dark, fetid space. I caught sight of brown paneling before he shoved me onto something low and lumpy, banging my shins against a hard edge. The stiff fabric under my face smelled dusty and rank. I coughed. Something jumped up next to my head and started sniffing around my ears and the back of my neck. Hot breath tickled my ear. After a moment, a coarse tongue swabbed my cheek.

"Ajax, get away from her! There'll be time later to do all the sniffin' you like."

He rolled me over onto my back. My bikini bra slid open and a breast spilled out. Nearby, I heard Lauren sobbing as if her grandmother had died.

"Ain't you a fine specimen? Too fine to keep from view." He leaned over and sawed through the tie of my bikini, before sitting back, his flat eyes glinting. I flung my arms over my chest.

He slapped me, hard. "Drop your hands, girlie. I want to look at you."

Panic raced through me, but I dropped my arms and closed my eyes. He stood up and I cringed, but he walked away. Through slit eyes, I watched him move down a dark hall and disappear through a door. In seconds he returned carrying a Polaroid camera and a package of film. He tore it open and loaded the camera.

"Say 'cheese!'" He snapped a photo and grinned. Evil smile lines cracked his thin face. He laid the photo down on the coffee table. Without waiting to see how it developed, he turned back. "Now open your legs."

I inched my legs apart.

"No!" He reached a hand between my thighs. "Like that, Sweetness."

A click, a whir, and the crinkle-snap of the photo paper.

"Take off them panties."

When I hesitated, he slapped me again. My ears rang and warm blood trickled into the corner of my mouth. I kept my eyes closed and removed my last piece of clothing.

"Ah." He panted. "Open your eyes, girlie. You ain't asleep or dead. Yet."

I opened my eyes and looked away. The stranger circled around me, clicking, grunting, and panting. The dog sat on the far end of the worn sofa watching, his tongue lolling. At last the stranger set the Polaroid down on the table.

"I'll take more later." He began to unbuckle his belt.

* * *

Outside hell's screen door, crickets chirruped along with the throaty strumming of bullfrogs around Sugar Lake. Fireflies flickered in the deep-blue June night. I watched them, wondering if I could discern a pattern or timing, but their flashes appeared unpredictable. After some time studying these tiny luminaries, I myself floated outside the cramped room on gentle air currents. Higher and higher I rose away from the winking lights and the symphony of night sounds until starlight flooded my vision and I forgot everything.

A tongue lapped at my chin.

A whimper followed.

A cold nose nudged my hand where it dangled over the edge of the sofa.

I noted these things and still I floated, although no longer star-struck. Ajax whimpered again and laid down on the floor between the sofa and coffee table, the top of his head positioned under my limp fingers.

After a while, the fireflies no longer lit the rectangle of sky framed by the screen door and even the bullfrogs and crickets hushed. I closed my eyes and slept.

***

I'm sobbing and running in rain as warm as blood. Rough pavement abrades my soles, pulling me back into myself. I'm not eleven anymore. I'm twenty-six. I'm alive.

Up ahead, dim orange lights gleam behind dark glass. A bar. I swerve and pull up short under a green awning. Hunched over and heaving, I become aware that my sexy black dress clings to me like a caul or perhaps a shroud. Something pokes the flesh between my breasts. Puzzled, I reach in and withdraw Kurt's note. I unfold it with shaking fingers to read a phone number.

Yanking the door open and ignoring stares from the bar's customers, I limp inside to the bar. The bartender, a bald man wearing a black shirt and a blank expression, watches as I cross to him.

"Where's the phone?"

"There been an accident?"

"No." I stop and hold his gaze. "Where's the phone?"

He gestures behind and to my right. I see the hallway to the bathrooms and set off for it. The payphone waits on the far wall. I call Kurt collect.

"To what do I owe the pleasure?" His voice purrs through the receiver.

"I'm looking for a degenerate cynic."

He laughs. It's a harsh caress in my ear. I shudder. "Aren't you worried about your immortal soul?"

"I told you, evil's already marked me."

"Where can I meet you?"

"Do you know Slim Jim's? Two blocks off Harvard Square?"

"I know it."

"Can you hurry? I got caught in the rain and I left my purse at the gallery."

"Ah. I see. I'll be right over. My place is nearby."

I return to the bar. Baldy eyes me but says nothing.

"Bring me a Royal Crown Crown Royal."

"You look like you've already had enough."

"And how would you know that? Can't you see I've already had a shitty night?"

"Got money? ID?"

"That how it is? Fuck you." I glare at him. He breaks first. "My date's arriving any moment. Card him."

Baldy brings my RCCR without a word, but I know he's keeping an eye on me. He's pegged me as either a drunk or a whore. Or both. I saw my fair share when I tended bar during college.

I sip my drink, ignoring him and the guys at the pool table who keep throwing speculative glances my way. I sit up straight, throwing my chest forward. The RCCR courses through my veins like a Jekyll-and-Hyde potion. I'm almost done when I'm disturbed.

"Hey, beautiful. What happened to you?" It's one of the pool players. "You're soaking." He laughs and looks over his shoulder at his friend.

I refuse to look at him. He's bold, but I'll let him hang himself before I react.

"That's a *very* attractive dress you got on." Genius steps closer and lowers his voice. His beer-laced breath fouls my air. "Looks torn. I bet you'd like a hot shower and some dry clothes. I've got some back at my place." He chuckles in my ear.

"Go away." My hand grips my drink, now mostly ice.

"Just trying to be a Good Samaritan." His hand lands on my thigh and slides up toward my crotch.

I whirl on my stool, my fist connecting with his unprotected jaw. He drops like a dead weight to the floor. "Keep your hands to yourself."

"Guess I didn't get here fast enough." Kurt stands inside the door, smiling. I notice how sleek he is, how glossy his short hair, how angular his jaw and shoulders. He could model for one of those hip young clothing stores in high-end malls.

I narrow my eyes and finish my drink before jumping off the stool. "Pay the man, Kurt."

Kurt grins and steps up to settle my tab. I wait under the awning, sniffing the warm, damp air which smells of clean pavement. Without turning around, I know when he's joined me. I lean back, letting him put his arms around me to cup my breasts.

"Come, my fallen angel. Let's see just how bad you are."

As he finishes speaking, the streetlight near us winks out.

Fifteen

WHEN I SHOW UP AT THE BEACH HOUSE ON CAPE COD for the annual July Fourth reunion of my BU friends, I bring Kurt. Only Marcie's inside when we arrive, laying out a platter of cheese and crackers. Jana, Laurie, and Elyse are already on the deck drinking and their giddy laughter is as raucous as the seagulls overhead. Terri, married and living outside D.C., always arrives later than the rest of us who drive. We've always left it open to bringing guys, but only Laurie or Elyse has ever brought anyone. Even in college, I kept as much of my sex life separate from my friends as I could—I knew better than to contrast my brief couplings with their tame dating lives. I don't care anymore.

Marcie looks up as I step into the kitchen. Her smile wavers when she takes in Kurt, but she's nothing if not gracious and warm. She wipes her hands on a towel and comes over to hug me. "Weeble, why haven't you returned my calls? I've been frantic about you. I didn't know if you were still coming or not." She swivels to Kurt. "You look familiar. Have we met?" I doubt he sees the sharpness in her gaze. I'll be quizzed later, if she can corner me.

"Marcie, this is Kurt. Kurt, Marcie."

Kurt holds out his hand and she takes it. I expect her to lean in and kiss his cheeks, but she astonishes me when she simply grips his hand and nods. Instead of 'nice to meet you,' she turns to me. "This is unexpected, Weeble. I thought you might bring someone else."

Kurt's glance snags mine. He knows, I realize. He must've seen her at the opening.

I shrug and step toward the bottles of beer, wine, and liquor sitting on the counter. "Don't know what gave you that idea." I look back at Kurt, who watches us. "Drink? There's enough booze and soda here I can make you almost anything. I paid my way through BU mixing up my share of drinks at Casey's."

He smiles the wolfish grin I love to hate. "I doubt you have the ingredients for a Tom Collins and I don't do fruity rum drinks."

I study him, ignoring Marcie's silence. "No, you don't look the type to drink girlie drinks." I look down at my options and pick up Laurie's bottle of Maker's Mark. "How about a *John* Collins?" The answering gleam in his eye rewards my clever suggestion.

As we're on the way out to the deck with our cocktails, Marcie lays a hand on my forearm and hisses, "What're you doing?"

I shake her hand off. "What I feel like."

Jana's eyes narrow a fraction when I introduce Kurt, but Laurie and Elyse smile and clasp his hand, letting him kiss their cheeks and compliment them. A surge of bitter pride twists my smile. Kurt, immaculate and crisp in a polo and khaki's, exudes respectability and confident male magnetism. He's more charismatic and charming than any of my friends' boyfriends. They'd be shocked to know what he likes to do in bed.

Not that he's all that unique in his tastes. He just thinks he is and I don't have any intention of setting him straight for now. Let him think his sordid games and sex toys are extreme, deviant even. He's no different than any other guy who looks at me, stripping my clothes off in his imagination before fantasizing about binding my hands, standing over me as I cower on my knees, and commanding me to suck him off. He's a petty sadist with a small mind, not much more terrifying or powerful than Tim, for all his sophistication and Harvard studies. Thinking of my half-brother makes me think of the message Mona left a week after I went home with Kurt.

"Weeble, it's Mom. I know you're not gonna call me back, but I gotta say what I gotta say to you anyway. Annie misses you. I don't know what happened between you two, but you got to forgive her. You got to." Her smoker's voice broke and grew watery. "*I* miss you. It ain't fair you holdin' what Tim did to Annie against me and your dad all these years. You know he kicked that asshole out. Wouldn't visit him in jail neither. Are you gonna let me go to my grave too without seein' or talkin' to you? You still talk to her grandmother, don't you? Don't you? She ain't your grandmother, Weeble. She ain't your family. Oh, God, Weeble, I'm sorry. I'm sorry Lauren died. I'm sorry that fucker raped and hurt you, but you can't let him ruin your life."

How like Mona to call on the anniversary of our kidnapping to berate me for my selfishness.

"So Kurt, how'd you two meet?" Laurie asks, bringing me back to the present. She's converted to a John Collins when she learns what Kurt and I are drinking. She grins at me. "Weeble always kept her conquests to herself in college. This is the first time we've seen her with a guy. Elyse and I had her pegged as either a Bible thumper or a lesbian."

Kurt laughs, throwing his head back. "Wow! Those are two *extremely* different options." His eyes slide toward me before he slips his arm around my waist. "It's not my experience that either is true, but she's a woman of many secrets. Maybe a female lover is one of them."

An acrid memory of captivity, of what Richard Lee Grady made Lauren and me do, coats my tongue. "You'd like that, wouldn't you?" I ask Kurt, not hiding a slight sneer.

Elyse gasps while Laurie laughs, a nervous edge sharpening it. Jana watches me drink but says nothing.

Kurt's grin increases in wolfishness. I suspect he finds my attitude arousing. "We met at the home of a mutual acquaintance."

We spend the afternoon drinking and chatting. I ignore Marcie and Jana, who stand to the side and talk too low for anyone else to hear. Overhead, the sun burns in a milky-blue sky too bright to look at for long. Beyond the radiant sand, the ocean glitters. Whenever the wind shifts, it brings the cool scent of fish and salt through the hot air. I refuse to think about anything but drinking and laughing and Kurt's possessive hand. Just before we head out for dinner, Terri arrives with her husband Mark. After a flurry of hugs and introductions, we separate into two groups to drive to a restaurant overlooking Cape Cod Bay. By now, I've had half a dozen John Collinses.

"Don't you think you oughtta slow down?" Jana asks when I order a drink at the restaurant's bar.

"No. Notatall." I hear the slur, but I don't care.

"It's not any different from college, is it?" Marcie gazes after Kurt as he heads to the bathroom. "You're self-medicating, aren't you, Weeble? When are you gonna tell us what's wrong?"

I drain my drink and look at her. "Why? Why should I tell you what's wrong, Marce? You think you can rescue me like all those poor drug addicts and battered women at Bea's Place? Did it ever occur to you I might be a lost cause?"

Marcie rears back, stunned, but she rallies anyway. "Is that what you think, Weeble? That you're a lost cause?"

"No." I gesture to a waitress with my glass. "I think shelters are a lost cause."

"Why? Why would you say that?" Laurie has overheard me and joined in the grilling. I swivel to look at her. "Don't you think Marcie's work has made a difference in the lives of many women?"

"She's only setting them up to get knocked down again."

"Look, not every woman breaks out of the cycle of poverty, abuse, and bad choices." Marcie's fervent voice riles me. And so does her hand gripping my forearm as she seeks to convince me. "But don't other women deserve the opportunity to have what we have?"

I laugh even though what she's said isn't funny. At all. "'What we have?' What the hell do you know about what I have, Marcie?"

"Why don't you tell me?"

Before I can retort, Jana says, "I can tell you what you threw away."

"What'd Weeble throw away?" Kurt asks, coming up behind me. He looks around our tense group, but no one answers. He turns to me and jokes, "You won't be invited back to the Freegan dinner co-op if you're throwing valuable stuff away."

I don't want to continue this here, so I shrug and tug a smile onto the corners of my mouth. "Not going to be invited back, anyway, am I?"

His answering smile agrees. "No, I don't think either of us is, actually."

For the first time since college, I wish I'd never met these women. I don't want to know them. I don't want to know Terri, soft and vulnerable and oh-so-doting on her husband now that they've managed to conceive. Laurie's highlighted-blond hair and tanned-cheerleader looks irritate the hell out of me, too. She keeps gazing at Kurt from under her eyelashes, smiling and complimenting his every contribution to the conversation. *Good luck with that*, I think. *His hand is on my thigh and he's barely listening to you.* Elyse, shy accountant, well she'd have a man in

276

her life if she'd stop trying to hide her bad teeth with her hand and her eyes with her hair. Beauty has little to do with it. Assurance. A willingness to look him in the face and sit a little closer. Those are the prime attractors. As it is, Elyse is the anti-Laurie and she annoys me too. I refuse to look at Jana and Marcie all night long, but their watchfulness digs at my vitals. I'm way beyond wishing I'd never met them.

Later, I leave Kurt in our stuffy room, sweaty and exhausted. In the dark, his naked spread-eagle reflects the moonlight from the slider to the deck. I pause at the door to look at him, my stomach hosting a fury of lightning in the midst of a rising black storm in my blood. The ache in my head isn't from drinking too much. No, on the contrary, I suspect I need more alcohol to drown out the storm. To keep me from jumping on his prone body and punching the back of his head until my knuckles bleed.

I stumble to the kitchen to mix another drink. Just as I feel the tang of rum and Coke sliding down my woolly throat, I hear someone talking on the deck. It's Jana.

"What the hell are we going to tell him now?"

"I warned you, Jayjay. I saw the signs at his opening. You should never've invited him here."

"Invited who, my lovelies?" I step onto the deck to an echo of gasps. "Come now, you couldn't think you'd have the deck all to yourselves on such a beautiful night."

The vivid full moon overhead throws Jana and Marcie's features into sharp relief, preventing me from reading their expressions. Still, Jana's quick shifting and Marcie's compressed lips say worlds to me. I sit down in the nearest chair and contemplate them through half my drink.

"Not sure how your silence makes this better." I press my icy, sweating glass against my temple. "I'm not an idiot. When does Tom Paul make an appearance? I'll be sure to be gone."

"That's not—" Marcie begins, but Jana overrides her. "What the hell's wrong with you? Why did you bring that asshole here?"

"Because assholes are my type."

"Is that what you think?" Marcie sounds calm, analytical. She's got me on her couch now. Sharp rage explodes behind my right eye.

"I *know* it." I launch myself into the kitchen for the rum. When I return, I sense I've interrupted hasty whispers. I answer them as I pour. "Nothing personal, ladies, but you're the ones who don't know what the hell you're doing. I can't blame you though. You don't really know me after all. But I've finally decided to quit pretending. To quit running from who I am. So I'm gonna tell you a little story about myself and then you'll see you don't know jack shit about anything."

I sit back in my chair and put my feet up on the wicker coffee table between us. Even though I've decided to spill my guts after all these years, I find that lead lines my chest. But I think about Kurt lying sated with upper-middle-class depravity. Gulping the rum, I replay Marcie's detached tone and Jana's righteous indignation. Molten ferocity softens the lead.

"Marcie, I told you a serial killer named Richard Lee Grady killed my best friend Lauren when I was eleven. I left out a few minor details, I'm afraid. One thing I didn't tell you: Richard Lee grabbed me, too. We'd been at the pool all afternoon when a storm closed it early." I can't see Jana and Marcie anymore as I call up that day again. I've played this memory over so many times you'd think its edges would've frayed, but it's as sharp and colorful as a beetle caught in amber.

"He had this wicked knife. Wicked. Wicked." I taste the pronunciation on my tongue. It sounds just the way Jana, who's from Maine, would say it. "Ah, yes, ladies. It was truly wicked. Cut a lot of interesting places with that knife. Jana, do you remember that scar on my inner thigh you asked me about when we were freshman?"

Jana makes a strangled sound.

"I told you I cut it on some glass while screwing a guy at the park. I lied. Sorry." A flaring heat rises through my chest and I have to stop for a few breaths. I swallow a huge mouthful of rum, but it scarcely dulls the fire. "Ol' Richard Lee, he looked like Dracula himself. You know, those dark dead eyes, a little red light in them? He brought us to his house, this mobile home near Sugar Lake. Had a mongrel dog named Ajax. Ajax took care of me after Richard Lee raped me. You know, I actually left my body when he did that?" I look at Marcie, sitting as still as stone in the glorious July night, and laugh.

"I don't know where I went, but that dog saved me from drowning—drowning in my own snot and tears. I came back to my body to find him licking my cheeks and nostrils. What an idiot." I can hear my affection for the black-and-white mutt, but then I clamp down on the scalding tears that start when I remember what happened to him after I escaped.

"Lauren didn't make it out of Richard Lee's room the first day we were there. He came out, saw I was awake, and told me to get his breakfast for him. It's a good thing I knew how to cook. If it'd been Lauren, I don't think she'd've lasted past his first mouthful. Then again, maybe that would've been for the best."

I can't go on when this occurs to me, so we sit there for who-knows-how-long until Marcie says, "What else happened?" I notice her voice shakes.

"Hm? Oh, yeah. What else." Now my voice flattens as it takes on the sing-song rhythm that got me through the later police interrogation and testimony. "It burned like hell when I urinated. There was so much blood I thought I'd started my period. I remember being frantic about what I was going to do to get some pads to keep from staining his furniture. He'd left purple handprints on my hips and fabric burns on my back and buttocks." I catch myself rubbing my free hand along my hipbone and quit.

"After he left to go somewhere, I scrubbed out the tub with steel wool and Comet." I turn and look at Jana, whose eyes are so large and dark I think she might be in shock. "Scrubbed myself with steel wool and Comet, too. In water so hot my body turned as red as a lobster. I couldn't scrub him off me, though. Too late."

I lift my glass to my mouth, but it's empty, so I'm forced to pull from the bottle instead. I heft its smooth weight against my palm, wondering how it'd feel to lob it against a wall. Or bring it against someone's head.

"When I got out, I didn't have anything to put on but my torn bikini. That's when I saw the sofa cushions. It's so funny. I'd been so worried about staining Richard Lee's furniture, but I'd already pissed and bled all over it. You probably wonder why I didn't try to run away while he was gone." I look at both of them, but only Marcie's head shakes a fraction. Jana hasn't moved or spoken since I started. My fingers curve into talons that itch to pry her wide hazel eyes from their sockets. Who the hell is *she* to look so devastated?

"I've asked myself that same question, over and over again, ladies. Turns out I don't know why. I've tried telling myself I knew Lauren was in bad shape and couldn't make it out, but I never thought about her. Selfish bitch, even then." I drink more rum to keep the prickling in my eyes under control.

"Richard Lee was one sick fucker. Took dozens of Polaroids of Lauren and me, some of us together—and I mean together. Don't go tellin' Elyse and Laurie, though. Somehow I doubt they'd really like to hear how right their suspicions are. They'd much rather have fun at my expense, no harm done. Right?"

"No, no they had no idea," Jana whispers.

"None of you has any idea." I spit these words at them. I look at Marcie now. "Just because you volunteer at a women's shelter doesn't mean you have any idea. Those women tell you sob stories about how awful it is to be with a man who punches them or kicks them. They're so terrified, they can't walk out. They can't call the cops or pick up a knife or gun to defend themselves until they've lost teeth or been admitted to the ER. Some of them have been on the streets since they're sixteen, selling their bodies and giving birth to babies they don't want. Some are addicted to heroin or crack or dolly or Peruvian marching powder. They can't help it. The drugs control them. They steal. They sell their bodies. Pity -poor women. Abused and taken advantage of. Highly educated social workers like you listen to these stories and tell them they've been dealt a bad hand, but they've got friends now. Some place to hide from the boogie man. Jobs and aid."

I stand up and my head reels. I've had enough. Enough to drink and enough baring my soul.

"Who are you to tell me I've been dealt a bad hand? Huh? You're both safe with loving men. Don't tell me assholes aren't my type. They are. They've been my only type for a very long time now."

Someone begins crying as I go back into the house, but I don't turn around to try to figure out who it is.

* * *

Around 6:30 the next morning, I get up and go to the kitchen to make coffee and wait for someone else to wake. An hour later Jana appears, looking as if she's suffering from the flu. Her honey-blond hair, pulled into a messy spray at the back of her head, adds little color to her wan, cosmetic-free complexion. Her red-rimmed eyes slide from mine, but she accepts the mug of coffee I hand her.

"I can't stay." I'm proud of my calm voice given how much I smolder, fueled by a pot of coffee on an empty stomach.

"I know." She sips her coffee, clears her throat, and then meets my eyes. "Weeble, I know you think you burned some bridges last night, but you didn't."

"Then I'm about to burn them." I slam my mug onto the counter. "Six sleepless hours in a bed next to a stranger who fancies himself a modern-day Marquis de Sade have a way of clarifying one's options."

"Those are?"

I shrug. "Maybe Mexico. Someplace sunny for sure. Someplace I don't have to try so hard to forget."

"What about your project? What about all those victims? Are you going to forget them too?"

"Told you I was a selfish bitch. Why else do you think I slept with every guy you wanted to date?"

"Not all of them."

I never slept with Julius. Still, I only look at her. She turns silver-green, the color of spoiled beef.

"No." Her manicured nails evoke the image of blood drops against her lips. "Not Julius."

"Bridge burned?"

I don't wait for her answer. Instead, I leave, passing Marcie in the kitchen doorway with a slight nod. If I'm lucky, my insinuation will buy me two burnt structures for the price of one. However, I suspect Marcie's tougher than that, even if it's a second-hand resiliency.

In the bedroom, Kurt still sleeps. Whatever attraction he held for me has evaporated. I toss his chinos at his head and growl. "Let's go."

I'll give the self-important prick this much. He read me from the start and this morning is no exception. He doesn't ask any questions, just drags on his clothes before stuffing his things into his bag. Even when I catch him tossing a sly glance at the newly risen Laurie, enticing in camisole and pajama bottoms with tousled hair and a just-been-laid languor, he interprets my expression and hurries after me.

When he drops me off at my apartment, I slam the car door without looking back.

Flat Stanley lurches to his feet, mewing his pleasure at seeing me. Guilt digs into my anger, stirring its banked embers. I shouldn't have left him alone to go to the Cape. I shouldn't have left. I'm the most selfish, spiritually stunted being on God's green Earth. Dropping my bag, I step forward and lift him into my arms. I'm shaking and crying, I'm too rough with him, but he's purring and pushing his head under my chin. Volcanic memories wait for me beneath the hard crust covering my wounded soul, but if I can just hold Flat Stanley long enough, I might be able to patch the fault lines in my composure.

The phone rings and an invisible hand wrings the vital juices of my heart.

"Hello?"

It's Claudine Prescott, the *Globe* reporter who interviewed me back in May. My hope withers.

"Kate? Kate Lonergan? Sorry to call on a holiday weekend. I was just going to leave another message for you. I'm glad I caught you in person."

As always, when I hear my given name, I go blank for several heartbeats and then I flinch. I close my eyes, take a breath, and answer.

"Claudine." I pull up an image of her from our interview. She's a thin woman, all angles and pale skin. Her fine hair, the color of tarnished silver threaded with white, hangs in a corrugated sheet to her shoulders. She'd smelled of burnt orange, stale coffee, and, oddly, motor oil. Over the phone, her voice sounds like ice cubes in a crystal tumbler. "Yeah, I've been really busy."

283

"How's the training going? Doing the sprint marathon, right?"

A warning buzz jolts the base of my spine. "I'm taking a little break right now as a matter of fact."

"Ah." Her pause implies that she's transcribing my answer. "Isn't the anniversary of Lauren Case's murder coming up?"

"Yes." Glacial fury threatens frostbite to my heart. "Is there some reason you called? I'm pretty sure it's not to check up on my training or whether I remember the date of my best friend's death. I thought you were running your story weeks ago."

She ignores my thrust. "Just following up on a few details. Why didn't you tell me before you were the one who led police to Richard Lee Grady's mobile home?"

I drop the receiver, Flat Stanley, and myself. The demons loom. I cover my head with my arms and cower where I've fallen. But they won't leave me alone. I lurch upright and rip the phone from its outlet before hurtling it at the blue-black devils who breathe out tongues of flame and ash. They lumber after me, unhampered by the staff-like tumescence between their legs. Their claws score my back in a thousand places.

This time I fight. I pull books from shelves, throw pictures and paperweights, toss CDs, sneakers, plants, cushions, dog squeaky toys—anything I can grab and fling. I scream. Hot tears burn frenzied tracks down my cheeks. I tear my hair and beat my head against everything. As hard as I fight, I lose. Molten images of that last morning, the day Lauren died, erupt.

"We gotta go. *Now*. There's no tellin' when he'll be back."

"No." Lauren looked at me. Her eyes were two pewter bruises against her swollen cheeks. "NO."

"Please. Please come with me."

She twisted her face away, aiming her gaze at the wood paneling next to the bed. "No, the hero has to rescue the heroine. Remember?"

"That's just what we read in books, Lauren. It's not true. We gotta save ourselves. Ain't no hero comin' for us."

She didn't look at me. When she spoke, she sounded dreamy. "He's got emerald-green eyes and a cleft chin. And an aquiline nose. He'll flatten *him*—" she spit the pronoun with enough venom to kill if her target had been the wall—"and then scoop me up and carry me in his strong arms."

"Lauren, I'm goin'. Come with me."

"You go without me. You'll miss your hero for sure. I'll tell him where to find you. Not *him* though. Never *him*. Don't worry."

Dismayed, I shook her shoulder, but she just twisted her fingers into the nasty stained blanket under her and ignored me. I stood up and straightened my spine.

"All right. Be that way. See if I care. I don't need you to find the police. And I don't need any damn hero, either. You both can go to hell."

That was the last thing I ever said to her.

I come to awareness some time after I remember what I'd done, slumped against my bed and holding the *planchette* from the Ouija game. My room looks like the aftermath of a hurricane. I crawl through the scattered papers, drifted down feathers, clumped clothes and sheets, and smashed cosmetics as I search for the Ouija board. When I find it, I set it on my dresser, kneeling as if in prayer to ask for benediction.

"Angel?"

YES.

"You haven't left me?"

NEVER.

"Will he come?"

YES. IF YOU CALL.

I close my eyes and try to hold the blessing of the Ouija angel's presence inside. To draw courage from it. Because I'd been wrong that day when I'd abandoned Lauren to her cruel fate. I do need a hero.

TOM PAUL

A SHADOW MOVED BEHIND TOM PAUL, and his hearing returned for the first time in eight hours.

Blinking, he laid his tools down on the bench in front of him as he adjusted to the small sounds around him, sounds at once strange and familiar. The raw edge sharpening his breath, the regular tick of the wall clock, the faint hum of the fluorescent lights, and the slight squeak of his soles on the linoleum disturbed him after such deep silence. He'd been submerged after Puck had led him into a world of variegated light and dark, filled with shifting shadows and a fractal sky. Against the mute beauty of Puck's vision, the clanging clarity of the real world hurt.

"Tom Paul."

He turned a reluctant gaze on Callista. "Hey. What's up?" Her aura, he saw now, had a thin steel-gray filament woven through it, fine and strong. An equally thin red line traced its edge.

"No one's heard from you since the night of your opening. Not Mom. Not Zandra. Not Jonah. Not Sharon. No one in your Freegan co-op."

He sighed. "No. I've been sleeping here. I've been experimenting with including metal in *pâte de verre*. Puck showed up after Weeble left that night and, if you'll excuse the expression, has been a monkey on my back ever since."

"Have you seen her?"

Tom Paul ducked his head and swiveled back to his workbench. "No. We sorta argued and she ran off." His gaze drifted to the clock. 10. Damn. He'd meant to be showered and on the road by now. Traffic on the Sagamore would be brutal.

"Your Freegan friends Angela and Yan said she met Kurt that night." When her soft voice sounded next to him, he started. She'd walked on cat's paws to stand beside him.

Tom Paul closed his eyes. Her news sent black sludge sliding down the slope of his spirit. Before it could suffocate him, he grabbed the tray of small pieces he'd pulled from the cooling rack to cold work and whirled to face her.

"Look at these. I've added aluminum powder to this row. Aluminum turns black when it's fired. See? This one has just a sprinkle. I increased the amount all the way across. The last couple didn't turn out so well." He picked up a piece and held it up to the light above them. "Too much metal overwhelms the glass."

Folding her arms, Callista took her gaze from his face to look at the glass he held. "What did you add to it? It's less textured in color than the others."

"Ah. Yes. Would you believe aluminum foil I balled up and straightened out before wedging between a layer of clear glass and a layer of black frit? And this one is a layer of black frit topped by a layer of aluminum wire I clipped into bits followed by a final layer of clear frit. What do you think?"

"They're stunning. And very different from what you've done before." She lifted her gaze back to his face. He ignored the question he saw there.

"Glasswork really takes too much time for Puck. He's been prodding me to try other materials like fiberglass. And he wants me to work on increasing bubbles, too. I've used baking soda before, so I'll give that a try next. That'll take me weeks to figure out. He's hinted that we'll include found objects after that. Something lightweight works best, like leaves. They'll burn off, of course, but I wonder if something will be left behind, a shadow or imprint?"

"Like an aura?" Callista's cool fingers slid across his, forcing him to stop equivocating. "You didn't know."

He set the piece he held next to its siblings. Their impassive surfaces gleamed under the harsh white light, but he knew that they'd reveal an internal fire when exposed to candlelight. He looked at Callista, whose expression had lost its old dreaminess and now looked pinched, with white apostrophes alongside her nostrils.

"No."

"I'm sorry."

He shrugged, closed his eyes, and pinched the bridge of his nose. "Don't be. We weren't dating. I don't even know what we were."

"She knew how you felt about her."

"Yes." He opened his eyes. "We argued the night of my opening about sex. She'd gone through the exhibit ahead of me. I found her in what looked like a catatonic state in front of St. Sebastian. When I put my hand on her shoulder, she screamed. You should've heard her. It wasn't out of surprise, Cally. It was terror. Then she took off. By the time I caught her out in the gallery, she was moaning. I took her in my arms to comfort her and she began kissing and rubbing against me. She wanted me to take her right there on the floor."

"She sounds possessed."

He stared at his sister. "Maybe she is."

Callista placed her palm on his cheek. "Then I'm glad you haven't seen her since."

"I'm not." His voice thickened.

Before she could respond, the phone rang. Their gazes locked and held even as he hurried across to the black wall phone, speckled with glaze and paint.

"Hello?"

"Tom Paul." At the sound of her voice, his heart lurched and knocked around his ribcage like a thrown gasket.

"Weeble?"

"It's Kate, actually. Kate Lonergan." Sobs made her almost incoherent. She rushed through her next words as though she feared that he'd interrupt her. "I'm sorry. I'm sorry. So sorry, Tom Paul. Please forgive me."

Sixteen

Suddenly little Gerda stepped through the great portal into the palace. The gate was formed of cutting winds; but Gerda repeated her evening prayer, and the winds were laid as though they slept; and the little maiden entered the vast, empty, cold halls. There she beheld Kay: she recognized him, flew to embrace him, and cried out, her arms firmly holding him the while, "Kay, sweet little Kay! Have I then found you at last?"

But he sat quite still, benumbed and cold. Then little Gerda shed burning tears; and they fell on his bosom, they penetrated to his heart, they thawed the lumps of ice, and consumed the splinters of the looking-glass; he looked at her, and she sang the hymn:

"The rose in the valley is blooming so sweet, And angels descend there the children to greet."

Hereupon Kay burst into tears; he wept so much that the splinter rolled out of his eye, and he recognized her, and shouted, "Gerda, sweet little Gerda! Where have you been so long? And where have I been?" He looked round him. "How cold it is here!" said he. "How empty and cold!" And he held fast by Gerda, who laughed and wept for joy. It was so beautiful, that even the blocks of ice danced about for joy; and when they were tired and laid themselves down, they formed exactly the letters which the Snow Queen had told him to find out; so now he was his own master, and he would have the whole world and a pair of new skates into the bargain.

Gerda kissed his cheeks, and they grew quite blooming; she kissed his eyes, and they shone like her own; she kissed his hands and feet, and he was again well and merry. The Snow Queen might come back as soon as she liked; there stood his discharge written in resplendent masses of ice.

I'VE TOLD MYSELF I DON'T REMEMBER ANYTHING from the year after Lauren died. But that's not quite true. I remember one moment from her funeral. The moment Grandma Nan said good-bye to the last member of her family.

In the red- and blue-tinted light of a stained-glass shepherd, the tea roses draping Lauren's closed coffin took on a festive, almost clownish appearance. Their heady fragrance hung in a cloying mist around the dusty sanctuary. Grandma Nan stood, her hands resting on the polished wood, her head bowed. For the first time since I'd met her, I thought she looked old. Fragile and crooked like a brittle branch snapped from a barren bush.

I sat in the front pew dressed in a stiff navy skirt suit made of polyester. My brand new black shoes pinched after weeks of flip flops and bare feet. Mona had relented when I pitched a fit over wearing pantyhose, but I stared at the bruises and burns on my calves, fascinated at the way the light through the church windows transformed them into something grotesquely comic.

As I kneel before my dresser in the wreck of my room, this image sideswipes me. It pulls a hidden inner chord I didn't know existed, releasing tears in a whoosh from the bucket of my eyes. I plunge into a tank of hot, salty grief, only to rise to the surface breathless and gasping. A firm hand pulls me to my feet and then two arms wrap around me. Familiar calloused fingers soothe my back and press me against hard muscles. I tuck my nose into his warm male musk, scented with the contradictory smells of balsam, lemon-basil, glass dust, and harsh chemicals. For the first time in my life, I feel safe. The tremors rolling through me weaken and fade away, but we don't speak until my body has stilled.

Speaking into his chest, I say, "I–I've been with Kurt."

He steps away and tilts my chin, bringing my eyes up. He looks as exhausted as I feel. "I know."

I start to cry again, but these tears are slow. I look away, but he doesn't let go. I nod. "I deserve this."

"Deserve what?" It's sharp enough to snap my gaze back. His own gaze is as keen as his tone. I know where the gold glints that used to dance in his eyes have gone. "Deserve me coming here and confronting you? Deserve me rejecting you for hurting me? Would you like it if I hit you too? Would you understand that better than the fact that I'm here despite my pain, still in love with you?"

I choke a bit. I have no idea what I'm feeling in the wake of his assault.

Now he drops my hands. Two weeks ago, I would've sworn he could never look cold. I was wrong. "*I* deserve to know the truth. The whole truth. What happened in *The Soul Illuminated* that night? Why did you run from me and into Kurt's bed?"

I sweep my gaze over the destruction around me. When it crosses the Ouija board, I reach and take the *planchette*. Palming it, I fix my eyes on the far corner.

"Do you know who I am?" It's a whisper—all that I can force from my dry mouth. I don't wait for his answer. "I'm Judas. I betrayed my best friend."

When I can't go on, he asks, "Lauren?"

I nod.

"You said she'd been killed by a serial killer when you were eleven."

I nod again.

An expectant silence settles over us. The Ouija angel stands next to me. I can almost see his diaphanous wings. The attar of roses fills my nostrils.

"That's not your fault, Kate."

"It is. I escaped. When she wouldn't come with me, I told her to go to hell and left her there."

A strangling sound reaches me, but I can't turn around. "'Escaped'? You mean he took you too?"

At his words, I'm inundated by a black tidal wave of shame, fear, guilt, anger, nausea, and a conviction of brokenness and filth. I would have crumpled onto my bed if Tom Paul hadn't caught me and taken me with him. His hot tears soak my already soggy shirt. And then he's kissing me, kissing me so hard I grow dizzy, and his fingers root through my hair as if searching for entrance into my skull. Instead of terror at his efforts to subsume me, I relinquish myself to him. Only now do I recognize that I've been treading air over a chasm so deep and dark it would have ripped me to shreds and ground my bones to dust if I'd realized I had nothing to keep me up but my willful ignorance.

Tom Paul never lets me go as he lowers me to my bed. He never takes his eyes from mine. In them, I see myself, transformed into something beautiful and whole. When at last he enters me, I'm not afraid anymore.

Epilogue

▼

As the other runners flow and part around me like a school of fish, I pass the final race volunteers holding their placards scrawled with encouragement. Ahead, spectators gather around the finish line, cheering and clapping. I ignore all of them, scanning instead for Tom Paul. He's standing about fifty feet down on the right behind two enthusiastically screaming women. I wave at him, relishing the strength remaining in my arm after swimming and biking under a brutal early September sun. He smiles. I'll never grow tired of seeing that, I decide.

Someone stands at his elbow, I realize as I draw nearer. She's too short and slight to be either Jana or Marcie, who materialize among the crowd waving a banner.

I draw near a timer, who bends in to tell me my middle-of-the-pack finish, when I hear my name.

Startled, I study the stranger, who holds Hero's leash. She's got shoulder-length fine brown hair and wears a hot-pink sundress. On her left shoulder, a tattoo of a red rose stands out against her pale, freckled skin. My energy and strength drain out of me when I scan her face.

"Annie."

She bites her lip and her eyes shift toward Tom Paul. Whatever she sees there, she squares her shoulders and looks back at me. "Weeble."

For a moment, I'm aware of the fatigue in my calves, of the sweat trickling down my spine and along the creases between my pelvis and thighs, and of the parchment lining my mouth and throat. Then I say, "Kate. It's Kate, Annie. I don't go by Weeble anymore."

She nods, little diamonds glistening in the corners of her eyes. Something—a word or a groan or a cry from my childhood— escapes me and I grab her and hug her hard. She's laughing in odd, jerky breaths, saying how much she missed me while Hero insinuates himself between us, pushing and leaning until Tom Paul tugs him free.

Finally, my post-race thirst and hunger assert themselves.

Laughing, I begin to jog backwards. "Last one to the awards tent is a rotten egg."